To Gareth

Death in a
Scarlet Gown

by

Lexie Conyngham

Lexie Ca...

First published in 2011 by The Kellas Cat Press, Aberdeen.

Dramatis Personae

Charles Murray of Letho, gentleman of Fife
Charles Balfour Murray, younger of Letho, his son, fourth year
    student at St. Andrews
George Murray, his younger son, gentleman of leisure
Daniel, putatively capable of becoming a decent manservant

Students at St. Andrews:
Thomas Seaton, bursary student of humble origins
Picket Irving, Boxie Skene and Rab Fisher, the Sporting Set –
    fashionable but bored
Sundry others, all wearers of the red gown and reluctant
    consumers of rabbit

Staff at St. Andrews:
Professor Helenus Keith, Natural Philosophy
Professor David Shaw, Moral Philosophy
Professor Christopher Urquhart, Humanity
Allan Bonar, assistant to Professor Keith
Mungo Dalzell, teacher of Hebrew
Ramsay Rickarton, bedellus
The Principal and the Chancellor, gentlemen of great
    importance but characters of little significance

Professor Keith's household:
Mrs. Keith, a matron who had a mind
Alison Keith, a lively maid
Peter Keith, an indecisive young man
Barbara, a distressed maidservant

Mrs. Walker, a bunkwife
Patience Walker, her forthright daughter
Lord Scoggie, a peer of notable dental endowment
Sybie, a beloved grand-daughter

Chapter One

When the black crow flapped in from the sea, it was like a cloud in a perfect sky. For a moment, as it perched, deliberately, on the heavy straw roundel, it looked like a crow-shaped hole slashed out of the tinsel-blue sea behind it. Then the breeze caught it and it jerked out ragged wings for balance, and the sea glittered and wrinkled, and the moment passed, but Charles had lost his aim and lowered the bow to start again.

'Shoot the crow,' said Picket, with casual coldness.

'We could hang the carcass outside Keith's chamber window tonight,' said Boxie, then looked as if he regretted it. Rab, fair hair swept back by the breeze, suffered a flicker of enthusiasm on his otherwise vacant face, and Picket lifted an eyebrow, considering the idea. Charles raised the bow again, drew the feathers back cleanly to a point beneath his jawbone, breathed in, breathed out, and allowed the arrow to find a satisfying path to a point about an inch from the very centre of the bull. The crow flapped away.

'Nice shot!' cried Boxie, almost keeping the relief out of his voice.

'But what about the crow?' Rab objected.

'Didn't want to spoil my arrow,' said Charles, briefly. He knew the crow's carcass would not have bothered Professor Keith in the least, but it would have given his maid hysterics. He turned and stepped back from the line. Now that he had his back to the sparkling sea, the wind caught the bare skin just above his high collar. It was fresh and cool, mild with springtime. The exposed headland on which the butts were placed was greened over and sprinkled with gulls and sheep, but not far away was the edge of the town, long rig-lands stretching out towards them from solid little sandstone houses. To the east, the great square tower of St. Salvator's Chapel marked the site of United College, where they all studied, and further south was the lower squatting spire of Holy Trinity, the parish church. At the far end of the town the broken tracery of the ruined cathedral and St. Rule's Tower were blotchy brown and yellow in the sunlight. The sky was a vast arc of enamel

1

blue, and the crow swooped and flapped across it again, bringing Charles' attention back to the butts.

'I like the idea, though,' said Picket, taking his turn at the line. He was almost as tall as Charles, but had the air of a plant that had grown too fast to reach a distant light. His hair was thin and colourless, and his face was drawn, his eyes, even now as he squinted at the target, looped with sagging lines, older than his seventeen years. He drew back the string and took aim, but his left wrist, though braced tight with leather, wobbled as if suddenly weak. The other three quickly pretended that they had not noticed. Picket muttered an oath, scowling like a devil, and tried again. This time the arrow left the bow but loosely, and skimmed to an uncertain halt in the grass beneath the target. Picket flung down his bow and stamped over to fetch it, thus preventing anyone else from shooting until he was clear again. The others were painfully silent, not watching him, and Charles scrabbled in his mind for something to say to start a harmless conversation. He wished he had not come: he had a book he wanted to finish and this morning's lecture notes to copy fairly, and either task, however dull the subject, was more appealing than spending time with this party of sportsmen. But it was a beautiful day, and Boxie had particularly asked him to come and make up a second team of two with the kind of gentle flattery to which any eighteen year old would be susceptible. Anyway, no doubt it would please his father to hear that he had been practising his archery: his father would smile that quick, proud smile, perhaps cuff him across the shoulder, mention it to his friends over the dinner table or at his fencing class ...

'Murray, step back, old man. It's Boxie's turn.' Rab's voice broke into his thoughts. Picket had returned to the line, picking grass off his arrow's feathers and checking it with unnecessary meticulousness to see if the line of balance had been spoiled. It was unlikely: the arrow had been travelling so slowly he would have needed to step on it to damage it. Apart from Rab's purely practical few words, the awkward silence still prevailed, and it was with a sense of deep relief that Boxie, slipping a quick arrow into the inner, turned and said,

'Oh, Charles! Here's your brother!'

Charles spun eagerly. There, indeed, with the heraldic green of the grass at his feet and the azure sky above him, came his big cheerful brother George, younger by a year and a half but the same height and nearly twice the width. Fair-haired and green-eyed, the very image of his father, George walked with an easy physical confidence and an open, innocent face. The brothers embraced while George tried simultaneously to wave at the others. He was a sociable man.

'You have the butts to yourselves, then, eh?' he remarked at once. 'Good day, Boxie, good day to you, Picket. Rab, take your shot, please, sir!'

Rab took aim and casually slid his arrow into the dead centre of the target, making Charles' arrow look untidy by comparison. They strolled down the range to collect their arrows, and George came too.

'Bit of a breeze, though, eh?'

'Not sure why they put the butts beside the sea,' said Rab, easing his two arrows out of the bull.

'So we'd be damn' good when we went into battle,' Boxie said.

'I'm sure that would impress Bonaparte,' Charles remarked, 'a few lines of British archers. Would we put them out with the Marines, do you think, or send them over to the Peninsula?'

It made Picket laugh, which was a good thing, but his revived spirits lasted only until George stupidly said,

'So where's your second shot, then, Picket?' and Boxie began talking loudly about gusting winds and intrusive birdlife. This unfortunately drew the conversation back to the idea of dangling corpses, avian or otherwise – Rab favoured rats – outside the windows of academics. George gave the notion his full consideration, though Charles wondered if the others particularly valued his opinion.

'It's a grand idea,' said George at last, 'but why Professor Keith? I would go for Professor Urquhart, myself.'

George was not a student at the university – nor had he any intention of being so, if he could possibly help it – but their father's Fife home was near enough by for him to pay frequent visits and not only to get to know Charles' friends and

3

acquaintances but also to indulge in the gossip of the academic community almost as if he were a part of it. Professor Keith might be hated, but Professor Urquhart was more easily ridiculed, and it was the latter activity that came more easily to George, a fact which might, Charles had sometimes felt, be the saving of him.

'Professor Urquhart might scream,' said Boxie, slowly.

'And that in itself might be rather gratifying,' Picket said, a nasty look in his eyes. Charles shivered slightly and thought with longing of his book and the peace of his lodgings – though now, with George here, all chance of that peace seemed to have gone. It was not that he was entirely against practical jokes, but Picket's schemes always seemed to take on a vindictive edge that made other people uneasy about associating themselves with them. 'However,' Picket went on as they reached the road, 'I have particular reasons for wishing to bring a little unease into Professor Keith's life. Master Skene's idea is a good one,' he said, clapping Boxie on the shoulder, 'but I think we might elaborate on it a little. Will you come with us for a walk on West Sands? We could debate the matter further,' he said to the Murray brothers. Charles doubted there would be much debate involved. He was trying, quickly, to think of an excuse, but to his surprise George spoke up immediately.

'Thank you most heartily, Picket, but my brother and I have other fish to fry,' he said, with an elaborate wink that took any offence away from the refusal.

'Do you stay long in the town?' Picket asked.

'A few days, perhaps,' said George.

'Then no doubt we shall see you again before you go. Farewell, gentlemen.' They all bowed, though Picket managed to give the action a hint of irony. Boxie added a small, slightly shameful wave, as if he was not sure which way he should be going. The three sporting gentlemen turned down right for the sands they could already see in the near distance. From the look of it some hardy souls were bathing, and a heavy rowing boat ploughed along parallel to the shore. Charles and George turned left instead, to return to the centre of the town, Charles stooping to pick up his scarlet gown and black trencher.

'Why *is* he called Boxie? asked George suddenly.

4

'Short for Snotterbox,' Charles explained.

'Oh. But his nose is hardly larger than – well, yours, for instance.'

'Thank you kindly, George. But it is, actually, or his head is smaller, or something like that. Anyway, I shan't fight him over it.'

'No, indeed,' George agreed, glancing down cross-eyed at his own more modestly-formed nose. There is nothing like a younger brother, Charles thought, for helping you to see yourself as others see you.

'Did you come by coach or horse?' he asked, looking about him for some means of transport.

'Oh, the horse!' cried George. 'I left it with some kind of infant down by the links. I thought you might be golfing, but when I saw you were not I asked myself how else I should spend a fine afternoon like this were I in St. Andrews, and straightaway walked up here.'

Charles smiled, thinking of his own preferences.

'Well, we had better go and fetch the horse, then.'

'Must we? The lad looked honest enough.'

'He might have better things to do with his time. And you know Father doesn't like them left long with strangers. Come on, we'll do it now.'

He turned back and followed in the now-distant wake of the sporting set. Inland from the West Sands was the links, dotted with players in their navy and red coats, and beyond them the Cupar road along which George would lately have ridden. At the near end was a small group of men and children, and by them was a horse, which even at this distance Charles recognised as Tam o'Shanter from his father's stable. The gelding was nuzzling the close seaside grass, passing the time. He strode quickly down the hill, hearing George puffing and blowing his discontent behind him, sounding quite like a horse himself.

One of the men, wearing the livery of the college bedellus or chief janitor, detached himself from the group and stepped a little toward them, hands clasped behind his back, while at the same time one of the boys made an anxious grab for Tam's bridle. The man's grey hair was thin on his bare head, and his nose was beaked between careful blue eyes. He had a broad forehead, but his cheeks sagged gently. Charles lifted his trencher and grinned.

'Ramsay Rickarton! Is this how you spend your days of leisure?'

The man gave a little bow.

'Mr. Murray, sir.' He had a broad Fife accent, an accent Charles and George had shared for a few years till it was beaten out of them at Edinburgh High School. 'No, this is no day of leisure, sir. Professor Shaw sent me a message down to the house thereby, and on my way back I find these two rapscallions on the loose. Aye,' he added severely, seizing one little girl by an affectionate pinch of the ear, and nodding at the boy with the horse. 'You'll ken wee Ramsay, my daughter's second boy? And this wee lassie is Sybie.'

He swung the girl up into his arms, a giggling, skinny child of about three years with her grandfather's blue eyes. Rickarton had the look of a man in love, though the child's bare muddy feet were streeling muck down his livery coat.

'Your father's horse, aye?' he added, nodding at Tam.

'Well, I brought it,' said George, keen to emphasise that he was allowed out on his own.

'Aye. Well, Ramsay's kept an eye on it, right enough.'

Charles glanced round at his brother, and with a sense of inevitability felt in his own pockets for some coins. He gave them to young Ramsay, who solemnly exchanged the handful for Tam's bridle. Then he scampered off, heading for the town.

'Aye, your brother's abandoned you, Sybie,' said Rickarton, watching the scruffy shirt and breeches of his grandson disappear into the distance. 'You'd best come back with this old fellow. I've the Senate meeting's tea to attend to.'

They walked together down the hill to the bottom of North Street, one of the three, almost parallel, broad main streets, while Rickarton regaled them easily with tales of Sybie's unusual genius and the compliments that had been paid to her. He told them over with pride, though half-laughing at himself as he did so. Sybie herself, alternately in her grandfather's arms and marching independently clutching only his fingertips, chattered too, and her grandfather listened and responded, paying her the attention he would have done to an adult. George sighed and meandered now ahead, now behind, but Charles was mildly cross with him and chose not to indulge him, though he was making the horse nervous.

The road, though called North Street, was almost rural at first, then was quickly lined with houses, some smart and newly-built, on either side. Families and servants busied themselves at the doors, returning with the shopping, setting out in carriages or on horseback or on foot, and further along a few students in their red wool gowns caught the afternoon sunlight, some of the few still living in College. The street rose slowly and broadly to the flat hill top on which the town was built, and a short way along this fine causeway they left Mr. Rickarton in view of United College. He and Sybie disappeared inside, and George, with renewed vigour in his stride, hurried down College Wynd, a much narrower passage. Charles followed him, tugging Tam into a half-hearted trot.

'What's your plan, then, George?' he asked, catching up.

'I intend to brush off my dusty clothes in your lodgings, stable Tam there, accept the reviving cup of wine you mean to offer me, and set off on a visit.'

'A visit,' Charles repeated.

'Indeed.'

Charles reflected, and stopped as they reached the end of the lane where it debouched on to Market Street. He held his hand over Tam's muzzle, calming his head-tossing, as they waited for a gap in the Monday afternoon bustle to cross to the Town House.

'This wouldn't, by any chance, be a visit to do with a girl?' he asked at last, as they worked their way round the tall block of the town house. George halted abruptly.

'Hush!' he hissed, and nodded down the street. Charles looked. He could see no attractive young women at all, of whatever class – and George had fallen for most. Instead, the most notable sight was that of the proposed victim of the sporting set, Professor Keith. Tall, majestically built, with lead-grey hair and immaculate coat and breeches, his heavy jowls nestled in his high collar like a toad in mud. He swept through

7

the crowd like a frigate through a fishing fleet, paying no attention to them and little to the man following him.

'Who's that?' asked George urgently.

'Professor Keith.'

'I know that,' George snapped. 'Who's that with him?'

'Oh, that's Mungo Dalzell. He teaches Hebrew.' Mungo Dalzell was an aimiable, thin man with a very red nose and the beginnings of a web of crimson veins over his cheeks. At the moment it gave him a flushed, anxious look – or it may just have been the effect of talking to Professor Keith, in whose wake he bobbed and splashed inconsequentially, glancing back apologetically at those townspeople who dared to show their feelings for Professor Keith as he passed.

'Do you think he's heading home?' George asked.

'Who – Dalzell or Keith?'

'Keith, of course. Why should I care where the other one is going?'

Why should you care about either? Charles thought, puzzled.

'Maybe – no, actually, I doubt it. There is a Senate meeting this afternoon in the college, and I expect they are both going there.'

'Good, good ...' George watched Keith and Mungo Dalzell pass, half-hiding behind Tam. Charles tried not to laugh: George looked like a hero from one of the more ridiculous Gothic novels.

'So, is it to do with a girl?' asked Charles as they started off again, crossing the rest of Market Street and heading down an even narrower wynd. Tam, even lowering his well-mannered head, took up all the space and several people had to stand waiting until they had led him to a wider part. Charles tipped his hat to them and they smiled forgivingly.

'What?'

'Your visit. Is it to do with a girl?'

George drew himself up, transferring his width to his shoulders.

'It is to do with a lady,' he corrected his brother.

'I beg your pardon. Might I be allowed to discover which lady it is for the purpose of a visit to whom I have the honour

8

of placing my humble bunk at Mr. George Murray's disposal for the cleansing of his boots?'

George scowled.

'Don't try to be funny. And I have a clean pair of boots in the saddlebags, anyway – do you think I would appear before her in these old things?'

The riding boots he wore were, indeed, three months old at least, Charles knew. Charles was not sure that he himself had anything less than three months old – except, perhaps, books. They passed the town kirk and turned right, out on to South Street. George walked with authority: Charles might have been his groom, he thought, bringing Tam along behind. Certainly his dark hair and brown eyes were nothing like George's. Nearly opposite the Grammar School and the tatty old apse of Blackfriars there was a well, not busy at this time of day as all the water would have been drawn for the laundry that morning. George led the way down a close beside it, and came out in a rig-garden with a stable yard at the end of it. He unbuckled the heavy leather saddlebags and stood clutching them, waiting impatiently when Charles handed Tam over to the stable boy, then led him back to the front of the house on the street. Charles stepped ahead to open the door and wave him in. He was just about to follow George inside, when he heard from nearby,

'Murray! Wait.'

He looked back into the street, and saw after a moment a solidly-built young man of middle height, wearing his red woollen gown in awkward tatters. He had hair the colour of last year's straw, a face unevenly shaved, and a complexion that spoke of airless rooms and unnourishing food.

'Thomas! What are you doing here?' Charles asked in some concern. 'You do remember you're supposed to be at the Senate meeting.'

'Remember? Of course I remember,' Thomas said belligerently. 'I've just been turned away at the door.'

'What?'

Thomas looked around, suddenly cautious.

'Maybe we should go up to your rooms,' he said in a lower voice, though his hands twitched as if he could control his voice but his emotions had to show themselves somehow.

'George is here,' Charles warned him.

'That's all right: he's not University. He'll not say anything.'

Charles was less certain of his brother's discretion, but allowed Thomas to lead him into the house and up the narrow staircase to the first floor. There was no particular sign of Charles' bunkwife or her daughter, but the thick smell of Monday washday from the kitchen quarters indicated their whereabouts and he left them to their own devices.

On the first floor Charles had a sitting room and a bedchamber, with a ceiling so low he and George had to walk hunched, or with their knees bent. Thomas could just fit under the beams except in one corner, where the whole building had sagged slightly and the gap between floor and ceiling was even smaller. George looked round in surprise when Thomas followed him up the stairs, and gave an awkward little bow, which Thomas returned even less elegantly. Charles waved them to the available seating: George secured the small upholstered armchair Charles had brought from Letho, and Thomas took one end of the hard bench by the front window, while Charles unlocked a cupboard and brought out cheap student claret and glasses.

'Thomas wants to tell us about the Senate,' he explained briefly to George as he poured. George nodded, without encouragement. Thomas did not look at him, but began even before Charles had taken the other end of the bench.

'You know the Senate was meeting with Lord Scoggie today and Professor Keith had asked me to come along as his amanuensis?' Charles nodded: George, at the mention of Professor Keith, blinked and sat up. Charles glanced at him and expounded.

'Lord Scoggie has – how many? – about half a dozen parishes in his gift, and someone told Thomas he might have a chance at one of them that's coming up soon.'

10

'A parish?' said George in disgust. 'What do you want one of those for? More trouble than it's worth, I'd have said. You should see our minister at Letho –'

'George,' said Charles with emphasis, and George shut his mouth.

'It was my only chance to meet Lord Scoggie. I have no family connexions and my father has no powerful friends, you know. All I can hope for is a bit of help from my tutors. Well, now I know where I stand with them. Apparently Peter Keith expressed some passing interest in the Church, and the Professor whisked him off to the meeting instead,' he said bitterly. 'When I turned up, the janitors at the door said they had no directions to admit me, and wouldn't let me in.'

'Well, you can't blame him for favouring his own son,' said George, not unreasonably.

'I wouldn't mind,' said Thomas, 'but Peter Keith wants to be something different every week. Last week he was going to take a midshipman's place in the navy, and next week he'll probably want to be an architect or a pig farmer or a pantomime dancer. I've been aiming for a parish since I sat my bursary exam at school, and I can't go back home without one. Everyone at school would say I had wasted the bursary, and my father would never apprentice me now. He'd say I had airs. It's not fair.'

'You're right, it's not,' agreed Charles, 'but it was almost inevitable something would go wrong. What made you ask Professor Keith in the first place? Urquhart or Shaw would have been much better.'

'But Keith asked me. And I thought, well, he's the man that will be able to approach someone as great as Lord Scoggie and have the nerve to introduce someone as low as me. Shaw would bumble away in the crowd and Urquhart would catch sight of some painting in the senate room and forget all about me.'

'If I were you,' said Charles, slowly, 'I should go back to the Senate room at the end of the meeting and see if Keith will introduce you then. If he thinks his son is likely to take the parish, he will think you no threat and not grudge it. He has a

11

high opinion of his own children, when they are not listening, anyway.'

Thomas looked unsure.

'Yes, do it,' said George, with enthusiasm. 'Only get rid of that awful old gown. Here, borrow Charles'.' He snatched Charles' gown off the back of the chair he was sitting in and flung it across at Thomas, where it knocked his wine glass and spilled the contents over Thomas' old gown. 'The deciding factor,' George declared with a laugh as Thomas looked down, dismayed. 'You must wear Charles' gown. It won't be much too long for you.'

'Very well, I'll do it,' said Thomas, standing up as if he was going to challenge George. 'I'll damn' well do it.'

'Sit down and have some more wine, first,' said Charles, cross with George and his insensitivity. Thomas barely survived on his bursary, and could not afford a new gown.

'No, I've had enough,' Thomas declared. 'Thank you, Charles. And if Professor Keith refuses … well, bad cess to the breed of him!'

'Do take my gown, though,' Charles said hurriedly. Thomas would have to learn to control his temper a little more if he was to become a minister: the anger in his eyes was alarming. 'And leave yours here: I'll ask Mrs. Walker if she can get the stain out.'

Thomas quickly changed gowns and left, clattering down the stairs. George stretched his legs out with a happy sigh.

'What a ridiculous man!' he exclaimed. 'A parish, and a run-down manse, and sermons to write every week, and having to set an example … oh, it's horrible!'

'Leave him alone, George,' said Charles. 'He has to earn a living, after all, and that is something you don't have to contemplate.'

'No, but maybe you do,' said George, then stopped abruptly. Charles turned to stare at him, as his brother turned slowly crimson.

Chapter Two

'Is that something you'd care to elaborate on?' Charles asked, sitting carefully on the bench. It was so low that his legs bent up at the knee like a spider's, but though he was uncomfortable he sat very still. George was useless at secrets.

'I daresay you were expecting me to be bringing up your allowance,' he said, not meeting Charles' eye.

'It had crossed my mind Father might send it with you.' He stopped, and stared at George. 'What – you mean he hasn't?'

'I mean he says he's not going to, either.'

'But ... why not?' Charles was bewildered. He knew his father was not exactly a supporter of what he termed 'excessive education', but he had thought that he would be allowed at least to finish his fourth year and try for his Master of Arts. He knew, too, that when he came to inherit Letho and the Edinburgh house and all his father's other concerns that there would be little call for Hebrew or natural philosophy, but like other young men sowing their wild oats or, like George, flinging money around on new boots and coats for visiting young ladies, he wanted to enjoy himself a little while he could, and he had thought that his father understood that much, at least.

'He says we have a perfectly good house at Letho, where you could at least hunt and shoot – not at this time of the year, I'm not sure why he said that – and another in Edinburgh, where you could be taking your place in society and meeting the right people, and he could see no good reason why you would choose to live in a hovel in St. Andrews just to read books, it wasn't natural.'

George was no mimic, but Charles could hear their father's voice behind his words even as George's voice grew more and more reluctant. Charles tried to take it in.

'But I have to pay my rent here: I have promised Mrs. Walker.'

'Father wants you to pack up and come home, at least for a while.'

13

'Won't he at least let me finish the term?' If he could finish the term, Charles might be able to give his father time to come round, and then persuade him to let him complete the year and his examinations.

'Oh, look, I don't know,' said George, crossly, but his tone was belied by the anxious look on his face. 'Lord knows, I don't want you to leave St. Andrews. I like visiting you up here, and you seem to be enjoying it – can't say it would appeal to me, but if it's your kind of thing … Anyway, I think you should come back to Letho with me and talk to him.'

'I might not be able to get leave of absence,' Charles objected.

'But if you're leaving anyway …'

'I'm not. I can't see why … What set him off? Why was he so cross?'

'I think it was the bill from the bookbinders.'

'But that should have come here. I pay that out of my allowance. I don't ask him for anything more.' Charles was less angry than desperate. His father could be very stubborn when the mood took him: it could be impossible to persuade him out of this humour. He sat for a long moment, wondering what he could do before his mind had really recovered fully from the shock of the news enough to reason clearly.

George took out his watch, and cleared his throat apologetically.

'Look,' he said, 'I should wash and change. So should you, if you're coming with me.'

'Coming with you where?' asked Charles, draining his glass and trying to shake his mind on to other things.

'To Professor Keith's. I want to visit his daughter, Alison.'

'Alison Keith? Why on earth?'

'Because she's an extremely fine young woman, and it is normally considered a pleasure for any man to sit with an extremely fine young woman on a bright spring afternoon and talk with her of this and that.'

Charles looked at his brother in amazement.

'You know what her father's like?'

14

'Oh, yes: but I also know he's at a Senate meeting, isn't he?'

'Yes, but – oh, well, I suppose I'll come, if only to keep an eye on you. George, you really have a taste for difficult women, you know that?'

George assumed a look intended to convey hurt dignity, and Charles gave an exasperated laugh as he headed back downstairs to ask Mrs. Walker for hot water.

The kitchens at the back of the house had a cold northern aspect not helped by the traditional duck-egg green walls, but as usual they were hot and busy. They were full to choking of the smell of soap and soda, and in the midst of the steam Mrs. Walker, a woman of the middle height and a red face, was exercising her not inconsiderable arm muscles in plunging sheets into hot water. She was helped by her daughter, both of them with their sleeves rolled up and their hair flat with sweat and steam, while their maid who did general work about the place scraped at a washboard in a small tub beside the blessedly open back door. The breeze, fresh outside, seemed however unusually reluctant to enter this netherworld of terrible industry, and the hot air surged from fire and laundry vats unmolested.

'Oh, Mr. Murray!' cried Mrs. Walker, seeing him at last. 'One moment, my dear: you have caught us just at a bad time. We'll just get this last one in to soak – steady now, Patience dear, and back a wee bit to the fire – that's lovely, and now a quick stir and make sure it's all under the water, my love.'

Patience Walker rolled her eyes a little, being of an age when she knew more about laundry and the life in which it occurred than her mother could ever teach her, but she set to willingly enough to stir up the sheets with an enormous paddle. Mrs. Walker, unaware of the eye-rolling, wiped her hands on a cloth and brushed at her apron before crossing the kitchen to Charles. Motherless from an early age, Charles was never entirely sure what the rules were in kitchens, and had instead imposed two on himself – if possible avoid, and if impossible, touch nothing. So far it had served him well.

'Now, Mr. Murray, dear, what is it?'

15

'I was looking for some hot water to wash with, Mrs. Walker, but I think I have chosen my time badly.'

'Och, no, not at all, dear. Katie's just put some fresh on to boil for the lace and we won't need it just yet, will we?' She looked round at her helpers, and Katie jumped up to fetch the water – less eager to please, Charles thought, than to be away from the finger-bruising washboard. She began to scoop water from a broad copper basin into a jug, and vanished briefly into clouds of thicker steam. Charles looked back at Mrs. Walker and noticed for the first time that her eyes were as red as her face. In addition, there was something a little different about her. She was wearing one of her two comfortable winter day dresses of dark grey wool with a little pattern of white in it, but the collar with its white starched inset looked somehow different. He could not put his finger on it: perhaps it was simply that the steam had taken out the starch.

'Are you going out, then, dear, that you're wanting a wash? Somewhere nice?'

'Oh,' said Charles, 'my brother George is come up from Letho unexpectedly, and we are to – meet a friend of his for tea.' He was not sure why he had chosen not to name Alison Keith: Patience had already glanced round at him and away again, and he felt oddly watched.

'That's lovely, dear.' Mrs. Walker looked across to where Katie, who was only about twelve, was still spooning hot water with slow concentration. 'Did you say your brother George was up?' She turned back suddenly with a strangely embarrassed expression on her face. 'From Letho? Perhaps –' she reddened, if anything, even more than she already had. 'Perhaps your father will have sent you something,' she finished, the words coming out in a lump like sweets all stuck together in a bag. She did not meet his eye, but then, in a second as Charles realised what she meant, it was his turn to blush.

'Oh, I am so sorry, Mrs. Walker – he has not yet sent me my allowance for the rent! Oh, dear,' he went on, fumbling for the words that would neither disgrace his father nor offend Mrs. Walker, and would at the same time not sound heartless. 'I hope to receive it any day ...' It was not quite a lie. 'Is – is

16

there a difficulty? I mean, has someone been ... only you look – upset.'

Patience Walker gave her mother a ferocious look, which Mrs. Walker ignored or did not see.

'Upset? No, no, dear, not at all. Oh, you mean my eyes? Well, that's the soda, my dear. See, Patience's and Katie's eyes are just as red!'

They were, too, he could see: it was quite true. Still, he thought, as he took the jug from little Katie with a smile, there was something about Mrs. Walker's manner, and something, in particular, about the way she fingered her strangely unfamiliar collar, that made Charles wonder if they were all only affected by the soda.

The cloth that Katie had given him with the jug was a thin one, and he hurried upstairs with it to where George had removed his coat and cravat and was waiting, passing the time by fingering the stunning boots he had pulled reverently out of his saddlebags on the floor. They were like horse chestnuts, leather burnished till it shone, buckles silver and bright without being too ornamental, and a soft white kid lining that simply cried out to be touched. No Fife cordiner had made these: George must have been down in Edinburgh, taking his place in society – wasn't that what their father had said? – and meeting the right people. An ungracious little though crept into Charles' mind: what was his bookbinding bill, compared with these glorious boots?

It was not something he wanted to raise at the moment, and as he set the jug of water down beside its basin he cast about for something else to talk about. George set the boots gently down on the chair he was vacating, and rolled up his shirt sleeves as he followed Charles into the bedchamber. With the two of them in it, it seemed even smaller than usual, with its heavy, dark furnishings and ornately-curtained bed. The little casement window looked out over the garden to the stable. George crossed to the washstand and poured the water out, and Charles, moving out of his way, caught sight of the book he had wanted to spend his peaceful afternoon reading. Bound in a smooth brown calf like the rest of his books, just as pleasing to him as the chestnut glow of George's boots, was his

17

copy of the book they were reading in class with Professor Urquhart. He caught it up and turned back to George, who had just swept half the soapy contents of the basin up over his head, soaking the thin carpet.

'Careful!' Charles exclaimed. 'The floor's thin, and the Walkers can't afford to replace their ceiling plaster downstairs.' The less so if I cannot pay my rent, he thought, but managed not to say. It was not George's fault, after all, if he happened to have the interests their father took seriously and Charles had the ones he did not understand.

George mumbled an apology through the towel with which he was vigorously rubbing his face and head, and emerged looking more cheerful than ever. He saw Charles holding the book.

'What's that, then? Lecture notes?'

'No, it's Suetonius' *Lives of the Caesars*. Have you ever read it?'

George shrugged.

'It sounds political. Is it political?' he asked, in the tone of one who boards a ship in the full expectation of seasickness. Charles laughed.

'In places.'

'Girls in it?' asked George.

'Not many,' Charles admitted. He thought that George would enjoy the book, all the same, but doubted that he would ever bring himself to read it. He sighed, and sat on the bed, undoing his neck cloth and pulling a fresh one from a drawer. The room was so small it was possible to reach almost anything one required from the bed, particularly if one was Charles' height.

'I've been reading a bit of poetry, myself, recently,' said George, his casual tone spoilt by the way he looked sideways at Charles to see his reaction.

'Poetry?' Charles was impressed. 'Whose?'

'Oh, a bit of Robert Fergusson,' George tossed off the name as if he had drunk with the fellow himself, 'and some Burns, of course. I like *Holy Willie's Prayer*, don't you?'

18

Charles had read some of Burns' work, but by no means all: modern verse could leave him cold. He made a face at George to tell him to continue.

'It's just a poem all said by Holy Willie himself, like a prayer, you know? I don't think the minister would care for it much. Holy Willie's a terrible old fellow, though, and he just gives himself away line by line. He's one of these ones – here, wait, I think I can remember a bit: 'Yet I am here a chosen sample To show Thy grace is great and ample', you know, thinking he's chosen and can do no wrong, you see? He's one of those predestined types. And all the time he's at it with the girls and cursing the Presbytery, and saying that if he looks good God's glory will be all the greater! Oh, it's a great laugh!'

Charles grinned: he had met the type himself a few times, and wondered how they could look themselves in the eye in a glass. But at the moment, he had more curious matters on his mind, and he thought they would not be unpleasant to George, either.

'So how long have you been taken by Alison Keith, then?'

George grew solemn again at the thought, trying to look older than his years. He was all of seventeen, Charles reflected: he would change his mind a few times yet, anyway.

'Well, it was the last time I was up, you know, in January, when it started snowing. Do you remember? We met her and her brother on the Scores, just as the snow was starting, whipping in from the sea like a burst pillow, and I held my hat out over her head as we escorted them home, and I caught an awful cold.' This act of extreme heroism on his own part seemed to have been enough in George's eyes to bind her to him for eternity, and his broad chest swelled with pride at the memory. 'I've never sneezed so much in my life, and Mrs. Chambers had to make me hot punch for a fortnight before the cough went. Miss Keith was wearing a brown velvet bonnet and a matching pelisse thing, and she looked like a heroine from a Gothic romance, pale and beautiful in the snow, with the snowflakes catching on her sleeves and her skirts.' He gave a sigh of considerable wistfulness: he had obviously been

19

practising. Charles hoped he had not been trying his hand at poetry himself.

'Her father is – not popular,' Charles amended. Professor Keith had never been particularly vindictive to him, saving his strength for the poor, the uninfluential, and the not over-bright.

'I'm sure there are lots of professors whom their students hate, but who are kind and loving husbands and parents.'

'Probably. I have a feeling that Professor Keith is rather more consistent in his behaviour, though. You know he sacked one of his maids for stealing a cravat-pin, though she was of impeccable character and the pin turned up stuck in the dining room carpet later the same day. He wouldn't take her back, either.'

'Maybe he had his reasons,' said George, blandly. 'How is it that so many maids seem to have impeccable characters after they are sacked?'

'This maid had one both before and after: she is the daughter of Ramsay Rickarton, the janitor at United College, whom we met earlier, a most honourable man, as you know, and there is no doubting her side of the story.'

George shrugged reluctantly, as one whose nature would be to believe him but whose feelings were not his own to command.

'He is a proud man, no doubt, and not anxious to admit his own mistakes. It shows he is human, anyway.'

Charles sighed, and finished tying his cravat. George was combing his damp hair with one hand and smoothing his eyebrows with the other. Charles tried not to laugh.

'Anyway, how did you come to be invited to tea by Mrs. Keith?' he asked.

'Oh, after I had recovered from my terrible cold,' George was constrained to refer to his heroic struggle once again, 'I wrote a note to Mrs. Keith to ask after Miss Keith and her brother and hope that they had taken no harm from their chilling, and she wrote me a very kind reply, and I took the liberty of sending some fruit from the hothouses at Letho, and she asked me to tea, and I asked if I might bring my brother, and she said yes. Quite a little flurry of correspondence, you know: she is a charming lady. One can see from whom Miss Keith has her own charms.'

'Is that something you said in one of your notes, then?' Charles asked sarcastically. George blushed.

'A little flattery goes a very great distance with mothers, and does no harm to the daughters, either,' he said, as though he had been expert for many years in the matter of seduction. Charles did laugh this time, and wondered where on earth George found his ideas.

As far as he himself was concerned, he was not particularly struck by the Gothic beauty of Alison Keith. She was certainly elegant, perhaps a little too thin, but pretty enough. There was that in her face, though, which, charmingly Gothic though it might have been, made Charles anxious. It was a nerviness, a spiritedness that was a little too wild to be a good sign of a stable character underneath. It reminded Charles of a horse his father had had some years before, sold to him as fine and indeed spirited. His father, liking a bit of a challenge in his horseflesh, had bought it readily, but had found that the beast was dangerously sensitive, springing wildly away at the slightest noise, and with no steadiness or staying power beneath to make it worth calming and training. He sold it again quickly, but the impression of the horse's blinking eyes and nervous muzzle had stayed with Charles and he seemed to see them again in the face of Alison Keith, though a less horse-like human it might be hard to find.

'Good heavens – is that the time?' cried George, catching sight of the little clock on the mantelpiece. 'We shall be late. What kind of impression will that create?'

They hurried down the stairs, George's boots winking like melted toffee in the dim light and his footsteps resounding hollowly. In the hall, not surprisingly, Mrs. Walker appeared suddenly, to see what the racket was. She was wafted towards them on a cloud of washing soda, and George involuntarily reeled back, trying not to let the smell attach to him.

'Oh! Charles, my dear, and my dear Mr. George: you look so splendid!' George smiled and made a tight little bow, edging towards the door and fresh air. 'Where can you two be off to, looking so fine, at this hour of the day?' Her voice was nervous still, hurried, as if she was trying to fill a certain time before something important she had to say.

'We are engaged to tea at Professor Keith's house, with Mrs. Keith and Miss Keith,' said George splendidly. Mrs. Walker visibly winced, so much so that Charles found he had put out a hand to support her in case she fainted.

'At Professor Keith's?' she repeated slowly, and as if seeing it for the first time she observed in detail all the glory of George's outfit, the brushed coat, the snow-pale breeches, the well-tended cravat, and the marvellous boots. She swallowed, a little too noisily.

'Mrs. Walker,' said Charles gently, 'please tell me what is the matter. If I can help at all …' He tailed away, sure that the only way he could help would be by paying his rent as soon as possible. She seemed to be trying to decide whether or not to say this, her mouth working as she stared at the floor. George edged again towards the front door, and Charles turned quickly to glare at him before looking back to Mrs. Walker. She drew a long breath.

'It was only,' she said quietly, 'that I have lost my brooch – you know, the one I always wear, here?' She pointed to her collar, and at last Murray realised what he had failed to miss earlier. She always wore a fine miniature at her throat of a clergyman, bewigged in the style of twenty years before, framed in old gold, and it was not there. 'It is a beautiful thing, and of some value in money, but it is of my dear late husband, you know, and no money could replace it.' She seemed to hear a noise from the kitchens, gave a little gasp, and went on. 'If you should see it – in the gutter, perhaps, when you are walking along the street, or perhaps in the house somewhere – you will know it, Charles dear, won't you, and will pick it up for me?'

There was something in her eyes, when she said this, that gave Charles the impression that she was trying to tell him more than she was saying, and that she was praying that he would understand. He frowned for a moment, and then gave her a little nod, trying to reassure her without really knowing if he could.

'If we find it, we shall make sure it is returned to you,' he said firmly, sure he could at least promise that. She smiled a little distantly, and at that moment Patience emerged quickly from the kitchens.

'Mother, here you are!' she said. 'I wondered what you had found out here to detain you so long.' She turned and curtseyed to George and Charles. 'Gentlemen,' she said, quite self-possessed. George and Charles bowed back.

'Now, if you will excuse us,' said George, his hand already on the door handle, 'we are already late, Charles. Ladies,' he finished, bowing again, and stepped grandly out of the doorway. Charles was left to bid mother and daughter a slightly apologetic farewell, before hurrying to catch up with his little brother.

Chapter Three

The customs of the past had changed considerably in St. Andrews. Once all those associated with the University, staff and students alike, had lived in the colleges of St. Salvator, St. Leonard and St. Mary, but now St. Salvator and St. Leonard had united and the St. Leonard's buildings were abandoned near the Cathedral. St. Salvator's premises were hardly less ramshackle, but were still in use on the United College site in North Street. Only fifty years ago, things had been so bad at the university and relations with the townspeople had deteriorated so much that there was talk of moving the whole affair to Perth and trying again, but the usual St. Andrean apathy had overcome, and here they still were. Married professors had probably been the first to eschew the accommodation provided by the colleges, but now few lived in the old dilapidated rooms at all.

Professor Keith had had every excuse to leave. His house, near the ruins of the Castle on the Scores Walk, was large, but friendly and rambling in appearance. It was understood in the university that he had acquired his property from his wife's family, and the house was seen as evidence of this, since it was assumed by all the students that nothing which had originated with the dreaded Keith would have appeared in the least bit friendly, or indeed rambling. The house was perhaps a couple of hundred years old, but with rooms attached whimsically here and there as required or desired, built of bumbling great balls of sandstone or little bits and pieces with more mortar than stone, roofed at odd angles with stone or slate or tile and with every shape and fashion of window or door. The whole was well-maintained, however: a type of unity had been forced on it by the application of bright white paint to every inch of woodwork and the creepers that seem irresistibly drawn to such a building were kept clipped and neat, and were just now showing the unbelievably fresh green of their new leaves. The gravel to the front door was swept and smooth behind a stern gate – a sign, no doubt, of Professor Keith's governance – and it seemed almost a crime to step on it. George, however, who had stalked through the humble streets of St. Andrews in the full confidence that his outfit was infinitely superior to everyone else's in the burgh, now strode ahead with some determination, the sunlight flashing off the calves of his boots, and Charles had to step up to catch up with him. They arrived together at the low, shiny white, front door, where George tugged the doorbell with the air of one who is expected. A maid came and collected their cards – probably the same one who would have opened the curtains to find the dead crow outside the window, Charles thought – and in a moment, true to George's expectations, they were ushered into a small, sunny parlour at the back of the house, overlooking a pretty garden within old sandstone walls. Already in the parlour were Mrs. Keith and her daughter, who seemed surprisingly delighted to see them. Charles wondered if they really considered George to be such a suitable match for Miss Alison that they were keen to snare him even at his young age: all modesty aside, George was a younger son, and it was Charles who might have expected to be considered the more promising candidate.

Mrs. Keith was a thin but neatly made woman of just an age to have grown-up children. Her hair still showed a little of its original chestnut in the curls at the front of her cap, though it was threaded through and through with grey till the effect was that of a dappled horse, and no less attractive for that, Charles thought. She wore, with good taste, a deep blue gown with Egyptian trimmings, neither too humble for her station nor too flamboyant for her age, though she had a penchant for rings, chiefly with cabochon stones, which cluttered her long fingers. Miss Keith, making a pretty curtsey just now to George, was also thin, but took more after her father for looks: he was a handsome man, whatever his faults, and it had done her no harm. She had light brown hair with an almost reddish hint to it and eyes of a remarkable dark blue, flecked like the sea at dusk as if the stars had risen to reflect themselves in it. They laughed easily, and her mouth, if a little wide, joined in to complete the effect. Charles glanced quickly at his brother: it was clear straightaway that George was smitten.

'Sit, do,' Mrs. Keith was saying, gesturing to several appropriate chairs as if to give them a choice. 'We are just at our embroidery here, as you see. I shall call for tea at once, I think, don't you, Alison? For sometimes the maid can be slow, or the kitchen fire won't draw properly for the water, and then we could be waiting an age ...' She looked slightly helplessly at her daughter, who obediently rose and pulled the bell. Charles and George selected two of the offered chairs and sat when she had returned to her seat, and George slid his chair over closer to Alison Keith so that he could more easily admire her embroidery – at least, that is what he said he was admiring.

'An exquisite pattern,' he remarked, almost as if he knew what he was talking about, 'and marvellously well worked. You must have extraordinary eyesight to work such fine stitches,' he carried on, taking the opportunity to check her eyesight personally by gazing into the flecked blue for a few significant seconds. Charles groaned inwardly. He had no wish whatsoever to be here, but he knew his place: talk to the mother, and allow George his way with the daughter. In his turn he shuffled a little closer to Mrs. Keith, and gave her a bright, affable smile which felt painfully artificial on his lips but, he hoped, impressed his professor's wife.

'And how are you, Mrs. Keith?' he asked, contriving to make it sound like the opening to a long conversation.

'Oh, passing well, passing well, thank you very much, Mr. Murray,' she replied rapidly. 'We have been busy for part of the morning with the spring pruning in the garden, and with checking over the summer sheets and pillowcases, but you can't want to know about all that, can you? You want to know about Cicero and Plato and natural philosophy and all kinds of excitement!'

Charles laughed and admitted that Cicero was indeed more his forte than summer sheets and pillowcases.

'I read them all, you know, when I was a girl, but it was so long ago!' she added, with a wistful smile. 'I think I could barely construe a sentence now.'

'Oh, you read them in the original languages?' Charles said, trying not to sound too surprised.

'Oh, indeed I did. My dear father was my dear husband's predecessor here, you know, and as I was his only child he taught me a very great deal. We were close, you know, and he

26

loved to teach, and I loved to learn ... I was not so interested in summer sheets and pillowcases then, either, I assure you!'

'But no doubt it has helped you in the education of your own children, and in helping Professor Keith with his work,' Charles said, because she seemed so sad at her lost learning.

'Oh, my dear husband is a different kind of professor altogether!' She gave a little nervous laugh, pleating the folds of her skirt between her cabochoned fingers. 'Peter, of course, has attended classes, but Alison – well, perhaps fashions have changed, but it seems that these days girls are not so encouraged to use their minds ... I do not know. Perhaps it is all a waste of our time, but I did enjoy it so ...' She tailed away, her gaze wandering out into the garden. Charles glanced round the parlour, wondering what to say. There were, he noticed, no books whatsoever in the room: instead the walls were covered with amateur drawings and paintings and every table top had its own embroidered cover.

'The tea will be ages, Mama,' said Alison suddenly, breaking out of George's conversation. 'Shall we walk for a little in the garden? It seems such a lovely day to be sitting indoors.' She flashed a smile at Charles, and he was quite happy to agree.

'Well, if you really think ... I don't want to put Barbara out if she brings the tea in and finds we are outside, dear.'

'If she find we are outside she will come and call us, Mama,' said Alison quickly. 'Let us go out, even if it is only for a few moments.' She skipped across to the french doors and opened them, stepping out on to a little terrace and breathing in the fresh spring air.

'Oh, your shawl, Alison, dear!' cried Mrs. Keith, seizing her own as if the breeze was wintry. George, keen to be attentive, caught up Alison's own shawl, silky and rose-sprinkled, from the back of her chair and hurried after her, leaving Charles to organize Mrs. Keith in a swathe of paisley and encourage her to brave the alarming outdoors.

Outside Alison and George were waiting for them on the little terrace, though Charles thought George looked as if he would rather have established some distance between himself and Alison and the others: the smile on his face was a little fixed. Charles offered his arm to Mrs. Keith who took it delicately, as though she was a bird perching there. They led the way down two or three uneven stone steps on to a path along the lawn, where it lay between waiting fruit trees and impatient daffodils, showing the way to a small grove with a summerhouse by the high garden wall.

'The wall protects us, you see,' Mrs. Keith explained to Charles, 'and it means we can grow a good deal despite the proximity of the sea.'

'Let us show them the summerhouse, Mama,' called Alison from behind them.

'My dear, I fear it would be damp,' Mrs. Keith stopped and turned back to her.

'No, not to sit down, Mama. I want to show them the view.'

'Oh, very well, Alison dear.' She gave an anxious little sigh. 'Come along, Mr. Murray,' she added, leading Charles gently towards the grove.

It was of yew trees, so dark they were almost black against the blue of the sky beyond the wall, and around them a few crows circled, cawing at the seagulls high above them. As they neared it, Charles could see one or two tiny red berries left on the trees, battered by the winter storms but seeming to shine against the darkness like little lanterns showing the way to the summerhouse. In the midst of the grove, it was of stone, the same creamy sandstone as the garden wall, and had a wide empty doorway and two windows facing towards the garden. Inside, however, it was not dark as Charles had expected, and after he had ushered Mrs. Keith in before him he followed to find a large, unglazed, window in the facing wall, high up but accessible by a broad, shallow staircase. She guided him up to the top of the steps and he found he had to stoop a little to look out at a vista of the sea, laid out flat in front of him, sprinkled with gulls and wavelets, just beyond a little green headland. Fishing boats, nets spread, were scattered in the bay, with the ruins of the Castle golden brown on the headland just to his left.

'What a lovely surprise!' he remarked. As he turned, Alison and his brother arrived in the doorway. 'George, come and see this: a remarkable construction.' George scrambled up beside him, and stood carefully, avoiding touching the gritty stone window frame with his elegant gloves.

'It is very old, isn't it, Mama?' said Alison, pleased with the effect. 'We think it might have been some kind of watchtower, perhaps with a light for guiding the ships.'

'It makes a superb summerhouse,' George said, 'whatever its original use.' He turned to beam at Alison.

'It is rather draughty when the wind is in the wrong direction,' Mrs. Keith said mildly. 'Alison, dear, we must remember to have the furniture in here scrubbed before the summer.'

'It is not too bad, Mama,' Alison objected, running a gloved finger along the top of a white wirework chair, slightly green from the damp.

'It is not fit to sit on, dear,' said her mother.

'Here,' said Charles, dragging himself away from the seaward window, 'Miss Keith, do you wish to see the lovely view you brought us here to appreciate?' He stepped back down to the floor level and handed her up the steps to stand between George and her mother. Looking back at the entrance, he saw how well the garden had been constructed to be appreciated from this angle, with the dark frame of the yews around the pretty fruit trees, borders and lawns beyond, finishing with the back of the house with its neat creepers and fresh white paint. He tried hard to picture a domesticated Professor Keith resting in this pleasant spot, contemplating the planting of a new rose, perhaps, or thoughtful over a book, in quiet contentment alone or with his family about him, and failed utterly. Professor Keith and happy quietude did not fit together, and the struggle was too much for him.

'We had better return to the house, Alison dear, before we all catch a chill,' said Mrs. Keith, unable to descend from the steps until her daughter had done so and moved out of the way. Alison looked expectantly to Charles, who felt obliged to put an arm out for her to steady her, and she skipped down the steps to him and took it properly. George was left to help her mother, the smile on his face slightly stiffer than it had been before. Charles was quite prepared to exchange partners with him when they were all outside again, but Alison had his arm held quite determinedly and smiled up at him.

'I should not like to neglect one brother in favour of the other,' she said softly, softly enough, Charles prayed, that George had not heard. He smiled back at her noncommittally, and guided her back towards the lawns and the path. George followed behind with Mrs. Keith, virtually on Charles' heels, and intent on joining in with any conversation Charles and Alison started, which suited Charles' own purposes very well. Alison, however, seemed to feel differently.

'Oh, Mr. Murray,' she exclaimed as they reached the path, smiling up at him again – her mouth was so wide it seemed disturbingly like a split across her face, 'there is something I would show you that we found this morning. I would show it to Mr. George Murray,' she said, combining formality and flirtation in a glance at George, 'but it is a muddy path and his boots are far too fine to be spoiled by it. Come, Mr. Murray – we shall be back in a moment, Mama.'

The look on George's face was a picture. Alison, seizing Charles' arm near the wrist, like a nurse with a disobedient child, turned swiftly and had him whisked away behind a hedge before either he or George could protest. The path was indeed muddy, and slippery, and it took all Charles' concentration not to slip in his old boots: his were definitely not far too fine to be spoiled, but they would take a good deal of polishing after this to return them even to their usual condition. Alison, relinquishing his arm as the path was also narrow, tugged her skirts up above her ankles, keeping the hems fairly clean while allowing him a glimpse of calf which was, to be honest, too thin to be appealing. He decided not to mention it to George.

After scurrying along for a few minutes they were nearly at the gate to the kitchen garden, and Alison stopped abruptly so that Charles had to slither a little to regain his balance.

'Here we are,' she said brightly, and pointed to a freshly clipped bush that even Charles, with his somewhat limited horticultural expertise, could identify as a rose. One of its stems had been left long, however, presumably because of the burden it bore: an early, perfect, yellow rose, golden in its centre, its petal tips blushing pink in the warm spring sunshine. 'Isn't it lovely? We found it this morning when we were pruning: the first of the season.'

'Very fine,' said Charles. 'George would indeed have appreciated it: he is very fond of roses.' It was a lie, but a valiant one. Alison smiled.

'It is even scented. Try it.' She took a quick breath of the scent herself, and then tilted the flower towards Charles, letting him inhale. The fragrance was heavy, too heavy for the season: it looked forward to long summer days, heat and dust, languor, fatigue. This bright spring afternoon was too crisp for it, too clean and new. He looked away, shaking his head to clear it, and saw signs of fresh digging beneath the bushes.

'Have you been trying to move the bush nearer to the house, then, where the flowers can be appreciated?' he asked.

'What?' She looked down at the soil at which he was pointing. 'No, no: it is not a good time of year to move roses, anyway. No, I was planting lily of the valley. Mama loves that scent, too, and the flowers are so pretty and delicate. See, the leaves are just bursting out of the bulbs.' She crouched down to point them out to him, little green blades slicing through the soil. 'It's terribly poisonous, though, you know. One has to be very careful.'

'Alison, dear!' came her mother's voice, from somewhere beyond the hedge. 'Come along, my dear, and bring Mr. Murray in: you will both catch chills, and I am sure the tea will be ready at any minute.'

'Coming, Mama,' Alison called obediently, springing up and squeezing past Charles to lead him back the way they had come. Again there were the flashes of undesirable calf, and again he slithered and slipped his way along, trying not to splash her. They regained the lawns at last, where Charles met his brother's eye with a look of complete innocence, in which George clearly did not believe. He ran his gaze down Charles from trencher to gloves to filthy boots, and stared at the last items with marked disgust. His own boots were still perfect.

'I've been showing Mr. George the lovely daffodils, dear,' said Mrs. Keith to her daughter, waving vaguely at the long strappy leaves under the fruit trees. 'He says he's very interested in gardening.'

'That's nice, Mama,' said Alison. 'I showed Mr. Murray the rose we found this morning. It's still perfect.' George had somehow come adrift from Mrs. Keith, in their perusal of the daffodils, and Alison now took possession of him once again, leaving her mother to reattach herself to Charles, a thin little bird returning to her perch. Despite her previous warnings about chills, Mrs. Keith no longer seemed disposed to hurry, and caused them to lag behind a little as Alison and George headed up the garden in front of them. If this was a scheme to leave them on their own for a little, it barely succeeded, as at that moment the maid, Barbara, appeared at the french doors and bobbed a little curtsey to catch Mrs. Keith's attention.

'Oh, tea!' said Mrs. Keith, quite surprised, and immediately sped up, tripping along beside Charles' long-legged stride.

Tea was indeed served, along with some excellent breads and cakes, making Charles feel that the afternoon had not been entirely wasted. They sat around the tea table evenly spaced, so that conversation was now general, rather than divided, and Charles realised he had been remiss in one thing.

'And how is Peter?' he asked as soon as he could.

'Oh, he is very well!' said Mrs. Keith, much gratified. 'He is taking some responsibility now for his father's properties and has been touring some of them this afternoon – seeing what needs repair and who needs help, you know.' She made it sound like a charitable concern, but Charles knew very well that the Keith estate was run very much on business lines. His knowledge was first hand: Mrs. Walker, his landlady, leased her house from Professor Keith, and had been heard to complain – gently, for it was not generally her way – of his impatience with rent and his slowness when it came to repairs. 'It is good to see him happily employed, for you know he has spent some time in trying to find what path in life he would like to follow. He will be sorry to have missed you, though.'

Charles was also sorry to have missed Peter, though he found Peter unsettling. The Professor's son, a year older than Charles, had graduated MA the year before but even before

32

that had flitted from scheme to scheme, from intentions of the army, of the church, of the law, of architecture … Some of the drawings on the parlour wall were his, and he had thought for a while of devoting himself entirely to art, studying with Professor Urquhart, the Humanity professor, for a month or two before the next idea came along. He could flit from excitement to misery in a few seconds, and was exhausting company, but he could be entertaining when he was in the grip of his latest enthusiasm, and keen to impart interesting information. His relations with his father were unpredictable, to say the least: they veered wildly from warm affection to stony silence and back in the course of a month, sometimes of a week, but he was always fond of his mother, though the pair of them could work each other up into a fit of nerves seldom paralleled.

'And does he find that the property takes up much of his time?' Charles asked politely.

'Our father has a very good factor for his estate,' George added with unnecessary grandeur, and Charles kicked him lightly under the table. He reckoned that the Senate meeting would be over by now, and he had no wish to prolong their visit much if Professor Keith reappeared.

'It is not full employment,' Mrs. Keith admitted. 'He still has time to pursue his other interests – and he is still contemplating returning to his studies and reading for the Bar in Edinburgh.'

'The profession would suit him, I think,' said Charles, who had thought so the last time Peter had contemplated it. His nerviness would have some dramatic impact there, and he would certainly commit himself body and soul to his cases – if that was necessarily a good thing. How he would cope with losing a case was another matter.

'I think so, but I should not want him so far away from us,' Mrs. Keith said sadly.

'What do you think your brother should do, Miss Keith?' asked George.

'Oh! Whatever makes him truly happy, of course,' she said, as if everyone had that choice. 'He is an artist at heart, you know, and needs to be where there is beauty. I do not think that the lawcourts would be the best place for him. He thought of architecture, and I think he would be better there. But he must decide for himself, you know.'

'Very wisely said,' agreed George solemnly, as if he had any idea himself what he was going to do with his life. Charles, with a view to the future financial security of Letho, hoped privately that George's existence would not revolve solely around the purchase of fine outfits and perfect boots. If it was going to, they would have to find him a richer wife than Alison Keith.

He had just bitten into a slice of moist gingerbread when there came a crash from the hall. He and George leapt up, and even the ladies pushed their chairs back in alarm. Mrs. Keith eyed the open french door as if assessing it as an escape route. Then the ladies heard a voice which seemed to relieve them, and in a moment Peter Keith himself burst into the parlour, flinging the door back on its hinges. He looked directly at his mother and sister, seeming not to see the Murrays, and casting his hat down hard on the sofa he cried:

'I'll kill him!'

Chapter Four

'Obstructive, self-serving, obnoxious toad,' Professor Urquhart remarked, without emphasis. 'Such gentlemen as Professor Keith make our fine old repositories of erudition what they are. We should be grateful.' He unlaced one fine, long hand from his teacup, and proferred it to Ramsay Rickarton to be refilled. Ramsay, on whose livery there were still minute traces of his grand-daughter's muddy progress, wore a large white apron and stood guard over the silver tea urn. On its stand it was nearly his own height, the gift of a grateful graduate, and it towered over little Professor Shaw at Professor Urquhart's side. Professor Shaw, mildly frog-like and completely aimiable, smiled at Ramsay and gently propelled Christopher Urquhart further down the Senate room where his analyses might be less audible. Urquhart, drifting like the breeze through a willow grove, allowed himself to be thus manoeuvred but kept talking. 'I mean to say, what is the University beside him? A mere nothing, four centuries of sheer frivolity and a few cramped buildings of little current worth. Whereas he –'

'Yes, yes, quite so,' said little Professor Shaw hurriedly. The room was still busy, and he had no wish for Urquhart to put himself in the way of any trouble. By moving in this direction, therefore, he had managed to distance both of them from the Principal, the Chancellor, and the mighty Professor Keith, who had taken their tea to the other end of the room. There there was a tray of bread and cakes on the table that had so recently been thumped so hard by certain disputants that the heavy minute book had leapt in its place. The Principal seemed inclined to continue the dispute, and Professor Keith showed no signs of yielding. Professor Shaw shuddered slightly at the idea of conflict, and wondered if staying in his parish would have been any easier. It had seemed such a pleasant idea, when it was offered to him, to return to his alma mater as Professor of Moral Philosophy, leaving behind the bickerings of the Kirk Session and the efforts of the parish matrons to provide him with a series of alarming candidates to be his wife. He had taken the opportunity of the move to marry instead his young cook, presenting her to the University as a *fait accompli*, and the couple lived in gentle obscurity by the mill lade in the town. Lectures were, with him, kindly affairs, the students for the most part his beloved sons, examinations a matter of tact and diplomacy. Senate meetings, however, broke into the pleasant pattern of his life, and left him with an uncomfortably brisk heartbeat and a spate of burning indigestion that bore no relation to his wife's excellent cooking.

Christopher Urquhart, Professor of Humanity, who taught some of the less Christian Latin with marked glee, despised Senate disputes with a showy carelessness that alarmed Professor Shaw. There were few, however high their station, about whom Urquhart would not make his feelings quite clear, even if it was only by a twitch of his eyebrows or a flickering gesture from those long, white fingers.

A few others, not strictly on the Senate, had attended the meeting, but of those only one or two had had the nerve, or the level of desperation to impress, to remain. One of course was Lord Scoggie, an honoured guest, whom the tactful Chancellor had drawn away from Professor Keith and the Principal.

'Discussing the portraits of old principals, I see,' remarked Urquhart, a little too loudly in his thinly sliced voice. 'I hope the Chancellor is not expecting him to be impressed: they are without exception despicable.'

Professor Shaw smiled nervously and swallowed too large a mouthful of tea. He continued to look around the room. Peter Keith, the Professor's son, had left immediately after the meeting – one of his quarrels with his father again, Shaw supposed. He was an edgy young man. Allan Bonar was still here: as assistant to Professor Keith and as his elected successor he had the confidence to remain and circulate with the others. How much longer that would be the case was anyone's guess. Professor Keith had hinted, during the course of the meeting, that the only way of persuading him to let to the University the lands it wanted would be to relieve him of Allan Bonar altogether. Shaw was privately astonished that the pair had worked together for as long as they had: Bonar was a pale young man with lank dark hair and the kind of eyes that saw clearly past what you were saying. Professor Shaw was sure

36

that Allan Bonar considered him a complete fraud: a country minister here as a professor! But how his strong personality had not previously clashed with Keith's own arrogance was beyond Shaw to understand.

'I hope this is a nice, peaceful corner,' came a voice, and Shaw turned with pleasure to find Mungo Dalzell standing nearby.

'I hope so, too,' he agreed heartily, 'but in any case you are very welcome to it.'

'Aye, if you can bear to stay in the same room at all,' added Urquhart, though he showed no signs of leaving it himself. Mungo smiled politely, and stepped forward to form a little circle with them, fortifying them against the rest of the room. He checked to see that everyone had enough tea. He was of slightly less than the middle height, with a calm, almost self-satisfied appearance, a smooth face, and a neatness of clothing which Professor Shaw rather envied. Though he strictly abstained from alcoholic liquor, he was a frequent appreciator of Mrs. Shaw's cooking and would sit contentedly in their little house long into the night in friendly debate of scholarship or politics, and Professor Shaw found him more comfortable company than any of his other colleagues.

'And how are matters Hebraical?' asked Professor Urquhart languidly, his gaze flickering between Mungo Dalzell, the Chancellor and Lord Scoggie, and the Principal and Professor Keith.

'They're no too bad, thank you, Professor,' Mungo Dalzell replied with a smile. There was currently no Professor of Hebrew: the work but not the honour had devolved upon Mungo, who had accepted it without rancour. Such was the way of things that he would probably find he was still doing it at his death. 'There has been a little more interest in the modern languages, too: I find I have a number of enthusiastic students for German and Italian.'

Professor Urquhart looked down his thin nose, his mouth twitching expressively.

'Modern, indeed,' he said. 'I'm not sure how you can thole it, when you have Hebrew and Latin to compare them with.'

37

Mungo Dalzell smiled.

'To love the parents is often to love the children, I find. Don't you?'

Urquhart's reply, which would no doubt have had something witty to do with barrenness or celibacy, was cut short by the arrival, in his well-mannered circulation, of Allan Bonar, Assistant in Natural Philosophy.

'Good afternoon, gentlemen,' said Bonar. His voice was thin and low, and Professor Shaw always had difficulty in hearing him. He wondered how his students ever managed to follow his lectures.

'Good afternoon, Bonar,' said Mungo Dalzell with a welcoming smile, and Professor Urquhart nodded, pausing for a moment in his study of the room to take in Allan Bonar's long black form and considered movements. Bonar's sharp gaze met his and Urquhart looked away quickly. Shaw wondered what to say, his mind entirely taken up now with Professor Keith's unfriendly efforts to rid himself of this ambitious assistant. He knew that he would find himself broaching the subject, however much he did not wish to, and therefore found himself reluctant to open his mouth at all. He forced his lips into a friendly, harmless smile, and tried to forget all about it, then found himself spilling his tea as he tried to smile and sip at the same time.

'Oh, dear,' he ventured, looking down at the drips on his gown. Urquhart offered him a handkerchief with a flourish, and Mungo Dalzell, taking it discreetly when Shaw seemed not to notice it, dabbed the drips away before they soaked in. Allan Bonar looked away.

Order was soon established, and Mungo Dalzell had cheerfully refilled Professor Shaw's teacup – politely not noticing the small form of Sybie inadequately concealed behind a door curtain next to Ramsay Rickarton and his tea urn. Allan Bonar had started a quiet little conversation with Urquhart concerning the inarguable merits of Latin. If Professor Shaw had been a little less innocent himself, he might have assumed that Allan Bonar was trying to reinforce his friendships: since he had been elected by the Senate as Professor Keith's assistant and successor, it would be difficult

38

for Keith to be rid of him, particularly if Bonar had plenty of supporters amongst the Senate members. Unfortunately, he was only halfway into his efforts when there was a billowing of gowns, like the Devil arriving in a fairy tale, and in a flash Professor Keith was amongst them. Professor Shaw almost fancied he could smell the brimstone.

'Professor Shaw!' Keith greeted him specifically, and Shaw's heart sank.

'Y – yes, Professor Keith?'

'We must have a word. I have already mentioned the subject to Mungo Dalzell here. It is a question which affects two students we both teach: a question of plagiarism.'

'Oh.' The others had gone quiet: Professor Shaw felt almost as if he were under accusation himself.

'The pair were set to do a short dissertation, in written form. A paragraph in the middle of the piece was almost identical in each one. Worse still, they had each copied it from a similar dissertation submitted by another boy, who doubtless allowed them to borrow his work for the purpose.'

'Collusion *and* plagiarism – oh, dear, oh, dear,' said Professor Shaw nervously.

'Moreover, they had not even copied it accurately,' Professor Keith went on, building himself up grandly. 'They had failed to include a crucial negative, which, when omitted, rendered the whole paragraph senseless.'

'Collusion, plagiarism and stupidity,' commented Christopher Urquhart. 'My, oh my. Are we sure that was all? No fire-setting on University property, for example?' He smiled sweetly, even in the face of Professor Keith's awful frown.

'I should not be in the least surprised,' he growled. 'We are talking about Skene, Irving and Fisher.'

'Oh, I see,' said Professor Shaw in bewilderment. 'Oh, dear.'

'Boxie, Picket and Rab,' added Mungo Dalzell quickly, seeing that Professor Shaw had no idea who these mere surnames were. Professor Shaw smiled his gratitude, but not for long.

39

'You call these boys by their pet names?' Professor Keith sneered.

'I like to get to know them,' said Professor Shaw, very quietly indeed.

'Get to know them?' Keith was a good deal louder, and the Principal and Lord Scoggie had turned to look. 'No wonder there is no discipline in the place! Plagiarism? I should be grateful not to have been murdered in my bed!'

'Yet,' added Professor Urquhart irresistibly, but covered it with a cough.

'How anyone,' Professor Keith went on oblivious, eyes only on Professor Shaw's beetroot face, 'could imagine that a country minister would find himself qualified to teach in a University is only slightly more surprising than that the minister himself should think such an elevation either reasonable or suitable.'

At this, Professor Shaw bolted, but found himself held by long, strong hands.

'No, Professor Shaw,' said Urquhart firmly, 'I feel quite strongly that if anyone is to leave our happy little circle, it should really be Professor Keith here. After all, at least Professor Shaw manages to deter his students from plagiarising.'

Professor Shaw struggled a little, not looking up, through hot, embarrassed tears, at the basilisk match going on above his head. He had had many painful moments in his life, but he had a strong feeling that even in retrospect this one would stand out.

'Ah, Professor Urquhart,' Keith was saying now, a nasty little smile on his face. 'Perhaps more qualified to be here in the first place, teaching your naughty Latin books, eh? But how much longer would you be allowed to teach the darling lads, eh? If their parents knew – oh, if their fathers knew the half of it! In fact, now I come to think of it,' he added, studying Urquhart's white face with pleasure, 'I'm surprised you don't prefer a little Greek ...'

'You disgust me, Keith,' Urquhart spat. 'What would you know about the boys? You wouldn't sully your fine gowns with being in the same room as them! Here, you have an assistant, forsooth! Who did you ever hear needed an assistant, unless he was sick or decrepit? But the boys are better off without you, anyway – after all, look at how your own son has turned out!'

Just at that moment, there was a crash at the door. They all turned, half-expecting to see Peter Keith stride into the room. Instead, tripping over his own gown-tails, was a rough-looking student in the scarlet of an undergraduate.

'It's Thomas Seaton,' said Mungo Dalzell in surprise. 'What on earth is he doing here?'

Allan Bonar glanced quickly at Professor Keith, but the professor did not meet his eye. Instead he was looking, lips curling in amusement, at Thomas, whose patched and shiny clothes looked worse than usual beneath the bright, fresh wool of his gown – except that he had managed to trail the over-long gown in the mud and it was starting to look more like his own.

'More to the point, where on earth did that peasant find a new gown?' asked Keith, at his usual volume. 'He's one of yours, isn't he, Professor Shaw?'

The little professor sniffed hard and wiped his eyes on his cuff, then nodded. He liked Thomas: the boy reminded him of himself at the same age, though a little more grumpy. He wished him a peaceful parish, with a moderate stipend, and would probably draw him aside one day to warn him against accepting tempting offers from his old University. Greeks bearing gifts, something like that, he would say – then he thought of the quarrel between Keith and Urquhart, and sobbed again suddenly.

Meanwhile, Thomas was standing where he had stopped, a few feet from the door, and was looking about him, frowning with determination. In a second, he had caught sight of Professor Keith, and was heading towards their group, head down and neck out as though he would have to fight his way through the hosts of Midian with his bare fists. Keith's smile turned to a frown of annoyance, and his hands twitched at the edges of his gown as if he were preparing to make a grand exit. But Thomas, red and solid, blocked any path he might have thought of taking.

41

'Sir,' he said, without preamble, 'you offered to present me to my Lord Scoggie. I should be very grateful if you would do that now.'

It was clearly rehearsed: Professor Shaw, whose gaze was still mostly directed downwards, saw that Thomas' boots were sandy, and had a sudden vision of him pacing the sands beneath the Castle, choosing and practising his words – and biting his nails, too, if Shaw was any judge.

'You would be grateful if I were to present you to Lord Scoggie, would you?' asked Professor Keith, his tone dangerously mild.

'Yes, sir. You offered, sir.'

'And you have the effrontery to remind me, have you?' asked Keith, still calm. Thomas was slow to take this in: his neck was still belligerent with purpose.

'You offered, sir,' he repeated.

'And if I had the courtesy to offer,' said Professor Keith, his voice growing effortlessly louder, like an approaching river-wave, 'perhaps I had the right to expect you to have the courtesy to arrive at the appointed time?'

Thomas stopped: hit by the wave, he lost his breath and gasped for a second.

'But sir,' he went on again, with a bravery that shocked Professor Shaw, 'I *was* here. I was here on time – I waited for half an hour before. The – the janitors would not let me in.'

'And is that any wonder,' said Professor Keith, 'when you arrive looking like that? Like a pleuchie in his rich master's hand-me-downs? Look at yourself, man: you're a disgrace!'

'They said –' began Thomas, but Professor Keith had had enough of this easy target. He started to move off, Thomas turning to run alongside him. 'They said you didn't want me, that Peter – oh!'

There was a sudden tumble of scarlet wool, and a devastating crash. Professor Keith drew quickly back, holding his gown tails away from the heap on the floor, while Professor Shaw and Mungo Dalzell hurried forward in concern. Thomas, in his rush, had finally tripped over his borrowed gown and had

42

fallen, bringing the colossal silver tea urn down on to the tray of cups and saucers on his way.

'I cannot imagine,' said Professor Keith, enunciating into the silence with extreme distaste, 'what earthly use you think you could be to my Lord Scoggie. You're a shabby, shoddy, useless lump of earth. And just remember, lad: *I* did not invite you to make this disgrace of yourself.'

With that, Keith turned and stalked off to where the Principal was standing still talking to Lord Scoggie. Ramsay Rickarton shook himself out of the shock he had had, and pulled the tea urn and its stand back up out of the wreckage, inspecting it for dents. Mungo Dalzell and Professor Shaw helped Thomas into a sitting position, plucking broken crockery from his hair and clothes, trying to hold one scalding tea-soaked sleeve of his gown away from his arm. Thomas' face was dripping with blood and milk, a pale pink mixture that was starting to congeal about his collar. He seemed to be mumbling something, but general conversation had resumed and they could not hear.

'What is it, lad?' asked Mungo kindly. 'Have you broken anything? Any bones, I mean,' he added quickly, looking round at all the smashed cups and saucers. Thomas shook his head, which seemed to cause him some pain. 'Then what is it?'

'I can't ...' Thomas tried, though his lip was split, 'can't afford ...' He waved a hand vaguely around him. 'I can't.'

'I know that well,' said Professor Shaw gently. 'We'll sort something out later. It was just an accident, you know.'

Thomas frowned, and put a hand to his cut face, wincing.

'He'll go to hell, you know,' he said indistinctly, nodding at the distant figure of Professor Keith. Mungo looked awkward, and said nothing.

'Can you stand?' Professor Shaw asked. 'I think we should take you back to your bunk and find some water for those cuts.'

'No, I can manage,' said Thomas, then added ungraciously. 'Thank you, sir.' He rose out of the crockery heap like a cow from a ditch, and fragments dropped off round him with little clicks and chinks. He bent carefully to remove a cup handle from the laces of his boot, then straightened again and walked unsteadily from the Senate room alone, as he had arrived. His gown, soaked with tea and splashes of milk, trailed dejectedly after him as he vanished from sight.

Ramsay Rickarton had left and returned with cloths and a sack, and was kneeling resignedly to pick up all the broken pieces and rescue what could be saved, though Thomas' weight had ground some of the pieces too small to be anything but brushed up. For a moment, a little face, full of girlish shock at the scene, appeared from behind the door curtain, then vanished again. The brief appearance, however, brought a smile to Ramsay's face, even as he frowned his disapproval at her, and he set to his task faster than before.

Professor Shaw and Mungo Dalzell returned to stand with Allan Bonar and Professor Urquhart, who had been holding their teacups for them.

'The man is no longer human: he's a beast,' Urquhart said, with more venom than usual.

'He certainly grows worse and worse,' agreed Bonar, staring at his superior's back as Keith laid down some more personal law with the Principal and Lord Scoggie.

'I quite like animals,' Professor Shaw said. 'And Francis of Assissi, though a Romish –'

'All right, all right,' snapped Urquhart. 'A monster, then.'

'Sorry,' said Professor Shaw. Urquhart grunted acknowledgement.

'It's true, though,' said Mungo Dalzell, 'he has very little to do with the students at all.'

'Unless one is from a rich or noble family,' Urquhart added.

'But even then,' said Bonar. 'Picket Irving is as rich as Croesus, or will be when he comes of age and his guardian hands it over.'

'As he never tires of pointing out,' Urquhart interjected again.

'Aye,' Bonar agreed. Shaw studied him for a moment, wondering. Bonar said all the right things, and sounded friendly, but that look in his eyes was so alien to Shaw that it frightened him a little. It was a very cold ambition. What must it be like, he wondered, to rely for one's advancement on the retirement – or death – of someone so universally disliked?

Something caught his eye, and he looked round. Sybie, overcoming her shyness and doubtless her grandfather's strictures, had crept out from behind the door curtain and was crouching beside her grandfather, helping him, her little fingers solemnly picking the crockery fragments out of the threadbare carpet.

She had caught the eye of one or two others, and several, thinking fondly perhaps of their own daughters or granddaughters, were watching indulgently, smiles playing on more than a few faces. For a few minutes, all was peace and tranquillity.

'What is that?' came a sharp, familiar voice. Professor Keith, noting Lord Scoggie's gaze, had turned to see what was catching everyone's attention. 'Rickarton! What is the meaning of this?'

Ramsay Rickarton creaked to his feet, turning to shield Sybie from Keith's hostility.

'It's my grand-daughter, sir. She's helping me.'

'It's a *child*, Rickarton. It has no place here.' Professor Keith's voice was as hard as granite. 'Get it out.'

A look almost as stony passed across Ramsay Rickarton's face, but he turned and knelt down by his grand-daughter.

'You're doing a grand job, there, Sybie,' he said softly, 'but I need you to wait outside for me now, hen. I'll be out in a minute, all right?'

Sybie looked uncertainly from her grandfather to the carpet, and across to Professor Keith. Then she looked back at her grandfather, and gave him a sunny smile.

'Aye right,' she said, all in one word, and ran back behind the door curtain. Ramsay bent again to the crockery, his back suddenly tired.

'I've had about as much as I can take,' Urquhart announced generally, and set his cup and saucer down on the table. The others followed, and Urquhart led them out in a body, nodding coldly in the direction of the Principal and Keith. Outside, Professor Shaw took great gulps of the fresh air, trying to relieve his nausea. Bonar vanished quickly towards his lodgings, and Urquhart drifted like angry smoke into the college buildings where he had a set of rooms. Shaw and Mungo Dalzell were left at the side of North Street, in momentary silence. Dalzell filled the moment by fiddling with the reins of his pony and trap, waiting there for him.

'You're not to worry about what he said,' said Dalzell at last. 'About any of it. You ken what he's like: he's good at finding Achilles' heels and tweaking them till they greet.'

'I greeted,' said Shaw quietly, still feeling the hot tears on his face.

'That's because you're sensitive, and you let him bully you. Has anyone else ever said you shouldn't be here?'

Shaw thought.

'Apart from me, no, I don't think so.'

'And who has more old students coming back to see their old Professor than anyone else I know? Aye, you! So don't help him by being hard on yourself, eh?'

'Aye, right,' agreed Shaw, smiling reluctantly. Dalzell was the one who could cheer him up. That, and in a minute he would be heading home to his own sweet hearth and his own sweet wife, and that mattered more than any professors or Senates.

Mungo Dalzell swung himself up into the trap, self-sufficient as ever, and sat as neat as he could wish with the reins gathered.

'I shall see you tomorrow, then,' he said, and set off with a cheery wave.

Professor Shaw stood to watch him go, and for a long time afterwards he remembered what happened next, though for the life of him he could never swear to the order. Ramsay Rickarton came out of the side door of the Senate room, looking around for his grand-daughter. A goat meandered out of Butts Wynd, dangerously close to Mungo's narrow trap. Sybie ran out from College Street across the road, calling to her grandfather. And Mungo Dalzell, avoiding the goat, swerved.

There was no doubt that Sybie was dead.

Even before her grandfather had reached her, before Mungo Dalzell had slithered, grey-faced, from the trap: before

Shaw himself had turned and vomited in the gutter and Ramsay Rickarton had cried her name into the blue sky, he knew the little girl was dead.

Chapter Five

No one in the University had worked much over the last two days: in fact, the little town itself seemed to be in shocked mourning. Everyone knew the dignified figure of Ramsay Rickarton in his smart University livery, and most knew, by sight at least, his little grand-daughter on whom the weight of such adoration had fallen very lightly.

Only Professor Keith's classes, the few he took, ran exactly as usual. Professor Urquhart, sensitive to the atmosphere around him, limited the usual frivolity of his own classes, and neither Professor Shaw nor Mungo Dalzell was fit to teach at all. Professor Shaw had not slept for two nights, seeing all the time that little broken body in the mud, the long black shadow of the grandfather laid out on the road, the edgy wheels of the trap as the pony jerked and tossed. He had not spoken of this to Mungo Dalzell, but then no one had spoken to Mungo Dalzell at all. He had left the scene of the accident on foot and nobody had seen him since. It had been up to the town's constable, happening on the accident within a few minutes, to sooth the distressed pony and ease the trap away through the sudden crowd to leave it in the University's stables.

Everyone agreed that it was not Mungo Dalzell's fault, that it could not possibly have been helped: they all agreed that, many times. If that alone could have lifted the load from Mungo Dalzell's shoulders, he would have been walking with a step as light as an angel, but it could not be.

The bellman had announced the funeral the next day: the death was news to no one and his ringing was greeted with silence in the three main streets. On the following day, by only a few minutes past ten, there was such a crush at the little house in Heukster's Wynd that no one could get in, and eventually a sort of system resolved itself so that people took it in turns to enter, pay their respects to Sybie's parents and brothers, bend to kiss the little white figure in the bed recess, and leave, taking their customary ale and oatcakes with them, to stand in the street outside. The house was rig-built, with outside steps to the first floor, for Sybie's father was a fisherman and the little room they had all tramped through had an underlying odour of herring, dragging at the black hangings and seeping into the guests' clothes. Neighbours hurried in and out, bringing more bannocks and ale, seeing that the family were all right: to judge by the look of the place, Charles thought with pity, they could never afford a funeral like this without such help.

Charles was on his own, in correct black a little too small for him: it was a while since he had been to a funeral and he was feeling thrifty. George had stayed one night with him and had then vanished home to Letho, leaving the grieving town to its own devices. Charles had thought fleetingly of his father and the problems he would shortly have to face in that quarter, and then put them out of his mind for now.

He stooped into the little cottage and allowed himself to be taken through the soothing formalities of the dead-room, feeling he was taking up too much space, but quickly he was back in the open air with a measuring-stoop of ale – the neighbourhood was running out of receptacles, but it would have been the pit of bad manners to refuse – and a handful of bannock crumbs. Just outside the door, he found Mungo Dalzell with Professor Shaw.

Mungo Dalzell was as grey as a rag, arms wrapped round himself as though the faint drizzle was blizzarding snow. He hesitated at the doorstep, clearly as reluctant to go near the place as if he thought the very building would burn him. Professor Shaw, gentle but firm, pushed him on and watched him disappear into the darkness inside. Then he turned to Charles.

'Good morning,' he said, turning on him a watery gaze where old tears mixed with new rain. 'How are you, this dismal morning?'

'Quite well, thank you, sir,' said Charles, and they made each other half-hearted little bows. 'Are you not going in?'

Professor Shaw gave a little shudder.

'I have already been in, early this morning,' he said, without the least hint of self-conscious virtue. 'I wanted to persuade them to meet Mungo Dalzell: an easy thing to do, and a good deal easier than persuading him that they wanted to see him. It will be good for him, though, I hope.' He frowned, worried.

'He has not been seen for days, I believe,' Charles said, more as a question than a statement.

'He has not been out. He will not drive, so this morning I walked out to Strathkinness and walked him back into town, as slow as taking a pig to market. He would keep turning back, or sitting on the side of the road – his breeches are quite muddy, unfortunately, but the good people in there will not mind. And little Sybie would have laughed, I am quite sure.' He gave a little smile, which soon passed. 'But I do not know what he thinks about the whole thing. He is a dreadful antinomian, you know – you do know what an antinomian is?' His gaze sharpened, as professor took over from friend.

'Someone who believes that God has already chosen his flock and condemned the rest, and that our actions on earth, good or bad, count for nothing,' Charles recited from Professor Shaw's lecture notes, and this time they both grinned. Charles did not mention Burns' Holy Willie, though it flashed through his mind: anyone less like him than Mungo Dalzell it would have been hard to find.

'Good boy,' said Shaw. 'But I do wonder, because if he thinks that Sybie was not a chosen one, then he has sent her straight to Hell, you know, and he would find that very upsetting.'

'Indeed,' said Charles, trying not to think about it in detail. 'But does he believe that he himself is one of the saved? If he does it must be very reassuring at a time like this.'

'Indeed I have never had the courage to ask him,' Professor Shaw admitted. 'It is a difficult thing to ask even a friend – 'By the way, are you off to Hell?' But I assume he believes he is chosen: it is harsh to say it, but every antinomian I have every met believes himself chosen. It appears to be a very comforting doctrine, from the inside.'

They both frowned, amused but feeling it inappropriate to show it on such a subject at such a time. The narrow wynd was becoming quite full now, and a number of students in their scarlet gowns clustered at one end, not quite mingling with the townspeople yet just as upset by Sybie's awful end.

50

'Where is your gown?' Professor Shaw asked after a moment, his gaze on the other students.

'Ah, I'm not quite sure,' Charles confessed. 'Someone borrowed it a couple of days ago and I have not seen them since.'

'Oh, dear,' said Professor Shaw, whose mind, quicker than he thought it was, presented him with a sudden image of Thomas Seaton tripping through the Senate room. 'I hope no harm has come to it.'

'So do I,' said Charles, reflecting that he might find it difficult just now to afford a new one. He had spent some spare moments yesterday selecting, with extreme reluctance, one or two books he might be able to part with to pay the rent: he knew his father would never miss them, whereas if he sold something of more intrinsic value but less important to him, like his watch chain, his father would immediately ask questions. Whatever he did, he would have to do it quickly, and save the Walkers any further embarrassment.

His thoughts were interrupted by the impact of a solid body against his ribs: it overbalanced him and he clutched at the rig steps beside him.

'Sorry, sorry,' slurred an untidy man in what were probably his best clothes. 'Sorry, sorry, sorry.' He lurched round Charles and was caught again by two friends, who gathered him into an upright position and propelled him gently further down the street to where there was a space by the wall to prop him up.

'Who on earth is that?' Charles asked, knowing the face but not the name.

'Ah, alas,' said Professor Shaw, 'it is another sorrowful penitent, who blames himself for poor Sybie's death.'

'How could he be to blame?' asked Charles.

'He owned the goat.'

At that moment, they were distracted by the sound of footsteps on the rig stair, and looked up. Mungo Dalzell, looking more corpse-like than an upright man had a right to at a funeral, came down towards them, and waved back.

'They're coming out now,' he said shakily, and as he spoke the line of mourners turned and flooded out of the little

51

house, forming a kind of guard of honour on either side of the wynd. The others, waiting outside, disposed of the last of their bannocks, brushed their crummy fingers on their breeches or their gowns, and straightened up to watch. In a moment, the little coffin, smothered by the kirk's mortcloth, was carried carefully out of the door, followed by Sybie's father, by Ramsay Rickarton, as grim as death himself, and by her eldest brother, hardly old enough but bearing his part well. As the bearers and the mourners arranged themselves in the wynd, Sybie's mother, her smaller brothers and the minister appeared at the door, and in that moment the drizzle eased and a bleak sun emerged from behind the clouds.

'There,' said the mother, looking up, 'My wee Sybie will get away in the sunlight, all the same!'

It was not far to the graveyard near the old Cathedral, and the sun held, turning the old grey sandstone cream, as the long procession wound out on to South Street and along to the east. Charles and Professor Shaw dropped back and joined the students and staff, letting the townsfolk go first. Even Professor Keith had made an appearance, walking at some distance behind Allan Bonar and nodding to his more important acquaintance.

The little grave was ready, the diggers standing by respectfully, and the interment was quickly done. As the crowd took sips of the few bottles of whisky expected to go round so many, the sun discreetly faded again, and in a moment they were scattering out of the drizzle. As he passed one of the close friends who would be returning to the house for the funeral repast, Charles distinctly heard him say something about looking forward to roast goat.

'A good turn-out,' said a voice behind him, and he turned to see Allan Bonar, his black gown drab with damp. He slowed to walk with him.

'A very good turn-out. And some fine weather, too.' He had been to very few funerals, but felt that these were appropriate things for a man to say afterwards.

'Aye.'

Charles was not sure if he liked Allan Bonar, but he was pleased enough that so important a person as Professor Keith's assistant should wish to be friendly with him, and so they frequently had stiff little chats, and very occasionally had rather more relaxed conversations in a convenient tavern, along with other of the more senior students. Bonar never seemed to remember these occasions afterwards, but returned to the same rigidity of acquaintance as before, as if progress towards actual friendship were something that could not happen.

'You're off home, then?' Bonar asked, after a moment's silent walking.

'Back to my lodgings, aye,' Charles agreed.

'I'll come along with you, if you don't mind,' Bonar said. 'I have a mind to call on your good landlady, Mrs. Walker.'

'I'm sure she'll be delighted to see you,' said Charles dutifully, not really knowing one way or the other. They had reached South Street by now, and it was a straight and easy walk down the broad commercial road: the atmosphere of general misery that Sybie's death had brought on the small town had lifted a little now that the funeral was done, but the rain still cast a damp heaviness over the place and the street traders huddled under their awnings, muttering darkly to their neighbours and not meeting their customers' eyes.

At the narrow little house on the north side, Charles and Bonar stopped and went in, and Charles coughed in the hallway to let the Walkers know they had a visitor. After a moment, Mrs Walker appeared from the direction of the parlour, and did not, contrary to Charles' words, seem that delighted to see Allan Bonar in her hall. She curtseyed to his bow, however, and managed a slightly empty smile, the habitual politeness of a minister's wife.

'Mr. Bonar, how lovely to see you. We were just taking tea in the parlour, if you would care to join us – you, too, dear Charles, if you have the time.'

'Of course, I should be delighted,' Charles said at once, 'But the rent! The rent!' said a voice in his head.

'We have a friend of yours already here,' Mrs. Walker went on, leading the way. For a moment, Charles even fancied he detected a simper on her face, but quickly decided he had imagined it. 'Mr. Seaton was good enough to call – I believe he intended to see you, Charles dear, but he has very kindly kept us company for a little while, now.'

Charles was not entirely surprised. Thomas Seaton was not the person of his acquaintance most endowed with the social graces, but the chance of any food to eke out the miserable college pap he lived on would lead him into all kinds of otherwise forbidding territory.

The parlour was quite forbidding territory at the best of times. Last rearranged in the days of the late Reverend Mr. Walker, it seemed perpetually to be fixed on a long winter Sunday afternoon. Light penetrated dimly through heavy lace curtains, helped only by candles when it was officially dark. There was a glazed bookcase, containing the grimmest collections of sermons Charles had ever seen, and the walls, painted a nauseous green in panels between woodwork of tired white, were for the most part obscured by silhouettes of long-dead ministers and their decaying wives, and by black and white prints of Biblical scenes, mostly from the duller parts of the Old Testament. No useful industry or entertaining conversation, no reading of light books or dalliance with an admirer could be imagined in this room, and none had left any evidence of its passing. Occasionally, drawn in there by thoughts of Mrs. Walker's excellent tea bread, Charles had found Patience Walker twitching the lace curtains or fiddling with the prints as if she longed to red the place out entirely and make it a different room, but her mother would not permit it and Patience had yet to find the courage to bully her.

Thomas, red in the face partly from uneasiness and partly from careless shaving, was in the act of rising from a low, hard chair by the empty fireplace. Beside him on the floor was a grubby parcel, which he seemed to be trying to hide. Patience also rose to curtsey at their arrival, taking in the pair of them with a swift, appraising glance.

'You'll have been at the wee girl's funeral, then?' asked Mrs. Walker, noting Patience's glance.

'Aye. She had some sunshine to light her way,' said Allan Bonar, surprising Charles with this sentimental observation. It smacked of old-fashioned superstition, too: a good sign of the soul's destination.

'Of course she would,' agreed Mrs. Walker, 'and her only a bairn. We called yesterday,' she added, excusing their non-attendance today.

'I was surprised not to see you there, Thomas,' said Bonar abruptly, and Thomas blushed hard. 'There were several of your classmates.'

'I didn't know about it till this morning,' Thomas said, rather too loudly. 'I've been busy.'

Patience looked from one to the other of them with a curious little half-smile that vanished so quickly Charles began to doubt he had seen it. The little maid, concentrating hard, had brought a large pot of fresh tea, and Mrs. Walker poured cups for Charles and Bonar. Patience offered Bonar some cake, then turned with it to Charles. By some absent-mindedness, though, she left Thomas out completely and set the plate back on the table, leaving Thomas stupidly with his mouth open and one hand out.

'Dear, Mr. Seaton would like some more cake,' Mrs. Walker said pointedly. Patience managed to look surprised.

'Oh! So sorry, Mr. Seaton,' said Patience cheerfully, and twisted round so quickly with the plate that she hit his outstretched hand. Two seconds later the cake was in his lap and the plate on the floor – fortunately in one piece.

'Oh, my dear Mr. Seaton!' cried Mrs. Walker. 'Patience, you clumsy girl! No, it doesn't matter in the least, Mr. Seaton, as long as you are all right – Patience, go and fetch a dustpan and brush before you do any more damage. Here, Mr. Seaton, do have one of these biscuits instead.'

It was all very nicely done, and Thomas, more scarlet than ever, was probably oblivious to most of it. Charles, however, was quite convinced that Patience had dropped the plate quite deliberately, and that Mrs. Walker knew it, too. Certainly she was more flustered than her daughter, who rose with studied care from her seat and made sure she walked in front of Charles and Bonar on the way out of the room. Charles suppressed a grin: Patience was making a play for Allan Bonar.

He had to admit, on reflection, as a great fuss was made of brushing Thomas' crummy coat and retrieving the upturned plate, that he was slightly jealous. Patience Walker was a fine looking girl, quick of wit and lively in her character, and full of energy. As her mother's lodger, he felt he ought to have had some kind of precedence with her, though familiarity frequently bred contempt and she probably never even considered him. In any case, he knew, for Mrs. Walker had, probably wisely, confided it to him one day, that it had been the Reverend Mr. Walker's dying wish that his only child should be found a husband amongst the clergy of the Established Church, and Mrs. Walker was bound to accede to his request: the Reverend Mr. Walker featured perhaps more largely in the family since his death than before it. Anyway, it was probable that a Professor of Natural Philosophy would not do, but of course Thomas Seaton was aiming for the church ... at last Charles grasped the whole picture behind the little scene with the cake plate. Mother and daughter were establishing battle lines, and poor Thomas had only been the field of conflict.

All settled again, Mrs. Walker made sure that Thomas was well provided with biscuits and Patience smiled sweetly at Allan Bonar.

'And how do you find your studies these days?' she asked encouragingly.

'Extremely interesting,' Bonar responded. 'I have been able to acquire a little more equipment for my chemical experiments, and have been discovering some very interesting effects from certain plant extracts. Perhaps you will both be good enough to come along and see one or two experiments some time? I am sure you will find them fascinating.' Compete with that, he seemed to say, as his glance flashed over Thomas. Indeed it was not a fair fight: Bonar had the dark, dramatic looks and, when he chose to use it, the charm, to attract any young woman. In addition, he was well established (barring recent threats of which even Charles had heard rumours) in his position at the College, and when Professor Keith died Allan Bonar would be settled for life. It would appeal to almost any mother for her daughter. All Thomas Seaton had, sitting like a lump in his seat with his breeches inexpertly patched and his coat shiny at the elbows, was the faint possibility that someone, recognising his academic worth and ignoring the rest of him, would be willing to present him to a parish in the near future. The fact that he seemed distantly to realise this did nothing for his appeal: a deepening scowl was fixing itself on his rough features, beside which Bonar's well-groomed smooth good looks simply seemed even better. Mrs. Walker gave a tight-lipped little smile.

'What a lovely invitation, Mr. Bonar! It would be delightful to see the science of natural philosophy at work, and in the hands of so enthusiastic a guide. It's such a shame that I'm sure I don't know where we'll find time in the near future: the garden needs so much work done in the spring, as you'll know well, Mr. Bonar, and then the spring cleaning indoors, too: the state of this parlour, for instance. I've been meaning to red it out and redecorate for years, now.'

Patience Walker looked at her mother in complete disbelief, too taken aback to be annoyed for the moment. Mrs. Walker nervously fingered the front of her collar, where her missing brooch usually sat, and looked at the floor. Charles had a sudden horrid thought: maybe she had had to sell it, and was too embarrassed to admit it. Surely, though, she would have tried to dispose of something less dear to her, first: some of the depressing old china in the china cabinet, or some of the books of sermons. There was a long silence, during which Allan Bonar composedly sipped his tea and Thomas crunched on biscuits, eating far too many of them for complete politeness but, as usual, failing to realise.

'Perhaps, Mr. Seaton, you would like to take Patience out for a walk?' Mrs. Walker suggested at last. 'She has been expressing a wish to see the daffodils down by the mill lade, and I am sure you would be an ideal companion.'

This was a little too blatant even for Thomas to feel comfortable, and he mumbled something inaudible through the biscuit he was eating. Allan Bonar looked a little less pleased with himself, however, and Patience was patently disgusted.

'Mama, you expressly asked me to go through the linen cupboard with you this afternoon, and then I must write to our cousins in Perth. Besides, it is raining.'

'And we really must go to our classes, if they are now back in order,' said Charles amiably, finishing his tea. He did not care about Allan Bonar – he could look after himself – but he felt that Thomas needed rescuing before anything worse happened.

Once they were in the hall, Thomas asked Charles if he could have a private word, and bidding Bonar and the Walkers goodbye they went upstairs to Charles' parlour. Thomas was carrying the grubby parcel that had been at his feet during tea.

'I haven't seen you for a couple of days, either,' said Charles, waving him to the comfortable chair and settling on the bench. 'What have you been up to? Did Professor Keith have you busy with something after all, after the senate meeting?'

Thomas' face darkened at the name.

'Have you not heard?' he asked. 'I have been completely humiliated. No one will give me a parish now.'

'But what happened? He can't have given it to Peter Keith: we were there when Peter Keith came home, and he was not in the best of tempers with his father.'

'Oh, aye?' Thomas' curiosity was peaked, and he was not so willing to live through the events of Monday again that he was rushing to tell his story.

'Yes, but I don't know why. He burst in to where George and I were having tea with Mrs. Keith and his sister, said he was going to kill his father, or words to that effect, then saw us and went silent. You know that sort of nervy look he gets, when he is worked up? When you're not sure if he's going to burst into tears or burst out singing – that's what he looked like.'

'And he said nothing about the Senate meeting? That's a bit odd.'

'He said nothing at all, so it could have been about anything. We left shortly afterwards. Did you see him there?'

'No, I arrived after he had left, when they were all having tea. I had to go and talk myself into it first, even after George was so sure it was the right thing to do.'

'And what happened?' By now, Charles had realised that whatever it was, it had not been an unqualified success.

'He – Professor Keith – told me I was a peasant, and then I tripped up and knocked the tea urn over into the china, and everything fell on the floor, including me.' He looked completely miserable.

'The big silver tea urn?' Charles asked. Thomas nodded. 'That must have been spectacular!'

Thomas regarded him out of the corner of his eye, and shrugged.

'It made an unholy mess on the carpet, anyway,' he admitted, with the tiniest of smiles.

'How will you pay for the damage?' Charles asked.

'Oh, Professor Shaw was there, and he helped me up and said he'd help. He and Mungo Dalzell were all right about it. It was only really Professor Keith – he said he'd never inflict a clumsy lump like me on any patron, and then he just stalked off. Everyone was staring, and I was covered in bits of cups and saucers and tea and – ah, your gown,' he added, and at last proffered the grubby parcel to Charles. Charles untied it. Inside, smelling still of damp wool and tea, was his gown, still with shards of china sticking to it here and there like flecks of snow, inexplicably woven in with long brown hairs. Thomas must have tossed it aside when he returned to his room, and simply bundled it up later into the piece of old sacking he had brought it in. It would be a challenge to Mrs. Walker on laundry day, no doubt about it, and in the mean time it was unwearable. Charles stared at it, and swallowed hard.

'Thanks,' said Thomas. 'But it was really too long.'

'Let's go to our class,' said Charles abruptly, not wishing to comment further.

It seemed a good night to go out for a few drinks. Everyone – with the exception of Thomas, who seemed almost oblivious to the whole thing – seemed edgy after Sybie's funeral, and Charles was cross about his gown but anxious not to show it and seem ungracious. Thomas himself was not happy, having consumed his eighth college meal in a row in which rabbit had been the main ingredient, and the name of Keith, used with care, merely darkened his expression further. The teaching staff, particularly Professor Shaw and Mungo Dalzell, were still a little absent-minded in class, and had been trying to catch up on the work missed the previous day.

59

Professor Urquhart had an unusually grim expression on his face, and rumour had it that he had quarrelled with Professor Keith after the funeral. Counter-rumour, less exciting but more likely, said that he just disliked the post of hebdomadar, which it was soon his turn to hold again.

It was just dusk when Charles and Thomas arrived at the popular Black Bull inn in South Street, and found themselves the corner of a bench at which were already settled Picket, Boxie and Rab. The three sporting men had been leaning forward in a huddle, but at Charles' approach Picket casually straightened, smiling, and the other two followed suit. As it happened, they were holding cards in their hands, and a small amount of money was stacked discreetly at the edge of the table where it could be slid swiftly off into a pocket at the approach of anyone who might find cause to disapprove.

'Come and join us, Murray,' said Picket generously, 'though we should be going soon, lads, eh?' He nodded to Boxie and Rab. 'We have our studies tonight, and we are of a mind to be diligent, are we not?' He grinned again, and Boxie had the grace to blush. On Rab's perfect features, however, there was only an innocently stupid benevolence: Charles reckoned he had been given the looks of a minor Greek god to make up for the complete emptiness of his head. Charles himself smiled back slightly absently: he had no wish to know what they were up to, but gravely doubted it had anything to do with studying. A serving man, sliding past through the crowd, took his order for two tankards of ale, and in a few minutes he and Thomas had the refreshing brew in their hands, which for the moment was all that mattered.

'We could do with a little help in our studies, if you would care to join us, Murray,' Picket said slyly.

'Thank you, but I have every intention of getting as drunk as I can afford, this evening,' said Charles.

'I am shocked that you should consider inebriation a suitable substitute for academic labour,' said Picket in a saintly fashion, and everyone laughed obediently.

'It's an act of friendship to Thomas here,' Charles explained. 'I'm trying to cheer him up.'

Thomas was sunk so sombrely over his tankard that it seemed unlikely that anything would ever cheer him up, and Rab clapped him sympathetically on the shoulder. Thomas jumped: he had been paying no heed to the conversation at all. The sporting gentlemen laughed, clearly in high good humour.

'What about a few tales before we go?' asked Rab, with slow delight on his face. 'You're good at them, Boxie, aren't you? Tell us a ghost story.'

'Well,' said Boxie, reluctant but flattered.

'Go on,' said Picket, after a glance at his pocket watch. 'Tell us the one about the nun on the Pends.'

'Oh, you know that one,' said Boxie dismissively.

'But it's a good one,' said Charles. A product of the age of reason, he knew better than to be scared by ghosts, but he enjoyed a good yarn. He grinned at Thomas, and almost had an answering spark of a grin in reply.

'Well,' said Boxie again. 'There were two golfers going home from the links one night ... March it was, and a night like this.' He had them straight away. The noise of the inn faded into the background, and the tallow candles seemed to grow dim even as he spoke and they leaned in to listen. 'The moon was high, and a light wind blew, and it was very late, for they had called in to this very inn on their way home. They sat by the fire there, and talked of their day's play in the warmth and the light, and then they finished their drinks, and went out innocent into the bright, cold night.

'One of them lived down near the harbour, and the other down Eastburn Close, but he said he would walk with his friend down along the dark Pends, because he had had the foresight to bring a hurricane lamp. You know the Pends: you know how the hill leads steeply down to the harbour between high, shadowy walls, with the graveyard on one side and the old stone carvings arching above. The man who lived at the harbour was pleased enough to be seen down that road in good company.

'The wind was whipping up and down, and some say the hurricane lamp was an old one, and was cracked. The flame inside the lamp flickered and dived, and before they were halfway down the hill, it suddenly went out. The two men

61

looked at each other, white shadows in the dark, and a strange chill came over them, and they agreed to go their separate ways now that they had only the moon for light. But still they were reluctant to part, somehow, the one up the hill and the one down, and as they stood there they suddenly became aware of a figure, grey in the moonlight, standing a little uphill from them. It was a woman, robed in the dusty habit of a nun, and how they felt she was watching them they could not say, for her head was bowed and the sweep of her cowl covered her face.

'And then, as they stood there, their bodies turned to ice, she began to move towards them. And though the wind tugged at their own coats, they say that her garments were hardly stirred by it, as though she moved somewhere where there was no wind. As she neared them, the man who was to go up hill, who was bolder, put out a hand as if to stop her, and though he felt nothing but a chill she did seem to stop. As he stood there, hand outstretched, she raised her head, and for one, long, eternal moment, he saw ... *what was beneath her cowl*.

'The other man saw nothing. The nun paused, then bowed her head again and moved silently past him, down and away, vanishing between the dark walls of the Pends. He turned to his friend and as if his throat had suddenly thawed he cried out, and in that instant, as if felled by an axe, his friend fell to the ground. He was stone dead.

'And this is only one of many tales of the Grey Lady. She appears to many without harm, but if she allows you to look upon her face, you will be dead within the year.'

Boxie sat back, and the rest of the company let out a long breath. There was no doubt, he was the best amongst them for story-telling. Even Thomas looked as if his mind had been taken off more worldly matters for a minute or two.

'And now we really have to be going,' said Picket suddenly, looking again at his watch. 'Murray, you are left to give the tale of John Knox and his bodyguards, or the Protestant martyrs at the Chapel, or the strange lights at the Castle: we have work to do!'

Rab laughed, and Charles wondered again what they were setting off to do. Few were exempt from their escapades: even the college laundry woman had had a fit after her heap of bedsheets came alive and a ghostly figure swept after her, with, coincidentally, a curiously Rab-like laugh.

Picket scooped up the money and the playing cards and handed them to Boxie, and drained his tankard – you could see the effort of swallowing all around his scrawny neck as he tilted his head back. All three of them gave signs of being a little drunk, but nothing much to signify, which was yet more evidence that they were intending some devilment for which clear heads were needed.

'We shall see you tomorrow, Murray, Seaton,' said Picket, standing to lead his friends out. 'I am glad to see you so recovered from your bout with the tea urn, though, Seaton. I hear it got the upper hand.'

Grinning, he picked his way awkwardly through the crowded inn, followed by Rab and Boxie. Boxie did not look back, but his anxious, guilty look did not bode well for Picket's victim, whoever he or she might be.

'Another ale, Thomas?' Charles asked, waving his empty tankard. It was never Thomas' turn to pay. Thomas nodded and drained his own tankard in a long, messy draught, and Charles tried to catch the eye of the serving man.

It was an hour or so later when they left the inn. Thomas had not been good company, barely saying a word, and Charles had begun again to worry about money, thus counteracting the good effects of the ale. Thomas wandered off back to his College room, and Charles thought he would take a turn, now that the night was drier than the day had been, around the Scores. The moon was high and bright, and the sheep grazing in the pastures by the cliffs were peaceful. He tried not to think about Sybie, or about his father, or about the pranks of Picket, Boxie and Rab, and particularly not about grey-robed nuns and the proximity of the Pends. Instead he stared at the moon until he was dizzy, letting his mind wander around cosier thoughts of Patience Walker, comparing her favourably with Alison Keith, and the dustier delights of Latin and Hebrew. When he began to feel the cold a little, he turned and slithered away along the muddy track to pass Professor Keith's house on his circuitous way home.

The rambling house dozed like a curling cat under the moonlight, the white paintwork startling with its brightness in places. Charles meandered up to the gate, still thinking of Alison Keith and her wide mouth and unappealing ankles, and the way she had tried to play him off against his brother. He stood by one of the pillars, propped against the damp gritty sandstone, gazing at the house in the same dazed, slightly drunken way he had stared at the moon before. At last he pulled himself together, his mind heading straight back to his financial problems, and he started to walk on.

In the dim light, he tripped on something nearby, and clutched at the gate for support. There was a sudden movement above him. He looked up. A long white skeleton lunged at him out of the night, empty eyes burning.

He was a product of the age of reason, and knew better than to be scared by ghosts, so it can only have been in order to hurry home that at that precise moment, he turned and ran.

Chapter Six

Needless to say, Professor Keith was furious.

He had been alerted to the presence of the skeleton by the hysterics of his maid, Barbara, at half past five on Thursday morning, long after Charles had left the gates behind and run most of the way home. The effects of Professor Keith's rage were still being felt in the yard, such as it was, of United College, some four hours later. Professors Shaw and Urquhart, waiting quietly in the Cage by the Chapel, tried very hard to seem invisible as Helenus Keith ranted up and down outside. They had it on good authority that he had been ranting, without pause, since half past five, and had not stopped for breakfast, which doubtless did not help. Both Professor Shaw and Christopher Urquhart believed in the value of breakfasting well.

There was no doubt in either of their minds that Keith was quite right in finding Picket Irving, Boxie Skene and Rab Fisher guilty of the terrible crime: Professor Keith had accused them of plagiarism and collusion, and this was Picket's choice of revenge. Urquhart and Shaw felt that Boxie Skene's role in the drama was ambiguous, but they agreed that Rab Fisher was as thick as mince, and must have been led.

It was wet again, and the yard was silent and dull with damp, a rain-sodden patch of uneven paving between ramshackle buildings and St. Salvator's College Chapel, which had a gate beside it leading to North Street. Any interesting tracery faced North Street, as well: on this side all it offered was a steep roof, the foot of the bell tower and the sheltering cloister of the Cage. A few students in soaked scarlet wool crossed the paths, trying to keep their books and papers dry. Others, but not many, peered from the grubby windows of their rooms above the yard, the last few living in College. Professor Shaw and Professor Urquhart waited in the shelter to see their students gather in class rooms across the yard, not speaking but unwilling to give up a kind of mutual support against the rain, the town's misery and the rage of Professor Keith.

Naturally there was no sign of the scoundrels appearing for morning classes.

Professor Keith's anger seemed in danger of seeking out some other, more innocent target. He picked out a fat little bejant, wearing his gown correctly in the manner approved for a first year, and gave him a vicious little lecture on combing his hair properly. Shaw watched with his face screwed up in sympathetic pain.

'*Not* a nice man,' Urquhart remarked, watching too.

The door behind them swung heavily open, but not far, and a thin figure eased itself out into the Cage. Mungo Dalzell looked as if he had not eaten for a week, but there was about his face something nearer peace than there had been since Monday's awful accident, and some of the deep swooping lines that had developed around his eyes in the intervening days had eased a little. He did not look quite so old.

'Good morning, Mungo,' Shaw was brave enough to say, bowing to his old friend. Mungo even managed a faint smile.

'Good morning, Davie,' he replied, in a voice not unlike his own. With a slight effort, grown unused to speaking, he went on, nodding back at the door he had just come through. 'I've just been in the Chapel.'

'There's a surprise,' Urquhart remarked, but not too unkindly.

'I don't think I'd spent much time in it before now, except at services. It's a calming sort of place, is it not?'

Professor Shaw, who had always loved the dilapidated old building, smiled and nodded, reaching out a hand to finger the centuries-old stonework as if he were caressing a favourite dog.

'Perhaps our revered Professor of Natural Philosophy should take a few turns in it,' Urquhart suggested, adjusting his gloves carefully. 'He could do with a deal of calming.'

Mungo Dalzell seemed to refocus his gaze for a second, before turning to look for Professor Keith. Keith was still beating a path around the yard, evidently looking for someone or something. Shaw avidly did not want to be the someone, and was not even sure he wanted to be there when the someone was found.

'What's wrong with him?' Dalzell asked.

'Someone flung a skeleton outside his gate last night,' Urquhart informed him. 'As a very thoughtful touch they had put phosphorus inside the skull so that it seemed to glow from within, like a thing from the demon realms.' He enjoyed himself for a moment, adopting the kind of grim, terrifying voice more suited to ghost stories around a winter fire, then returned to more prosaic tones. 'It did not help the Professor's general mood that the feet had not been particularly well articulated – I believe he had to pick a number of small bones out of the gravel of his carriageway this morning, and reconstruct the feet on the kitchen table to ensure he had all of it, before his family would consent to walk on the drive at all. His maid has given notice again.'

'I'm not in the least surprised,' said Mungo. 'It would take a sturdy sort of character to work in that household, I should think.'

'Peter Keith is not speaking to his father again, I notice,' Professor Shaw said with a sigh. 'Such an unhappy household: I never meet Mrs. Keith or Miss Keith without thinking how much better life would have been for them if the Professor had been a different kind of man entirely.'

'Why limit your pity to Mrs. and Miss Keith?' asked Urquhart, arranging himself to lean against a pillar now that his gloves were perfect. 'What about those of us who have to work with the man?' Professor Shaw sighed again, heavily, and nodded. 'After all, those of us of a sensitive disposition have a great deal to put up with every day: I think Mrs. Keith and Miss Keith perhaps only see him for meals.'

'And imagine what that would do to the digestion,' said Shaw quite involuntarily, swallowing hard. His own digestion could certainly be said to be of a sensitive disposition.

'Someone should do the world a kindness and dispose of him. He's not doing anyone any good on earth, and the Devil must need a challenge every now and again,' said Urquhart. Shaw gave a shocked little intake of breath, and shot Mungo Dalzell a swift sideways glance. He was not sure if such a remark would upset an antinomian or not. Mungo Dalzell managed a slightly indulgent smile, and Shaw relaxed a little, only to feel every drop of blood stand stock still when he

67

realised that Professor Keith had finished his dissection of the miserable bejant, and was heading in their direction.

'I don't suppose you've seen them,' he snapped, as if everyone in the town should be devoting themselves to his self-appointed task.

'Neither hide nor hair of them, I regret to say,' said Urquhart, with so smooth a smile that Shaw almost believed that he had been looking for the miscreants.

'I'll have the little devils this time. I'll teach them respect for their elders and betters.'

'I understand that Picket Irving's guardian is a powerful man,' said Urquhart in gentle concern, so that even Professor Keith did not recognise the sarcasm. 'It might be better – for the University – not to offend him.'

'I take your point,' said Keith, his teeth clenched, 'but this has gone far enough. And neither Fisher nor Skene has any influence beyond what Irving can lend them. Perhaps it is time that Irving's powerful guardian knew the truth of his charge's behaviour, and set some limitations on him. Oh, is that them?'

He swept away, like an osprey spotting a fish, and Urquhart watched him dispassionately, removing his hat to run a delicate hand over his well-groomed wig.

'I doubt,' he said, 'that Picket's guardian has much control over him. That's why, I believe, he sent him to St. Andrews in the first place: out of the way of the temptations of Edinburgh. I think Picket might have been better off placed in the way of a few ordinary temptations. He might not have felt it necessary to go about looking for extraordinary ones.'

'And James and Rab would have been much better off without his influence,' added Professor Shaw, sadly. 'I think they are both quite good boys, on their own, but Picket will lead them astray.'

'Oh, here he comes again. A case of mistaken identity.' Urquhart grinned. Professor Shaw shuddered. 'So what will your punishment be, once you have them?' Urquhart asked meekly as Professor Keith returned to the Cage. Keith was angular and twitching with impatience.

'I should like to beat them senseless,' he hissed, then cleared his throat. 'What can I do? I shall fine them a substantial sum of money each, and confine them to their lodgings. I should send them down altogether, but I cannot help feeling that Irving, at least, would appreciate that. They will be escorted to their classes, and to the library should they wish it, but they will be allowed no other freedom. One of Ramsay Rickarton's underlings can mount guard at the door.'

'Have you told Ramsay?' asked Professor Shaw, sure that Rickarton would consider this beyond the duty of his few staff and possibly dangerous to them.

'I should, if I could find him,' Keith snapped. 'He might as well be in collusion with the little brats, for all I can see of him, either. He has been very lax in his work these past few days.'

'Well, there was the funeral ...' said Professor Shaw, bravely, but he went unheard. Keith had just spotted Ramsay Rickarton, who had emerged from the Chapel's other door and was crossing the Cage towards the yard, carrying a white packet.

'There you are, man! Where on earth have you been?'

Ramsay, a vacant, hollow look on his face, opened his mouth but no sound came out. Fortunately, Keith was not really expecting an answer.

'You'll know what happened at my house this morning.' Ramsay's blank look remained. Keith gave a quick breath of frustration, angry that the doings of his household were not the immediate concern of the whole town. 'Picket Irving and his crowd left a human skeleton outside my gate, bones all over the place, with a notice round its neck saying –' he looked round suddenly at Urquhart, Shaw and Mungo Dalzell standing politely watching him from the Cage. 'Well, never mind what it said. It is cleared up now. But I want to see those scoundrels punished, and punished well. I want them fined five guineas each – each, mind – and confined to their lodgings for a week. More if they misbehave, all right?'

'Sir,' said Ramsay Rickarton quietly.

'And I have to go out this afternoon: Lord Scoggie has invited me to dine at his home –' he said this bit quite loudly, and Urquhart was not the only one to smile a little '– and so I want you to collect the fine, inform them of the confinement,

69

appoint one of your men to watch the door of their lodging and escort them to classes, and bring the fine back here and place it,' his voice dropped again suddenly, but those in the Cage could still here him quite clearly, 'in my office upstairs. I shall collect it tomorrow.'

Thus dismissed, Ramsay Rickarton fumbled his way towards the janitor's lodge, the dazed look still on his face. Professor Shaw made a mental note to visit him there shortly and make sure that he had actually taken in Professor Keith's instructions: the man was clearly still stunned with grief and Shaw did not want him to draw more trouble on himself. Keith had returned to the Cage, and Shaw did not, either, feel courageous enough to follow Rickarton straight away when Keith could still see him.

'And while I think about it,' said Keith, half to himself, 'there are a few other things I should leave upstairs, too. When one's house is attacked,' he went on more loudly, making it sound as if there had been a solid bombardment against the building for at least a week, 'one starts to look around and see what vulnerable things might be removed to a place of greater safety.' He nodded approval at his own wisdom, and with a crack of his gown he swooped across the yard towards the stairs that would take him to the staff rooms.

'He still retains an office up there, then, does he?' Mungo Dalzell asked, as they watched him go.

'Oh, yes,' Urquhart replied in disgust. 'I should be quite happy living up there – indeed I am quite happy living up there – but I should have preferred to have the staff corridor to myself, particularly where Keith is involved. The man has no idea how to be quiet: he believes that it is everyone else's privilege to listen to him and his opinions.'

'Ah,' said Professor Shaw hurriedly, 'I believe I see two of my students now. I suppose it would be best if I went and taught them.'

'And I, too, must catch up with my classes,' said Mungo, a little shamefully.

'And I have Peter Keith coming to discuss fine art,' Professor Urquhart added, 'which completes the set. Off we all go, then.'

The students whom Professor Shaw could see were Charles and Thomas Seaton, crossing to a class room from the doorway that led to the students' quarters: Charles had gone to find Thomas earlier and make sure he was awake and fed and ready for his class. Thomas was a hard worker, but had a tendency to sleep late. Charles might also have had, but with a landlady eager to start the day early, he never had the chance to oversleep. In addition, Charles had been up and out more swiftly than usual, and standing outside his usual bookseller's shop before the shutters were off it, before he could change his mind about selling his books. Fortunately he kept his books well, even when they were much read: he had had them plainly but neatly bound and did not treat the pages the way a huntsman treats a hedge, so he managed to negotiate quite a good price for the half-dozen or so he could bear to part with. In his pocket now was just enough for Mrs. Walker's rent money, and he was able, in his imagination at least, to put off the prospect of a visit to his father for another little while. The story of Professor Keith and the dislocated skeleton had made the rounds of the town by an invisible process early in the morning and he had heard it quickly, thus saving himself the embarrassment of telling the story of how a skeletal form had attacked him on the Scores the night before, only to find that he had been the first victim of the Sporting Set's latest prank: he remained, therefore, silent on the experience, and reflected that at least his father would have been proud of the speed he had made from the far end of the Scores to the near end of South Street, in the dark, without injury. On the whole, he was in a cheerful mood, which was not diminished by the sight of his professor waving at them across the yard, and then, apparently, abandoning them to scuttle off in the direction of the janitor's lodge.

'Perhaps he wants us to follow him,' Charles suggested.

'Why on earth would he want us to do that?' Thomas scowled, still not recovered from his experience in the Senate Room and convinced that everyone around was laughing at him.

71

'I don't know: perhaps we have to study in a different room today. I'll just go and see, shall I?'

'If you really want to,' said Thomas.

Charles sighed at him.

'I'll wave if we need you,' he said, handing Thomas his books, and ran quickly across the yard to catch up with Professor Shaw just as he entered the little janitor's lodge. Ramsay Rickarton was seated on a stool behind the wide table, the white packet he had been carrying out of the chapel thrown in front of him, and the vacant expression still on his face.

'Ramsay,' Professor Shaw began cautiously, as though he were interrupting a train of serious thought. 'Ramsay, are you all right?'

The janitor looked up slowly, and nodded, though it was not convincing.

'Did you hear what Professor Keith wanted you to do?'

'Professor Keith?' said Rickarton, trying to find an image in his head to match the name. It came all too quickly, and his face darkened. 'Oh, aye, Professor Keith.' He spat the words out.

'Did you hear what he wanted you to do?' Shaw repeated.

'Something about punishing a few of the lads, aye, I got it. I've to fine them and keep them in their house.'

'Do you know what lads?' Shaw persisted, unwilling to see Ramsay make a mistake. The janitor thought for a moment, and nodded.

'His usual ones: Mr. Irving, Mr. Fisher and Mr. Skene,' he said, though Charles was tempted to think it had been a guess. Professor Shaw nodded encouragingly.

'You've to fine them five guineas each, and keep them at home for a week.'

Ouch, thought Charles, that was a hard punishment. Five guineas was probably more than Boxie Skene could afford, and certainly more than Rab Fisher could. He wondered what punishment Professor Keith would have devised if Charles himself had not sprung whatever trap the Sporting Set had laid, and the skeleton had not been discovered harmlessly on the ground this morning. He noticed that Thomas had caught up and was standing outside the low doorway: they exchanged looks of shock at the news, and looked back at Ramsay Rickarton.

'Aye, I'll do that,' said Ramsay, concentrating on committing it to his memory. His face was grainy and grey, and his eyes were red: his wiry hands at the cuffs of his livery coat were clenched but he seemed unaware of them.

'By the way,' Shaw asked, nodding at the table, 'what is in the packet?'

Ramsay looked at the white packet as though he had never seen it before, and then light dawned.

'Poison,' he said.

Shaw looked alarmed. Ramsay looked at him.

'For the rats in the Chapel. They're eating all the linen and they've started on the pews.'

'Oh, oh very good, very good,' said Shaw, looking relieved. 'Come and see me, Ramsay, if you need any help over the lads to be punished – I gather Professor Keith will be away this afternoon. Keep an eye on his office, too, for I believe he means to keep valuables there.'

A strange, half-absent smile crept suddenly over Ramsay Rickarton's worn face.

'Aye, that's the case,' he said, quietly. 'Professor Keith will be away.'

For a minute, silence fell in the little room. Then Professor Shaw cleared his throat nervously.

'Well, then, come along, gentlemen: we have a lecture to read, have we not?'

Charles and Thomas stood back to let him through, and followed him out into the yard.

'I am pleased to hear about the rats,' Professor Shaw murmured as soon as they were out of hearing distance. 'Professor Keith has been saying that Ramsay has been neglecting his duties, but of course he has been working perfectly well. It would not be like Ramsay, no, not at all ... whatever the provocation ...' He meandered away in his speech, and became silent. Thomas and Charles followed him back to the classroom, and went inside. Just at the door, Charles' eye was caught by a movement in the Cage, a flurry of light colour. He turned, just in time to see Alison Keith, fluttering in yellow and white striped muslin, emerge from the Chapel and disappear towards the college gateway. He could have sworn that as she hurried off, she was pushing something white into her reticule.

Chapter Seven

The satisfaction of paying off Mrs. Walker gave Charles a quiet night's sleep, all visions of pouncing skeletons laid to rest by the knowledge that it had simply been the Sporting Set's trap. He enjoyed his morning lectures, ate a cheap but hearty meal of broth and bread in a coffee house, and strolled back to his lodgings to spend the afternoon reading. The house was quiet as he let himself in, with no sign of either Walker or of the maid, and he climbed the stairs with his mind entirely on the pleasures of learning. Opening the door to his parlour, he stopped abruptly, and all thoughts of learning fled from his mind.

On the only adequate armchair, making it look like a piece of nursery furniture, sat his father.

Charles Murray of Letho, widower, was in his forty-sixth year but did not look it. Tall, strong and with an athletic deftness in his movements, he had a determined face, generously endowed nasally, with George's high fair colouring. He was generally considered a very handsome man, and had not been without opportunities for remarriage in the years since his wife's death: however, he found that he preferred the liberty of being single. He dressed according to fashion, and had very marked tastes: even now, in what he would have termed country clothes, the toffee brown of his gloves was exactly that of his coat, and his boots were almost as gorgeous as George's new ones. His hat, placed authoritatively on the table that Charles used as a desk, was large and well brushed, and he carried a cane with a silver top and showed discreetly on his waistcoat the fine gold chain of a watch.

When Charles remembered to breathe again, he found that in his mind he had shrunk to the size of a schoolboy, and his feet had forgotten how to move. He made an awkward bow, at which his father did not smile.

'Well, Charles, I hope I find you in good health,' he remarked, mildly.

'Indeed, sir, I hope the same of you.' Charles fumbled through the words.

'Aye, thank you, you do. And your good landlady, Mrs. Walker, and your tutors – they are all well?'

'They are, sir: I should be pleased to pass on your good wishes to them.'

'You may do so.' He flicked at a minuscule speck of dust on his breeches with the gloves in his hand. 'And what sports have you been practising in the last month? The weather has been very fine.'

Charles was ready for this question, and refrained from pointing out that, whatever the weather, he had studying to do.

'I practised in the butts on Monday, and played a round of golf on Saturday: both have been regular activities recently.'

'Good, if a little sedentary. How did you do?'

'I won three out of four golf games –' Charles did not mention that in two he had been playing against Thomas Seaton, who clutched at the golf club as though it was his last hope in a strong gale, '- and I shot quite well.' It always went against the grain to applaud his own achievements, but for his father it had to be done. 'I boxed several times with some of the other gentlemen students, and I attended my fencing class twice a week as arranged.'

'You may tell me the success of your bouts on the journey to Letho: I have already spoken to your fencing master, and he says that your progress has his full approval.' Mr Murray remained in the chair, doubtless realising that it was difficult to be authoritative with the hunched back that the low ceiling would inevitably give him. 'Well, Charles, since you are all well, and since everything in St. Andrews is in order, perhaps you would like to explain to me why you are here and not at Letho? Perhaps George did not make my wishes clear: I expected you home with him.'

'I had a funeral to attend, sir,' said Charles. It was a good excuse, but he knew he had managed to make it sound feeble.

'Whose?' his father asked sharply, taking Charles aback.

'The granddaughter of our janitor at the college. She was much loved, and died in a tragic accident.'

His father nodded, accepting the story for now, but apparently disappointed in some way.

76

'But the funeral is presumably over,' he said after a moment, 'so there is now no reason why you should not abandon your studies and return with me to Letho today. I have brought a horse for you – Cobweb, in fact.'

He laid out the horse's name casually, as if tossing it on to the table, but Charles knew it was a bribe. Cobweb, the lean grey hunter, was his father's second best horse, and the privilege of riding him was rarely bestowed on Mr. Murray's sons, let alone for such a mundane matter as riding from St. Andrews to Letho. Charles had to resist the temptation of going to the window overlooking the garden, and seeing if he could see the beautiful gelding in the little stable yard beyond. Instead, he tried to concentrate on his father's unusual tactics: normally Mr. Murray would regard his instructions as sufficient, and a bribe as superfluous and possibly showing weakness. For some reason he must be very eager to have Charles leave St. Andrews straight away. Charles could not, for the life of him, see what the urgency was.

'I wish you to return home for a week at least,' said his father, and Charles' heart leapt. This was not the final blow, then: he would be allowed to return. 'There is something I wish you to do for me, which will not wait. Then we can talk about your remaining here.'

Charles tried not to let the disappointment show on his face. There was a definite tone to the words 'remaining here' which demonstrated that as far as his father was concerned, Charles remaining here was not an option. He stood, hands clenched behind his back, as his father continued to talk, something lengthy about whatever it was he wanted Charles to do over the next week, and a great dark abyss opened in his mind. He would not be allowed to finish the year: he would not be allowed to try at his Master's examinations. He would be dragged back to Letho, and would spend his days being sociable with his father's friends, and battling with George over who was the smarter, the fitter, the stronger. And Charles would never have the chance to read or study, and George would always win.

'Are you listening to me at all, lad?'

His father's voice was scarcely raised, but the tone was enough to penetrate the bleakness of Charles' mind.

'I beg your pardon, sir: I was thinking about – about Cobweb.'

His father smiled briefly.

'Then we should be going soon. I hope you have eaten something: we shall not stop till Cupar at least.'

'I need to see my tutors and get their permission to leave,' Charles said quickly, knowing it would not please, but his father's face was still cheerful enough.

'I shall come with you,' he said with unexpected heartiness. 'I should be pleased to meet Professor Shaw again, and it is some time since I saw Urquhart and Keith. Come, let us waste no more time!'

He stood, seeming to tower above Charles in the tiny room, and Charles was quick to descend the stairs again and out into the spacious street. Even there, with his father close by, there seemed to be little room to breathe.

'Where first?' asked his father briskly.

'To the college,' Charles replied. 'Professor Urquhart is probably there in his rooms, and we may well catch Professor Shaw and Professor Keith, too.' He led the way along lanes between South Street and Market Street, and then between Market Street and North Street, emerging by the college near the spot where Sybie had met her awful end. The great gate of the College was open, and in a moment they were crossing the quadrangle to the doorway to the staff quarters. As they approached, Mungo Dalzell emerged, looking more peaceful than he had for days. He smiled at them, covering the awkward moment when one sees an acquaintance but is too far away to greet them properly, and bowed to Mr. Murray when Charles presented him.

'Delighted, sir,' Dalzell said, and appeared to mean it. Mr Murray, with his general views on scholarship, returned the bow with markedly less enthusiasm, and Charles was left to give Mungo Dalzell an apologetic smile which he hoped his father would not notice. Dalzell, not slow socially, understood at once and smiled back, explaining that he was sorry he could not wait. He hurried off and Charles saw him vanish into the shadows of the Chapel before they reached the doorway of the staff quarters.

Inside, there was a rich and full smell of damp. The stone walls were quite green in places, mostly beneath the inadequately sealed windows. The staircase was worn to the point of almost being a continuous slope, and was lit only by one or two slit windows: Charles and his father fumbled their way up, with Mr. Murray using a few choice words which Charles would not have dared to repeat in front of him. In the corridor at the top, Charles knew there was a candle sconce with a flint underneath: after a few attempts he managed to light a taper and bring the reluctant – and probably damp - candles to life. His father's face loomed out of the dusk, frowning.

'The staff live here?' he asked, clearly doubting their collective sanity.

'Only Professor Urquhart,' Charles explained. 'Professor Keith has an office up here, though: it's that door on the right at the end. All this side is Professor Urquhart's rooms.'

He decided to tackle the worst first, and knocked on Professor Keith's door. It was very slightly open – he could see dim light in the crack and feel a draught – but there was no reply.

'He must be at home,' he said to his father. 'We can walk round there later.' He turned and knocked again at Urquhart's door, and after a moment, heard a distant 'Enter!'

Urquhart had taken full advantage of the fact that no other staff members wished to live in the college any more. He had originally taken what had once been a fine corner room, with windows in two directions, to serve as his bedchamber and study, but as rooms had fallen vacant he had knocked through to the next room, and the next, and the next, so that now he had what constituted a suite on the old staff corridor. The original corner room was his main reception room: the others served as bedchamber, study and dining room. He had quietly made sound all his walls and floors, sealed the windows, hung curtains, laid carpets, replaced doors and introduced colour into the rooms, probably for the first time since they had been built: dark reds, rich golds, and vibrant

79

blues and greens in the detail gave the rooms a startling luxury after the dim stone passage outside. He had used much of the available wall space to display his fine collection of watercolours and prints. Three or four statues, all on classical themes, stood about in tasteful formation. A pair of pastel burners on the mantelpiece, lit even at this time of day, kept away the smell of damp and filled the air with heavy scent. He kept two cats to deter the rats that infested the rest of the college buildings, and these were often to be seen, as they were now, sprawled comfortably on velvet cushions on one of the sofas. Urquhart ordered food regularly from the best inn in the town, which was brought hot to his rooms, and he was known for intimate dinner parties which went on for more hours than was usual. No one quite knew where his money came from, but it was fairly obvious where it went, and amongst his colleagues, most of them married with families, there was for him a distinct, slightly envious, respect.

As Charles followed his father into the reception room, Urquhart appeared at its inner doorway, a book in his hand. At the sight of Charles and his father, he smiled, and bowed just too late to hide a look of sardonic surprise in his eyes. The Murrays returned the bow in a unison that Charles, at least, found awkward.

'Mr. Murray, how delightful!' Professor Urquhart advanced gracefully amongst the furnishings. 'To what do we owe the privilege of your visit?'

'I wish to take Charles out of his studies for a fortnight or so,' Mr. Murray said smoothly, wasting no time. 'I trust that this will inconvenience no one?'

The smile froze slightly on Professor Urquhart's face.

'Perhaps a small glass of something will help to keep out the damp. Can I offer you a glass of spiced wine? My speciality. I have a jug warming by the fire.'

'It is very kind of you,' said Mr. Murray, rattling off the civility, 'but I wish to get away promptly, so as to be home before it grows dark.'

'I see.' Urquhart propped himself thoughtfully against the back of a sofa, one white hand pensively brushing his chin.

'You do realise, do you not, Mr. Murray, that Charles here is one of our more promising young scholars?'

Oh, no, Charles groaned inwardly. This was not what his father wanted to hear. He could not bear to look round at his father's face, and found that he was listening for the sound of the strong hands clenching in annoyance, or teeth grinding.

'He has but a term and a half before he could be expected to be examined for his Master's, and any time lost now in his studies could be fatal for the result.'

'It is not necessary for Charles to graduate. He has an estate and a place in society: he has no need to earn his way.' Mr. Murray's words came out clipped tight.

'It is not a question of necessity, Mr. Murray ...' Urquhart looked up, and suddenly seemed to see something in Mr. Murray's face. 'I take it that the business for which you require his presence is both urgent and important?'

'It is,' snapped Mr. Murray.

'Perhaps a ... family funeral? In some distant part of the country?'

'Something of the kind, perhaps,' Mr. Murray agreed, without humour.

'Then go with my blessing, dear boy,' Professor Urquhart said to Charles. 'Travel safely, and come back to us soon, eh?'

He waved them out of his reception room with almost unseemly haste, sweeping his long hands about generously as if he were bestowing the gift of liberation on the pair of them, not sending Charles into temporary exile.

'Now Keith,' said his father firmly, as they found themselves once again outside in the quadrangle.

'He lives on the Scores,' Charles responded, and led the way back to North Street and east towards the Cathedral. The fact of his going had sunk in now: he accepted it, and wanted to have it over with, and if that meant finding and persuading Professor Keith, then he was content to do the finding and let his father do the persuading, which he was clearly very good at. He was not quite sure what Professor Urquhart had seen in his father's face to make him change his attitude so quickly, but the very thought of it made him shiver.

'Come on, lad, keep up!' said his father, two strides ahead as usual. Charles hurried on, trying to avoid being tripped up by the tail of his father's cane. Towards the end of the street, they turned left into Castle Wynd just as Mungo Dalzell came out of Heukster's Wynd opposite, where Sybie's funeral had started. He gave Charles a quick, anxious smile and vanished down North Street. My goodness, thought Charles, my father will have every lecturer in the place a bundle of nerves before the day is out. Let's see him tackle Professor Keith, though!

There was not a trace of human remains at the stern black gate, but Charles, looking up quickly at the gate post as they passed, thought he saw the end of a piece of string and a spike of wire, which might have formed part of the apparatus. He felt that the Sporting Set owed him a favour: if he had not sprung the trap before Professor Keith had the chance, they would have received an even worse punishment, he was sure.

The bright white door opened at his father's knock, and Mr. Murray handed in his card. They were ushered into a drawing room, not the ladies' parlour Charles and George had sat in on Monday, but still the view was of the garden, and in the distance Charles could just make out the dark peak of the summerhouse roof under the yew trees. Fresh daffodils and hyacinths from the Keiths' hothouse stood about the room in blue and white planters and scented the room with earth and moss and perfume, not, Charles thought, Professor Keith's choice of decoration. In a moment the door opened, and they both turned, not, as they had expected, to see Professor Keith, but to find Alison Keith making them a quick curtsey.

'My father is busy just at this moment,' she said, with a smile at Charles, 'but begs that you will wait and take tea, and he will be down as soon as he can be. Please be seated,' she added, and herself took a pretty little armchair that neither Murray would have fitted in. Charles went to sit near her, and glanced round to find that his father was staring at her as if he meant to memorise every detail of her appearance.

'So you are Miss Keith?' he said. 'Miss Alison Keith?'

Something in his tone surprised her, and she sat up straight, smiling her wide smile with less confidence.

'Yes, sir, I am. My mother will also be with us shortly,' she added, as if that would protect her from whatever threat she seemed to be feeling.

'I see,' said Mr. Murray, seating himself with dignity in the middle of a sofa. He did not take his eyes off her. Eventually, as if musing to himself, he said 'A happy period in a woman's life, is it not, Charles?'

'I beg your pardon, sir?' Charles jumped, completely bewildered by his father's remark.

'The moment when she can see herself with an establishment of her own, perhaps – forgive us, Miss Keith,' he added. 'It is simply a hypothetical question which has formed in my mind recently: the happiest period of life for a man or a woman. Perhaps you can enlighten me as to a woman's views on the subject?'

Charles looked at his father as if one of them must have gone mad. Alison Keith, red to the roots of her hair, sat with her hands clenched on her lap so hard that the knuckles shone white. Mr. Murray opened his mouth to speak again: Charles saw it with dread, but at that very second, the door opened, and Professor Keith strode in.

The battle between Mr. Murray of Letho and Professor Helenus Keith was not a pleasant one, and Charles spent most of its short duration wishing fervently that he was elsewhere. Phrases such as 'with the greatest respect, sir,' were flashed like newly-sharpened daggers. Though Professor Keith had no particular attachment to any of his students, he objected greatly to any interruption to university routine or to the removal of anyone from his sphere of influence. In addition, he suspected the students universally of laziness and stupidity, and thought none of them above talking their parents into making excuses for them. Mr. Murray, on the other hand, had several weapons at his disposal, not least of which was his son's general inclination to obey him in order to live a relatively quiet life. Another was a trust, of which he was the principal trustee, which had been set up many years before and which contributed money to the university. In the end, Professor Keith, deciding that Charles was probably intelligent enough to catch up after a fortnight's leave, granted permission and

83

immediately went into a sulk. The Murrays left, abandoning the Keith household to confusion and general grumpiness.

After that, Charles' only concern over Professor Shaw's consent was that he should not be too much injured in the granting of it. However, Professor Shaw knew well enough how much Charles enjoyed his studies, and that he was not encouraging his father to take him away: Shaw knew, too, that as soon as it was in Charles' power to return he would do so, and that Thomas Seaton would probably lend him his lecture notes. Consequently, the interview was swiftly over, and well before the dinner hour Charles and his father were on the road to Cupar, Charles, in spite of himself, thoroughly enjoying his reward of the use of the gelding Cobweb.

George was waiting for them at Letho, anxious on the shallow front door step with a collection of dogs about him. When he had Charles to himself, after dinner in the garden, it was not difficult for Charles to encourage him to talk. George was appalling at keeping things to himself.

'So what happened at St. Andrews? Has he made you leave?' was George's opening concern.

'Not definitely: not yet, anyway.'

'Oh, good!' George was breathless with relief, but not for long.

'I've paid my rent, too, which is a considerable weight off my mind. George, what's the matter?'

George had started swinging his stick and was taking the heads off the crocuses with an absent ruthlessness. He stopped when Charles spoke, and looked sheepish.

'Did you see Miss Keith?' he asked, watching Charles out of the corner of his eye.

'Oh, is that all! Yes, yes, we did.'

'*We* did? You mean our father was there, too? And met her?'

'Yes – though come to think of it, he was very odd when we were talking with her. He kept going on about the best time of a woman's life.'

'What?' George was genuinely bewildered.

'The time of life when she is setting up a home of her own, I think he meant,' Charles went on, though he was far from sure himself. 'She went absolutely scarlet: I think she must have some man in mind. It's not you, is it?' He turned to George with a laugh that was only half-humorous.

'Well, I haven't said anything to her, if that's what you mean.' George looked tetchy. 'I might have, but she didn't seem inclined to listen. But the problem is ... your problem, that is ...'

'What?' asked Charles, suspiciously.

'Well,' George began, toeing the gravel path and fidgeting again with his cane, 'it's just a stupid little thing, you know ...'

'What is?' Charles felt he was being remarkably patient.

'Oh! Well, when Father asked me why you hadn't come back with me on Tuesday morning, you know, as he wanted – well, he was gey angry.'

'With me, though, not with you.'

'Yes, well, that doesn't always make much difference. I was there, and you were not.'

'True, yes. I'm sorry about that. But you told him about the funeral?'

George gave a sick smile with eyes that almost met Charles'.

'I forgot. And anyway,' he added quickly, before Charles could interrupt, 'I didn't think it was a very good excuse. I know you'd rather just be reading books, but you know he wouldn't take that at all. So I told him you had a sweetheart.'

'You did *what*?'

'All right, all right, no need to shout!' George giggled nervously.

'And did you think to give this sweetheart a name?' Charles asked, though he was fairly sure he knew the answer.

'It was the first name in my head,' George admitted. 'It usually is, these days.'

'So now Father thinks I have it in mind to court Alison Keith,' Charles snapped, 'and presumably that isn't good enough for the heir to Letho. No wonder he was so peculiar. He probably thought he was wounding us with every jibe, and punishing her for her presumptuousness.'

George sighed.

'I probably haven't done my own cause much good, either,' he said. 'Now he'll feel ill-disposed to her as a wife for either of us. And she has quite a good portion, you know: her mother has lots of money.'

'I know. George, you aren't really determined on her, are you?'

He did not have the chance to hear the answer.

'Charles! George!' their father's voice interrupted from the terrace. 'Come along! No time for meandering amongst the flowerbeds: let's take the dogs out for a run!'

It was at supper that evening, a casual, usually relaxed meal, that Mr. Murray broached the superficial reason for his removing Charles at such short notice from St. Andrews.

'I want you to go down to Edinburgh, boy, and meet with Mr. Simpson, our man of business there. You remember him?'

Charles met George's eye: old Marmalade Head, they thought at once.

'Yes, sir,' Charles replied.

'I have papers to send him which I do not wish to entrust to the mails, and you may learn something of financial matters from them and from your dealings with him. You may stay in the Queen Street house, though do not expect it to be much opened up for you: you can take a manservant down with you. Daniel, perhaps, is the best suited: it will be good for him, too.'

'Yes, sir,' said Charles.

'You may attend the Assembly on Monday, and you can take my invitation to the Dundases on Tuesday for a reception: it is not as formal as a dinner and they will be pleased to see you. I have sent them a note to expect you. It is time you started to take your place in society, Charles. George is far in advance of you in that.'

'Yes, sir,' said Charles. George looked pleased with himself.

'The mail passes the village tomorrow at mid-day. Fenwick has acquired a ticket for you. You will have the

86

morning free to pass some time fencing and boxing with George: it will do you both good if you can pass on to each other what you have each learned from your teachers.'

'Indeed, sir,' said Charles. He did not wish to fence, box or go to Edinburgh, but at least he could try to read his copy of Vergil in the mail coach.

George evidently did not trust to Charles' enthusiasm for fencing or boxing either, for he knocked on the door of Charles' room late that night after the household had retired. Charles, taking advantage of his father's excellent lamps, was still reading, and hid the book under the pillow before calling out, 'Come in!'

George was clutching a torn piece of paper, which turned out to be a tailor's bill. He handed it, almost shyly, to Charles.

'Could – could you get me some of that when you're in town?' he asked, and cleared his throat noisily.

Charles looked at the bill: it was for silk cravats.

'Another silk cravat?' he said with a grin. 'All right: what colour?'

George looked agitated.

'No! No, the other side.'

Charles turned the paper over. On it, in George's careful hand, was one word: 'Cantharides'. He frowned, thinking 'Cantharus, canthari, tankard. Cantharis, cantharis, - beetle?' He looked up at George.

'What is it?'

'You can get it at an apothecary's, one of the big ones, maybe, that would be best.'

'A drug? George, what's wrong? Is something the matter with you?'

'No, no,' said George quickly, 'not with me. I mean –'

'With Father, then?'

'No, I mean, there's nothing the matter with anybody, and it's not for me, and it's not for Father. All right?' He sounded defiant, but he could not meet Charles' eye. Charles sighed.

'All right, then, I'll get it for you, whatever it is. Do you want the account send here?'

87

'No! Look,' George rummaged in his pocket and came up with a couple of shillings. 'Take these. I don't think you'll need more than that, no, I shouldn't think so.'

George paying cash was not a common phenomenon, let alone George volunteering cash before it was asked for. Charles' jaw dropped.

'Good night, then,' said George rapidly, and left the room. Charles sat with the tailor's bill in his had, staring at the closed door. What on earth was George up to this time?

The mail coach arrived at Letho's only, slightly ostentatious, inn at mid-day the next day, and Charles was waiting for it. No one had come to see him off, but Daniel, a somewhat haphazard boy in his father's household, carried his bags, not unpacked since they had arrived late the previous evening from St. Andrews. Charles, not entirely trusting Daniel, saw to him seeing to the stowing of Charles' bags on the roof, and then saw to Daniel finding his own perch in the fresh air: Charles handed him up a plaid to cover his knees, for the breeze stirred up by the mail horses' speed could chill even when the day was mild. Then, the only inside passenger to alight in Letho, he climbed into the body of the coach.

Inside, grinning in welcome, were Picket Irving, Boxie Skene and Rab Fisher, the Sporting Set.

Chapter Eight

'But how on earth did you get away?' asked Charles, when they had set off. 'The last I heard of you three, Ramsay Rickarton was to send someone round to Mutty's Wynd to keep you under arrest!'

Rab Fisher laughed good-naturedly, though a little frown crossed his perfect brow, and Charles wondered if Rab had realised how much trouble he and the others were in. He was not endowed with the sharpest of minds.

Picket, however, with a wicked gleam amidst the wrinkles of his eyelids, was only too happy to share his triumph.

'That would be Thursday morning, would it?' he asked, his thin voice dripping with glee. 'What a shame: we left on Wednesday night. I'm very sorry to have missed Ramsay's man. I'm sure we would all have got along just fine.'

'But if you left on Wednesday night,' said Charles, 'how are you only this far on Saturday?'

'We had to wait for the stage coach, of course,' Picket explained impatiently. 'We left our bunk on Wednesday night, set up our little surprise for dear Professor Keith, and strolled on to an empty bothy Boxie here knew of, and hid ourselves there for a while.' Boxie looked gratified that his contribution had been appreciated, though if any University officer had happened to glance into the coach at that moment in search of a fugitive, he would have chosen Boxie at once. The man was pale, hunched and tense, and seemed to expect to be caught at any second. Picket was too shiny with triumph to notice – or to care.

'We had our tickets in advance, and this morning we simply emerged from our comfortable priest's hole, waved the coach down just outside the town, near the Swilken Bridge. My one mild dissatisfaction with the affair,' Picket went on, a cool, self-critical campaigner after the battle, 'was that the trap somehow failed.' His gaze fell lightly on Boxie. Boxie went paler. 'You heard, I suppose, that he found a skeleton on the ground outside his gate in the morning?'

'Yes – he had great fun putting the whole thing back together. Where did you get it from? It's a shusy, I take it, but it's not as if we have a medical course at the University.' It was something that had been bothering him slightly – he did not like to think that the Sporting Set would stoop to grave-robbing, but he wanted to be reassured.

'No, but my guardian knows some of the senior anatomists at Surgeons' Hall in Edinburgh,' said Picket, with a smile. 'One of them obtained it for me – of course, he may not be aware of that just yet ...' His grin became wider, his narrow yellow teeth disconcertingly horrible, spaced in his mouth like the bars of an ivory cage. 'Probably the result of some resurrectionist's industrious excavations. Anyway, we had set it up to fall on him when he came home that night – we had phosphorus in the skull so that the eye sockets glowed, another of Boxie's excellent notions.' Boxie now looked faintly sick. 'It was wired to the gate, but it must have blown down or something, before he reached it, and then he didn't see it in the dark. Quite annoying, don't you think?'

'Frustrating,' Charles agreed. His heart still leapt when he thought of that ghostly skeletal face bearing down on him in the moonlight, but he was not going to tell Picket that. He wished to run no risk of finding Picket his enemy. 'So where are you off to now?' he asked at last, his mind so full of skeletons that he thought it would look less suspicious if he simply talked about something else.

'To Edinburgh, of course.' Picket sat back in satisfaction, though his gangly form was awkward on the coach's hard cushions, and he was clearly trying to look more comfortable than he was. 'We shall return in a few days, contrite, ready to receive any contrivable punishment – and with a banker's letter for a substantial sum from my guardian for the use and benefit of the University.'

'And the other!' said Rab, who had been exercising his intellect in the mean time by watching Picket's face and mouthing some of his longer words after he had said them. 'Tell him about the other!'

'Rab, Rab,' said Picket soothingly, 'you should be careful what you say when you are excited, eh? You leave no surprises! Mind you, Murray, he has his moments: you should have seen him shin up that gatepost with the skeleton like a monkey on his back, and never a bone broken! Yes, Rab, yes: we'll tell Murray about the other. I think we can wait, though, until we are sure of our facts, all right?' He gave Rab an indulgent pat, and looked to Charles as if for sympathy. 'Yes, we do have another little treat up our sleeves for dear Professor Keith, but it is uncertain as yet. We shall see, eh, Boxie? We shall see!'

Boxie's ordinary face was shot through with red for a second, then turned white again, like taffeta twisted in the light, and Charles, pitying him, wondered what Picket was landing them all in this time. What could they bring back from Edinburgh that was worse than a skeleton?

It was only as they were all leaving the coach later that another question occurred to Charles, but he decided not to ask it. If the Sporting Set had gone into hiding straight after planting the skeleton on Wednesday night, how did they know that Professor Keith had found it on the ground on Thursday morning?

Edinburgh was polished grey and black with rain as he showed Daniel how to hail a porter to help them with their bags. Daniel, too, was sodden from sitting outside the coach, and Charles was keen to get him home and into dry clothes before he caught cold. He led the way at a brisk pace, forgetting how much taller he was than either Daniel or the porter, up and out of the Grassmarket and the crowds around the coach.

The West Bow wound them up on to the steep ridge of the Lawnmarket, where Daniel, who had been growing almost dizzy looking about him at all the new and fascinating things he could see, drew in a deep breath and stared. The High Street sprawled before them, down and down again to the Canongate, swarming with people, bright with stalls and coloured clothes, and here and there sprouted an umbrella like a mushroom: Daniel had only seen one or two before, but here it was like a fairy ring. He gaped at the women, loud-voiced stall holders, non-committal shoppers and ladies aloof in chairs, alone or in pairs, gazing blandly out at the rain-soaked passersby: Daniel had set himself up as having quite an eye for the girls, but suddenly found that up to now his scope had been painfully limited. He stared and stared, until the crowd buffeted him back to his senses. Then, like a man who gazes at a picture and then sees the frame, Daniel looked up and from side to side. Tenements of unbelievable height rose at either side of the street, with shops at their ground floor, and windows above, where more signs hung to show where cobblers, hatmakers, musical instrument sellers, teachers, had their premises and probably their homes, too. As the rain eased, at one window a man leaned out, polishing the great gold boot that showed his trade – then twisted and let out a cry of profane alarm as a maid on the floor above tossed out a carpet to be beaten, the dust tumbling damp on to his head and the boot. Daniel laughed out loud, and Charles smiled, watching his amazement. The porter, hauling his load up the steep West Bow, finally caught up with them and Charles set off again down the hill.

A grand church stood formally at a cross-roads about halfway down the street, three or four times the size of the little Letho kirk and even larger than the one in Cupar, which was the biggest one Daniel had seen. Around it were market stalls, stacked with fruit and vegetables, making the air, full of the stink of wet wool, scented briefly with kale and well-stored apples. Two young ladies stopped to look, draped in the latest fashions: more for Daniel to stare at, and Charles had to poke him before they noticed – though Charles himself managed a more discreet assessment of their fairly obvious charms. One of them turned and noticed him, and gave a not unencouraging smile from beneath her bonnet even as she looked modestly away again. Charles grinned to himself, and guided Daniel reluctantly away to the left, to another wide road leading down off the main causeway.

'North Bridge Street,' he explained to Daniel. 'The church is the Tron Kirk. Down there,' he pointed further along the street they had been descending, 'is the Canongate, leading down to Holyrood Palace – you'll have heard of that.' Daniel nodded, not believing he could be so close to legends, straining to see though the road twisted too much, and was cluttered with overhanging storeys. 'Down here,' Charles pointed to the road into which they had turned, 'is the way to the New Town, which is where the house is. You'll need to remember all this: you may be sent out on your own.'

Daniel's eyes widened dramatically at such a thought, as he followed Charles down this new street. Again, tall buildings walled each side of the street, and a couple of sturdy horses strained to pull a laden cart up to the Tron Kirk. Two chair bearers, urged to hurry by their passenger, had run out of control on the hill and passed them, faces frantic, as the weight of the chair pushed them on almost faster than they could run. Just as it seemed they had the mastery of it again, the front bearer tripped and fell flat. The chair tipped over him, balanced for a precarious moment on the shafts, while the back bearer clung to his end, trying to drag it down. Then the chair smashed down to one side, and a large and angry passenger pulled himself from the wreckage, laying about him with his cane before he could even see what had happened. A crowd clustered, but Charles passed swiftly on, followed by Daniel and the porter, until they reached a point where the buildings ended on both sides of the street, and before them was a view so astonishing in its unfamiliarity that Daniel nearly sat down on the spot. Heedless of his open mouth, he looked about him. High up to the left, on a green hill but bursting out of it with rock like a tooth in a gum, was a Castle. Even from here, Daniel could see the gleaming black of the guns, and drew a long, staggering breath. To the right was another hill, smaller but somehow striking, like another fortification to the town. Ahead, though, was another wonder: a long street, straight as a rod from east to west, with gardens in front and, on the far side, a row of perfect white houses, clean and exact, as if made out of china. Daniel had never seen anything like it.

A long, broad, bridge spanned the valley that divided the old town from the new, and Charles continued down it, trying not to slither on the damp cobbles. Daniel stopped him with a question.

'But what does it *do*, sir?' he asked, peering over the side of the bridge. 'What does it go over? It must be a mighty river.'

'No, just a valley,' said Charles, looking too as if something might have changed. The damp dregs of the

Nor'Loch lay beneath the splendid spans, and a grubby cluster of tenements huddled at the lower end. It did look a bit pointless.

They reached the other side at last, facing a grand square building with a dome: it did not look like a church, so Daniel thought it must be the house of some very great gentleman – Henry Dundas, perhaps, or even the King himself. Perhaps it was Holyrood Palace. Charles saw him looking.

'That's Register House,' he said, and seeing that this meant nothing he added, 'where they keep deeds and all kinds of documents, the whole history of Scotland. And that is the Shakespeare Theatre,' he turned to point to the square at one side of the bridge, 'and this,' he said, turning again, and waving at the street with the china houses, 'is Prince's Street. There are three main streets in the New Town, all lined up side by side like the streets in St. Andrews, remember? This is Prince's Street, the middle one is George Street and the far one is Queen Street, and our house is on Queen Street. You'll soon get to know it – though not this time, I hope,' he added half to himself, 'if I can get away again quickly.' It was not that he did not like Edinburgh: he was fond enough of the house, and he liked some of the entertainment and some of his father's friends, for he had gone to school here himself and knew their families, but it was no good praising one place when you really wanted to be somewhere else.

The Queen Street house was not officially open, but a woman called Grant lived in the basement and kept an eye on the place. She was also a fair cook, and could manage to make a few simple meals if Mr. Murray or either of his sons needed accommodation. She had been warned of Charles' arrival, fortunately: it would have been easy enough to find supper in some respectable tavern, but breakfast the next morning, on the Sabbath, would have been harder to obtain and Charles would not have had the remotest notion how to do more than make himself a jug of coffee even if there had been food in the kitchen. Supper, however, was nearly ready when they arrived, and Charles found that his usual room, a bedchamber on the first floor, had been aired and warmed for his use. He loved this room: at the front of the house it faced north, over the gardens at the other side of Queen Street, and the soft green hangings and curtains, embroidered by his mother, echoed the fields that led from the gardens down to the dark Forth and the hills of Fife beyond. The trees opposite were just coming into leaf, tender buds braving the Edinburgh weather, and when he opened the window the breeze blew in cold and determined from the sea. It was dusk, however, and he did not linger long, washing and changing before going down to his solitary supper in the dining room on the ground floor.

The next day, Sunday, between the usual church services at Greyfriars, he managed to spend reading. It was raining heavily, and only a few people knew he was in town, so he felt no social obligations. He supposed, as he was reading books which were for his studies, that he was properly speaking working on the Sabbath, but he felt he was enjoying it too much for it to be sinful in that respect, anyway, though some of the subjects he was reading about were only rendered respectable by the fact that they were in Latin, that great bringer of decency to the most decadent of literature. Mrs. Grant cooked him dinner and supper, and forcibly persuaded Daniel to escort her to morning service, which did him no harm at all.

On Monday he called on Mr. Simpson, Marmalade Head, and found that an appointment had been arranged for him for the following day. He was attended by Daniel, who had quickly developed a look of supercilious disdain worn by the Edinburgh servants he saw and tried to hide his curiosity behind a cool, blank stare: Charles decided to march him down to stare in at the gates of Holyrood Palace, nestling below the skirts of Salisbury Crags, and then to walk him the length of the Royal Mile to see the Castle at closer quarters, to wonder at the uniforms of the soldiers on duty outside the stockade, and to stand amidst the gorse bushes and long grass and survey the whole of the New Town laid out beyond the ditch of the old Nor'Loch, three straight streets, gardens beyond, and linking side streets, as neat as a griddle. Grand coaches and busy sedan chairs moved like insects along the streets, and tinier people promenaded together, shopping or just walking to be seen.

Charles drew him back down the hill and showed him St. Giles' High Kirk with its crown tower, and let him wonder at the coloured glass and the carvings inside; pointed out the Law Courts behind the church, the lawyers that ruled the city in their black gowns, the City Guard in their cocked hats, their long red coats faced with faded blue, their Lochaber axes to attention at their sides. They moved away, further down the hill, before stopping at a coffee shop for dinner. Daniel spooned thick broth into his mouth while his eyes never stopped moving, watching lawyers talk secretly with their clients in booths, merchants making deals with careful joviality over a few jugs of claret, potboys in stained aprons running back and forth, bringing them roast beef and boiled vegetables and refilling the salt dish from a great earthenware pot, sticky with damp. Daniel had ale: Charles allowed himself half a jug of Leith claret, nothing to what the lawyers and merchants were consuming, but he was trying to save his cash. His father had given him a sum of money to spend while he was in Edinburgh, and he hoped he might be able to smuggle some of it back to St. Andrews to buy back one or two of his books. His father had also told him to go to their tailor and buy himself some smarter clothes - not something he was looking forward to – but that payment would be on account, so he could save nothing from it.

He went to the tailor that afternoon, in the lane behind Prince's Street. It was as tedious as he had expected, and after that he returned to bathe and change for the Assembly.

The Assembly Rooms were in George Street, not far to walk, and he felt suitably formal in his finest coat with its large, shiny buttons, his palest breeches and his dancing slippers: it had been dry all day, but he wore a heavy evening cloak. Daniel, eyes like saucers and stiff in full livery, attended him, and they were escorted by a link-boy, though darkness had only just fallen. It was easy to see where the Assembly Rooms were, for carriages were stopping and crowding together, drivers swearing as they tried to reverse reluctant horses to extract themselves from behind other vehicles, grooms dancing out of the way of hooves and wheels, footmen busy with steps and doors, pretending their liveries were everyday wear. Light from the tall doorway splashed over silk and satin, and pooled on pale gowns and waistcoats.

Charles left Daniel in the hallway with the rest of the servants, hoping that he would behave, and ascended the curving forked stairway with everyone else to the rooms above. It was drawing towards the end of the season and there was not the air of excitement that would have attended the autumn assemblies: many couples were already engaged, some married, and the few chaperones who were still alert had an air of desperation lest their charges should have to be carried over to next year like winter clothes in a press. Charles walked over to the side of the room where single young men predominated, and eyed the available women for a suitable partner for the first dances: he very much enjoyed dancing, and though his attendance here had been one of his father's strictures he was determined to have an excellent evening's entertainment.

He danced solidly until suppertime with a wide variety of partners, some good, some truly awful, most daughters of his father's social circle whom he had known for years. He was in demand, for as usual most of the mothers knew the size of his father's income and the extent of his estate, and Charles himself was tall and not at all unacceptable in the eyes of most of the daughters: occasionally he felt like a pig at Cupar market, prodded by the mothers' gaze, his pedigree passed around the hall.

In particular he was introduced to one Mawis Skirving, a young lady of reportedly large fortune and blatantly large teeth, who was built like a farmer but tried to compensate by the practised daintiness of her movements and speech, and by the optimistic daisies in her hair. Charles found himself obliged to lead her into supper, and lost her almost at once in the crush. He fought his way to the food tables in the hope that if he collected some food for her he might be able to track her down, and found, instead, Picket, Boxie and Rab Fisher, tucked into a window embrasure with three well-heaped plates and busy forks. Picket swallowed, his angular Adam's apple jerking against his cravat, before greeting him.

'What are you doing here, then, Murray?' he croaked.

'Dancing, mostly,' Charles replied innocently.

'Yes, there's not a great deal to look at,' Picket agreed, with a fairly offensive glance round at the ladies in the supper room. 'Rab and I have found only a few to admire, and Boxie here, of course, his heart is already spoken for.'

Boxie blushed hotly, and concentrated on his food. Charles grinned.

'Anyone I know?' he asked.

'Maybe,' said Picket, with a knowing sneer.

'But you don't know, either, do you?' Rab asked Picket guilelessly, and Picket had to revise his stance. He gave a twisted smile.

'He's refusing to tell anyone. But of course, we have our suspicions ...' He was clearly angry with Rab, and Charles decided to change the subject.

'Have you managed to achieve what you came to Edinburgh for? When do you go back to Fife?'

'Oh,' said Picket, in disgust, 'it's taking ages. My revered guardian fell out of a chair on Saturday and has been in a foul temper ever since, so this banker's draft is proving more trouble than I thought it would be. We came out this evening to give him a chance to calm down.'

Charles wondered if Picket's guardian might have fallen out of his chair on North Bridge Street, but chose not to ask.

'What about yourself?' asked Rab, oblivious to the admiring gazes washing over him from most of the females within range. Though his evening coat was of a cheapish cut and his breeches were ungenerous, he managed to look like the height of fashion.

'Oh, I have a couple of engagements tomorrow, and then I shall see,' said Charles carelessly. He had no wish to say anything about the boring dinner party he had to attend, or the business he had to complete: he did not wish to seem entirely under his father's thumb at his age.

'Yes, we have a little work to do tomorrow,' said Picket absently, watching a promising girl with diamond earrings pass them coquettishly. 'You know, for our little project.'

'Ah,' said Charles, trying to sound knowledgeable and interested without pandering to Picket's love of secrecy. A movement nearby caught his eye: it was Mawis Skirling, coyly waving to him. He set a courteous smile on his face, and returned to her.

He went obediently to his appointment at Mr. Simpson's the next day, finding that the business his father had sent him on was trivial and not particularly confidential, and could easily have been committed to the mails. Mr. Simpson seemed to assume that Charles had deliberately used the business as an excuse to spend three or four term-time days in Edinburgh, and spent the half-hour the matter took making jovial half-jokes about Charles' tastes and inclinations. None of them was very funny.

Simpson's office was in the Canongate, and Charles, who had come out on his own this morning, left in a bad mood and allowed himself to be buffeted gently to the junction at the Tron Kirk while he thought dark thoughts about Simpson and his marmalade hair. He turned left, on to South Bridge, thinking about finding a tavern and a jug of claret, which led him to wonder how he was going to manage if his father continued to refuse to support him through his last term. There was a jewellery shop on the corner behind the Tron Kirk and he drifted over to look at the window, trying to determine what price might be fetched by his watch chain. The prices of chains were not encouraging, but a pair of bracelets caught his eye, linked flat stones set in gold. They were handsome, brown as toffee, and according to the label were Roman: he wondered if it was true, that something so old could be lying in a shop on South Bridge, and tried to picture them adorning the graceful arms of Augustus' granddaughter Julia, or some Vestal Virgin.

There was an apothecary's dark little shop next to the jeweller's, and as he was standing in gloomy contemplation, he noticed – as if they were the only other people in the city that week – Picket and Rab emerge from the dark shop. He thought at first that they had seen him and he was about to wave back, a smile halfway to his lips, when out of the corner of his eye he saw, inevitably, Boxie appear from somewhere and join his friends. Picket, with a wide, nasty grin on his face, carefully handed a small but bulky white packet to Boxie. Even Boxie had a slight smile, and Rab seemed as vague and content as ever. Charles thought of going over to them, but hesitated, he was not sure why. Even though it was best to get on with them while they were all at St. Andrews, he often wondered if he liked any of them at all.

He watched them disappear down South Bridge towards Brown Square where he seemed to remember Picket lived. Once they were out of sight, he turned and passed the Tron again, still not happy, trying to make plans for contingencies which might never happen, trying to guess how he could achieve what he wanted and still please his father.

Chapter Nine

Though he had grown up so near the place, the unexpectedness of it always delighted him: the little fishing town on the promontory that held at its heart traces of government, fragments of a mighty cathedral, and dearest and best such an ancient seat of learning. To return, to follow the long shore road and see in the distance the spires of Sallies, of the Town Kirk and the Cathedral, was to move outside and inside the real world, with its wars, its estates, its constricted society, and to find oneself once more amongst a conflux of strangers, a cross-section of the sons of ministers, of fishermen, of shopkeepers, of soldiers, some he would never have met as equals in the outside world. What brought them together he was not sure: a shared suffering? or a shared privilege? He only knew that if the French invaded tomorrow, he and his fellow magistrands, tertians, semis and bejants would take up any weapon to hand and fight to the death for the little grey town and the invisible, matchless treasure it contained.

Charles sneaked back into St. Andrews on Thursday like a fugitive. He had brought his father's papers back to Letho but managed to deliver them while his father was out somewhere on the estate. He left Daniel to talk of the wonders of Edinburgh to the other servants, and took a groom and a couple of horses and departed again for St. Andrews before his father reappeared. He did not see George, either: he did not ask Fenwick, the butler, and was not told where his brother was.

At his lodging, Mrs. Walker brought him tea and gingerbread but professed herself too busy to stay and talk, which suited him quite well. He sent the groom back with the horses and sat in his little parlour, propped on the bench with his elbows on the narrow windowsill, watching the crowds on South Street and reviewing his situation.

It was not a good one. When his father found out what he had done he would almost certainly be furious, which might not have been a good idea strategically: a furious father now was less likely to be one who in the future would be receptive to plans about Charles staying in St. Andrews for the rest of the term. He pictured his father's face – possibly at that very minute – finding the papers from Edinburgh and discovering that Charles had fled. It had seemed such a clever idea at the time, but now he shuddered at the thought.

He tried to cut his problems down to size. He wanted to stay at St. Andrews at least to finish his term, and his father did not want him to. A daily ride from Letho for classes was out of the question, and even if it were practical to stay at Letho, while he was there, under his father's watchful gaze, his father would be constantly thinking of excuses to keep him at home for the day. No, he had to stay in St. Andrews, whatever his father's thoughts on the subject. Well, his father could not cut him off altogether, but if he did stop his allowance – and his father could be extremely stubborn – then Charles would just have to find money somewhere else. But where? Pocket watches and chains would not fund him forever, and nor would books, which in any case he needed. He had to find a source of income, not necessarily a large one, but enough to cover his living and his fees. After all, Thomas survived on very little, and surely Charles could manage it, too. He did a quick calculation, and reckoned that about seventy pounds would cover a whole session, including fees. All he needed was a job of some kind.

He managed to say it casually enough inside his head, but he had not much idea of what he could do or how he could find someone to pay him for doing it. He decided to discuss it with Thomas later in the day.

The trouble, the main problem, the real difficulty with all this, though, was his father. Charles sighed heavily, misting up the window in front of him. He wiped it with his sleeve. He had never gone against his father before, and he did not want to. It was not that his father could disinherit him, or thrash him – he probably could do the latter, even now, but the former was dealt with by a tailzie on the estate and it had by law to come to him. But to go against his father … actively, deliberately, planning to do something that would earn his father's disapproval – that went completely against the grain.

Since his mother had died, when Charles was very young, his father had brought up the boys and had brought them up as much as possible in his own image. Charles, and soon George too, were required to be active, able, fit and busy. They were required to run and swim, to ride and drive, to shoot with guns and bows, to dance and fight, all in the interest of their physical selves, made to compete with each other and with anyone else fool enough to join in. Mr. Murray was no more proud than when his sons won wapinshaws or were commended by their fencing masters or their boxing instructors, and Charles and George, like any normal boys, enjoyed his approval as much as they could, fighting each other for it, struggling against the odds. Mr. Murray liked society, and therefore expected his sons to like it, too: he was fashionable in his appearance, and therefore thought it no waste of time or money when George appeared in his glossy Edinburgh boots, or when they spent hours at the sales at Leith to acquire well-matched horses for the grey and blue carriage, or fine hunters or hackers to ride in the Meadows where they could be admired. George, his father's son to the very life, entered into all this like clay poured into a mould, filling it to perfection. Charles, on the other hand, did not.

He enjoyed some of it: he was proud of his abilities with a foil or a bow, he liked dancing, and he thought George and his father looked very fine in their silk waistcoats or their kid breeches. He loved them both dearly, and when he could spare the time, he had no objection to looking just as fine himself. But he needed more: he needed to focus his mind on more purely mental pursuits, and to exercise his mind in the same way as his father constrained them to exercise their bodies, and because his father could not understand this need Charles had found himself working twice as hard as George, for one thing because his father would not allow him to stint on his physical training to spare time for reading, and for another because his father, deeply distrustful of academia, was convinced that Charles was softer than George and demanded much more frequent proof of Charles' physical attainments that he ever required of George.

Outside, cut off from him by the thick glass, the crowds mingled and meandered back and forth, chattering and calling. Up here, above them, there was silence, as if the rooms themselves were waiting for some kind of decision. Even the

103

mice behind the panelling paused. Charles sighed again, and wondered if his father would summon him to Letho or appear, like Faust's demon, to drub him on the spot and drag him home in person. He looked at the empty spaces on his bookshelf where the much-loved, carefully bound volumes had been that were now in the bookshop, vulnerable to anyone's thoughtless fingers. He shook his head. Perhaps it would be better to give up. He could go now, tell the Walkers he would send someone for his furniture, hire a horse, and be back at Letho in time for supper. It would be easy: he could tell his father that he had simply gone on in order to collect some things – clothes, it had better be, not books. His father would be quietly satisfied, though perhaps a little suspicious. He need not speak to his tutors, for they were not expecting him back yet anyway. He could abandon all this for the easy option, and spend his days as he did in the vacation, in sports and hard work, and in learning how to run the estate and behave in society. He need not come to St. Andrews again except to bathe or play golf, and his father would be a happy man. He could even read, in the evenings, in the very early mornings, or whenever he had the chance.

It was not enough. He knew it, even as part of him longed for the quiet life that acquiescence would bring. He had never in his life felt part of something the way he felt part of his college, part of the life they all led here. He had never in his life wanted anything so much as he wanted to learn, to be taught, to read books that never appeared in his father's library, to have, at last, the chance to sit and earn his M.A. For that privilege, for that fellowship, he would give up a great deal. For that, he would give up even Letho, and even, if he really had to, his father and George.

He groaned and rubbed his eyes with the heels of his hands, a curiously therapeutic action. After a moment of that he felt almost recovered: he put the thought of earning his living to the back of his mind to stew, and turned his attention to the present.

Mrs. Walker had brought back his gown, which looked less than perfect but a good deal better than it had when Thomas had handed it back to him. She had also left him his

104

mail, which was not extensive. It included a note from Professor Shaw, sent shortly after his departure, welcoming him back, and an invitation from Professor Keith, printed, inviting him to a soirée for all of Keith's students on Friday night. For just a moment, he wished he had not returned quite so quickly: Professor Keith's soirées, though occasional, could be very painful. However, there was always the possibility that he might meet someone there who could point him in the right direction to find an income of some sort – perhaps someone who needed a tutor, or a secretary – some local work that he could do while he finished his studies, and perhaps, if his father was really annoyed, for some time afterwards.

He wrote a quick reply to the invitation, and reflected that he could save himself a particularly small sum by taking it to the Keiths instead of having it delivered. He pulled on his gloves and gown and picked up his trencher, and headed out into the March sunshine.

South Street was busy but broad and free moving, less congested than Market Street could be. Charles decided to walk its length up to the east end, allowing his imagination to dwell on incomes and positions, passing tall through the crowds with ease. Boys scuttled about outside the Grammar School opposite, but there were few other students about: they were either in late afternoon lectures or sequestered in the library. He glanced at the gateway to St. Mary's College, the other half of the university, and at the stern stone wall of the university library beside it, and wanted to go in, but he knew it was just to avoid thinking about his future, and made himself walk on.

He should move out of his nice, comfortable bunk, anyway, and find himself something a little less luxurious. He certainly did not need two rooms, and while Mrs. Walker fed him extremely well, he could probably fend for himself on more humble food, kale and brose, with a bit of fish, perhaps. But then, how much did Mrs. Walker rely on the money he brought in? Though she ran an excellent bunk, it was not a good time of year to look for new tenants. She might have to wait until the beginning of the new academic year, if she was unlucky.

At the east end of South Street he reached the wall of the Cathedral and the graveyard where little Sybie had been buried the previous week. He did not look towards the modern graves but ahead to the old tombs and to the ruined arches and spires of the Cathedral itself, golden-grey sandstone against the blue sky. A few well-mannered sheep kept the grass low, and a clean white gull perched on a table tomb, watching them disdainfully. More gulls circled above, swooping and calling in the clear air, and crows flapped back and forth amongst the ruins.

It was a popular place for local walkers and appreciators of the picturesque, and Charles could see more than one young lady practising her drawing on the view of the great double spire and arch. Amongst them, fifty yards away or so, he noticed the thin form of Alison Keith, walking arm in arm with her mother, without, Charles thought, her usual energy. She was carrying a folding easel and case, presumably holding her drawing papers. The wind caught at their shawls and bonnets, and they paused to rearrange themselves before slipping their thin arms around each other's waists, walking in a kind of moving hug. Charles looked away, something hurting inside. He could hardly remember his mother.

He walked on slowly, rounding the corner of the cathedral precinct and walking on to the cliffs that bordered it, a broad pathway in between the walls and the cliff edge. Here it was no longer sheltered, and the wind, slapping him hard in the face, whipped the tails and wide sleeves of his gown, lashing at his legs and arms. He grabbed the edges and folded them close across his chest, head down into the wind, one hand on his trencher, and staggered forwards. The path, if he followed it, would take him down towards the shelter of the harbour and its pooled smells of fish, salt, tar and rope. Working its way out round the little headland was the same rowing boat he had seen before near West Sands, and he remembered now what it was: an awful accident off East Sands had led to a public subscription for a lifeboat, and this was it with the crew, practising. Even at this distance he could see the men, local fishermen, mostly, sweating and straining at the oars. Up here, though, the air was bright and fresh, beating at him and hissing in his ears, and he balanced near the cliff edge and looked down at the waters hurled against the rocks below, the gulls spinning and tumbling in the air, and the rocks wet and glistening.

A hand landing hard on his shoulder made him jump, and he nearly went over. He spun round, catching his balance again, to find Rab Fisher laughing at him. Behind him, inevitably, were Boxie and Picket, equally amused. Charles was beginning to feel that he was being followed.

'You're back, then?' he shouted above the wind. 'I hope you were received as well as you hoped you would be.'

'Oh, aye,' said Picket, grinning. Even the wind could raise no colour on his sallow cheeks, though his red lips seemed to shine more bloodily than ever. 'The Principal was thrilled to see us – or more importantly, to see the banker's draft in my hand. Professor Keith was maybe a wee bit more reluctant to take us back into the arms of our alma mater, but what could he do?'

'He was fair scunnered,' giggled Rab. Picket's face froze when he was interrupted, but he carried on as soon as Rab had stopped again.

'He was overruled and undercut,' Picket went on grandly. 'He had no hope in the face of the powerful goddess Pecunia: she waved her little bag of coins and he fell helpless at her feet, gnashing and wailing. I almost felt sorry for the man.'

'But we're leaving that till Friday,' added Rab. Boxie gave a secret little grin, and looked uncomfortable. His face was growing spotty.

'So what's happening on Friday, or should I not ask?' asked Charles, half-dreading finding out. Picket, he suddenly thought, reminded him of some of the nastier Roman emperors, the ones they studied in Suetonius. Perhaps one day they would wake to find orders had been issued for the execution of the entire university Senate, who would be expected to fall on their – swords? No: well-sharpened pens, perhaps.

'Don't tell me Professor Keith hasn't invited you to his little party?' said Picket smoothly.

107

'Oh, yes, he has: I have the acceptance in my pocket. I was just on my way there.'

Boxie looked suspicious, and half-turned to Picket, but said nothing. Charles tried to remember when he had last heard Boxie speak. Picket was smiling.

'Oh, we're going too, but I don't think we need to send an acceptance. Not the way we're going.' His claw-like hands clutched at the ends of his gown, trying to control its flapping but fumbling as if they were cold.

'Oh?'

'No: you could call it a paperless kind of correspondence. There was no invitation, and there'll be no acceptance, and I very much doubt there'll be a thank-you letter on Saturday morning, either!'

'No, indeed,' said Boxie suddenly, and Rab laughed loudly.

'And your plans are all going well?' asked Charles, against his better judgement. They must be intending to sneak into the party by some back door: Professor Keith would not be pleased. He wondered if he wanted to be there to see it or not.

'Oh, very much so,' said Picket, 'very much so. Thanks, as always, to Boxie here – our talented man of knowledge! If you ever need help with any of your academic work, you know, Murray, Boxie here charges very reasonably.'

'I'll bear it in mind,' said Charles, laughing. 'Now I must go, I'm afraid: I shall be expected for supper soon.'

'At the Keiths'?' asked Boxie quickly. Picket looked round at him with interest.

'No, not at all!' said Charles. 'Don't worry: anything you've said is safe with me. It's just my bunkwife who likes me to be there in good time.'

They bowed goodbye to each other, and Charles, pushed by the wind, was quickly back in the street. He turned the corner into Castle Wynd, and in a few moments was handing his acceptance in to the maid Barbara at Professor Keith's front door. She seemed surprised that he was simply leaving it in, but said that the family were out, anyway, and he escaped.

What he had said about Mrs. Walker and her preference for his promptness when supper was ready was true, and he headed back straight away for South Street. He had no wish to meet the Sporting Set again, and he cut straight through Heukster's Wynd rather than go past the Cathedral. In the wynd, he noticed a small boy sitting on one of the rig stairs, and recognised him as the boy George had had look after his horse on the links the day of his arrival, Sybie's older brother. The child had a self-conscious air as Charles nodded at him, and he noticed that the boy's breeches were uncharacteristically whole and had an appearance of stiff newness about them. It was only as he passed further down the narrow lane that he was aware, too, of a particularly fine smell of stew coming from the open front door of Sybie's family's house. He was soon out in South Street again, but the scent of the stew lingered in his nostrils, heavy and warm and full of rich gravy. He had walked on a hundred yards or so when it occurred to him that the stew had had meat in it, and good meat, too, by the smell. There was probably little enough meat to be had in a household like that, where fish would be much more common. And new breeches, as well ... He wondered, without thinking about it much, if the family had come into some money. Perhaps Ramsay Rickarton was helping his daughter a bit out of sympathy – but then, janitors were almost certainly not paid much, either. He considered it a mystery, and dismissed it from his mind.

Chapter Ten

'I've been robbed, damn it!'

Professor Keith swept across the quadrangle to the Cage like an avenging raven, crying his misfortune to the wind. In the Cage, his daughter Alison was waiting, pale and nervy, not helped by her father's exclamation. Professor Shaw, timid as a frog in a pond when he spies a heron, shook in his black gown and edged behind a pillar. Charles, who was sitting on one of the stone benches at the end of the Cage near the vestry door, looked up from his book with interest at Professor Keith's shout, and saw him spring into the Cage with his gown tails flapping in the wind, a raven coming to rest on his perch.

'I knew I should never have trusted my possessions to the miserable security of that derelict over there, though I only moved them because I thought they were not safe at home, with skeletons and crow's corpses and all kinds of things happening.' Keith waved across the quadrangle to where his office lay next to Professor Urquhart's luxurious apartments. 'A child could take that lock off with a butter knife, the door is so rotten. The man who did it – well, it must have been easy for him, of all people.'

'You know who did it, father?' asked Alison in surprise. She was wreathed in scarves and shawls, which twitched around her as she jittered.

'Of course I know: who else would have any reason to steal from me? It is quite ridiculous to expect honesty from anyone these days: dishonesty passes from father to child like syphilis, and weakens the next generations to the father's everlasting disgrace.' He spat the words out, glaring around him as if demanding a challenge to his words, someone to shout down. Charles wondered at his choice of words. The comparison with syphilis was a bit on the violent side, particularly in front of his daughter, but why had he said 'father to child', instead of the more usual 'father to son'? Clearly he had some specific example in mind. Charles tried to think of any dishonest women he knew, but reflected sadly that he had led a sheltered life.

'But if you know who it is,' said Shaw, wrapping his gown around him like woollen armour, and tangling his short fingers in its fraying edges, 'if you know who it is, shouldn't you say?'

Professor Keith turned on him, and Shaw quailed.

'Say? Say? Oh, I shall say, indeed, in good time. I shall bring it up at the next Senate meeting on Monday, and as God is my judge *someone*, someone who has deserved it for some time, will lose his position.'

Ramsay Rickarton, appearing in the Cage at that moment with his livery coat buttons done up wrongly, stopped at these words and stared at Professor Keith, alarm in his red eyes. Charles, as unnoticed in his corner as Ramsay was at the other end of the Cage, watched as Ramsay straightened his shoulders, his head bobbing on his thin neck, a nasty angle to his chin, fists forming hard and solid at his cuffs. Then he seemed to change his mind, and before Keith had even seen that he was there behind him, Ramsay had disappeared through the heavy wooden doorway into the Chapel, taking his white package of rat poison out of his pocket as he went.

'But just now I have more urgent matters to attend to,' Keith was saying.

'Oh, you have a lecture to give?' Shaw asked, with a tentative smile. Keith frowned, dismissing such a foolish idea.

'No, not at all. I have the much more important task of punishing some students for their misdeeds. Your sporting set again, Professor Shaw: Picket Irving, Rab Fisher and James Skene. They thought they could walk back into the university unpunished just because Irving's guardian made a substantial donation to the Principal, but I am not so soft. The Principal thinks only of money, and is more easily swayed by a parent or guardian's influence than by the honour of the University, but you and I, Shaw, you and I must have the welfare of the students at heart, and the common good of all. These three are the most disruptive, disrespectful boys I have ever had the misfortune to teach, and they must be punished soundly for all they have done. Last time they evaded me: this time I shall take them unawares.'

111

'How – how will you do that?' asked Shaw, but Keith no longer trusted anyone.

'That we shall see, Professor Shaw, that we shall see.' He gave a thin-lipped smile, and his chins settled firmly into his high collar as if to signify his determination. 'Alison, are you ready to go?'

'Oh!' said his daughter, 'just a moment, Father. I must just –' She adjusted her little square reticule and skipped into the Chapel. Keith, mouth open to say something, frowned, but not with much anger.

'You'll be coming this evening, won't you, Shaw?' he turned instead to his colleague. Shaw managed to smile.

'Oh, yes, yes, we're looking forward to it. At least – I hope you won't mind – my wife, you know ... delicate condition ... might not ... though she'll be dreadfully disappointed, but you do understand ...?'

'Oh, of course, of course,' said Keith quickly. Charles was not sure, in the shade of the Cage, but he thought for a moment that Keith blushed suddenly, and as quickly returned to his normal complexion.

Alison reappeared at the door of the Chapel with Ramsay Rickarton close behind her as she turned to bid him farewell. She hurried over to her father, smiling her wide smile, and took his arm quite as if he were not the most frightening man in the town. They left the Cage together and vanished towards North Street, and Professor Shaw visibly sagged as if the tension had gone out of his body. Charles was about to call out to him when the chapel door opened once again, and Mungo Dalzell came out, a look of serenity on his face. Charles had noticed that he had been spending a good deal of time in the chapel recently, and others had remarked on it, too: he was not sure if antinomians usually prayed in established churches, but at any rate it seemed to be doing Mungo good, for he seemed more cheerful than he had done for months, even before Sybie's tragic death. Only when his gaze fell on Ramsay Rickarton did a deep sorrow pass across his expression, and Charles wondered if Mungo was assured that he himself was one of the Lord's Chosen, but was not so sure about Sybie. He tried to remember Burns' 'Holy Willie's Prayer', but could not quite fit the pattern of the sanctimonious Willie on to Mungo Dalzell, whose serenity seemed to come less from self-satisfaction than from the pleasure of duty done. He glided up to his friend Professor Shaw, and bowed.

'Our colleague Professor Keith has some further concerns?' he asked, nodding in the direction in which the Keiths had departed. 'I met Miss Keith in the Chapel, talking with Ramsay Rickarton. She said her father was waiting for her, and not in great form.'

'Well, and is that anything unusual?' Shaw responded, with a sorry shrug. 'He says he's been robbed: apparently he left some valuables in his office over there, and they've gone. Those rooms have never been very secure, though.'

'True enough,' agreed Mungo smoothly. 'Maybe he should have left them at home.'

'He says he knows who did it, though,' said Shaw sadly. 'That is my chief concern: he says he's going to lose someone their place when he condemns them on Monday at the Senate meeting. I do worry about him, you know. He will really damage someone soon, and that is not good for him, let alone the person he damages. He says he's doing it for the sake of the University, but I am sure he never really considers the consequences.' He sighed heavily.

'Did he say who he thought it was?' asked Mungo.

'No, but I think he thinks it was Picket or Boxie or Rab, one of those three boys. They are terrible, you know. He's quite likely right. But now I come to think of it, maybe it wasn't them he had in mind, for he said that the culprit would lose his place, and he has plenty of reason to send the boys away from the University if he wanted to, and he says he doesn't. Am I making any sense, do you think?' he asked with a watery smile, and Mungo grinned, patting him on the shoulder.

'Very little, my dear Davie! Never mind, I'm sure we shall soon find out. Senate meetings are much less dull with Professor Keith about, anyway!'

'True, true, Mungo, but do you know I much prefer dullness. Oh!' He turned, and spotted Charles packing his book into his book-satchel. 'Here is one of my students already. I must go, but I shall see you tonight, Mungo, shall I not? At Professor Keith's?'

'Yes, yes, of course,' said Mungo, though he seemed already to be thinking about other things. 'I shall look forward to it.'

When Charles arrived back at his bunk at the end of the morning's lessons, he was tired and hungry and looking forward to a meal. He expected to see Mrs. Walker or her daughter about the place, going to set the table, popping out into the hall to see if he was back. What he did not expect was a snatched-open door, an 'Oh!' of surprise, and a small, scruffy individual shooting out into the hall to present himself before him. It was Daniel.

'I thought I left you at Letho,' said Charles, somewhat ungraciously. 'What are you doing here? Father isn't here, is he?' he added hurriedly, glancing at the stairs.

'Mr. Murray? No, sir, he's no,' said Daniel with a cheery grin. 'I'm here by mysel.'

'Availing yourself of Mrs. Walker's hospitality in the kitchen, no doubt,' said Charles, noticing fresh soup stains on Daniel's livery. Daniel nodded with enthusiasm.

'And what else?'

'Bread, sir, and ale,' Daniel explained.

'No,' Charles suppressed a sigh. 'What else are you here for? Who sent you?'

'Oh, Mr. George sent me, sir. He sent me off pretty quick, once he found me. He made me hide in his room, and then he took me off to the stagecoach himself, and watched me go.'

'And what was the purpose of this urgency? Did he give you a message, or anything?' If this was George's idea of a joke, Charles was unimpressed: he was worried enough about feeding himself, without having to find fuel for this eating machine, too. 'Oh,' he said suddenly, remembering something. 'He didn't send you for a small parcel, did he?' The cantharides, or whatever it was, that George had asked him to buy in Edinburgh, was upstairs in his bedchamber: he had been

114

in such a hurry to leave Letho undetected that he had forgotten to leave it there. Daniel, however, looked blank.

'No, sir. He gave me this note, though.' Out of his pocket he drew a crumpled scrap of paper which did, however, bear George's seal, messily applied as if in great haste. Charles unpicked it carefully, and opened out the page.

'My dear Charles,' it began. 'Herewith Daniel. I hid the papers you returned here. Father thinks you are still in Edinburgh and is pleased. No one saw Daniel who will tell and I gave the groom a sovereign not to blab – he thinks it's some kind of joke. Keep Daniel till I see you – not far behind,
'George'.

That would explain, at least, why his father in the form of an avenging angel had not yet descended upon him at St. Andrews and dragged him back to Letho. He suddenly realised how much he had been dreading that happening, as a wave of grateful relief swept over him. Good old George! It was really very impressive: George did not always think things through very competently, but this just showed what he could do when he tried. Charles was delighted. Suddenly the future seemed brighter – he was not alone, he had an ally. He clapped Daniel on the shoulder, for want of George, and grinned happily.

The afternoon seemed to bear out his mood, for as he walked back, attended by Daniel, to his lectures, the sun shone with the first real warmth of the spring, drying out the muddy streets so that the ridges turned powdery even as the ruts stayed damp. People lingered at the wells he passed in South Street and North Street, chatting and exchanging news, content to spend a few extra minutes lingering out of doors.

There were several possible routes that would take Charles from Mrs. Walker's to United College, and today he chose Mutty's Wynd as his path between Market Street and North Street. It was narrow and shady, and halfway along it was a bun shop. Charles had emerged, followed by Daniel, on to North Street when a thought occurred to him. He had brought Daniel with him rather than leave him back at his bunk on the grounds that Daniel was less likely to get into trouble the nearer he was to Charles. However, there was little for him to do while Charles sat in his lecture, and feeding him seemed to be a good way to encourage his good behaviour. Charles fished in his pocket for a penny, and handed it to Daniel.

'Run back to the bakery there and buy yourself a good big bun, then catch up with me.'

Daniel was not slow to follow basic commands of this kind. The bow of acknowledgement he gave was in one flowing motion with his departure, and Charles laughed at the speed he could show when it was important. However, he had hardly gone two paces when Daniel, panting with excitement, reappeared, tugging his gown.

'Mr. Charles, sir! Mr. Charles! There's a fight! Come and see!'

Almost at once he was away again, running back to Mutty's Wynd, and Charles was only a step or two behind him. He expected to see a couple of fishermen – or even their wives – settling some dispute with their fists. He was astonished, though, to see Boxie Skene, alone for once, with a look of complete surprise on his face. Opposite him in the narrow lane, flailing like a tree in a gale, was Peter Keith, son of the eminent professor.

Charles ran up, Daniel close by his side and grinning from ear to ear. Boxie, caution taking over from shock, had his guard up now and had started to strike back. Peter Keith, his face white with passion, lashed out at Boxie's well-protected chest, and Boxie easily pushed the blow aside, turning the action into a strike to Peter's shoulder that spun him round.

A crowd was starting to gather, beginning with the owner of the bun shop and her assistant. One of the University janitors sidled up and started trying to gauge the odds on the two men: both were well-enough kent faces in the small town, even though Boxie was a student, and each had his supporters. Boxie was by far the better fighter, but he was encumbered by his gown. His book satchel, leather and heavy, lay at his feet with the buckle burst, just where it must have fallen. Peter, speechless with fury, seemed to have some reason to attack Boxie, and that impetus was keeping him on his feet despite his own lack of skill.

Recovering from the shoulder-blow, Peter lunged again, putting his whole strength into it. Seeing it, Boxie tried to

116

sidestep. He tripped on his satchel, falling hard against the wall. He scrabbled to regain his balance, but Peter was on him, clawing and punching whatever bit of Boxie he could reach. His lips were drawn back, showing clenched teeth, his breath hissing. Boxie yelped and swore, struggling against Peter's irresistible force.

Charles decided it was time to intervene. He stepped forward and grabbed Peter's shoulders, and received an elbow in the stomach for his trouble. Doubled up, he struck out with his foot at Peter's ankle. His boot hit the ankle bone with a satisfying solidity. Peter shrieked. Boxie squirmed to free himself, but lost his balance and toppled over. He fell against Charles' leg, knocking him sideways across the lane to crash against the opposite wall. Peter, his targets thus divided, stood in the middle of the lane for a second, staring wildly from one to the other of them, then dived again at Boxie. Boxie, in a better position now to retaliate, waited for precisely the right point of Peter's dive, and socked him hard in the face. Peter was flung across the lane, into Charles' arms, and was seized from behind. Boxie grabbed his feet, and held them down. Peter struggled furiously for a moment.

'You filthy, selfish, dog!' he spat at Boxie. 'You disgusting, filthy, evil ...' Overcome by the effort of trying to think of fresh insults, Peter collapsed, trying to reach his bloody nose with one of his trapped, flapping hands. Charles could feel him shuddering.

The crowd, clapping their hands in mock applause, laughed and dispersed, leaving the students to mete out their own punishment. Only Daniel still stood watching, delighted that his master should have added to his entertainment so generously, even the penny in his hand forgotten. Charles, still keeping tight hold of Peter Keith, nodded to him.

'Go on and buy your bun, Daniel: the excitement is over.' Daniel reluctantly disappeared into the warm bakery, and Charles gave Peter a little shake. 'What was all that about, eh?' he asked.

'I – I can't say, Murray,' said Peter. Now that the fight had gone out of him, he had reverted to his usual nervy self, more like his sister Alison than ever. He flicked a look at

117

Boxie, who had let go of his legs and was propped against the other wall, wiping his forehead. His gown was liberally covered in the usual rubbish that accumulates against the walls of narrow lanes, including one or two fragments of buns. His mortarboard had one corner bent, and he did not look his best.

'Boxie?' asked Charles. 'Are you all right?'

'Yes, yes,' said Boxie, wearily, though he was rubbing his shoulder where it had hit the wall. 'Never worry about it, Murray. He was just a bit upset, weren't you, Peter?'

'Aye, that's right,' agreed Peter, a look of relief suddenly washing his bloody face. 'I'm sorry, and all that, Skene.'

'Och,' said Boxie with a grin, 'for the matter of that I think you came off the worse. I bunk just here. Come on upstairs and let's get a cold cloth for your nose, eh?'

Charles let Peter go, and he staggered across the lane where Boxie caught him. Peter's eyes had started to swell and close, and his nose had a distinctly unfamiliar shape. Puzzled, Charles watched them go, and saw Boxie turn to give him a nod of thanks just before they disappeared into a doorway, Boxie supporting Peter with an arm round his shoulders.

Daniel sauntered out of the bakery with a bun the size of a small plate clutched between his two hands, one bite already in his mouth.

'That was just brilliant, sir, wasn't it?' he asked, spewing crumbs around him. It was already ranking as the most exciting week of his short life.

'Don't speak with your mouth full, Daniel,' said Charles absently, turning back towards North Street. It was past time for his lecture, and he would have the opportunity to puzzle over Boxie and Peter Keith later. Daniel followed dutifully behind. Torn between speaking and eating, Daniel quickly decided to devote his full attention to the bun. It did not long survive the experience.

Chapter Eleven

Mrs. Walker let it be known, during the course of the afternoon, that she and her daughter had also been invited to the reception at Professor and Mrs. Keith's house and would be glad of an escort, and Charles willingly agreed. When they could not afford a carriage, it was undoubtedly more desirable for ladies to be escorted to a social function: it made it look as if the walk itself were part of the evening's entertainment and infinitely to be preferred to a dull slog in a stuffy barouche, whatever the damage to one's skirts and slippers. Charles, his evening dress quite in keeping with his father's expectations, with a clotted cream silk waistcoat and new buckles on his shoes, gave an arm to each of them and trotted them along South Street and round the corner, keeping to the wider, cleaner roads. Mrs. Walker had clearly found the absence of her husband's portrait very trying at her collar, and was wearing some smaller, cheaper brooch in its place: her white hair was covered, under her velvet bonnet, with her best black lace cap, and a little busy stitching had modified the shape of her sleeves into a more fashionable style. Miss Walker was practical and pretty in yellow muslin with short sleeves, trimmed with blue ribbon purchased only last week from the chapman, and never before seen in public. The evening was cool, and she wore her ordinary everyday long-tailed spencer over the dress. Life in the Walker establishment did not include so many evening entertainments as to admit of specially purchased evening cloaks. It did not cross Charles' mind to be ashamed of them, however: Miss Walker glowed with happy anticipation of the evening ahead, and Mrs. Walker was pleased enough to have an excuse to put on her finery for the occasion. He felt fond of them both, and had to crush the qualms he was suffering about having to tell them he was leaving their comfortable home. Daniel went ahead of them with the torch he was to use later, and added depth, if not grandeur, to their progress.

Though it was only just dusk, the drive at the Keiths' house, short as it was, was lit on either side by torches, which also flared on the gateposts and at each doorpost. The door was

119

open, and the maid Barbara welcomed them in, taking their coats and hats until she seemed ready to disappear under the heap. She deposited them quickly on a settle and hurried upstairs ahead of them to announce the new guests at the drawing room door before going back to sort the coats out.

The drawing room was fine, with yellow draperies and a good fire going in the plain marble fireplace. Already several guests, students and staff, were gathered in small groups about the room. Professor Keith and his wife held these soirées a few times during each academic year, inviting only the most senior of students, the intent being to prepare them for the outside world by introducing them to polite society and encouraging them to regard their tutors as pleasant acquaintances rather than slave-drivers of evil intent. That the success of these social occasions varied tremendously was something that passed by the Keiths' consciousness: they had done their duty, honed their lucky subjects to their idea of perfection, and felt the satisfaction of the charitable. A few suitably marriageable girls would be asked to provide musical entertainment. Often, too, some patron of a parish would be invited, and appropriate candidates introduced to him or her, or some advocate in need of an apprentice, or minor noble anxious for a tutor for his sons. The magistrands would be paraded like ponies in a sales ring, sometimes tested for their learning, sometimes observed for their sobriety, more often questioned about their background, parentage and station. It was not a happy experience, and on previous occasions Charles had felt uncomfortable watching its progress, but this time he himself was hoping to find some position in the same way and found the prospect daunting, as well as distasteful.

Charles was not surprised to see Thomas there with his hair brushed and his uneven jaw shaved quite neatly, for once: he hoped to have a second chance with Lord Scoggie, and was determined, in the face of all obstacles, to make the most of it this time. For the moment, however, Lord Scoggie had not arrived, and Thomas was standing peaceably with Allan Bonar. Charles, determined to have a reasonable conversation with them both before they noticed that Patience Walker had

120

arrived, excused himself from the Walkers and their hostess and went to join the men.

'Few people realise that lily of the valley is actually quite poisonous,' Bonar was saying as Charles approached. 'Oh, good evening, Murray, good to see you.' They bowed to each other.

'We were just talking about Mr. Bonar's researches,' Thomas explained. He had a glass of wine in his hand, and was looking much more cheerful than usual, if a little nervous. 'He's working on the extraction of certain substances from plants – just ordinary plants!'

'And lily of the valley is poisonous, is it?' Charles asked, quite interested. He thought he had seen some somewhere, recently, but could not call it to mind.

'Oh, yes: it is sometimes used in small quantities for medicinal purposes, but in larger doses it is quite deadly.' Bonar, his dark eyes alight, had the look of a man just checking the saddle girth on his hobby horse, and preparing to mount. 'It's not unlike arsenic, in that respect, of course: many people take very small doses of arsenic for stomach complaints, and find a palliative effect, but of course we use it for all kinds of deadly purposes, too. Rat-killing, for example.'

'Indeed. I think I would have to suffer from very bad stomach pains before I would risk taking even a small dose of arsenic,' Charles laughed, and Thomas and Bonar agreed. 'But arsenic is not taken from plants, is it?'

But the conversation, promising as it was, was not destined to continue, for at that very moment both Thomas and Bonar spotted Patience Walker, and she saw them. Thomas and Bonar instantly shifted slightly further apart, as if driven by an electrical charge, and the air of mutual intellectual discussion was gone for good. Charles waited until Miss Walker had approached and joined the conversation, and gently manoeuvred himself out of it.

He looked around the room, which was already quite busy. Peter Keith, jittering beside his mother and sister, tried to look as if he was unaware that he had two neat black eyes on either side of an uncomfortably bulky nose. Alison Keith was also fluttery, clinging to her father's arm. She was wearing a soft cream silk dress, very pretty, with a paisley shawl in brown and cream, and on her bare arms was a pair of bracelets. They caught Charles' eye and he stared at them for a moment: they were of an unusual design, of dark brown stones chained together, and made him think instantly of Imperial Rome. He wondered why, and then remembered where he had seen such bracelets before: they had been in the window of the jeweller's shop behind the Tron in Edinburgh on Tuesday. He wondered how common they were, and how Alison Keith had come by them. They suited her.

The drawing room door opened again, and another guest arrived. Charles turned to see – and was astonished to find his brother George, splendid in the most fashionable of evening waistcoats, striding in with beaming face to greet his hostess. His cravat was so extravagantly tied that his head seemed to ride on a seafroth of linen, and as he bowed to Mrs. Keith Charles half-expected to see it float away.

George had flowers for Mrs. Keith, straight from the hothouses at Letho, and to Alison he presented, with eager anxiety, a tray of what Charles could just see were crystallised fruits. He wondered if the poor Letho cook had had to make them to George's specifications, and grinned at the idea. George was disposed to linger around Alison, but she set the fruits aside with a wide, noncommittal smile, and seemed to dismiss him. Professor Keith, close beside his daughter, also nodded at him, as though kindly to reinforce the dismissal. Still beaming, as one who feels there is hope yet, George turned to survey the room, and immediately saw his brother.

'Charles!' he exclaimed. 'Excellent! Did Daniel arrive all right?'

'He did,' Charles admitted, 'though I'm still not quite clear about what is going on. Where exactly does Father think I am?'

'In Edinburgh, of course,' said George proudly. 'I worked it all out. As long as you were in Edinburgh, he would be pleased, and he would not forbid you to return to St. Andrews. If he forbade you to return here, he would not look favourably on me coming up here, for whatever purpose, and just at present, Charles, I really do need to come up here.

Persistence is all-important in these matters, isn't it? So I hid Daniel, and sent him to you, and I hid the papers – they were not really important, anyway, he just used them as an excuse to send you to town –'

'I suspected as much.'

'- and there we are!' George was shining with self-satisfaction.

'But don't you think,' said Charles gently, 'that when he finds out he has been deceived, that he might be even more angry and inclined to forbid me to come back?'

'How could he find out? I bribed the groom to say nothing about bringing you back up here.'

'Well, old Marmalade Head could write to him, or old Mrs. Grant, or he could ask me straight out – and I wouldn't lie to him, George, I don't think I could – or he might come up here for some other reason and happen to see me.'

George dismissed such possibilities.

'None of those will happen for ages, and by then who knows what might have happened? You might manage to graduate, or make a rich marriage, or Father might just find something else to worry about.'

'Like you not making a rich marriage, eh?'

George turned irresistibly to look again at Alison Keith.

'She is lovely, isn't she? So much life!'

Charles made an ambiguous noise, which seemed to be enough for George.

'Come on,' Charles tugged at his brother's arm, 'we'd better do the rounds a bit. If you spend the evening staring at the host's daughter you'll be thrown out.'

'Oh, well, then: who's here?'

'Thomas is, and Allan Bonar.'

'Thomas is very dreary,' George objected.

'He is at the moment, anyway: he and Bonar are battling for the affection of Patience Walker, and all they do is score points against one another and grow irritable. Look, there's Professor Shaw and Mungo Dalzell: are they good enough for you?'

'I suppose so, though I did not come all the way up here to talk about philosophy or theology,' George grumbled. 'I want to talk to pretty girls.'

Unrepentant, Charles guided his brother over to where Professor Shaw was standing near the fire with Mungo Dalzell, each of them nursing a glass of wine as if they did not intend to drink. Professor Shaw beamed up at Charles as he came over.

'I believe you may have met my brother, George.' Charles presented him just in case, and all three men bowed low. Beside George's splendour, the two academics looked very shabby, but rather more comfortable. 'May I enquire after Mrs. Shaw, sir?' Charles asked. Professor Shaw looked pleased.

'She is very well, very well indeed, in general,' he said, 'but disappointed not to be here this evening. She has had much discomfort today, and is constrained to stay at home with her feet up. Her mother is with her, though.'

'I believe that is a great comfort at a time like this,' Mungo Dalzell said sagely, and they all nodded, three bachelors and a man to be a father for the first time.

'Her time of trial is at hand,' Professor Shaw went on, 'but she is young and healthy, and there is no reason, no reason at all why she should not survive it well.' Again they nodded, and George added a little sigh, as of sympathy with the whole female race.

'Cats are so much more simple,' came a voice, and they looked about to find Professor Urquhart hovering at the edge of their circle. 'They vanish into a corner, and within a day or two are hunting again, and in the mean time have produced any number of offspring at one go. Have you seen this extraordinary watercolour, Mungo?'

He led Mungo Dalzell off to view, with apparent derision, some work of art on Professor Keith's drawing room wall, leaving George and Charles with Professor Shaw. Charles nodded towards Mungo's back.

'Is he all right now, sir?' he asked.

Professor Shaw frowned.

'I think so,' he said. 'He has gloomy moments, but they seem to be overcome by a visit to the College Chapel. I do not

124

think I have ever seen him there so much before: I think before he considered it a somewhat Papist edifice, but just now it seems to give him great consolation. Perhaps he will be drawn back into the fold of the established Church, and good will have come of the whole thing in the end.'

'Excuse me,' said George suddenly, '- an acquaintance.' He bowed hurriedly to Professor Shaw, and vanished.

The drawing room was really very crowded now, and there were few seats to be had. Charles glanced round to see where George could have gone, and to his surprise realised that the Sporting Set were amongst the guests.

Alison must have strayed from the door into the body of the room, and at that moment Picket Irving was presenting her with a box of sweetmeats. He was on his own: Rab Fisher was near one of the windows, smiling his vague but handsome smile at George, and Boxie was near the fireplace, watching Picket with burning eyes. Picket seemed to feel his gaze: he smiled his lupine smile and turned to wave Boxie over. He seemed to be trying to persuade Alison to eat one of the sweetmeats there and then, but she, with a polite smile, was flapping her hand in denial. Boxie, too, was refusing to yield to Picket's will, and half-turned away, though he watched still. Alison had not noticed Boxie, for she was concentrating on trying to escape from Picket without being actually rude. Charles could see the broad smile fix on her face, stiffly, while she turned and twisted the bracelets on her arms, eyes downcast, feet edging away.

Charles turned to look at Boxie again, and was surprised to see Peter Keith hurrying over towards his erstwhile sparring-partner with a welcoming hand outstretched. Since Picket had made it clear to Charles that he, Rab and Boxie were not invited to Professor Keith's soirée, Peter Keith's clear enthusiasm seemed even more unlikely, and Charles moved over to his brother George to share the gossip about the fight.

No supper as such was to be served, but little trays were laid about the room containing pastries and other manageable food, and they were occasionally replenished by the maid under Professor Keith's watchful eye: it was not unknown for impoverished students to starve themselves for a few days to

125

make the most of his largesse, a practice he had no wish to encourage. George, who had no excuse, had annexed one of the plates and he and Rab were making neat surgical excursions into its contents at an unnatural rate, gossiping as they went. Charles broke in at a good moment, when they both had their mouths full.

'You see Peter Keith's fine nose?'

George glanced around, trying to locate Peter. Rab had no need to, and laughed.

'Aye, a grand one, is it not?'

'Did you hear how it happened?' Charles asked.

'Ouch,' said George, catching a glimpse of it. 'That looks fresh. What was it?'

Charles looked at Rab to confirm his story.

'Peter attacked Boxie this afternoon in Mutty's Wynd, and had to be dragged off him. What was it all about, Rab?'

Rab looked completely blank.

'Boxie did it?' he said. 'He never told us. Why would he do that?'

'Well, Peter was giving him laldy,' said Charles. 'He had no choice. He was down on the ground with his back against the wall.'

'Grand!' said George. 'I wish I'd seen that!'

'I'm surprised you didn't know,' said Charles to Rab. 'Boxie took him up to your lodgings to wash his face –'

'Boxie did what? To a man who had just laid into him?'

'The wind seemed to go out of Peter after a minute or two, and he apologised to Boxie, and all was sweetness and light,' Charles explained, though he did not understand it himself. 'Anyway, you mustn't have been in. There was blood everywhere. You were sure to have noticed.'

'No, I was out this afternoon – with Picket. We were out,' said Rab, with slightly unnecessary emphasis.

'They seem friendly enough now, anyway,' said George, watching the two men talking together near the fire. Peter had his hand on Boxie's shoulder in an affectionate manner, but the talk seemed to be of a serious nature: they were staring at the floor, frowning, and talking out of the corners of their mouths at each other. No one nearby was paying them any attention.

126

Nor was George, after a second or two, for there was a piano in the bay of the big window, and Alison Keith was turning the pages as Patience Walker began to play.

There was nothing frivolous about Patience Walker's performance. She had the air of a girl who knew she had to have some accomplishment and had chosen this one, had devoted to it precisely the amount of time it took for her to be proficient, and had then spent her time on more useful things. She played a suitable piece of music, as it had been written on the paper with neither error nor embellishment, smiling pleasantly but not excessively as she did it, and did not sing. When she had finished, she thanked Alison for her help, raised an eyebrow and gave a small curtsey at the applause she received, and returned to her seat between her mamma and Thomas Seaton. If she tossed a little glance at Allan Bonar as she passed him, it was probably also for purely practical purposes.

Bonar, presumably instructed as her father's assistant, was to turn the pages for Alison Keith's performance, though there were other more eager candidates for the role: George was almost panting to dash to the piano, but Charles, trying to teach him decorum as he would teach a spaniel restraint, had both hands on his arm. Instead George had to content himself by watching adoringly from the other window, resting his head on the full curtain, and tapping one discreet foot in time to the music.

This in itself was a feat of devotion, as Miss Keith did not choose to allow exact rhythm to cramp her sense of expression. She sang as well as she played, in a thready soprano that reminded Charles of the wind on sand dunes, hissing slightly when she went too fast. Her eyes were mostly on Boxie, though her expression was ambiguous. He noticed that the sweetmeat box and George's tray of crystallised fruit were both on top of the piano, both untouched. No wonder Alison was thin. He smiled.

Other girls took Alison's place when she had finished, and played on, but conversation had started quietly again amongst the less musically inclined. Professor Keith had watched his daughter from the doorway, and was about to go

127

over to her now but he was intercepted by his son, Peter, and Boxie. Charles watched, letting his mind drift to a German flute solo. Professor Keith looked astonished, and then managed a strained smile as he acknowledged Boxie's bow. Charles wondered what was going on, particularly when the three men, after a moment's discussion, turned and left the room.

He looked round further. Professor Shaw, now seated beside Mungo Dalzell, was trying a discreet look at his pocket watch, probably wanting to return to his expectant wife. Mungo Dalzell appeared to be enjoying the music, a slight smile on his face, arms folded as he leaned back in his chair with his long legs sticking out in front of him. Professor Urquhart was poised by the mantelpiece, a glass of wine in his elegant hand, adjusting some invisible imperfection in his wig as the firelight twinkled on his coat buttons. He seemed to have been in conversation with Lord Scoggie, who was at the other side of the fireplace like the other half of the fire irons, gazing into the distance. Thomas had left Patience Walker and was propped against the wall, staring hungrily at Lord Scoggie as if he himself was the living he had it in his power to bestow. Mrs. Walker, observing that Allan Bonar had returned not to his own seat but to Thomas', beside her daughter, did not look pleased, but was not in a position to do much about it, and Bonar and her daughter talked quietly between themselves as the music played on.

The music was reasonably good, and Charles was enjoying it. He would have liked a dance, but there were too many people and not enough room, and he could not see anyone in the Keith family suggesting it. He had his wine glass refilled by the maid, and wondered if he should try to approach anyone about becoming a tutor, but the only prospective employer he could see in the room was Lord Scoggie, and his life would not be worth living if he beat Thomas to that particular golden goose. He bit thoughtfully into a chicken pastry, and tried to calculate how long it might be before his father found out that he was back in St. Andrews. George was always over-optimistic.

He was thus lost in thought when he felt his arm tapped, and Professor Shaw was standing at his elbow.

'Excuse me, Charles, but if you don't mind – Lord Scoggie has just asked if you would be good enough to come and be presented.'

Astonished, Charles straightened smartly and disposed of the chicken pastry. He followed the little Professor over to the fireplace.

'Lord Scoggie, may I have the honour to present one of my fourth-year students, Mr. Charles Murray, younger of Letho?' Professor Shaw said, with great exactness. Charles bowed very low, but Lord Scoggie aimiably claimed not to need such worship, and urged him to straighten up at once lest he injure his back. Lord Scoggie was a little shorter than Charles but above the middle height, with teeth so prominent that they seemed to act on their own account, and a little of his own grey hair showing indecorously at the temples of his powdered wig.

'I hope you are taking great benefit from your studies?' said his Lordship.

'I am, my lord, indeed,' Charles replied. 'I am very fortunate in my tutors, of course.'

Lord Scoggie smiled broadly, allowing his teeth a freedom of expression that was fascinating. Charles tried not to stare.

'You are indeed, as I was in my days here – not surprisingly, as Professors Urquhart and Shaw were among them even then. You are a young man, and probably do not find it surprising that such ancient relics as these gentlemen should have taught Methuselah in his youth, let alone me, but when you reach my age you will realise that indeed they must have begun with lecturing in their very cradles to have produced so many satisfied students. And do you hope to graduate?'

'If the examiners are generous, my lord, I do!' said Charles, hiding his concern over that very issue. 'But even if I do not, it will never diminish, I think, my affection for the place and for what I have learned here.'

'I am glad to hear it,' said Lord Scoggie, more solemn now. 'For Master of Arts is not a title conferred lightly: it is a great honour. Money or privilege may bring you here, may fund your studies and make your life comfortable, but it will abandon you in that examination chair, as I found to my cost!' Here he smiled again, at trials long past. 'Hard work and native wit, in almost whatever proportion you please – that is the mixture to apply. Before the examiner, we are all equal, except in those two things. But here: this is a social occasion, and I see from your face you are eager to apply yourself at present more to admiring the endless line of young beauties entertaining us than to listen to a tedious old man, however remarkable he might be in the dental line, eh?'

Charles did not know what to say, and was spared by the general laughter of Lord Scoggie and Professor Shaw at his lordship's own expense.

'Never mind, Mr. Murray,' said Lord Scoggie at last: 'go back to your friends. I am heartily glad we have had this little talk, sir.'

'Thank you, my lord,' said Charles, hesitating to bow low, and feeling himself completely dismissed. Turning, he saw Thomas at once, glowering at him, and thought it best to go straight to him.

'What, precisely, was going on there?' Thomas asked, in a voice almost entirely acid.

'I have no idea, Thomas,' said Charles, trying to soothe. 'Professor Shaw called me over. I promise you, though: if he offers me a parish, I shall decline it with thanks, and lay your name before him. But Thomas – we must talk some time, though not here. There may be other reasons why I should like, if I could, to meet Lord Scoggie and his like at the moment.'

'If it were anyone but you, with your money and position, I should not trust them an inch with the man,' said Thomas with grim sincerity. 'But I swear to you, he is my only chance of advancement, if I am not to be a miserable village schoolmaster for twenty years, waiting for preferment before I can think of – marriage, or anything beyond scraping a pathetic living for myself.'

'I know, I know,' Charles agreed. 'If I could do anything to help you, I would: just be assured I shall not knowingly do anything to hinder you.'

They fell silent on this compromise, and listened again to the music, currently a pair of violins unhappily married and fallen on bad times. The door opened again and Professor Keith returned, on his own. Extra chairs had been brought in before the music started, and it was now easier for him to survey his guests than it had been when they were mostly standing. He had entered the drawing room with an unaccustomed smile on his face, and stood for a second with his gaze on his daughter, seated in the front of the informal rows waiting, presumably, to be asked to play again. Then, unfortunately, his gaze lifted and scanned the rest of the room, and the first person he saw was Rab Fisher.

Rab was lost in what might, in anyone else, have been thought. He did not see Professor Keith notice him, and had no idea that anything was about to happen, but munched contently on yet another of his hostess's excellent pastries. The first he knew of his fate was when Professor Keith's hand landed heavily on his shoulder, and the last mouthful of pastry shot out to land messily on the back of Alison Keith's bare bony neck. She gave a shriek. The better violinist, faltering at Professor Keith's progress across the room, stopped altogether. Rab dropped his wine glass, leaving a red trail down the yellow curtains, but he had no chance to do anything about it. Professor Keith, in grim silence, marched him to the door. What happened to him in the hall was a matter for conjecture: the silent guests shortly heard the front door slam, and Professor Keith returned in splendid isolation, just in time to see Picket flinging open one of the windows, one hand full of pastries. He darted across the room. Picket leapt through the window, crashed into a bush, and was heard rolling free, laughing and calling back at Keith something that was fortunately indistinct. Professor Keith slammed the window shut, and ran for the door, calling for the servants. He vanished into the hall, and silence returned once more.

'Charlotte, dear,' said Mrs Keith into the quavering hush, 'do start that lovely piece again. I'm sure we should all like to hear it uninterrupted.' She continued wiping her daughter's neck free of pastry.

The page-turner scuffled back the pages, and the violinists, now even more shaky, began the piece again, but the guests, contrary to Mrs. Keith's expectations, were more intent on listening to the shouts and laughter from the grounds outside. By the time they had eventually died away the piece was finished again, and in a moment or two Professor Keith returned to the drawing room, decorated with shards of pastry and bringing Peter and a pale-faced Boxie with him. By their muddy shoes, they had all three had a good run in the grounds, and Charles wondered how Boxie felt about that, chasing his friends.

Professor Shaw looked at his watch again, less discreetly this time, and suddenly it seemed like time to leave. There was a general upsurge of people from the seats, and a polite queue formed in front of Mrs. Keith, thanking her for a lovely evening. Professor Shaw, with the good excuse of his wife's health, escaped first, and Mungo Dalzell was left to help with the little things at the end of an evening, the gathering of shawls or the locating of lost reticules. The maid Barbara came upstairs with a tray holding a jug of claret and a plate of biscuits, which she set on the top of a low kist before hurrying back down again to help everyone with their coats: Charles saw her anxious look as she passed the door, while he stood near the head of the queue. It must not be an enviable place, working for Professor Keith, he thought. Hadn't he heard that Ramsay Rickarton's daughter had once worked here, too, and had been fired? Professor Urquhart, keen aesthete that he was, paused on the way out to admire the jug, which was silver, elegantly chased. Charles could not catch the remark he made to Lord Scoggie by his side, but could guess the tone from the sardonic twist of Urquhart's thin lips.

At last Charles and George were at the head of the queue, and giving their thanks and farewells. Boxie, just ahead of them, was holding Alison's hand for what seemed an unnecessary time, but fortunately George was looking the other way. Alison seemed particularly panicky as Boxie left her, her bracelets jingling, and Charles thought again that if she were a

132

horse he would get off and walk before she had him killed. He bowed to her, smiling politely. George followed him, and impulsively she put out her hand to him, too, as she had done to Boxie. She looked as if she were about to cry, but George's face lit up as he took the long, thin hand in his and put it to his lips. Charles nearly choked as he watched George torn between gallant anxiety and ecstasy, drawn up to his full height and width as if saying, 'I can protect you. Shelter behind me.'

Even then, Charles could not see how soon she would need it.

Chapter Twelve

The crow flapped lazily across the dunes, paused for a moment on the edge of the wind, and swooped down to the sand where a dead seal had been abandoned by the high tide. Two gulls, already gouging the seal's innards with yellow beaks streaked red, moved round generously to let the crow in, eying him warily. There was enough of the corpse to satisfy everyone.

George and Charles watched for a moment before strolling on, feeling the wind whip at their faces and tempt their headgear to freedom. George had his third-best boots on: there was no sense in sacrificing your best ones on the salty sand. They walked on the half-damp sand where it was firm, but the wind flicked waves of dry sand from high up the beach across in front of them, pale against the dark beneath, and made them feel loose at the knees, as if they were walking on water. The little waves of low tide, nervous frills of the sea, trickled up the shallow beach and were immediately deterred by the wind, flipping over on themselves and falling backwards in their eagerness to flow back to the sea.

If the Walkers had wanted an escort home as well as to Professor Keith's unfortunate soirée the night before, they had not been disappointed: they were accompanied on their walk by Allan Bonar and Thomas Seaton, silently competing for Miss Walker's arm, as well as by Charles and George. Daniel, very full of himself, walked ahead with his torch lit from the one outside the Keiths' front gate, once he had been deterred from making patterns with it by swirling it round his head. The evening had ended so abruptly at the Keiths' that Mrs. Walker seemed to feel that something more was required, and she and Patience quickly found some bottles of their elderflower wine while Charles lit the lamps in the parlour, and Allan Bonar set to to light a small fire in the grate. The elderflower wine was plentiful and very good indeed, and they had all drunk perhaps too appreciatively of it: Allan Bonar had left in uncharacteristic anger about eleven o'clock, Thomas had started to sing ballads of indeterminate tune, and Mrs. Walker had grown quite tearful, expatiating to George about the death of her reverend husband. Patience had brought out her violin and played German airs which did not consort – quite deliberately, Charles decided – with Thomas' endless, meandering songs, and Charles found himself as a music lover quite unable to bear the contrast, and began to hum something else entirely under his breath. Thomas, feeling that he had made a grand contribution to the evening, finally left well after midnight, and the ladies retired to their chambers. Charles found that his legs were not as reliable as he would have liked, but once he had sorted them out he discovered that George was in an even worse way, having been unable to speak during Mrs. Walker's soliloquy and therefore having drunk even more than the rest. Charles hauled him to his feet and pushed and dragged him to the bottom of the stairs, whereupon George fell to his knees and crawled the rest of the way. At the top, incapable of further movement, he rolled on to his back and began to laugh, and Charles in the end had to climb over him and leave him there, though he himself was almost helpless with laughter. Through the open window to the street, in the distance, he could still hear Thomas singing his tuneless way home.

The consequence of such entertainment was, naturally, that neither Charles nor George was particularly communicative this morning, and had a tendency to wince at sharp noises. The sands seemed the obvious place to go, particularly when breakfast smells began to waft up from the kitchens, and despite their delicacy both brothers were surprisingly quick to dress and leave the house, pausing for a moment to gasp in the fresh dawn air of South Street.

The sands were long and broad, and at that time of the morning were quiet. The scavengers who worked the tideline had long gone, but there were grooms exercising their horses along the water's edge, a few boats hauled in and up for repair, and a dozen or so hardy sorts bathing. Up on the links an occasional golfer could be heard, playing before breakfast. There were five or six red gowns to be seen, worn by students probably very like themselves, whose happy Friday night had led to a rather more miserable Saturday morning. Not far ahead of them were three gowns in particular, clutched against the wind around three fairly familiar figures: one well-set and

135

elegant, one stocky, and one so thin the wind seemed to go through it rather than round it. It was the Sporting Set.

Despite himself, George called out to them the moment he recognised them, then scowled at the sound of his own voice. Rab turned first, eagerly, but it took a moment for the other two to quit their intense conversation, move a little further apart, and turn to see who had hailed them. Picket was as pale as limewash, but was grinning from ear to ear as he waited for the Murrays to catch up with him and his friends. His teeth looked so weak Charles was slightly surprised not to see them blown out by the wind.

'Good morning, dear friends!' Picket exclaimed, with a deep and flourishing bow. 'And how does the world treat you, this fine morning?' His grin seemed already to know the answer, and when George explained briefly about the elderflower wine, Picket laughed out loud in delight. Rab, too, had the face of a very contented angel this morning, glowing with the wind and with something internal, too: perhaps the vision of a greater than usual number of sinners saved, Charles thought, ironically. If that were so, then Boxie had not heard the news, anyway. He looked - Charles was not quite sure what – unhappy, yes, and perhaps confused. Picket saw where Charles was looking, and slapped Boxie on the back.

'Professor Keith's new favourite here, eh? Maybe our new man on the inside, eh, Boxie? He's good at keeping secrets, is Boxie: he had a little fight with the Professor's son, and never mentioned it to anyone. And now he and the Professor's son are all friends again, and he's been taken to meet Papa.' Picket made a face meant to represent some kind of lovesick charmer, all smile and wide eyes. The effect was horrible. 'I think maybe Peter Keith thinks Boxie will make him a good husband – what do you think, Boxie? What's his dowry like? You have to ask the Professor, you know: it's very important to sort out things like that before you grow too fond of poor Peter. Isn't that right, George? You know the right order of things, I think!'

George, who was sometimes a little slow on the uptake, laughed heartily at this joke, and did not blush until Picket had turned away. Boxie, however, was purple with embarrassment, and looked as if he would have run away from them like a fox from the hounds if Picket had not been keeping tight hold of his sleeve. Charles remembered, suddenly, a rumour that he had heard, that Professor Keith had accused Professor Urquhart of corrupting his son – was that what they had meant? Like all those dreadful but entertaining emperors in Suetonius? It was not something he wanted to think about just now: he had a nasty feeling that Picket was good at reading minds.

'You gave them a good run for their money last night, anyway,' he suggested, and both Rab and Picket cackled delightedly.

'Didn't we just?' Picket cried.

'All over his daffodils!' Rab added in excitement. 'Broke a hedge and damn' near broke a tree! Up and down, and out the gate, and away!' It was not hard to imagine Rab, athletic and strong, leading the stout Professor and his willowy son out into the darkness of the street and losing them, but Picket, weak and tiring more easily than he would admit, would have had to have been cunning. That was not hard to imagine, either. Charles was only a little surprised that the Professor and his son had come back uninjured, and had not been the victims of some kind of trap.

'You should have seen the old fool, huffing and puffing around his rose beds,' Picket added.

'Aye, he was a sight,' Boxie said at last, and Picket looked at him approvingly. 'But how did you ever manage to get in in the first place?' Charles asked.

'Barbara, the maid,' said Picket, grinning again. 'It's damn' handy having a man like Rab around: the ladies – and their less elegant sisters – take one look at Rab and think the Angel Gabriel has bred with Apollo and sent his offspring to woo them. Anything, just any little thing they can do to oblige him – och! It's lovely, so it is! It would probably have worked just as well on Peter,' he added, thoughtfully, and fingered his long chin.

'It's an excellent joke,' said George, recovered now from his embarrassment. 'If I'd been asked I should have given a guinea to see Professor Keith's face when you went out the window!'

'Next time we'll take up a collection,' Picket said solemnly, and at that even Boxie laughed. 'But that wasn't all the joke, was it, Boxie? There's more to come!'

'Oh, what?' asked George eagerly, but Picket tapped the side of his thin nose, eyes half-closed. He looked remarkably like an underfed goat, and for a second Charles shivered. Picket glanced at him and grinned, as if he knew.

'We'd better be getting back for our breakfast, George,' Charles suggested, feeling like a coward but unable to persuade himself to stay. There was something about Picket this morning that was even worse than usual. George frowned, but Charles took him by the elbow. 'Mrs. Walker will be eager to see you. Remember how good her oatcakes are?' A beatific light, rarely associated with anything but food, spread abruptly over George's face, and it was suddenly easy to bow to the Sporting Set and guide George away along the damp sand and back to the town. Charles could feel Picket watching them all the way, though he knew it made no sense, and he would not look back. He only relaxed when they were safely round the corner and out of sight, heading for the town gate at the bottom of North Street.

Even North Street seemed quiet and still in the early morning: a few maids scrubbed steps, and those sent out to the wells for water did not linger, eyes still full of sleep. A cart taking flour to the bakery in Mutty's Wynd sat in a little white cloud of its own by the side of the road, while the driver hauled the sacks in silence into the lane. Hens wandered undisturbed across the highway, sharing forgotten food scraps with rock doves from the trees nearby. A dog on a doorstep did not even look up as they passed, but hid his nose under one paw, and a cat, pacing along a high stone wall, ignored a sparrow as it flew just above it. Only the crows disturbed the peace: a flock beat across the sky, cawing urgently, and as one detached himself from his fellows they cried out to it in alarm. Charles looked up. The crow flew over, close to their heads, then swerved and swept over the wall where the cat was. It vanished from sight.

Just at that moment, Charles noticed a figure in the distance, tall and narrow, sweeping down the street towards them in a black gown. For a second, he thought it was another crow, leaving the flock. Instead, it was Professor Urquhart. He was beside them in an instant.

'Good morning,' he said, bowing almost without stopping as they paused to greet him.

'Good morning, sir,' Charles replied. 'Is anything the matter?'

'Matter? Well, now, that's a moot point.' The Professor had overshot them and now stood facing up the street, back the way he had come. His feet were eager to be away. 'Matter enough, I suppose, and it'll be round the town by dinner, if not before. It concerns Professor Keith.'

'What has he done now?' asked George, incautiously: his mind was on Mrs. Walker's oatcakes.

'Well, he's died, that's what he's done, not to put too fine a point on it.'

'Died?' said Charles.

'But he can't have,' added George. 'We were at his party last night.'

'I'm afraid that even such an honour as that could not protect him,' said Professor Urquhart sarcastically. 'He is indeed dead. I am on my way for the physician – why on earth do we not have a medical professor? – and in the mean time, Professor Shaw is with Mrs. Keith. He might be grateful for a little help, you know.'

'Of course: we shall go at once,' Charles agreed.

'Farewell, then. I shall be back directly – *tam vicina iubent nos vivere Mausolea, cum doceant ipsos posse perire deos!*' he added, bowing as he swept on down the street.

'I suppose that was Greek,' said George, looking grumpy.

'Latin. Martial. 'The neighbouring tombs order us to live, since they teach us that the gods themselves can die.' I think we can take it he meant it ironically.' He watched the Humanist for a second, and then turned back up the hill.

'We don't really have to go now, do we?' George pleaded. 'After all, Keith won't be going anywhere.'

'Alison may be in want of comfort, of course,' Charles murmured, quite as if he had not heard his brother, and walked on. He was not surprised to find that George was right beside him.

To anyone who did not know, the rambling white house with its shutters closed looked as if it was still undisturbed after the excitement of the night before. The daffodils in the garden were a little battered, but the wind was combing them out again and it would not be long until the damage done by Picket and Rab would be gone. Charles knocked quietly on the door, and then thought that mourning did not necessarily make servants more acute of hearing. He was about to knock again at a more normal volume, when the door opened, and Barbara the maid, her apron untied, appeared.

'Yes?' she said, apparently unable to recognise them.

Charles tried to look sympathetic.

'I am very sorry to hear about the misfortune which has affected the family, and we should like to present our cards.' He nudged George hard, and they both presented the little scraps of pasteboard that could intrude where they could not. 'Also,' Charles added, as she accepted them, 'Professor Urquhart said that Professor Shaw was here, and might be in need of our assistance.'

For a moment she looked even more blank, then her face cleared.

'He's in the parlour,' she said, with a sense of achievement, and stepped back to let them in. In the pleasant little room in which they had met Mrs Keith and her daughter only a couple of weeks ago, Professor Shaw was waiting.

'Oh, my dear Charles,' said Shaw, as Barbara backed out. 'My dear George. This is a very terrible thing!'

'How are the family?' George asked hurriedly.

'That is another matter again. Mrs. Keith is terribly shocked, of course. Peter is with her constantly.'

'And Miss Keith?' George persisted. Professor Shaw looked at him strangely for a second, and then quickly turned to the window. One blind had been lifted, and in the distance they could see the summer house.

'Christopher Urquhart offered to go for the doctor – did you meet him?' They nodded. 'It seemed the best thing.'

'But for whom? Who is sick?' George's broad face was ashen. Professor Shaw looked up at him again, nervously.

'For Miss Keith. Did not Professor Urquhart say? She has been poisoned, too.'

'Poisoned!' Charles exclaimed, as George sagged on to a chair. 'Steady, George: we may be needed. But Professor Urquhart said nothing about poison!'

'Well, that's what it looks like,' said Professor Shaw, apologetically, as though it had all been his own idea. Charles found his head was swimming, and touched the back of George's chair to steady himself. It did not help: the chair was shaking.

'But what kind of poison? And how? And how do they know?'

Professor Shaw signalled to him to sit down, and perched himself on the very edge of the sofa. He fidgeted with his hands.

'Christopher Urquhart and I were supposed to be meeting him this morning to talk about – about some students. The maid said he was in his study, and we should go up. When we knocked on the door there was no reply, and Christopher – Professor Urquhart – tried the handle. I did say he shouldn't,' he added longingly, as though none of this would have happened if Professor Urquhart had paid more attention to his manners. 'There's a kind of campaign bed in the study, and he's lying on it. Mostly.'

Charles swallowed hard. Professor Shaw met his eye, and they shared a horrified look.

'Was he – already dead?' George asked, unexpectedly. He did not look up from the floor, and Charles wondered if he was going to be sick.

'Oh, yes, very much so,' Professor Shaw assured him.

'But what had done it? Had he eaten something, or what?' Charles asked.

'We're not sure,' said Professor Shaw. 'I asked Mrs. Keith, very gently, because, you know, it could be in anything, and anyone else could take some – well, Miss Alison must have, I suppose, too.' Here George groaned softly, and Charles put out a hand to rest on his shoulder. Professor Keith looked curiously at him. 'I hope – is there an understanding? If so, I am very sorry to have broken the news so badly.'

'There is nothing fixed,' Charles reassured him. 'You could not have known. But he has – hopes, I suppose.' George's head sank lower between his hands. 'What did both Professor Keith and his daughter eat that no one else touched, not even the servants?' he asked, his mind already past the shock and on to questions.

'As to that, I don't know,' said Professor Shaw. 'As I said, Mrs. Keith is not – at her best at the moment, and with -' he lowered his voice and nodded towards George 'with her daughter so ill, too. But Peter said he saw someone give Alison a box of something during the evening, and there are sweetmeats and candied fruits, both in pretty boxes, on Professor Keith's study desk.'

George flung up his head and gasped. Charles stared at him, and then remembered: when George had arrived, he had presented Alison Keith with a box of candied fruits. But surely they had been harmless? He remembered thinking that the Letho cook had probably made them, and nothing unwholesome came out of Letho's kitchens. Then he remembered something else: Picket Irving, bowing very low, proffering a pretty box of sweetmeats to Alison Keith, and trying to persuade her to take one. He thought of Picket's hideous grin that morning, and felt sick.

'You were there, Charles,' Professor Shaw was saying quietly. 'Do you remember anything? Did anyone give him the sweets?'

Charles stood up slowly, thinking hard. George was his brother. The Sporting Set, however unappealing, were his fellow students. He could not believe that they had intended murder – injury, perhaps, but that was all. What would happen to them if they had accidentally killed Professor Keith as part of one of their pranks? They were only young, only his age. He avoided looking at Professor Shaw, but he knew that the lecturer was watching him. He glanced at George, and wondered what he knew. He remembered the Sporting Set on the sands, remembered Boxie's look of dismay, guilt, confusion: Boxie's look, the same look, last night when he saw

142

Picket offer the box of sweetmeats to Alison. He remembered Rab's delight, half-innocent, half-vicious, not a strong enough mind to know truly the difference between entertainment and evil; and he remembered Picket's face, Picket's sick, laughing, leering face, as he pressed the sweetmeats on Alison, as he gloated this morning, as he read the very thoughts in Charles' mind. If Picket could be guilty, but not the others, he thought ... could he? He did not know the niceties of the law. A judge would take one look at Picket and send for the hangman. Perhaps he would be right. Charles went to the window and stared out at the summerhouse, remembering the day he and George had stood there with Alison and Mrs. Keith – with a widow, and a fatherless daughter, herself perhaps near death. He saw the crows again, swooping in a low cloud across the garden, black against the beaten daffodils, and then up into the dark yew trees that nearly hid them but for their ceaseless cawing. They seemed to be waiting for something.

He turned back to Professor Shaw.

'I saw Picket Irving giving the sweetmeats to Miss Alison, so I suppose he brought them,' he said, and sat down again near his brother.

'Oh, dear,' said Professor Shaw.

Charles nodded. He folded his fingers in front of him, elbows on his knees, half in prayer. George stared at him, expressionless.

'Picket Irving was no admirer of Professor Keith, but I cannot see him intending to kill him – can you?' Professor Shaw asked. Charles shook his head. 'It may have been an accident, I suppose,' Professor Shaw went on, a little hope entering his voice. 'He worked on natural philosophy – some poisonous substance, perhaps? Arsenic, now: they say that's very poisonous ...'

He had a look of optimistic desperation in his eye, and Charles suddenly realised that Shaw was out of his depth. It was a shock. He had always recognised that Shaw was a little reluctant to be part of the real world, but to find him thus adrift in it, without direction, was distressing: Professor Shaw actually seemed to be looking to him for reassurance, which

143

Charles did not feel ready to give. It did not seem right: he was only a student.

George was not being very helpful, sitting heaped like a misbuilt stookie with his arms flopping down between his knees, a look of fear on his face. Professor Shaw, little vulnerable frog, perched on the sofa, twiddling his fingers and looking helpless. What did they want him to do? What could he do?

'Maybe I should go and see Picket and friends,' he said at last, into a mature silence. Instantly Professor Shaw brightened.

'That's a splendid idea. That's really a very good idea, Charles: you know where they live, and everything.'

'Are you sure it's a good idea?' Charles asked, suddenly not at all sure it was. What on earth would he say to them?

'Of course it is,' said Professor Shaw happily. 'Far better you than the town sergeant: it's more of a University matter, isn't it?' Charles forbore to point out that if it were a University matter, it might be better to send Ramsay Rickarton, maybe with some of his janitors with large sticks. What if Picket attacked him?

'Will you come with me, George?' he asked instead, but George looked up at him blankly.

'No, thank you, I shall stay here.' He stood up, slowly, shaking his heavy head as if the contents would settle down into some more manageable form. 'I shall stay here,' he repeated, 'in case they can make use of me. I should consider it a very great honour – a very great honour – if I can be of service in any small way.' He blundered his way to the end of the sentence without seeming to have much awareness of having started it, and stopped. Then he turned to Charles with a pleading stare that shook Charles to the heart. 'If her father is dead already, then it must be quick acting, must it not?' he said quickly. 'So if she isn't dead already,' his voice shook at the words, 'then maybe – maybe she will be all right? Isn't that so?' He gasped, as if he found breathing hard. 'I shall stay here, in case she needs me.'

144

Chapter Thirteen

Charles was hurrying back down North Street towards the sands when he saw Boxie, Picket and Rab just turning in to the end of Mutty's Wynd where their bunk was. He broke into a run, and caught up with them at the bottom of the stairs leading to their rooms.

'Murray! Here amongst us again so soon?' said Picket grandly. 'Come in for a bite of breakfast, do: we have just bought bread, and our bunkwife is grand with the cold ham and beef.'

'I –' Charles hesitated. He was starving, he suddenly realised, but was he in a position to accept their hospitality, given what he had come to say to them? He decided quickly that it all depended on how he said it, and nodded. 'I should be delighted.'

The little house was dark and hot after the cool fresh light outdoors, and Charles was glad to see Boxie open a window. The air did not move much in the lane outside, though, and it provided little relief. Indoors, their shared living room's dirty white-washed walls were bare except for a series of political cartoons, less notable for their consistent support of any particular party than for the liberal portrayal of unlikely women which they shared. There were no curtains, only shutters, and the floor was decorated by a carpet so small Charles assumed it had been made as a cover for a chest of drawers. The whole room echoed sharply. Charles stood, awkward, while they disposed of their trenchers and rearranged the sparse furniture to have four seats at the small round table, and Rab ducked quickly underneath it to replace the folded newspaper that held it steady. In a few moments their bunkwife, an angry-looking woman with movements like a Fife coalhewar's pick, flicked a cloth on to the table and distributed the ham, beef and mustard before them, followed by a tall pot of coffee. She left them again like a blade withdrawn, and slammed the door.

'Dear Mrs. Mutch,' said Picket with a smile. 'The sweetest of landladies.'

'She's not too keen on having us about, that's the trouble,' said Boxie, who seemed if anything more relaxed than he had earlier. 'Here, take a seat, Murray.'

Charles sat, finding the table a little too low for his frame. Picket seemed to have the same problem.

'And to what do we owe this honour?' he asked, passing Charles the bread which he had now sliced. Charles took a piece.

'Well,' he said, trying to decide how to begin, 'I come with some news, though you may already have heard it: if you have not, you should hear it, for it may nearly affect you.' How would Cicero have tackled this? That was easy, he thought, on reflection: that wily old conspirator-catcher would point a bold accusing finger at the party, outline the case against them in an eloquent, well-rounded and probably pre-written speech, and then call in the heavily-armed guard he had sensibly arranged outside. He would, of course, also be sure that his accusation was just.

'Oh, aye?' said Picket, with a brief glance at Charles. 'Pass the mustard, would you, Rab?'

'It concerns,' said Charles, trying to look at them all at the same time, 'the Keith household.'

Picket laughed.

'News from there? How can that nearly affect us, unless he is on his way here with Ramsay Rickarton and the town sergeant together?'

Boxie, however, had paled.

'They are – all well, are they?' he asked, as if it was an effort to get the words out. Rab and Picket doubled up with laughter.

'Is Peter well, he means!' cried Rab. 'Poor Peter – is he lovesick?'

At this extraordinary example of Rab's ready wit, Picket laughed even harder, and had to lay down his knife and fork, fanning himself with his napkin. Boxie went scarlet, but kept his gaze on Charles, who for a moment did not know how to answer him. What was Boxie expecting? He waited for Picket and Rab to recover.

146

'As it happens,' he said, 'only Mrs. Keith and Peter could be considered to be well.'

'It's worked!' shrieked Rab. 'She ate it!'

Picket tried to glare at him for his indiscretion, but he was too intent on his own satisfaction.

'I knew it,' he said simply. 'The only question is, when should we strike?'

His face took on a calculating look, which was reflected, as in a distorting mirror, in Rab's brainless beauty. But they were not left long to reflect. Boxie shoved his chair back with a crash. He was across the room before they knew it. He stood, staring at them. He swallowed hard several times, as if he was trying not to vomit.

'You did do it,' he gasped at last. 'You gave it to her.'

'Of course we did, Boxie dear,' said Picket coolly. 'You came up with such a delicious idea, and we simply had to use it.'

'But not on her!' cried Boxie.

'Who else would be so deserving?'

'She – *she* does not deserve something like that!' Boxie was almost hysterical. 'You have – she – how could – '

'Oh, come, Boxie: surely some oratorical style has rubbed off on you from all those grubby old Romans! How will you take your place as an advocate if you cannot construct a simple sentence?'

Boxie, unable to say another word, lunged at Picket. Rab sprang up. Picket's chair toppled backwards. Boxie caught his balance on the table and tipped it, and though Charles tried to save it the ham and beef slid on to the floor in a clatter of cutlery. Rab snatched at Boxie's collar and dragged him back, punching him hard on the jaw. Boxie shot backwards, sprawling on the floor. Rab helped Picket up: Picket was breathing hard, but he managed to make Charles a little bow.

'You see us at our best, of course, this morning,' he explained with a tight smile. 'Rab, see to Boxie.'

'He's only had the wind knocked out of him,' said Rab sulkily, but he went and knelt by Boxie, helping him into a sitting position.

147

'May I ask,' Charles said at last, 'just what Miss Keith is supposed to have eaten?'

Rab and Boxie both looked at Picket. Picket glanced back, and then turned to Charles.

'Spanish fly, of course.'

'Of course,' said Charles. He had heard of it, but only vaguely: he tried to remember where.

'Excellent stuff, according to Boxie here,' said Picket. He stood up, a little weakly, but trying hard not to show it. One bony hand clutched at the back of his chair. 'It was Boxie that recommended its use.'

'But not on Miss Keith,' Boxie insisted indistinctly. There was blood on his lips, possibly from loose teeth. 'I thought you were going to use it on the maid.'

'On Barbara? What possible use could that be? Keith would simply sack her, and anyway, there's no need to use Spanish fly to make old Barbara rumpish – one look at Rab here usually does the trick.'

Of course, Charles remembered now: Spanish fly, the legendary aphrodisiac. Schoolboy stories of unlikely conquests and nights of wild passion came flooding back, told in hushed voices in the schoolyard or on the long walk home. But good heavens, to give it to Professor Keith's daughter!

'No: we had to give it to Miss Alison,' Picket was continuing, half to Boxie, half to Charles himself. 'We wanted ructions in the Keith household: all our tricks were simply making them huddle together like rabbits in a hole. We needed to put a terrier down there, and shake them up a bit!'

'What … what happened?' Boxie asked. He sounded as if he no longer had control over his own voice. His face was the colour of ash. Picket pushed away the chair he had been holding, and stamped on the floorboards.

'That's what we're trying to find out!' he snapped, a nasty fire in his eye. 'Murray here has come to bring us news, news of our success, and have we even paid him the least attention? No! Right, let's hear it.'

Every eye was on Charles. He sat back from the table.

'Miss Keith is gravely ill,' said Charles.

'What?' cried Boxie. He pushed Rab away and staggered to his feet, spitting blood on the floor.

'Ill? You didn't tell us that might happen,' said Picket, but he did not seem particularly distressed. 'She's not much use to us in that state, is she?'

'There is – worse,' Charles went on.

'Worse? What worse? The silly girl didn't go and tell, did she?'

'I think she is too ill, but it was generally known that the sweetmeats came from you,' Charles said, distracted again from his principal news. Picket swore, and kicked the table. The mustard, which had been saved when the table tipped, fell off and spattered the carpet.

'Professor Keith –'

'Is furious, no doubt,' Picket finished for him. 'We may as well start packing our things, lads: we'll be off sooner than we can think. Why is he not round here already?'

He turned on Charles with a suspicious look. Charles sighed: Cicero would never have allowed them to get a word in sideways.

'Because he's dead.'

The silence, at last, was gratifying. He let it lie.

'So she did it,' said Boxie suddenly, and then shut his bruised mouth so sharply he made a grunt of pain.

'How, dead?' asked Picket at last. 'Rab, wipe the smile off your face: we may have hated the ground he walked on but we could be in serious trouble now.'

'Poisoned, I hear,' said Charles. 'He was found in his study this morning. And Miss Keith is assumed to have taken the same thing. The sweetmeats you gave her' - he saw no need to mention George's fruits – 'were on his desk.'

Picket swore again, an oath that made them all turn in shock. He paid them no attention.

'What did you mean, 'She did it'?' Charles asked Boxie, but Boxie, standing bolt upright against the window, would not meet his eye.

'Boxie, is this possible?' Picket asked sharply. 'Could the stuff have killed him?'

Boxie glanced at him and looked away.

'I don't know. I told you all I knew about it.'

'I thought you'd read a book!'

'No! Someone I knew at school told me about it.'

'Devil take it,' muttered Picket. 'So for all we know it's possible. We could have killed him.'

'Excellent!' said Rab, rubbing his hands together. 'Best joke ever!'

'Rab!' Picket took two strides across the room, and slapped Rab across the face. Rab sat hard down on one of the chairs, less injured than shocked. 'Listen: we could be hanged for this. Hanged, do you hear?'

'But your guardian ...' said Rab slowly, as the words sank in. 'He can pay them, can't he?'

'Pay? Whom should he pay?' Picket's voice was acid, searing through the room. 'You can't buy yourself off a murder charge – particularly when the victim is a university professor! It's not as if we can keep it quiet, is it? Oh, why do I even bother? You might have been in the front of the queue for the looks, Rab Fisher, but when the sense was handed out you were away eating parritch.'

'Look, I'd better go,' Charles said. 'I should –'

'Go! Yes, so should we. Let's get packing, lads,' said Picket. 'We can hide out in the usual place for a few days, see what's happening. Murray, you'll have to send us word –'

'Don't you think if you run people will think you guilty?' Charles asked. Picket swore again.

'They'll think us guilty enough as it is,' he said, 'and we are. How in the devil's name could this have happened? The damn' man wasn't supposed to touch the stuff. What would he have to do with it? It was only for her.'

'Aye, and she's gravely ill,' Boxie broke in. 'It doesn't seem to have worked on either of them, does it? Are you sure you bought the right thing?'

'Do you think my mammy knitted me? Of course I bought the right thing,' Picket was furious. 'If you were so convinced I'd get it wrong maybe you should have come into the apothecary's, too, instead of wandering off on mysterious errands of your own!'

150

Suddenly Charles was back in Edinburgh, on the South Bridge Street, seeing Picket and Rab come out of the apothecary's next to the jeweller's with a white packet, and seeing Boxie join them. It must have been then.

'Do you have any of it left?' he asked. 'You should probably get rid of it, in case it hurts someone else.'

Picket looked at Boxie, and Boxie gave a half-nod. He left the room by one of the doors at the far end: Charles could just see that it led into a small bedchamber. After a moment he was back with, as far as Charles could tell, the same white packet.

'That's the stuff,' he said, as Charles pulled back the wrappings carefully to see. The paper was folded around a little mound of sticky black balls, like miniature fish roe. Charles sniffed it cautiously. 'That's Spanish fly. You're sure –' he turned back to Picket.

'I'm dead sure. I didn't ask for Spanish fly, just as you told me. I asked for cantharides.'

'What!' cried Charles.

'Cantharides. That's its other name – what's the matter?'

But Charles was already gone.

His long legs carried him down the short stairway in two strides, and out into the lane. It was empty, and another three strides brought him into Market Street. By now the street was busy, with housewives making their last provisions for the Sabbath and students enjoying a day of comparative freedom. He slowed down, suddenly realising that it might not be a good idea to attract attention to himself. His agitation must have been clear, though: people ducked out of his way, glancing back at him, every eye burning into him: he could feel it, he was sure. He darted across the street, and down Logie's Lane, skipping around playing children and lazy dogs. Out into South Street, he tried to limit himself to a brisk stride, but it seemed that his bunk was teasing him, as far away as ever every time he looked up. At last he was there. He fumbled the door open, and ran upstairs. George had not been back: the rooms were the way they had left them that morning, except that Mrs. Walker had made the bed and tidied George's clothes. There was no sign of Daniel. Charles dived across the room to his desk, and snatched a drawer open. Inside, the white package lay, innocent and bland. He took it to the table where the light was better. It had clearly been disturbed. The outer layers came off quickly, like old onion skin. Inside was a closely wrapped little parcel, with part broken off one end. Black sticky balls like miniature fish roe spilled out into the outer wrapping. He pulled off his gloves, and used only the tips of his long fingers, delicately undoing the apothecary's work. He lifted back the final layer, and the black heap stood revealed.

'George!' He could have wept. What was he going to do? He turned to the little fireplace: Mrs. Walker had laid a fire there already. He struck a light from the tinder box on the mantelpiece, and crouched by the hearth, coaxing the flames into life, trying not to hurry them. It seemed an age, but he finally had enough of a fire going, and fed it another few sticks from the basket nearby. Then he slid the whole package from the table, outer wrappings as well as inner, and tucked them into the fire.

He sat motionless, watching it burn, making sure that the whole thing was completely destroyed, hoping that no noxious airs would escape into the room. When it was all gone, gone without a shadow of a doubt, he took the poker and riddled at the fire until it was out, then poked amongst the ashes, searching for any possible trace of the packet or its contents. There was none, though it took him long enough to convince himself. He rubbed the soot from his hands, and stood up, pulling his gloves back on.

He was half-surprised to find that it was still daylight outside, and when he pulled out his watch he saw that it was only half an hour since he had left the Sporting Set. He wondered if they had decided what to do. As for him, he should go back to the Keiths' house, and see if Professor Shaw needed him.

He trod lightly down the stairs, but Mrs. Walker heard him. She shot out of the kitchen door.

'Have you heard the news?' she gasped. 'Do you want breakfast?'

Suddenly, the smell of bannocks assailed him, and even more potently, the scent of bacon and onions. His stomach seemed to melt within him.

'I'll take a bit of breakfast, Mrs. Walker, but I must be quick. What news?' he added cautiously.

'About Professor Keith? Whose very house we were in last night?'

'Oh, yes,' said Charles. 'I've been over there. It's all very bad.'

'It's terrible, the poor man. And his daughter so ill! It could have been any of us!'

The truth of this struck Charles suddenly: Alison could easily have taken a sweetmeat and passed the rest round. Picket was – well, not an idiot, but thoughtless to the point of evil.

'Who do you think did it?' Mrs. Walker was asking.

'Aye, that's a good question,' said Patience Walker, who was standing guard over the frying pan. She lifted out six bacon slices and a whole onion, and passed the plate to her mother to add the bannocks from the girdle. 'Who indeed? If the circumstances had been otherwise …'

'What do you mean?' Charles asked, filling his fork with bannock and bacon.

'Hush, dear: it's not a nice thing to repeat,' said Mrs. Walker, but Patience shrugged.

'It's only that Alison herself hated him as much as any,' she said. 'The way she was watching him last night, even when she was turning the pages for me: I thought he would burn up on the spot.'

'Well, it can't have been Alison, dear,' said Mrs. Walker definitely, 'with her so ill herself, so don't go saying that any more. It's not nice for her mother.'

'It's not nice for her mother anyway,' Patience retorted, but she said no more on the subject.

Charles ate quickly, and was soon finished, ready to return to the Keiths' house. Mrs. Walker gave him a basket as he was going out the door.

'Bannocks, my dear,' she explained. 'A death in the house does nothing for the cooking, as I know to my own cost!'

153

'You're very kind,' said Charles sincerely, and took the basket with him.

He flew back to the Keiths' house and knocked on the door. The whole place looked exactly as he had left it: he was not sure why he should have expected it to be otherwise. He was shown back into the parlour. He was about to greet Professor Shaw when the doorbell rang again and the maid gave a little 'Oh!' of surprise and disappeared.

'What success, Charles, what success?' asked Professor Shaw, anxiously twisting his hands around themselves. George was slumped on the sofa, wordless.

'Limited, I think,' said Charles, trying not to look at his brother. 'They say they put something in the sweetmeats that was intended for Miss Alison alone, but was certainly not meant to kill her. When I left them they were contemplating flight.'

George twitched and looked up at Alison's name.

'What did they put in them?'

Charles turned to look fully at him.

'Cantharides,' he said clearly. 'Spanish fly.'

The blood drained from George's face, and his mouth dropped open.

'Spanish fly, eh?' said Professor Shaw sadly. 'I might have guessed they would do something like that.'

'They are not all equally guilty, I think, though they were all involved,' Charles went on. 'It was Boxie's idea, but he had no notion they were going to give it to Alison. Rab is, of course, not very bright.'

'Well, Charles, I think Boxie is probably just as guilty as Picket if he thought they were going to give it to anyone at all,' Professor Shaw said kindly, and Charles blushed.

'You're right, of course, sir. Picket told Boxie that they were going to give it to the maid.'

At that very moment, Barbara herself entered, to announce the physician and Professor Urquhart.

'Ah, at last!' cried Professor Shaw in relief.

'Dr. Pagan here,' said Professor Urquhart languidly, 'had some important details of attire to attend to before we could set out.'

154

Dr. Pagan, so neat and clean he looked like something done up for sale, nodded in satisfaction. He gave the impression of being hung up by the ears: his features were drawn higher than normal on his face, and the corners of his mouth stretched unprofessionally up to his tight cheekbones.

'I like to make my patients feel I have made the effort,' he added.

'No doubt Miss Keith will appreciate it, through the pain,' said Urquhart blandly. 'I take it her mother is still up there?' he asked Professor Shaw.

'Oh, yes, I think so: maybe Barbara will know,' Professor Shaw answered. 'Certainly she has not been down here.'

'We should go upstairs, then,' Urquhart said. 'There is no point in delaying any further. Where is Peter?'

'With his mother, I believe,' said Shaw. 'She needs someone with her to comfort her at the moment.'

'Indeed,' said Urquhart, with a strange little smile. 'And perhaps it is as well that there is someone with him, too. Come along, then: you and I, Shaw, shall stand outside the door in moral support.'

George stood up, and Charles said quickly,

'George and I shall stay down here, then, for the moment.'

'I'm sure you can come up if you want to,' said Shaw, anxious not to lose part of his web of support.

'In a moment, then, sir,' said Charles with a smile, trying not to make much of it. The two professors and the neat doctor left the room with Barbara, and Charles took a deep breath.

'Well, George,' he said. 'What have you been up to this time?'

Chapter Fourteen

At that precise moment, the door slammed open, and Peter Keith ran in.

The hooded look on George's face vanished in an instant, and he turned in relief. Peter staggered to a halt and stared at them.

'What are you doing here?' he asked, less in hostility than in bewilderment. His hands scrabbled at the back of the sofa, as if he was clutching at it for protection.

'We came to help Professor Shaw, and to be of any service we can,' said George eagerly. 'I am very sorry for your loss.'

'Indeed,' added Charles. 'If we can be of any help ...'

'Oh, well – if old Shaw wants you here, then I don't see ...' Peter tailed off, not, apparently, much conscious of what he was saying. His gaze flickered away from them, feverish in its nerviness. George cleared his throat.

'I beg your pardon – your sister – Miss Keith – I hope she is ... recovering?'

Peter's eyes swooped back to meet his.

'I have no idea. Mother is in with her, talking to her.'

'So she's awake, anyway?' George snatched at the hope.

'Awake and moaning and groaning fit to shake the house,' Peter snapped. 'I'm not going in if she's like that.'

'The doctor's gone up to her now,' Charles said.

'I saw him,' Peter said. 'A shiny wee man. Professor Urquhart was looking at him as if he smelt bad.'

'Didn't you want to study medicine at one stage, Peter?' Charles asked, remembering. It took a second for Peter to catch up.

'Oh, yes, I did. I read a few books, anyway: Father always has books like that round the house. It comes from doing natural philosophy.' He sighed sharply, and shoved his hands hard into his waistband as he strode to the window. He stared out at the garden, but did not relax. 'He's dead, you know!' He turned suddenly with a breathless laugh. 'Out cold on the study floor, like – like a fish! I bet he never expected that! I bet he wanted pomp and grandeur and the whole family

156

round the bed weeping as he spoke his final significant words!' He gabbled so fast it was all they could do to understand him: he was as white as chalk.

'I'll ring for some brandy,' said George, pulling himself together and going to the bell. Barbara appeared again, looking more exhausted each time they saw her, and brought a bottle of brandy and a glass. When she had gone again, they found it was still corked, and it took George a minute or two with his knife to open it. Peter, throughout the process, said nothing, but stared out of the window, breathing heavily. Occasionally he fumbled with the window catch, as though he remembered some reason for going into the garden, then forgot again.

'I think I'll go up and see if Professor Shaw needs any help,' Charles said at last. George could cope with Peter, and should not leave him for a while until he was settled. The expression on George's face, anyway, seemed to say that even if they were left alone, he was not going to tell Charles anything about the cantharides. Charles went out into the hall, found himself alone, and rubbed his face hard right up to the line of his hair. It was only eleven o'clock, but already the world seemed to be upside down.

Upstairs, Professors Urquhart and Shaw were waiting on the landing outside the drawing room where the party had been the night before. Shaw was perched on a hard hall chair with a knobbly back, while Urquhart had disposed himself against the old wooden kist on which Charles remembered seeing Barbara set a jug and tray last night. Now it only held a narrow glass vase of daffodils, shining against the white plaster wall in an unsuitably cheerful fashion, and even the old family portraits around the walls seemed to be laughing. It was unnerving. Shaw and Urquhart greeted Charles in silence, with the kind of half-smile appropriate to a house of mourning.

'Has the doctor given his verdict yet?' Charles asked, in a low voice.

'No: he threatened to start sniffing urine, and we thought it prudent to leave.' Urquhart's nose wrinkled fastidiously. 'Mrs. Keith seems to have kept jugs of the stuff for the purpose.'

157

'He's going to blister her, he said,' Shaw added sadly. His hands were clasped closely on his lap, and he sat in a dejected heap, like a schoolboy awaiting the rector's verdict, and knowing it would involve tawses. Distantly, Charles became aware of a breathless groaning, very much alive, but certainly miserable, and punctuated by the occasional squeal. A murmur, almost soothing except for a hint in it of anxiety, susurrated like a contralto accompaniment to the soprano groans: Mrs. Keith's motherly comfort.

In a moment or two, a door opened and shut. The doctor appeared at the top of the next flight of stairs, paused theatrically to adjust his waistcoat and straighten his wig, and then descended the stairs trying to control his compulsive smirk. His smart shoes clicked on the bare wooden treads, and it was a relief when he reached one of the rugs on the landing and could move in comparative silence. Shaw stood up, but Urquhart did not straighten.

'Well?' asked Shaw anxiously. The doctor was gratified by this, and allowed a heavy sigh to escape his lips.

'She is not at all well,' he pronounced. His polished face was as solemn as it could be.

'Of course she isn't,' snapped Urquhart. 'What's your diagnosis and prognosis, man?'

'My diagnosis is that she has been poisoned,' stated the doctor, his dignity offended. 'It is gravely affecting her kidneys, and I have purged her quite heavily.'

'Cantharides,' muttered Shaw, wide-eyed. He sat down again as if he had been folded.

'What's that?' said the doctor.

'We think,' whispered Shaw, not looking at him, 'that she was given cantharides.'

'Spanish fly? Well, why did no one tell me?'

'*I* didn't know,' said Urquhart, in a dangerous tone. 'Which is why I did not tell you: no one told me, either.' Shaw met his eye.

'We only worked it out when you went for Dr. Pagan,' he explained. 'Charles here saw who gave Miss Keith the sweetmeats we found on Professor Keith's desk, you see.'

158

'Well, who the devil –' Urquhart began, then broke off. 'Never mind,' he said, with a half-nod indicating that they should wait until they were in private. 'We shall speak about it later.'

'Oh, certainly, certainly.' Shaw was eager not to be the only academic with this burden of knowledge.

The doctor breathed out sharply, trying to regain the lead in the conversation.

'We use Spanish fly professionally, you know, for blistering,' he said brightly. 'Some fools think it has other powers, but what blisters the skin outside will blister the flesh inside, you know. It can kill.'

Professor Shaw swallowed hard, and Urquhart drawled,

'And obviously it has.' The doctor looked dismayed: he had forgotten that there had been more than one victim in the case.

'And your prognosis, Doctor, in the case of Miss Keith?' Charles quietly reminded him. Urquhart paid attention to the doctor again.

'Well, she is young and strong.' At this point a little frown crinkled Dr. Pagan's face. 'However,' he added, 'in her interesting position ... I think, on the whole, it is likely that *she* will survive. I have told her mother to make her drink a good deal of milk. Milk is always soothing. I shall return later to apply leeches, which will relieve the pressure of the discomfort within. And, of course, she needs to calm herself, which again is where her mother can help. She keeps calling out a name – Peter.'

'That's her brother,' said Charles. 'He's downstairs: shall I fetch him?'

'No! Not at all,' cried Dr. Pagan hurriedly. 'She is crying out that he should not be admitted, on any account. She is half-delirious, and does not know what she is saying, but it would only upset her further if we went against her requests at this stage.'

'Well, it is of no matter,' said Urquhart smoothly. 'Now to the father, I suppose. The study where we found him is along this corridor, here. We directed that he should be left as we found him.'

159

He led the way, followed by the doctor. Charles brought up the rear, in a state of mild anxiety: he had seen corpses before, of course, for you could not go to a funeral without paying your respects, but he had never seen anyone who had been poisoned, or who was still … *in situ*. What on earth was he to expect?

'Apparently he often slept in here if he was working late,' Urquhart was explaining to Dr. Pagan, ducking under a low beam. Charles did the same in his turn. 'As you can see, he has a species of campaign bed – well, usually made up.'

Urquhart opened a low door, and, crowded in the doorway, all four of them reeled at the stench that swept out over them. Professor Shaw choked and buried his face in his sleeve. Urquhart and Charles drew out handkerchiefs, but Dr. Pagan, screwing up his nose professionally, stepped a pace or two into the room unmasked. He was followed by Urquhart, and the pair of them stopped abruptly, blocking most of the view. Charles, buoyed up to confront the corpse, had to hold himself in check and make do with what was visible to him.

The part of the room that Charles could see was lined with books, all the books that were missing in the rest of the house. He could see a few familiar titles, and suppressed the desire to examine them further for the moment: it was the largest private library he had had the chance to see, outside Letho where his grandfather had been a bit of a collector. His father would not have contributed much to it beyond pedigree books and estate manuals … he shook himself and tried to concentrate on the room he was in. There was, so far as he could tell, one window, a rounded corner one, in a little turret, over a window seat padded with a cushion, panelled below. The window curtain had been tugged back, probably by Urquhart and Shaw earlier, for on the corner of the great oak desk was a candlestick covered in icicles of wax where the candle had burned right down. Beside it were an open notebook, with Professor Keith's sharp black writing on half of one page, and a small wooden tray. Charles recognised it: it was the one Barbara the maid had left on the landing the night before, holding a plate of biscuits, now somewhat diminished in number, a used wine glass, with a fine spiral stem and a bud-shaped bowl, and the chased silver claret jug. Someone had added the sweetmeats, the box now rather crumpled. By straining round the corner Charles could just see the edge of what he thought was George's box of candied fruit.

At that moment, Urquhart and the doctor moved forward into the room and bent over, and Professor Shaw shifted slightly to one side. Charles could easily see over his shoulder. Against the wall he had been unable to see before was a set of shelves, high up, containing scientific apparatus. Below them was a kind of campaign bed, set into the wall, low and flat with a hard pillow, and covered with a couple of rumpled plaids and a grey English blanket. Tangled up with them, as if forgotten in a rush to leave the bed, was a leg.

Swallowing hard, Charles followed it with his eyes. It was not, as it had at first appeared, detached. Professor Keith, grand, fiercesome and relentless, lay upside down like a clown in a pantomime, swinging from a trapeze.

The most striking thing was his look of shock. He seemed to be saying, upside down, 'What, me? Now?' The eyes were still open, the folds of flesh around them sagging into strange, unnatural shapes, and the chin rested awkwardly out of place. There was a thick trail of vomit from one side of his mouth, splashing down over his shoulder and on to the bare boards of the floor where he must have tried to turn his head away and not to choke. Incongruously, its substance was raspberry pink, with little flecks of scarlet.

Professor Urquhart stepped delicately across the room and opened one casement of the window, relieving the stench considerably. Everyone tested the air with cautious sniffs, then breathed normally. Dr. Pagan peered at the body from a standing position, then reluctantly crouched down beside it, finally covering his own mouth and nose with a handkerchief. He pulled a flat object like a blunt knife from his pocket, and gently pressed back the corpse's lower lip to open his mouth wider. Charles tensed: he half-expected Professor Keith to choke and struggle up, in the worst of all his tempers. Peter's words downstairs came back to him: 'I bet he wanted pomp and grandeur!' Maybe: he would have wanted dignity, at least.

161

This was far from that, and Charles suddenly felt embarrassed, as if he had walked in on his professor in his bath.

'Now,' said the doctor, standing again to ease the knees of his skin-tight breeches, 'in a case of cantharides poisoning we would expect to see evidence of the victim having suffered great thirst as the poison took effect.'

'What about the claret jug?' Charles suggested. Professor Urquhart stepped back to the desk and flipped the silver lid back. He squinted inside, then lifted the jug and shook it, to make sure.

'Empty,' he said, setting the jug carefully back.

'And the vomit is pink,' added Dr. Pagan, as if he would not have expected the uninitiated to notice. 'I think we can assume that he ingested it – though of course we don't know how much was in the jug.'

'It was full,' said Urquhart. He stopped and looked at them. 'I saw the jug last night as we left. I was admiring it, and lifted it to look at the chasing nearer the candles. It was full.' He said all this flatly, as something that could not possibly be of interest to them. But Dr. Pagan, his attention drawn to the little supper tray, had begun to examine the biscuits and the sweetmeats. The biscuits were dry, and had probably been dipped into the claret: there was no trace of anything strange about them, but the doctor sniffed them cautiously, turning them over and over. Professor Shaw nodded at the sweetmeats.

'Those,' he said uneasily, 'are what we believe the cantharides was brought in. They were a present for the young lady, you see.'

'Then I wonder what they are doing here?' Dr. Pagan mused.

The box, now that Charles could see it better, showed itself to be the work of a local confectioner who had his shop in Market Street. The sweetmeats seemed to be irregular lumps of something treacly with a dusted sugar coating. The doctor poked at them cautiously with the blunt blade.

'Just a little, pressed into the bottom of each piece,' he murmured. Charles thought of the cantharides in his own bunk, and the missing piece, and felt sick. 'The young lady upstairs says she took one piece and bit into it, but it tasted strange so she did not finish it.'

'Would a little be enough to kill someone, sir?' Charles asked. He found he was shivering. The doctor bit his lip.

'I should not have thought so, not so quickly. He was a large, strong man.'

They all glanced involuntarily down, noting as if for the first time the heavy, slumping jaw, the powerful arms and legs, the broad shoulders pressed into the floor.

'But there is room for only one missing sweetmeat in the box,' said Charles, unsteadily, 'and presumably that was the one that Alison took.' Professor Shaw was standing by the desk. Charles could not see George's tray of candied fruits, to see whether or not it was full.

'Perhaps there was a lot of poison just in that one,' suggested Professor Shaw, but without much hope. He sounded confused: it would have been a bit of a coincidence. Urquhart frowned. Dr. Pagan met Charles' eye, and looked away, fidgeting with his blunt blade.

There was a distant sound of footsteps in the silence, and Professor Shaw said,

'Shut the door, Charles: someone might pass by.'

Charles shut it and leaned on it. Still he could not see George's candied fruits. He stared down at Professor Keith, at his tousled, sweaty hair, at his hand tangled in his cravat. It seemed to be grasping something, but when he bent over to look more closely, he saw that it was only the missing button from his coat, glinting between the fingers. The doctor saw where he was looking.

'Is that his button?' he asked. 'Let's see if we can get it out.'

Professor Keith's thick fingers were stiff with death, but not so much so that Dr. Pagan could not prise them open.

'He must have died late last night, I think,' the doctor remarked, then added, 'My goodness!'

It was in a tone that made them all lean over to see. Dr. Pagan showed them Professor Keith's half-open hand with the button in it. It was bloody: the edges of the metal circle had dug hard into his flesh as he clutched it.

163

'Is that from rigor mortis?' asked Professor Shaw in amazement.

'No,' said the doctor, straightening, 'no, I don't think it is.' He cleared his throat, and put the button on the desk with an air of importance.

'There's something wrong, isn't there?' Professor Shaw asked timidly. Professor Urquhart, stony-faced, folded his arms, but his fingers twitched. The doctor looked round them all, then glanced down at the body as though his host might have given him permission to proceed.

'Well,' he began, 'the matter is this. I'm quite convinced that Miss Keith upstairs is suffering from cantharides poisoning: it is a typical case, and you seem to know who brought the poison into the house.' He managed to keep most of the irritation at his exclusion from this knowledge out of his voice, but a taste of it remained. 'If she does not die, and I think it likely she will not, that will be a simple matter for your poisoners.

'However,' he went on, 'Professor Keith here has only some of the symptoms of cantharides poisoning. They are, however, as are his other symptoms, also signs of something quite different. The flecks of blood in his vomit, for instance, and the convulsions that led to the cuts from the button in his hand. Something quite different.'

'And what is that?' snapped Urquhart. Shaw looked as if he did not want to know.

'Arsenic poisoning,' pronounced the doctor.

Urquhart gasped. Professor Shaw swayed, and sat hard in the chair behind him, and Charles could at last see the box of candied fruit.

There was one missing.

Chapter Fifteen

Professor Shaw cleared his throat for longer than seemed necessary, but eventually managed to speak.

'Did – did our friends say anything about arsenic?' he asked. Even then, Charles did not hear him for a moment, and Urquhart, his tone sarcastic as he had not been told who the 'friends' were, repeated the question loudly. Charles jumped.

'Oh! Our friends! Ahh ...' he thought, trying to put cantharides out of his mind, trying not to imagine how George could have got hold of arsenic. 'Arsenic,' he repeated, 'No, no, they did not. Their aim was not to kill, I am sure. It was only to make Miss Keith, er ... well, rumpish was the word they used.' He felt awkward using it himself in front of his tutors.

Dr. Pagan nodded.

'The common misconception I was telling you about. But a burning feeling in one's nether regions is much more rarely the effect of passion, in my experience, and much more commonly a result of something you've eaten.' Something about this suddenly seemed to embarrass him, and he turned away, rearranging his cravat with a few anxious touches. Urquhart smirked.

'So perhaps ... if he died from arsenic and not from cantharides,' Professor Shaw said tentatively, 'and there is only one sweetmeat missing, then presumably that is the one that Miss Keith took, and we must discover where the arsenic was, before anyone else takes any.'

'And find out who the poisoner is,' added Urquhart, with an edge to his voice.

'It is harder to see than cantharides,' Dr. Pagan said carefully, looking about him. 'It could have been in the wine, in which case we may well find some deposit at the bottom of the jug, or even at the bottom of the glass.'

There was a sudden crunch and a tinkle.

'Oh, dear,' said Christopher Urquhart, 'I'm afraid I have trodden on the glass.'

They all looked down at the pieces as he moved his long, elegant foot back. Urquhart gave a helpless little shrug, which

Charles suddenly realised would have looked more at home on Professor Shaw, as if Urquhart had borrowed it for a moment.

'We must talk to Mrs. Keith, and to Barbara, and to Peter, and see what Professor Keith had that no one else had,' Shaw began again. 'How long would it have ... taken?' he asked the doctor, who spread his hands out.

'It seems to have been a massive dose,' he said. 'It would have taken effect quite quickly. It may have depended on how much he had eaten already, though. Sometimes a lot of food in the stomach draws the poison out.' He seemed struck by an idea, and knelt again with caution to feel under the campaign bed, first on one side of Professor Keith, and then, stepping over his corpse with a kind of curtsey of respect, on the other side. There he drew out, with some satisfaction, a chamber pot, over which the white cloth was still starched and fresh. Shaw blanched a little: Urquhart choked and turned away. Dr. Pagan drew off the cloth.

'Well, he had partly emptied his stomach, anyway,' he remarked, swishing the contents round the pot like someone about to read the tealeaves. 'This is all very healthy in appearance, and I think must have been expelled before the onset of the poison.'

'Enough! Enough!' cried Urquhart, his handkerchief muffling his words. Dr. Pagan looked at him for a moment, then replaced the cloth and the pot with what Charles could have sworn was a sly smile. Urquhart went to stand by the window, and took several gulps of fresh air. The breeze as he opened it wider flicked at the papers on the desk, turning the notebook pages, and ruffled the edges of Professor Keith's cravat and the handkerchief over his face, as if he were sighing. Charles did not think he was the only one to shiver, this time.

'The burgh sergeant will no doubt be along soon,' Dr. Pagan reminded them, 'and I shall ask Mrs. Nicolson to pop in to help with the laying-out – in cases such as this, particularly in a gentle household, it is often difficult and distressing for the ladies of the house to deal with the matter unaided, and Mrs. Nicolson has seen everything.'

'She is to be with my wife, when her time comes!' Professor Shaw was a little distressed at the thought of his midwife laying out murder victims, however gentle the household.

'Oh, she is entirely respectable, my dear sir,' Dr. Pagan reassured him. 'She is a very good person, moreover. Now, I have an appointment with a patient at one o'clock, and I'm afraid I must be going. I have told Mrs. Keith that I shall call again to see Miss Keith this evening, to see how she has managed the day, and as I say I shall send a message to Mrs. Nicolson to wait upon Mrs. Keith. If you need me, you have only to send word, of course.'

He bowed, and left the room, closing the door behind him. In a moment they heard him ring downstairs for his hat and gloves, and the distant thud of the front door closing. In the study, Professor Keith moved as much as any of them for a long moment. Then,

'Well, what now?' asked Urquhart. 'Will you tell me who it is who has admitted to the cantharides? though I think I can guess.'

'I expect you can,' said Shaw mildly. 'Shall we go downstairs? I am not sure that I want to stay in this room any longer.'

'That is something I can agree with,' said Urquhart with feeling. Charles shifted to open the door for them. 'There's a thing, though,' said Urquhart, as he passed the desk. 'This other box – what is it, crystallised fruits? Are they from the same source? For look, there is one missing there.'

Professor Shaw looked at Charles.

'They did not mention fruit,' Charles said, as blandly as he could. 'Only the treacle things, I think.'

Urquhart poked at and then lifted the box.

'No confectioner's name – yet I cannot see a student diligently standing over a pot of sugar and orange peel. Well! You must tell me all you know, downstairs.'

He ushered Professor Shaw through the door first, and followed him, while Charles brought up the rear. He glanced back into the room as he closed the door, and for a second stopped, as Urquhart reached past him to turn and remove the key.

The notebook on the desk had disappeared.

167

Urquhart presented the key to Professor Shaw, who took it with an anxious look and slipped it into his waistcoat pocket. Then, without another word, they set off downstairs. His mind racing, Charles followed.

George was alone in the parlour, examining the modest watercolours on the wall with all the interest of a starving man asked to examine silk for an evening dress. On the whole, he seemed pleased to see them return, and even before they said anything he tipped his head towards the French window.

'He's gone,' he said, succinctly. Then, feeling he needed to do more to relieve himself of this responsibility, he added, 'I couldn't stop him. He said he needed to look for something in the garden. I left the window open in case he came back – didn't feel right, locking a man out of his own house.'

'Well, never mind that now,' said Urquhart. 'Let us all sit down so that you can tell me who your poisoners are.'

Charles met George's eye as his brother turned pale, and gestured him to sit on the sofa. When the Professors had found chairs, Charles sat on the sofa too, far enough from his brother to see his face, but near enough to feel like a support. With academic economy, Professor Shaw summarised for Professor Urquhart Charles' own summary of his visit to Picket, Boxie and Rab, while Urquhart made a face that said he had expected as much. George, on the other hand, seemed increasingly relaxed, and Charles, tense as he was himself, wanted to shake him.

'Well, it is clear enough that the Sporting Set, in whatever combination, is responsible for what has happened to Miss Alison,' said Urquhart at the end of Shaw's account. 'But I am not convinced that they had anything to do directly with Keith's death. Picket is as thoroughly nasty a student as I have taught in many a long year, but his kind of nastiness does not consist in the elimination of his enemy. He would prefer instead to keep Keith in his power, angry, frustrated, and if possible afraid. Do you not agree?'

Looking faintly sick, Shaw nodded his innocent, froglike head. His eyes were large and anxious.

'And arsenic is not the weapon of one who means only to frighten,' Urquhart went on, 'it is the weapon of one wishing to eliminate the victim quickly. They would know that: I explained about arsenic-eating and so on when we read the Lives of the Caesars in their first year. I remember even then Picket took a particular delight in that book. Nero was a special favourite of his.'

There was a long pause as they reflected on this: even George had heard of Nero.

'Well,' Urquhart seemed to have taken charge. 'The physician as good as said he was sending round the town sergeant, so we had better decide what we want to tell him.'

'Oh! The truth, I would have thought,' said Shaw simply.

'Oh, of course.' Urquhart's voice was smooth and easy. 'But it would be easier for him if we could straighten things out a little, first. And he will wish to hear from Mrs. Keith, which obviously is not something the dear lady would be comfortable with at the moment. It would be better if we talked with her ourselves and then passed on what she had to say to the sergeant when he comes.'

'Of course,' Shaw agreed. 'She would find it very distressing, being questioned by a virtual stranger at a time like this.'

Charles almost opened his mouth to offer to call the maid to find Mrs. Keith, but caution kept him quiet. He was desperate now to find out what was going on and, if necessary, to protect his wretched brother. He wanted to hear what Mrs. Keith had to say, but a mere student might well be asked to leave, if he happened to draw attention to himself. He felt awkward, though, when Professor Urquhart levered himself elegantly off his chair and went to pull the bell. He stayed standing, touching at his cravat in front of a pier glass, until Barbara had fetched Mrs. Keith. They all stood then as she entered, and bowed very formally, though her answering curtsey was slight and automatic.

'My dear Mrs. Keith,' Urquhart advanced and led her to her usual upright armchair. 'How are you? And how is Miss Keith?'

'My daughter is – bearing up a little, I think, I thank you –'

169

At that there was a step at the French window, and Peter burst in. It occurred to Charles that he had rarely seen Peter Keith enter a room in a reasonable fashion: he was always on the crest of some emotion, almost as if it was brought on by the change of the surroundings itself.

'Mamma!' he cried, and fell to his knees beside her chair, taking her hand in his. 'How is Alison? She has not – has not ...'

'She is resting just now.' Mrs. Keith seemed to draw some strength from reassuring her son. 'She has taken a little tea, but she is still very weak indeed. Dr. Pagan has said that he will return this evening.' The rings on her fingers scraped and clicked together as she gathered her son's hands together. 'We must be patient, Peter dear.'

There seemed, overnight, to be nothing of her: she was a huddle of bones, and the skin of her face and neck sagged. Urquhart sat near her, forward in his seat with his arms across his knees, and began with surprising gentleness.

'Madam,' he said, 'we believe we know what poison Miss Keith has taken, and who gave it to her, and why.' Charles, standing against the wall, could see her face clearly: it was blank and stupid, but somewhere at the back of her eyes the girl who had read and learned and loved to think was stirring, and realising that she was needed.

'Will you tell me?'

'Some foolish students – the same who disturbed the party last night, with whom Professor Keith has been displeased for some time – they gave Miss Keith sweetmeats with Spanish fly in them.'

'Spanish fly? But that is for blistering!' Her mind's eye seemed instantly to be seeing what blistering might do if applied internally to her daughter, and her face was wrung with pain.

'Yes: but they did not know. They thought – forgive me, madam, but you know what boys can be – they thought that it would – ah, encourage her to flirt with them.'

Her gaze, which had wandered with her imagination, came back sharply to meet his eye.

170

'I take your meaning, sir,' she said shortly. 'So, they were wrong and my daughter, though sick, has her honour intact.' Peter raised his head from the arm of her chair, and she patted it like a child's head, smoothing and soothing his tousled hair.

'Indeed,' agreed Professor Urquhart. 'Now, I am afraid, to Professor Keith.'

'Yes,' she said, and you could almost feel the strain as she pushed her long-disused mind to work. 'You said – you only said – Miss Keith, that you knew what and who and why.'

Urquhart drew breath, and looked at the floor, and then, eyebrows raised, at Professor Shaw. George, seated nearby to be helpful at the least opportunity, squinted as he tried to follow this: the arsenic had not been explained in front of him, and George was not a reasoner. Professor Shaw blushed and shrugged helplessly.

'Dear Mrs. Keith,' he said at last, 'We have spoken with Dr. Pagan, and he believes that it was not Spanish fly that killed your husband: it was arsenic.'

'Arsenic!' Mrs. Keith went white, but she did not faint. 'He has brought this on himself!' she gasped. 'On himself and on his daughter! He drove these students to hate us, taunting us and leaving bones at the gate and dead crows outside the windows and breaking the garden plants! And now he is dead, and Alison so ill, and in so much pain! Foolish, foolish man! Foolish, short-sighted ...' She gulped another great breath of air, and Charles thought she was going to cry: both Urquhart and George had hands hovering over their handkerchief pockets. But she took another, gentler breath, and straightened as if she had been poked in the back.

'Forgive me, gentlemen,' she said with an effort. 'I –'

'Say no more, madam: it is quite understandable,' said Urquhart. 'But we think it would be a good idea if we talked over, here between ourselves, what happened when everybody left last night, what Professor Keith might have eaten that no one else did, when he went off to his study. Just so that we can have it straight in our minds.'

Whether this reasoning made sense to her or not, she obediently began to think.

171

'He was very angry, you know,' she said after a moment. 'Angry that the party had been so broken up. Not that he had been enjoying it, I think, for he seemed to have a good deal on his mind. Maybe he suspected that these boys would do something.' She looked up, testing their reaction, and Shaw and Urquhart nodded encouragingly. 'He went off to his study almost as soon as the last guest had left. You – you came back for your gloves, did you not?'

Professor Shaw nodded and blushed again.

'It was after that. He was like a bear with a sore head. He took his supper tray – Barbara leaves him a supper tray on the landing upstairs, so that he can decide whether he will go to his study or into the drawing room or up to his chamber, though mostly it is his study.' She sighed, an old sigh. 'He went off to his study as usual.'

'And mightily relieved we all were,' added Peter, straightening.

'Peter,' warned his mother, as if used to it.

'Well, we were, Mamma. You called for a tray of tea, and I tidied some of the chairs back and dealt some cards, and Alison and I sat down for a game of rummy, and we all generally behaved as if the storm had passed.'

He spoke too loudly still, but at least he seemed more coherent. Charles wondered if he had found what he had been looking for in the garden.

'Well,' Mrs. Keith turned up her hands, 'perhaps we relaxed a little. Then I said, "Oh, what about one of those nice sweets you were given, Alison?" and she said, "That's a good idea," and fetched them from the piano, where they had been left. But when I looked at them, I realised they were both kinds I don't like, and Peter never eats sweet things, do you, dear? So Alison took one of the toffee treacly ones and bit into it, but she said it didn't taste very nice. She swallowed the bit she had, I think, but she threw some of it into the fire, didn't she?'

'I thought she swallowed all of it, and it was the paper she threw into the fire,' said Peter, but not as if it mattered. Mrs. Keith looked anxiously at Urquhart, and he nodded again.

'So you sat up for a while?' he prompted her.

172

'Yes: Peter and Alison played a few hands, and I drank my tea, and then Alison said she wasn't feeling very well, and she would go to bed. Peter and I weren't long after, were we, dear?'

'But you did not think that it was the sweetmeat that made Miss Keith feel sick, or did you?'

'No, not at all, it never crossed my mind, anyway. Did you think it, dear?'

Peter shook his head slowly, meeting his mother's gaze.

'So when did you realise that it was more serious?'

Mrs. Keith's brow creased upwards.

'I heard her bell ring – I'm not sure when it was. I had certainly been asleep for a little, at least. I went along to see what the matter was so I was there before Barbara. Alison was looking very ill – I should be with her now,' she said anxiously, glancing at the bracket clock.

'She needs to rest, my dear madam,' said Urquhart quickly. Mrs. Keith looked only partly reassured.

'She was terribly, terribly thirsty. She said her mouth and her throat were burning, and when I looked closely with the candle, there were little blisters. I asked her if she had drunk something hot, I didn't think of Spanish fly, but of course it's obvious now. Barbara brought warmed milk with honey and thyme in it, and she gulped it down but she screamed with the pain, and I gave her a little wine then with laudanum in it, or was that before the milk? There was so much noise and rushing to and fro. That quietened her, the laudanum, a little in the end, and she slept for a while, and I stayed with her and slept too, I don't doubt. But she was awake again – it was light, then, but only just – and crying, so we gave her all the same things again but it didn't ease her so much – she slept, but she was tossing and turning and clutching her stomach, and – well, I'm sure you don't want to hear everything,' she finished slightly primly, and Charles assumed that the account had been going to include the infamous chamber pots that Dr. Pagan was so keen to sniff.

'And, er, where was Professor Keith in all this?' asked Professor Shaw diffidently.

Mrs. Keith looked surprised, and at a loss.

173

'But you said there was a great deal of noise and confusion,' said Urquhart. 'Did he not appear? Was he not roused?'

'Did anyone go to look for him?' added Shaw. Charles could imagine that if anyone had been ill in Professor Shaw's house, he would have been there in his nightcap, fretting and confused with everyone else, and liked him the better for it. Mrs. Keith, however, still looked bewildered.

'He hates to be disturbed by this kind of thing. We were trying to keep quiet.'

'But would he normally have come out of his study to ask for less noise?' Urquhart chose his words delicately, though they could probably all picture the scene quite well.

'Oh,' Mrs. Keith gave a high little laugh, 'yes, he often does that. I was pleased that we were not disturbing him too much – I believe I thought he must be asleep.'

Shaw and Urquhart exchanged glances. Mrs. Keith was still catching up, and a curious expression crept over her face.

'You mean that by then, he was already ...'

'My dear madam,' said Urquhart, 'I fear we must believe it.'

There was silence while she digested this. Charles could not see Peter's face, for his head was again bent over his mother's lap. Professor Keith had still been in the clothes he had worn for the party – even his shoes had still been in place and his cravat knotted. It was probably true: he had died very soon after entering his study.

'We thought she was past the worst, perhaps, just after breakfast time,' Mrs. Keith went on absently, her eyes miles away, her mind back on her daughter. 'It was only when you came – when you found him – that we thought it might be – that she might ...'

'But we know now that it was two different things, Mamma,' said Peter, raising his head again. 'She'll be grand again soon, you'll see.'

'And where were you when all this was happening?' Urquhart asked suddenly. It was impossible not to take it as some kind of accusation, and Peter spun angrily on his knees to face Urquhart.

'Outside my sister's room, anxious for news of her! Where should a brother be? I was ready to run for the doctor on the instant, if I was asked.' George nodded enthusiastic approval. He was ready even now. 'I always look after her.'

'You're a good boy, Peter,' said his mother, but there was a strange sadness in her voice.

'I even helped Barbara fetching the milk and buckets and the clean sheets,' he went on, sulky now that his hard work was going unappreciated. 'What more could I have done? And now I know who did it – Picket Irving and Rab Fisher, *I* know – I'll see to it that they don't go unpunished! I can fight, you know! I've been in a fight before!'

'My dear boy, there is no need for that!' said Urquhart, one slim hand out to calm him. 'The law will take its course, which is both more certain in this case, and more dignified. You are not some common fisherman to go scrapping on the pier.'

Peter closed his mouth abruptly on his next outburst, and sat staring at Urquhart. The effect of Urquhart's words was impressive, and reminded Charles of the rumours he had heard once or twice – that Urquhart had corrupted Peter during the course of those classes on art and architecture. He clearly had some influence over him.

The doorbell rang, and they all jumped.

'That may well be the town sergeant, madam.' Urquhart rose like silk unfolding. 'Will you allow us to deal with him?'

Mrs. Keith rose stiffly, patting the creases automatically out of her skirt.

'Oh, yes, yes, if you please. I can't – I must go back to my daughter. Please, just tell him whatever you need to.'

She hurried out of the room, and Peter, with a long look back at Urquhart, followed. Barbara met them at the door, her face sagging with tiredness, and announced the town sergeant as if she was not quite sure that the parlour was the place for him.

Charles pushed himself away from the wall, and shook George by the shoulder.

'Come on, we're off,' he muttered.

'What?'

175

'I have an idea.' Bowing a hasty farewell they let themselves out the front door, and started towards the gate, leaving the town sergeant, in his best uniform, to the mercy of the professors.

'But I wanted to stay ...' George protested.

'You're not staying out of my sight,' Charles announced. 'And I want to go to North Street. I've just realised where the arsenic might have come from.'

Chapter Sixteen

They eased the heavy wooden door open, slowly at first. Charles stopped and listened. There seemed to be nothing going on, and he pushed back the thick velvet curtain at the top of the steps and entered the dim antechapel with the assurance of old familiarity.

He had heard, as every proud student had, that Dr. Johnson on his disgruntled tour of Scotland had called this 'the neatest place of worship he had seen': this, despite the general air of dilapidation, the soft smell of mould from the leather cushions on the staff seats, the blurred outlines of the oak furnishings, black with age and abundant polish from generations of janitors. It was a wide, bright chapel, its long windows facing south on to North Street, and the simple chancel formed the round east end, open and light. To one side of it, in the depth of the sandstone wall, was the chipped and battered tomb of Prior Kennedy, the college's founder, adorned in an un-Presbyterian gesture with a jug of daffodils. The whole place had a curiously happy mixture of the Papist and the Reformed, with both altar and pulpit prominent, as if the college had secretly taken the best of both and blended them to everyone's quiet satisfaction. Certainly the feeling of peace and content in the place did nothing to reflect the religious struggles of the country for the past two centuries.

George followed him, tutting, his boots clipping on the tiled floor. Charles had left the antechapel and was heading up the aisle. There was someone in the staff seats, he noticed, kneeling in prayer, and he half-turned to give George a warning look. Ramsay Rickarton, however, was up in the chancel. Cloth and brass ball in hand, he was polishing anything that seemed to need it for tomorrow's Sunday services. He had already finished some silver: the gilded silver mace he would carry in the academic procession was lying on Kennedy's tomb, all its details, its lions, angels, arches and pinnacles glittering. He wore the same apron over his livery as he had on the day of little Sybie's death, and in his eyes was the same dead look he had worn there ever since.

177

'Ramsay,' said Charles, going close enough so as not to disturb the man praying in the staff seats, 'How are you doing?'

Rickarton looked at him, but his hands polished on, the cloth feeling its way round the familiar details of the brass candlesticks.

'Aye,' he said, with a slight nod.

Taking this as some kind of encouragement, Charles smiled and nodded back.

'Ramsay, you know that poison you were putting down for the rats in here a while ago?'

'Aye,' agreed Ramsay, though Charles was not sure if he had understood the question.

'Do you know,' he went on, more slowly now, 'is it arsenic? Only – well, do you know if it is?'

'Aye,' said Ramsay again, and then, after a moment's thought, added, 'It is.'

Charles nodded and grinned again, and then remembered the gravity of the question.

'Have you seen anyone meddling with it? Or doing anything, well, suspicious near it?'

Ramsay Rickarton frowned.

'What for would you be asking that?'

'Just – just because ...' Charles trailed away. He did not know how much was common knowledge yet, and he had suddenly realised how hard it was to ask questions without giving away nearly as much information as you could obtain. 'Have you heard about what happened at Professor Keith's last night?' he asked.

'Oh, aye.' Something that might once have been a smile skirted past Ramsay's face. 'I heared that young Picket and Rab made a fine mess of his wee pairty and his flowerbeds, anyway.'

'Ah,' said Charles. 'Well –'

'Look, Professor Keith's dead and his daughter is gravely ill,' George broke in, so unexpectedly that Charles turned and stared at him. George's fair face was scarlet with impatience. 'Well, just get on, you know?' he said to Charles. Astonished, Charles turned back to Ramsay Rickarton.

'Look,' said the bedellus, a wariness creeping into his eyes. 'Look, I dinna ken whit ye're thinking to accuse me of ...'

Charles' hands flew out in front of him, instantly placatory.

'We're not! We're not accusing you of anything, Ramsay ...'

''Cause there are folks that say, ye ken, after Sybie died, that I blamed Professor Keith, that he had sent Sybie away out to play on the road ...'

'But you don't think that, do you?' Charles asked quickly. He had heard the same theories himself. Rickarton stared at him steadily for a long moment. When he drew breath to speak, he sounded infinitely weary.

'Thinking won't bring my wee lassie back, Mr. Murray, whether the thoughts are right or wrong.'

'Well, now, the same could be said of Professor Keith,' said Charles tentatively, 'but someone killed him, and maybe they won't stop there. You wouldn't want to see Mrs. Keith hurt, or one of the other professors, would you?'

Ramsay shook his head slowly.

'Ye said Miss Keith was poorly, though?'

'That was by another hand, a coincidence.'

'I see.' There was a pause, while he thought. 'I hope she's better soon. She's a kind young lady, and very good to me and mine.'

Charles felt ashamed. Despite George's involvement, he had not thought much one way or the other about Alison Keith's survival, nor much about her character beyond her vulpine grins and nervy laughter. Ramsay Rickarton knew her virtues better than he did.

'Dr. Pagan says she stands every chance of making a good recovery,' he said firmly, as if his best apology to Alison would be by consoling someone who liked her. 'The thing is,' he went on, 'we need to find out if anyone has been – well, have you seen anyone near the poison you put down for the rats? Or noticed some of it missing?'

He barely heard the footsteps behind him, though Ramsay Rickarton's expression gave him some warning.

179

'My dear Mr. Murray,' said Mungo Dalzell smoothly, 'could we have a word? You will excuse us, Ramsay, won't you?'

Before Charles knew what was happening, he, George and Mungo Dalzell were outside in the Cage, and Ramsay Rickarton was left in peace to polish his brasses. Charles, bewildered, was left to gabble through the social rituals.

'I believe you met my brother George on Friday night, Mr. Dalzell. George, you know Mr. Dalzell.'

'Oh, yes!' George looked surprised, but bowed and said roughly the right things while Mungo Dalzell smiled politely.

'I am sorry to have whisked you away so precipitately,' he said when George had finished. 'I'm not sure you realise just how upset Ramsay Rickarton has been recently.'

'Well, of course ...' Charles tailed off. He had been about to mention Sybie, but had remembered, just in time, Mungo's own tragic part in Sybie's death.

'Professor Keith was never the most tactful of men. You have probably heard that he had found money missing from his office across the yard? He was determined that Ramsay had stolen it.'

'No!'

'I'm afraid so. The rumours of his accusation had reached Ramsay, though Professor Keith had not had the opportunity to confront him with it. Ramsay was as upset as an honest man can be in such circumstances: he values his character very highly, as well he might.'

Mungo had in his own character that enviable trait of kindness that never makes anyone else feel awkward or reprimanded in receiving or seeing it. Charles nodded thoughtfully, feeling he had been let in on a charitable conspiracy.

'How is Miss Keith?' Dalzell added, shifting the focus of his concern. 'What befell her?'

'She is improving, we gather,' said Charles, 'though it has been a nasty fright.'

'I think I heard you say that it was unconnected with Professor Keith's fate.'

'That seems to be true. A different poison was used.'

180

Mungo Dalzell blew out a long sigh.

'A dreadful shock, the whole business.'

'I regret that you should have heard about it in such a way,' Charles added, not looking at George. 'We should have kept our voices lower.'

'No matter,' said Dalzell, waving one hand softly. 'I heard about it early this morning, before I came here. You know what rumour in this town is like! Ah, Ramsay – finished all that polishing?'

The bedellus emerged from the dark Chapel doorway with his brass ball and cloths in a basket.

'Aye, all done for another Sabbath,' he grunted. 'I'm away home for my dinner.'

'Oh, Lord, dinner!' cried Charles. 'Mrs. Walker will think all kinds of dreadful things. Come on, George. Excuse us, Mr. Dalzell, please, and thank you!'

Dinner was overcooked. Mrs. Walker insisted that she was not in the least displeased, though she and Patience were both edgy. Afterwards, Charles and George escaped gratefully to Charles' parlour upstairs. George did not look quite so grateful when Charles insisted that they stay there for a while, rather than rushing back straight away to be at the service of Alison Keith.

'There are a few things I want to have a think about first,' said Charles.

'But you don't need me to think. You've often said it: you're the thinker, and I'm the doer. I'd just be in the way.'

'George.' Charles propelled his brother gently into the Letho armchair, and sat himself down on the bench, long legs crooked in front of him to support his elbows. 'You are not going anywhere until you have told me what is going on.'

'I don't know what you mean.' George was good at appearing stupid, but for once Charles was not convinced.

'George!' Charles glared at his brother, but George looked at the coffered ceiling as if he had always had a compelling interest in such things. 'George, you sent me to buy cantharides for you in Edinburgh, and I see you giving sweetmeats to Alison Keith, and then she nearly dies of

181

cantharides poisoning. Her father does die, by a different poison, the same night. Surely you must have something to say for yourself?'

George, lips pursed into ostentatious secrecy, transferred his gaze from the ceiling to the open window, through which came the post-dinner noise from South Street. The greasy smell of chilling pastry wafted in from the pie stall on the other side of the road. Charles reached out a long arm and pulled the casement closed, without looking away from his brother.

'George ... I know the Sporting Set poisoned the treacle sweetmeats, and I know why, but were you up to the same thing? Did you think Alison might look on you more favourably if she'd been drugged?'

George, shocked, met Charles' eye at last.

'No! It was just – I thought it might help. I didn't know what it really did, honestly.' He shut his mouth again as if he had pulled the drawstrings tight on a purse. Charles waited a moment, then sighed.

'All right,' he said, as he stood up. 'I'm going to go and see the Sporting Set again and let them know they're probably off the murder charge, though Heaven knows it did me good to see Picket off his balance for a bit. I think Boxie knows a good deal more than he is saying, and if I could get him on his own, he might be tempted to tell me a few things. More than you, anyway!'

George sat in obstinate silence while Charles fetched his gown and trencher. From downstairs came the clattering and scrubbing that went with redding out the house for the Sabbath, but it was not clear that George heard them. When Charles emerged in his less than perfect gown, George did not move.

'Two things to think about, George.' He turned to go, one hand on the latch. 'I know there was cantharides missing from the packet I bought for you – I saw it earlier today in this room. The sweetmeats you gave Alison Keith were found in Professor Keith's study, along with his corpse. One of them was also missing.'

On this, Charles opened the door and left the room. Only when he glanced back did he see George's white and shaken face.

182

Charles escorted the Walkers and Daniel to Holy Trinity next morning before going on across Market Street to St. Salvator's Chapel, but his mind was not devoutly on either church. He had not been able to separate Boxie from Rab and Picket until quite late in the evening, by which time all three of the Sporting Set were drunk on a mixture of relief and a barrel of ale rolled along from the Black Bull – even now they had no particular wish to be seen drinking in public. Boxie had fallen asleep before Charles could question him. Charles had a few pints with them but was not drunk, and nor was George when he returned from his vigil at the Keiths', much later than politeness dictated. When Charles had stepped softly past him this morning as he lay across the armchair and the desk chair, Charles was sure that his snores were fake, but did not bother to test his thesis.

St. Salvator's Chapel was already nearly full, packed with the hundred or so undergraduates, the junior staff without families, and the town congregation of St. Leonard's who were currently churchless and seemed, on present evidence, likely to attend the Chapel until the Last Trump. The students were well used to the sight of women and children in the treacle-black pews, and the Sunday School learned half its lessons from the deep-carved misericords and high wall panels. Charles tucked himself in to the end of a pew on the left, and tried to concentrate as Ramsay Rickarton, his buttons polished to Sunday sheen, led in the academic procession holding the grand mace before him in steadfast, white-gloved hands.

The service wrapped around Charles like a familiar blanket, comforting but mostly unnoticed. The metrical psalms were set to tunes he had known from infancy, and the sermon was the same one that the Professor of New Testament had preached two weeks ago, but this time preached by the Professor of Biblical Exegesis, who must have read the same sermon book. The Professor of New Testament glowered from the staff seats. Bejants fidgeted in the front pews, and the young regents, who drilled them in their lectures, noted their names, then fidgeted themselves. Charles stared up at the dim painted patterns on the Gothic ceiling, and noticed a couple of pigeons perched on a crossbeam – Ramsay Rickarton would not be pleased.

The keen wind slicing its way round the college yard woke everyone when they finally went outside, pushing yesterday's broken clouds endlessly past the sun. Gulls glittered white as they soared by. Beneath the wind's hiss, you could hear the hushed conversations of both citizens and students – conversations in which the words 'Keith', 'Alison' and 'poisoned' seemed to echo from mouth to mouth. Moving through the groups, Charles recognised Thomas from his tatty gown, and realised that he had not seen him for what seemed like days – but was only, on reflection, since Friday evening. He went over, stepping with accustomed care on the uneven flags. Thomas, as usual, was on his own.

'You've heard the news, then?' Thomas said, with what even the charitable would have had to call a smirk.

'That Professor Keith is dead? Yes, I have. I was there yesterday, helping Professor Shaw to see to things.' Charles was only eighteen: he was not above a bit of glory-snatching.

'I hear it must have been bad for him.' Thomas was trying not to be impressed. 'Is it true he had half bitten his arm off with the pain?'

'Oh, aye, surely,' said Charles, 'and seven crows on the window sill waited to carry his soul away. Where did you hear that daft version?'

'It's going round.' He looked faintly disappointed. 'Is it true that all the rest of them are dying, too, though?'

'No. Miss Keith is ill, but that's not connected, and the doctor thinks she will make a full recovery. And as far as I know, Mrs. Keith and Peter are still quite all right.' A queer look passed over Thomas' rough face. 'What's wrong?'

Thomas' face went blank, then he scowled.

'Peter could still take Lord Scoggie's parish if he wanted to,' he muttered.

'You're a generous soul, Thomas,' said Charles mildly. 'Would you rather the whole family had been wiped out?'

Thomas managed to appear more shamefaced, but could not stop looking sulky at the same time.

184

'Well, the man did nothing for me, so I'd be hypocritical if I said anything else, wouldn't I? He's as well out of the world as in it, in my view.' He eyed Charles. 'So go on, then: what did he look like?'

Charles opened his mouth to describe the dreadful scene – and suddenly discovered that he did not want to. He tried to work out why: he remembered it vividly in his mind, and it had featured prominently in his dreams last night, and there was nothing to a young man like the glory of a first-hand account, yet ... Thomas was waiting, and Charles had to make do with a quick outline of the facts, proving that he really had been there but managing to turn it into a kind of illustration that he saw this sort of thing so often that one more poisoned professor squirming on his study floor was neither here nor there. Thomas seemed convinced, he thought. But still – why could he not find it in himself to give the full gruesome account?

'Why don't you come for dinner?' he asked Thomas as if by way of an apology. Thomas agreed at once.

'It'll be rabbit again in College,' he explained. 'I was nearly going to stand up at dinner yesterday and give the Rabbit Grace. You ken,

For rabbits young and for rabbits old,
For rabbits hot and for rabbits cold,
For rabbits tender and for rabbits tough
Our thanks we render – for we've had enough.

Charles laughed: the verse was passed down through the student generations, and legend had it that it had been invented by the poet Robert Fergusson when he was at the college.

'Robert Fergusson was gated for a whole term for saying that instead of the Latin grace,' came a leisurely voice, 'and I don't suggest you try it, however great the provocation. He at least had the virtue of originality.'

They turned to find Professor Urquhart next to them in his full Sunday gown and hood. They bowed.

'How did things go on yesterday, sir? With the town constable?'

'Oh, very well, I think.' Urquhart's voice was so polished it glistened as it left his mouth, yet Charles thought he could

185

sense just the least trace of discomfort somewhere. 'The little man went away quite satisfied with what we told him.'

'But will he investigate the matter? Is he going to find out who the killer is?'

'I doubt it. I think we may forget all about it: Keith had so many enemies, staff, students and citizens, that even if we caught the actual murderer, the *victor ludorum*, shall we say, there would be so many more dangerous people still about who had simply been beaten to the winning post that there would hardly be any point in punishing the one who had been quick enough to get there first.'

He smiled, bowed very slightly, and drifted away towards his rooms, anticipating the arrival of his excellent dinner. Reminded of it, Charles led Thomas out to the street and off to give Mrs. Walker fair warning of a not unwelcome guest.

The town smelled bland on a Sunday, with the shops and trades closed up for the Sabbath. Here you could catch a few threads of heady scent from the bookbinder's glue, and there you tasted thin shadows of leather, blood and bread from the cordiner, the flesher and the baxter, but gradually the faint everyday smells were overtaken at every pace by the wonderful odour of gravy, potatoes, roasting meat, and Mrs. Walker's excellent carrot pudding. They walked faster and faster as if on an uncontrollable slope, rushing towards Mrs. Walker's blessed kitchen and the welcome sight of her and Patience, aprons on over their Sunday best, coming to the kitchen door to greet them. Daniel, glimpsed behind them at the kitchen table, had the unnatural air of a saint gone to Heaven.

Patience, on seeing Thomas, had given a quick exasperated sigh, but her mother had applied a less than discreet sharp elbow to Patience's ribcage, and Patience managed a kind of smile before turning neatly to Charles.

'Did you by any chance see Mr. Bonar at the Chapel?'

'No, I didn't,' Charles said, thinking about it. Allan Bonar had not been amongst the staff in the congregation.

'No,' agreed Thomas shortly. The unshaveable patches of pale bristle stood out crossly on his face. Patience smiled at him with acid sweetness and took him into the parlour. Charles hesitated to follow.

'I should like to go up and see how my brother does,' he explained.

'Oh, he is out,' Mrs. Walker said. 'He said he was needed at the Keiths'.'

'I doubt it,' said Charles, and sighed. 'I hope he is not being a bother to them.' He watched absently as Mrs. Walker untied her apron strings and lifted the apron off over her head. Then he noticed something.

'Your brooch! It's back – where did you find it?'

Mrs. Walker blushed, one hand fluttering over the brooch at her collar. Her husband's face once again looked out from it in disapproval.

'Ah,' she said, lost for words, her eyes searching around the low ceiling. 'Ahm, I, er, found it. In the garden, yes. It must have dropped off when I was out there. In the garden, you see?'

'Of course,' said Charles, embarrassed by her obvious untruths. It was none of his business where she had found it, as long as she was happy to have it back. Feeling confused and tired, he left her in order to take his gown and trencher up to his rooms, then returned to join Patience and Thomas in the parlour.

They went for a walk after dinner, all four of them: Patience, glancing about her eagerly from the depths of her best bonnet, seemed to be looking for someone – probably Allan Bonar – but without success. Thomas, for whom possession was nine-tenths of the law, wanted to be seen with Miss Walker on his arm, but she was unco-operative and walked apart from him. Mrs. Walker wanted Thomas and Patience to be seen together in the hope that what was gossiped about might then become fact, though even she was beginning to think herself over-optimistic. Charles wanted simply to walk and think, but this was not possible. Mrs. Walker's conscience was not used to burdens, and hurried to rid itself of its present one.

'My dear Charles,' she began, as they entered the precinct of the ruined Cathedral, 'I fear I misled you before dinner, and I ought to tell you the truth. I was ashamed at first,

187

but now it seems likely that the situation will not recur I feel I can tell you everything.'

'Please do not feel obliged to, Mrs. Walker, if you do not wish to,' said Charles politely, though he was twitching with curiosity. 'I cannot oblige you to tell me anything you may regret to speak.'

'Oh, I must, I must!' Patience caught her mother's words and looked round in alarm, but Mrs. Walker gave her a reassuring smile and Patience looked away again, too far ahead to hear a normal level of conversation. Nevertheless, Mrs. Walker lowered her voice.

'The brooch was returned mysteriously, yesterday evening,' she explained. 'I didn't find it in the garden, as I told you I had, and nor did I really lose it in the first place. It was very wrong of me to deceive you, and to have you looking for it when I knew where it was all along, but you see you asked, and I couldn't tell you the truth, may the Lord forgive me!' She touched the brooch with the tips of her gloved fingers, as if the image of her husband had a more direct link to Heaven than it appeared. 'I knew you would pity me, and maybe even feel guilty about it yourself!' She gave a little laugh, and Charles slowly, with a creeping feeling of general awfulness, began to guess what was coming next.

'You know Professor Keith was our landlord – well, it was Mrs. Keith's property, you know, in her family. Well, last quarter we were late with the rent. It very rarely happens, you know, very rarely, but things have been so expensive lately, and the winter is always worse – more coal, more candles, that kind of thing.' And late rent coming in from your tenant, thought Charles, miserably. 'Anyway,' she cleared her throat, not looking at Charles. 'Professor Keith came to see us a couple of weeks ago – the day George came up to see you, remember, dear? – and he insisted on payment, and when I said we couldn't, not yet, not until – until something came in, he said he'd take something as a deposit. And I tried to offer him the silver spoons, or the tea caddy, but he insisted on taking my brooch. If Mr. Walker had ever known that his likeness ...' She fell silent, while Charles cursed and swore inwardly at himself.

Mrs. Keith took a few deep breaths, but she was not the weeping kind, and in a moment she was ready to continue.

'Anyway, Peter Keith was supposed to have been collecting the rent that afternoon. His father mustn't have spoken to him, because he arrived anyway and of course I had to tell him what had happened. Well, dear, he just went entirely hyte! He went storming off headlong saying the worst kind of things about his poor father – I had to put my hands over my ears! So then, of course, his poor father died yesterday, and yesterday evening back comes the brooch, and nothing else in or on the wrapper, so all I can think is that poor Peter thought of us even in his own grief, and brought it back. He's a grand boy – though a great deal too lively for my Patience, I think.'

Yet in her excitement at receiving back her treasure, Mrs. Walker had forgotten something. It would be far from proper for a gentleman in Peter Keith's position, with a dead parent in the house, to go walking about the town. Someone else must have returned the brooch. But who?

Chapter Seventeen

'So how is she?'

'As well as can be expected.' George sounded tired and short-tempered. Charles wondered if he had been allowed into the house at all, but if he had not, where had he been all this time? Charles wanted to press the repeater on his watch, but thought George would hear the chimes and think he was being reprimanded for being late home. It was late, anyway: Charles knew he had been asleep for some time before he had been woken by the footsteps on the stairs.

'But she's no worse, anyway?'

'Apparently not. She passed a better night last night, but she was uncomfortable today.' He was looking for something, blundering around the little room. Charles felt him stumble into the bedpost and swear.

'You mind if I strike a light?' he asked at last.

'Go ahead.'

George felt his way to the night table and found the candle. As soon as it was lit, Charles could not resist looking at his watch.

'Two o'clock! George, tell me you haven't been at the Keiths' all this time!'

George's face was in shadow as he recovered his nightshirt from a heap of his things on the floor. Daniel was not a manservant with much initiative. George pulled off his shirt and cravat and dragged his nightshirt over his head, all without speaking. Then he sat down on the side of the bed to remove his boots. Even in the dim light, Charles could see sand glittering on them.

'I left there about ten,' George said, 'then I went for a walk. I needed to think.'

Charles managed to say nothing.

'Have you ever been in love, Charles?'

'Well, there was that girl Geillis who came to stay a couple of summers ago ...'

'Old Jelly? Yes, but I mean real love, not puppy love.'

Charles winced at this description of what had at the time been undying adoration.

'You know, from the old stories, or from Shakespeare,' George went on, one boot forgotten in his hand. 'Where you would do anything for the woman you love, even kill someone who is hurting her – even give up your own life.'

'George,' said Charles quickly, 'please don't give up your life for Alison Keith.'

George gave him an odd look in the candlelight.

'I hope not to,' he said, and went off without another word to sleep in the parlour.

Charles could not rest so easily, even when he had blown out the candle again. What would their father do if George died? Or – almost worse – if he had killed Professor Keith? To kill someone who is hurting the woman you love: would George really be capable of that? Professor Keith was dead, there was no doubt, but surely George, young and fit and trained as he was, would rather fight a duel than use poison? It was illegal to duel, but then it was also illegal to murder. But perhaps that was the reason, perhaps he had challenged Professor Keith, and the Professor, feeling himself to be older and in worse condition, had refused to give him the satisfaction. But poison! But then again, George had asked Charles to buy the cantharides for him. What else might he have bought?

Charles was not sure about the distinctions between the effects of cantharides and arsenic, though the doctor had seemed so. *Difficilior legio est potior*, Professor Urquhart would have said: the more difficult reading is the preferable one. So, because Dr. Pagan could more easily have assumed that both Alison Keith and her father had been poisoned with the same substance, the fact that he had noticed differences was good evidence.

He saw the tumbled body of Professor Keith again in his mind's eye. It was odd, he thought: any number of people might have wanted Professor Keith to suffer, to die in a particularly nasty way, yet most of those he could think of – the Sporting Set, for example, or even Thomas – would have liked to have seen the results of their labours, not just heard the rumours, in the same way that the victims of crimes liked the satisfaction of going to the hangings. He did not like hangings,

191

himself: he hated the finality of it. He knew that it had to be done, that there was no effective alternative, but the helplessness of the criminal, however evil or depraved, made him ache. And suddenly he realised what had struck him most about seeing Professor Keith tossed like a broken marionette on the floor of his own study: it was the Professor's completely uncharacteristic helplessness. No more could he gate or expel, or punish with extra work or unpleasant examinations; no more could he sack his servants or accuse College staff. His murderer had rendered him useless, and might well because of that go free. Charles had not liked Professor Keith or his methods, but he could not stand by and see him so powerless, so unavenged. Professor Urquhart had reckoned that the town constable would not find the murderer, and that was not good enough. Cicero would not have approved. If no one else would work it out, then Charles decided he would.

And what if it turned out to be George?

Charles was really not convinced that Alison Keith was the love of George's life, but then even puppy love could make some very unreasonable demands. He remembered climbing far too high in far too tall a tree to rescue Geillis' shawl, blown there by an inconsiderate gust of wind ... But climbing trees and murdering professors were somewhat different, he was sure.

It was so dark he could not see whether or not his eyes were open. He turned over heavily in the bed, trying to find a cool patch on the pillow. Would George have been that stupid? That was a difficult question to answer. George was capable of great stupidity, and if he had decided to kill Professor Keith, then going about it in such a way actually as to attract Charles' attention was not at all unlikely. However, to be stupid enough to decide to kill in the first place, even in some cause he perceived to be noble ... surely that was beyond even George?

If George had not done it, Charles thought, turning again as he tried to look on the bright side, then who had? Professor Urquhart was right: there were plenty of people with reason, and if the poison had been slipped into the claret jug they had all passed as they left the party, plenty of people with the chance to do it, too. Ramsay Rickarton, of course, had not been

192

there. Professor Shaw, perhaps, had left too quickly – but then Mrs. Keith had said that Professor Shaw had returned later for his forgotten gloves ... but Professor Shaw was an even less likely murderer than George. But why had the notebook disappeared from Professor Keith's desk while they were all in the study? What had been written in it, and who had taken it? Had it gone before or after Dr. Pagan had left? If after, it must have been Shaw or Urquhart – and Charles' money had to be on Urquhart. And who had brought both boxes of sweetmeats to Professor Keith's study, and why?

Charles sank slowly into an unpeaceful sleep, and found he was dancing at a party. A huge version of an eightsome reel was in progress, and as each dancer danced his or her solo in the centre of the circle, he recognised them: Urquhart, Shaw, George, Mungo Dalzell, Allan Bonar, Thomas, the Keiths and the Walkers taking their turns. When it was his turn, the circle around him spun faster and faster, blurred with speed and music, and would not let him back in.

Next day lectures began again, as they always did on a Monday, though this Monday it seemed more of a shock than usual to the staff and students. For Charles and Thomas, the day normally consisted of classes in Latin, Greek, Mathematics, and, now that they were in their magistrand year, Natural Philosophy. In addition, on Monday mornings Charles and several other boys who could afford it took History with a barrell-shaped academic with whiskers, and sat in on Professor Shaw's tertian Moral Philosophy course. Thomas' bursary did not run to History but Allan Bonar's optional chemistry classes were cheaper. When Charles' history class was over, his head full of Tudors and Stuarts, he went to meet Thomas from his chemistry class. The chemistry class room, tucked away against Butts Wynd to the west of the college, was as redolent as ever but bore no signs of recent occupation, and Charles left the college by the back gate on to the Scores, walking between the neatly-walled pastures towards the Castle.

Almost opposite it, past the end of Castle Wynd, some well-meaning citizen had placed two large sandstone boulders and a partially-smoothed log, to serve as a seat. It was Thomas' favourite spot on a pleasant day: the wall against which the seat was set was a high one, with yew trees bundled at the top of it and dropping, in season, their jelly-red berries around his feet, and the view of the bay and the castle as the cliffs dropped away from the other side of the path was as calming as the breeze was refreshing. If he had ever taken the trouble to work out that the high wall in whose reflected warmth he basked was the wall of Professor Keith's garden, it seemed not to bother him, and here Charles found him now, notebook fluttering forgotten in his hand, head back, snoring gently with his gown wrapped round him.

'Chemistry cancelled, then?' asked Charles, rather more loudly than was kind. Thomas jumped, and dropped his notebook in the mud, and leaned forward, cursing, to pick it up before he replied.

'No chemistry. No Allan Bonar,' he explained briefly. 'We sat around for a bit then gave up. Is it time for Latin, then?'

'Nearly.' Charles sat at the other end of the rough bench and stared out at the sea. The sky was high and clear, the palest of blues, and the ruined castle had a bleak, battered look. Legend had it that there had been a great feast in the banqueting hall one night, as the storm blew and the rain lashed, and the whole banqueting hall, guests, feast and all, had crashed down the cliff into the sea. The ruins had the air, today at least, of having been taught a lesson.

'What do you know about arsenic, Thomas?' Charles asked eventually. He was not looking at him, but felt Thomas shift quickly in surprise.

'From Chemistry, you mean? Well, er ... it's poisonous, but some people take it in small doses for years for stomach troubles. Wait, though: that wasn't from Chemistry class, that was what Allan Bonar was saying the other night, at Professor Keith's party.'

'So he was.' Charles was thoughtful. 'So you haven't done any work in class on arsenic?' Both Picket and Boxie did Chemistry – Rab's father could not afford it.

'Not that I can remember. We did that bit in Latin, though, when we read Suetonius' *Lives of the Caesars*.'

194

'Yes.' Everyone did Latin, overseen by Professor Urquhart, no matter what year they were in. Everyone read Suetonius. How many people knew you could find arsenic in Sallies Chapel, though? The Sporting Set regarded the Chapel more as a prominent place with a good tower for hanging out embarrassing objects during their pranks than as a place of worship, but they were almost always there for Sunday services as they were expected to be. Thomas himself was always there, as if there were some exchange arranged whereby the more services he attended the more likely he was to become a minister himself. The staff, of course, had to set an example: Professor Urquhart, Allan Bonar, the Principal, the Chancellor, were all there week in, week out: Professor Shaw attended the Town Kirk with his wife, as Professor Keith had done. But the Chapel was there, central to their lives geographically, if not spiritually.

'You didn't happen to see,' he began slowly, 'a tray with a claret jug on it? On the landing at Professor Keith's, just as we were leaving the party.'

Thomas thought about it, wiry eyebrows drawn close together, his eyes half-closed against the wind.

'I think so,' he said at last. 'There was something else on the tray, too: biscuits. They looked nice. I nearly took one, thinking they were for the guests.'

Charles half-smiled: anything to eke out the College meals.

'You didn't notice anyone else near the tray, did you? Anyone touching it, or touching anything on it?'

'Oh, come on, it was last Friday! I never remember anything like that!'

'Well, where were you standing when you saw it? Were you waiting to say goodbye to Mrs. Keith, or were you on the landing waiting for your coat?'

'No, I didn't say goodbye to Mrs. Keith. I squeezed out round the queue. I was waiting for Miss Walker. Remember, we all walked back to your bunk together, a great procession of us!'

'Oh, yes.'

'So I just noticed the biscuits when I was looking round for Miss Walker, and then Mrs. Walker came out so I knew she couldn't be far behind, and then I remember seeing someone lifting the jug ... oh, who was it?'

The frown was back for half a second, before they heard footsteps above the hum of the wind, and both turned. It was Mungo Dalzell.

'Good day to you both, gentlemen! No Latin today?'

'Oh, heavens, is it that time already?' Charles scrambled to his feet, bowing to Mr. Dalzell. Thomas began to gather up his untidy notebook.

'I heard Sallies ring the hour five minutes ago at least,' Mungo looked on with kindly dismay. 'With everything in a guddle today, though, I'm sure Professor Urquhart will not be much concerned if you are a little late. Shall I walk with you?'

'Please do, sir,' said Charles politely, positive that Mungo Dalzell was only ensuring that they did go to class and did not fetch up in a coffee house. They set off at a smart pace back along the Scores.

'I have just been to pay my respects to poor Mrs. Keith,' said Mungo Dalzell. 'It is very difficult to know what to say on such occasions.'

Thomas and Charles nodded, each trying to look as if he had a wealth of experience of such adult things.

'Poor lady,' Dalzell went on. 'She has two kindly children, but they must be so overwhelmed themselves with their father's death, and Miss Alison so ill, even now ... I believe her own family are all dead. Who does she have to turn to?'

'Professor Urquhart and Professor Shaw were being very kind on Saturday,' Charles ventured.

'Of course, of course, I had forgotten. But Professor Shaw has his own worries: perhaps Professor Urquhart is better placed to help, but he is not – forgive my indiscretion! - perhaps the most sympathetic of men.' He smiled at them, knowing they were unlikely to betray him to Urquhart, and they smiled back, knowing it too. Mungo had time to be kinder than Professor Shaw, Charles thought. Professor Shaw spent so much time being anxious about whether or not he would do the right thing that he had no chance to do anything. Mungo Dalzell simply went ahead and did it, unselfconsciously.

'Is there much hope of finding the murderer, do you think, sir?' he asked. Thomas coughed. Mungo looked severe.

'Oh, yes, I should think so,' he said firmly. 'In a small town like this, it would be very difficult for anyone guilty of a serious crime to escape detection for very long, surely.'

Thomas dropped his notebook, and they had to stop while he gathered its errant pages once again.

'I'm pleased to hear it,' said Charles when they were moving again, though he was a little disappointed to think that someone else might solve the puzzle before he did. 'I should not like to think of others suffering the same way.' Then he thought of George. 'But what if it was an outsider, sir? Someone who did not belong to the town?'

'But Mr. Murray,' said Mungo kindly, 'as I understand it, the poison was introduced in a claret jug which was on the landing at the end of last Friday's party. The murderer must be of the Keith household, which is unthinkable, or among the party guests. Did you not study Logic in your Semi year?'

'Yes, sir, of course,' said Charles humbly.

'Maybe it was Lord Scoggie,' Thomas suggested, with a suspicion of bitterness.

'Now, Mr. Seaton, we should be very careful what we say in jest, should we not?' Mungo grinned, and so, after a moment, did Thomas.

'So they are sure the arsenic was in the claret jug.' Charles returned to his own concerns. Surely he would have noticed George tampering with the jug?

'I believe so. The town constable took it away for the apothecary to examine, I believe. The wine glass, I hear, was broken.'

'Yes,' said Charles blandly, 'Professor Urquhart stepped on it.'

'Indeed,' was Mungo's equally bland response. They did not look at each other. 'Well, here we are: no doubt Professor Urquhart is waiting for you. I shall see you later for Hebrew, Thomas, yes?'

197

Thomas nodded and bowed, and they scuttled in to the Latin classroom, to face Professor Urquhart's well-practised sarcasm.

Christopher Urquhart was not on form, however. He nodded at the two of them from his desk at the front of the room, and while they found spaces at the end of the back form he toed a coal in the dismally dark fireplace, as if the lesson had not even begun. He seemed abstracted. Thomas, dropping his notebook on the floor in his haste to be ready, made him jump, and he glanced up at the twenty or so magistrands before him, and down at his notes.

'Ah ... Juvenal. Yes,' he began, with none of his usual confidence. He looked out of the window. In the row in front of him, Charles noticed the three members of the Sporting Set seated in unaccustomed attentiveness, not even taking advantage of Professor Urquhart's distraction to pass a note or scribble an irreverent cartoon. It seemed that by being murdered, Professor Keith had, for a time at least, achieved a level of good behaviour he could never manage when he was alive.

'Little is known of Juvenal. He lived and worked in the period of the Emperors Trajan and Hadrian, and it is generally agreed that he spent some period of his life in exile, and was more prosperous in old age than he was in his younger years, a blessing, no doubt. No need to write that last bit.'

The class paused, pens over ink wells.

'His Satires are sixteen in number, and tradition divides them into five books. They are –' he stopped, as if searching for the right word, though he was as usual reading a prepared text. 'They are bitter and cynical, the work of a man to whom life has dealt nothing but the lower cards of a minor suit, to whom the rich and powerful are corrupt and vicious enemies, and to whom women have been sour, cruel and disdainful. In the sixth Satire you will find a full denunciation of women: a good woman is a *rara avis*, a rare bird. Consider this: there are twenty of you, and more in the first, second and third years. How likely is it that each of you will find a *rara avis* of your own? One untainted by nagging, possessiveness, small-mindedness, chronic stupidity or gross ugliness? And if you are

198

lucky enough to catch sight of such a fowl, who is neither too old nor too young, too high nor too low, too open with men or too shy, the chances are high that she is already in another man's cage, singing for him and eating seed from his fingers.'

Several members of the class looked up, grinning, Rab included, ready to laugh at one of Urquhart's frequent displays of wit. But Urquhart himself was not laughing. He pushed his chair back from his desk and rose in a movement too sharp to be graceful. Again he stared out of the window, hands clasped tightly behind him: the sun, smothered now by rain clouds that the wind was flinging at it, blurred his profile and picked out grey shadows amongst the white folds of his cravat and wig. The glass in the window shook and squeaked. He looked as if he were about to spit.

The slightest chink of a student's pen against his inkwell roused him, and he turned abruptly.

'The Principal has asked me to announce that Professor Keith's funeral will take place tomorrow from half past ten at his house. Morning classes will be cancelled. He – the Principal – expects all of you to be there and not to eat more than is polite.' He pressed his fingertips together close to his stomach, and avoided looking at anyone in particular. 'I, on the other hand, require a translation from each of you of Juvenal's third Satire, and a version in Latin of Dr. Johnson's poem, 'London', which was inspired by it. Points will be awarded for good vocabulary and deducted for untidy work: no doubt for some people the one will balance the other. Now, some further words about the first Satire.'

Pens were redipped and there was a collective shuffle as the class relaxed: whatever had been amiss with their lecturer seemed to have passed, and they copied out their dictata obediently as he explained the poem to them in the manner to which they were accustomed, occasionally grinning at his sarcasms. Latin class, for Charles anyway, usually passed quite quickly, and today was no exception. It was soon one o'clock, and the air was filled with the distinct scent of rabbit stew emanating from the college kitchens. The few who lived in college caught one another's eyes with looks of resignation, as Sallies rang the hour and Professor Urquhart wound up his remarks. Thomas packed up his notebooks very unenthusiastically, no doubt thinking of the rabbit stew, and Charles, waiting for him at the front of the classroom, nodded to Urquhart.

'I hope Mr. Bonar is well, Professor.'

'Bonar? Why?'

'Oh,' said Thomas, 'he didn't come to Chemistry today. No sign of him.'

Urquhart moved towards the door, ushering them out before him. He was frowning.

'I have no idea. I have not seen him since ... no, he was not even at Chapel yesterday, was he?'

'Not that I remember,' Charles agreed.

'Then I cannot have seen him since Friday night. He lodges near the West Port, does he not? Perhaps he has gone away for a few days: his bunkwife could tell you, no doubt.'

'Aye, probably,' said Charles, equally carelessly, though Urquhart looked worried as he left them to meet his dinner.

'He's the one I saw with the claret jug,' said Thomas suddenly.

'What, Urquhart? I know: he said he had admired it.'

'No, Allan Bonar. I remember now, because I realised he was waiting for Miss Walker, too.'

'Oh, dear,' said Charles.

'Why?'

'Because it is greatly to Allan Bonar's advantage that Professor Keith should be out of the way. Allan succeeds to the Chair of Natural Philosophy, has the money to carry out his experiments, and the position to marry Patience Walker.'

The scowl on Thomas' face would have turned milk sour.

'The blackyirtly, ill-deedit, meschantly gallow-breid,' he muttered.

'Oh, now, don't hold back, Thomas. You're among friends here,' Charles remarked.

'Huh.'

'And you should be getting along in case you miss your dinner. It smells good.'

Thomas sniffed bitterly.

'The last few rabbits in the kingdom must be running scared,' he said. 'Here, I have a notion – why don't we go and see if we can find Allan Bonar instead? If he's in, his bunkwife might give us a meal.'

Charles laughed.

'Is that concern for Allan Bonar speaking, or desperation for a good meal?'

'Why can't it be both? Just a minute, though: I want to see if I can catch Ramsay Rickarton. My window's coming out of its frame.'

He trotted over to the Chapel and disappeared inside, leaving Charles to hum to himself till he returned a moment later.

'Success?'

'Aye, all done. Come on, then.'

His enthusiasm increasing with every step he took away from the rabbit stew, Thomas led the way out of the gate and down the road. Allan Bonar lived near the West Port, the old gateway out of the city at the west end of South Street, and as they passed the Walkers' house Charles darted in to excuse himself from dinner and leave his book satchel upstairs. Three minutes further down the road, they found themselves outside a tiny confectionery shop, and went in. The smell of sugar and violets was delicious, and the woman behind the counter looked as if she seldom resisted sampling her merchandise: she was round and red and cheerful, with extraordinarily bad teeth. Charles winced to look at them.

'Mr. Bonar?' she said. 'Aye, he lives up the stair. I havena seen him since ... oh, Friday, I imagine, but he comes and goes as he pleases, ye ken.'

'Then you don't cook for him?' Thomas asked, disappointed.

'He doesna like to be bound to mealtimes, ye ken,' she explained, her smile undiminished. 'Do yous want to see if he's up there the now?'

'Would you mind?' Charles asked.

'Not a bit of it. On you go, it's no locked.'

They pushed past a curtain at the back of the shop, and found themselves at the foot of a narrow stair. On the landing there were two doors, one to each side. One turned out to lead to Allan Bonar's bedchamber, and one to his parlour. Though Charles had held his breath as they had opened each door, both rooms were empty of their occupant, dead or alive.

'I don't know whether to be relieved or disappointed,' he sighed, as they stood looking about the parlour. The bunkwife must have done little to try to mitigate the effects of her lodger's lifestyle: the place was a dusty mess, with jars of strange substances, branches covered in crispy leaves jammed upright in stone bottles, presumably for his experiments on plants, mashed-up leaves stinking on shallow dishes, books, open and closed, on every chair and shelf. As far as Charles could judge, there was no sign of a struggle in either the parlour or the bedroom. Allan Bonar must have left of his own accord: there was no sign of a coat or hat, but his gown was on the back of his bedroom door, and his usual boots were not to be seen.

'Well, no chance of a meal here, then,' said Thomas, looking about for any sign of edible remains.

'No,' Charles admitted. 'We'd better go and find ourselves a bowl of soup somewhere.'

Indecision and meandering led them back to Sallies again, with the intention of eating fish broth further up North Street at one of the places used by the fishermen. Thomas said he would leave his book satchel in his room first, and they went into the yard together.

'I suppose,' Thomas said, as if he had been considering the matter carefully, 'that Allan Bonar could have put something in that claret jug.'

'It seems to be a strong possibility. You're sure you didn't see him do it?'

Thomas turned thoughtfully and took two steps before tripping on one of the uneven flagstones. He went down solidly, and his book satchel flew open, spraying notebooks and library books over the yard. Charles sighed and went to help him up, and started to gather up the books while Thomas expressed his considered opinion about the state of the flagstones.

202

'It's time this college was just damn' well demolished and the land used as a midden – though whether the Senate could even manage that, I doubt.'

But Charles was not listening. He had picked up Thomas' Chemistry notebook where it lay face down on the worn flags, and turned it over. At the top of the page, in Thomas' brutal handwriting, was the heading:

'Yew – Poisonous Effects, Compared With Arsenic'.

Chapter Eighteen

Rain was not that common in St. Andrews, not proper pelting rain. On the morning of the funeral of Professor Helenus Keith, however, it poured. The gutters flowed, bobbing with the detritus of shops and houses. On the worn pavements, between the cobble stones, on the flags around the wells and in Sallies yard, the puddles flashed with busy rings of ripples, and a cat, ejected from one South Street doorway, moved with offended speed from door to door down the street, snatching shelter on its way, tail flicking.

Charles had lent George a sober cravat and waistcoat: the Walkers had mourning clothes to hand, and they set off together with Daniel in wary attendance, a black daylight parody of the night they had gone to the Keiths' soirée, only four days ago. It seemed, to Charles at least, a century away.

George, absently escorting Patience Walker, seemed happier than he had for days, and Charles had managed to work from him the information that Miss Keith was well enough to make an appearance at the funeral: it seemed hardly decent to be setting off for a burial feast in quite such a lively mood.

Everyone else, however, was damp and drab and properly dejected as they tramped in large numbers up the soggy gravel to the Keiths' white front door. A row of sodden crows watched dully from the garden wall as the great and good of St. Andrews came to pay some form of respect to the dead man. Inside everything had been done properly: the hall mirror was covered in smooth black cloth, and the drawing room as they passed it was quiet and subdued.

Up the narrow wooden stairs to the family apartments they clattered, embarrassed by the noise, following the general flow of mourners to the dead-room where Professor Keith was laid out. Charles came to the open door and closed his eyes, seeing suddenly the corpse tumbled in the study, but when he opened them again he saw the waxy, sagging face nested neatly in pristine linen Keith would not have been ashamed to wear in his lifetime, hands folded over his stomach almost as if he were content with his lot. Charles could not imagine that he could be so.

Mrs. Keith, supported by her son, sat beside the bed where the corpse lay already in its coffin. The minister from the Town Kirk stood by, and Professors Urquhart and Shaw, the latter red-eyed, the former with a mouth like an unpicked buttonhole, sat at the foot of the bed. Charles touched the corpse's hand with the back of his own, hardly feeling the customary touch he dreaded, then bowed to the professors and to the Keiths, muttering the usual formula. He was just another black figure to Mrs. Keith, though he half-expected her to sense that he planned to find her husband's murderer. George, following him, bent low over Mrs. Keith's hand but could not bring himself to ask about Alison. The silence, underlaid by the shuffling of feet on the carpets and the distant clattering as mourners came up the stairs and went down again, was muffling, gagging even the most talkative. Professor Shaw looked desperate, as though he had not spoken for hours.

They returned to the drawing room, trying to shrug off the suffocation of the dead-room, and Charles saw Mrs. Walker and Patience to seats near the fire to make what they could of drying their skirts, and then joined George and Thomas awkwardly stuck against a table by a pier glass. It too was draped in black, but George managed to detach one corner of cloth to check the arrangement of his cravat in the mirror, till Charles nudged him hard. They were close enough to the window to hear the rain tapping at it, hard, like the beaks of urgent crows.

The company consisted of worthy burgesses, Dr. Pagan, other professors and staff, and students, trying to look like grown-ups. Wives, sisters and daughters had most of the chairs: young Mrs. Shaw had a chair and a footstool to support her bulk, making the words 'In the midst of life we are in death' echo tinnily in Charles' head. Mungo Dalzell, who had evidently arrived early enough to help, had a seat and was just giving it up to the wife of one of the lecturers from St. Mary's College. He was smiling at her but looking pale, Charles thought. But then, it would be his first funeral – nearly everyone's first funeral – since little Sybie's burial. Just as the thought occurred to him, Ramsay Rickarton arrived in the room, grey but stoical. As if he were on duty, he took up a post near the door and stood like a sentry, meeting no one's eye.

Charles' thoughts wandered on, disjointed ... Ramsay with the rat poison in the Chapel when Professor Keith announced the theft of money from his office ... Professor Keith pouncing on some poor bejant, red gown crisp and new ... The students at the funeral wore red gowns, standing out amongst the black mourners liked redcoats on a winter battlefield, the velvet collars blood-dark around their necks. It seemed an age before the trail of mourners finally came to a halt. Charles imagined that more of them were there out of duty or desire for sensation than out of respect or liking for Keith himself. He hoped Mrs. Keith did not realise it.

She arrived at last, entering the room with Alison on her arm, and the sensation-seekers were satisfied. Alison was barely thinner than she had been, but there was about her an unmistakable air of illness, a worn, older look about her mouth. Black did not suit her: it draped dully on her, making her pallor grey. She clung to her mother, and did not raise her eyes. George let out a long, agonised breath, and Charles touched his arm, half in restraint and half in sympathy: if ever a girl looked as if she needed protecting, it was Alison at that moment.

They were followed into the room by Shaw and Urquhart, by the minister, and finally by Peter. The minister shuffled his way into a vacant space and cleared his throat in that universal way Charles thought must be taught to Divinity students, and all heads were bowed before the minister had even said 'Let us pray'.

When he had finished, the first course of the funerary meats was served to them there as they sat or stood, cold meat and cheese, and ale. Mrs. Keith had not stinted: there were large ashets with heaps of food, though little of it seemed to be being eaten. The Principal had warned the students not to eat embarrassingly well at the funeral, but what he had not taken into account – and only now seemed to be realising himself, as Charles saw him nibble uncertainly at a piece of cheese – was that in a house where two people had been poisoned, even students might find their appetites diminished. Of the people Charles could see, only Professor Urquhart was eating with anything approaching enthusiasm, though others may have had more than one reason for abstemiousness: Professor Shaw, for instance, clearly had his thoughts fixed more on his wife than on himself, and Alison Keith did not look up to facing more than gruel for a while yet. She sat quietly very close to her mother, with Peter Keith hovering protectively, eyes scanning the guests. If she felt the fencing-foil stare of George's gaze, focussed on her from the moment she had entered the room to the exclusion even of food, she did not react to it but kept her head down. No one approached or greeted her, and Charles presumed that like him they could think of nothing to say: eager professions of joy at seeing her recovered seemed out of place at her father's funeral, and expressions of sympathy would still have echoed with the unspoken reflection that at least it was only one funeral, when it could so easily have been two.

When the first course had been served to everyone and the ashets cleared away, Professor Urquhart rose and offered his arm to Mrs. Keith. They left to return to the dead-room, followed by Alison, Peter and the minister. Professor Shaw, on the receipt of a kindly nod from Urquhart, hurried over to join his wife and Mungo Dalzell. Conversation was almost non-existent and the guests remained where they had established themselves, and if things went on as they were no one would consume enough alcohol to relax. However, academics, drunk or sober, can rarely remain silent for long, and by the end of the mostly ignored second course there was a low hum of conversation, at least among the men in the room.

'Still no sign of Allan Bonar,' Charles murmured to George, if nothing else to nudge him out of his reverie.

'Why, is he missing?' George glanced around as if hoping to prove Charles wrong, but he could not.

'Well, not missing, exactly, I suppose. It's funny he's not here, though. No one saw him at Chapel on Sunday, and he didn't take his chemistry class yesterday.'

'Bit funny,' George agreed unemotionally, 'Seeing he was probably the last to see Professor Keith, and all.'

'The last? He left with us, remember?' Charles could not understand the expression on George's face.

'Aye, well, he wasn't with us all night, was he?' George looked around him again, this time for eavesdroppers. No one seemed to be listening, but he lowered his voice still further. 'Barbara says he came back here on Friday night – after Mrs. Keith and Alison had gone up to bed. She showed him up to Professor Keith's study.' The odd expression on George's face resolved itself into a smile. 'See? You're not the only one who can find things out.'

'But why didn't Barbara tell anyone? I mean, apart from you, whatever she told you for. Professor Urquhart, I mean.'

'Because he didn't ask her.'

'I wonder why not?'

'She told me because I was the only one there who was ready to listen to her. You know, waiting here for so long, sometimes I didn't see anyone for hours, so she talked to me.'

'Good heavens, George. Well done,' Charles added, a little grudgingly. From George's look of satisfaction he did not appear to have noticed.

'See? Intelligence and taste.' He fingered the hem of the waistcoat Charles had lent him for the funeral. 'Remind me to give you some advice, some time.' He grinned, and Charles had to remind himself firmly that they were both adults now and that giving his wee brother laldy at a funeral would not be calculated to impress.

'What are you two muttering about?' demanded Thomas. Unimaginative as ever, he had not held back with the funeral meats and drink so far, and his rough face was already a little pink.

'No Allan Bonar again, that's all,' said Charles quickly. Thomas never liked to think he had been missing anything important. No one else seemed to have noticed their conversation: the level of subdued chatter had risen gently since the Keith family had left the room, and now people were even moving about, leaving their seats to greet friends and acquaintances almost as if it were a party. Mungo Dalzell, who was helping to top up people's drinks, headed towards his friends Professor and Mrs. Shaw, but paused on the way to greet the Murrays and Thomas.

'Congratulations, Mr. Seaton,' he said to Thomas almost immediately. 'I have just been speaking with Lord Scoggie there, and it seems that your way is clear to your parish. It seems destined for you.' He gave a little grin, and looked much happier than he had when he came in. 'Excuse me: I must go and see how Mrs. Shaw does.' He bowed and left. Charles moved to look past Thomas, to where Lord Scoggie was now chatting easily with the Principal, his face long with the strong verticals of his side whiskers and front teeth. Charles looked back at Thomas, whose mouth was still hanging unattractively open.

'Thomas, well done,' he said.

'Though why you should want ...' George tailed off as Charles stepped on to his toe. George hurriedly polished the fine black leather on the back of his black stockings, then craned to see if he had left dust on them.

'I haven't even met him – not really,' said Thomas, his mouth moving numbly.

'I think you're about to now,' Charles whispered sharply, and Thomas looked up in shock.

'Mr. Murray,' said Lord Scoggie, having moved across the room with remarkable speed, 'we met last Friday. I am sorry that we are renewing our acquaintance under such tragic circumstances.'

'Indeed, my lord,' said Charles, bowing. 'It is a very sad occasion, though I am honoured to meet you again.'

'Perhaps you will be so good as to introduce me to your friends?'

'I should be happy to present them, my lord. Mr. Thomas Seaton, my fellow student, and Mr. George Murray, my younger brother.'

Thomas bowed as if he expected to be hit.

'I understand you intend a career in the Kirk, Mr. Seaton?' Lord Scoggie said, with a glint in his eye. Thomas swallowed noisily.

'I do, sir – my lord,' he gulped. 'But I have no patron and no family influence.'

'I see. A very distressing disadvantage. But not every minister in a country kirk has a degree from a university. How do you think your years here would help you deal with the problems of your congregation?'

Charles could see panic in Thomas' eyes: it looked as if he had not only no idea what answer to give, but that he had also forgotten the question. He thought frantically.

'You've often said, Thomas, what a broad section of society comes to St. Andrews, haven't you?'

'Ah, yes.' Thomas looked like a drowning man offered a thorn branch. 'Yes, my lord: university has given me a wider experience of the world than I would otherwise have had. I have often remarked on it. If I had more money I'd have lived in a bunk and met some women, too, but my bursary only went as far as college residence.'

'I see.' Lord Scoggie fingered his sidewhiskers, eyeing the servants as they brought in the third service of food.

'Thomas often comes to my bunk for dinner: Mrs. Walker and her daughter are very fond of him,' said Charles desperately.

'Well, *Mrs.* Walker is very fond of him,' added George, but Charles kicked him. Unfortunately, Lord Scoggie seemed to have noticed, and his lips twitched alarmingly.

'And your attitudes to the current – er, divisions within the church ... how do you feel about those?'

This was a tricky one: one of the major arguments within the Established church was over patronage. Ferocious debates raged amongst those who liked the church appointment system as it was, particularly with the financial interest that brought, and those who resented the influence that people like Lord Scoggie had on appointments to parishes. Charles winced inwardly, for Thomas, in his desperate search for a patron, had grown to despise patronage as much as he craved it. As Thomas wallowed in a prolonged and meaningless answer, Charles watched his friend, the bristly, panicking face, the bunched-up fists, the shabby gown and habitual black, and saw Thomas clearly, perhaps for the first time. He saw a man accustomed, almost born and bred, to be unhappy, to be powerless regardless of his circumstances, faced in this glittering, dangerous moment with the chance to break the habit of a lifetime and to be content, comfortable, prosperous.

210

The light in Thomas' eyes was one of snatching ambition, but also one of fear, fear that he could not do it, fear that he could not live it, fear even that he had gone too far now to turn back. There flashed into Charles' mind a vision of Thomas' chemistry notebook: 'Yew – Poisonous Effects'. Could Thomas have seized his opportunity? No: no, it was not a question of seizing an opportunity. If Thomas had slipped poison into Professor Keith's claret jug, he had to have prepared the poison and brought it with him. It could not have been a completely spontaneous murder. But Thomas' anger against Professor Keith had been boiling away since the disastrous day of the Senate meeting: he had had plenty of time.

What was he thinking? Thomas was his friend – they had sat together on their very first day at University, staring agog at Professor Urquhart's waistcoat, stunned by the strangeness of it all, Charles from his prosperous estate, Thomas from his carpenter's cottage in Dunkeld. Thomas could not have murdered Professor Keith.

Yet he had the means: his favourite seat was under those yew trees leaning over the Keiths' garden wall – Charles could see the irony appealing to Thomas. He knew they were poisonous. By his own admission Thomas had been on the landing outside the Keiths' soirée for some time, just where the claret jug had been waiting. Finally, he had a reason for wanting to hurt Keith, to kill him, even. Charles felt his pulse race. Could Thomas have murdered Professor Keith?

'And you are Mr. Murray's younger brother?' Lord Scoggie's voice broke into his thoughts. George was agreeing. Thomas, sweat in channels on his unlovely brow, seemed reprieved. 'And do you have a profession?'

'I have not thought of it as yet, my lord,' said George aimiably.

'The army would surely suit someone like you,' Lord Scoggie offered, and Charles wondered if he bought commissions, too, for hopeful young men. 'Your brother here will have his hands full with the estate, of course, when his time comes.'

'I pray it will be long delayed,' said Charles hurriedly. He was certainly in no mood to contemplate his father's death – nor even, really, his father at all. There was a noise from downstairs, and one or two people looked round at the door.

'And in the mean time, of course, there are your studies to complete.'

There were voices downstairs, and the guests exchanged glances. The undertakers were noisy: they must have started on the mandatory whisky.

'Of course, my lord. Fortunately I find them very enjoyable.'

'Ah, intellectual rewards, the sweetest kind, are they not?'

Thomas, George and Charles nodded sagely, each with his own opinion. There were footsteps on the stairs.

'Though I quite like boxing,' said George helpfully. Lord Scoggie, smiling, opened his toothy mouth to reply.

The door burst open like a thunderclap. On the doorstep, dressed in unfunereal green, stood Allan Bonar. He was breathless, staring about him.

'Will someone tell me,' he gasped, 'Where is Professor Keith?'

Chapter Nineteen

'So where exactly were you?' asked Thomas, unsympathetically.

Allan Bonar hunched over his tankard of ale at the end of the long table. The Black Bull had a good fire going, and steam rose slowly from each of them and from the heap of red wool gowns they had left on the settle beside them: gowns were not to be worn in ale houses. This, combined with an ancient statute that said students must wear their gowns in the town should have prevented them from entering the Black Bull at all, but that statute was in a state of decay and anyway, this was an emergency. Bonar's face was the colour of the yellowish whitewashed walls, making his hair and brows stand out coal-black. He had already, at Charles' specific instructions, disposed of one tankard of ale, and this one had emptied more slowly as they told him in detail about Professor Keith's death.

'I was ... but to arrive just in time for the funeral ... oh, my,' said Bonar faintly.

The funeral was over, anyway. When the reluctant feasting was finished Bonar had joined the men following the Professor's coffin to the town burying-ground beside the Cathedral, where Sybie had been laid so lately, too. The rain had made the clean grave cut a glinting brown cavern, a topaz turned inside out, and the bearers had slithered dangerously setting the coffin down in the mud. It had seemed wrong to let it be soiled like that, with the heavy raindrops turning the mortcloth soggy and soaking into the coffin cover, but after all, they were going to bury it. In a few minutes, it made no difference: the gravediggers heeled earth back in from the spoil heap, clods falling hollowly on the firwood box. The bearers folded the mortcloth with a few neat gestures: the mourners shared a few sips of rapidly-diluting brandy, and hurried away, parting almost in silence. How Thomas and the Murrays had ended up in the Black Bull with Allan Bonar was not clear, but Charles, at least, was determined to make the most of it.

'When did you last see Professor Keith?' he asked, trying to make the question sound casual, and failing. Bonar eyed him.

'At the party, just like you,' he said.

'But what about when you went back later?'

Bonar maintained his stare for a moment, then gave it up. His eyes were still bleak with shock.

'I don't know that I should talk about that,' he said. 'You say they have no one in mind for this murder, and I have no intention of giving them any reason to think of me. I have a reputation in this university, a good one: I've built up my position in spite of that bad-tempered old tulyier, and I've no intention of doing anything to endanger it now, just when I have the chance to take the next step up.'

Charles could not help glancing at Thomas: it was a similar situation for both of them. Professor Keith's death had been very timely.

'But we know you were there at Professor Keith's house after the party,' said George, keen for his information to be valuable. 'And if we know, the chances are half the town knows, too.'

Bonar scowled. His dark hair was lank with damp, and with his pale skin and black eyes Charles fancied that he looked like a demon that had accidentally slipped into a holy spring.

'It's true,' he added, supporting George. 'If everyone knows you were the last person to see him alive, they'll all think you killed him.'

'For pity's sake, can a man not have a reasoned discussion with his superior without some damned murderer creeping in and ruining his chances?'

'A reasoned discussion?' repeated Thomas. 'I thought this was Professor Keith you were talking about?'

Bonar sighed with frustration.

'Yes, it is, and no, of course it wasn't a reasoned discussion. Did whoever told you I was there not tell you we had a shouting match? Or is the Professor's study door too thick?'

Charles and George exchanged glances.

'I think there was probably too much else going on in the house,' Charles ventured. 'But what were you arguing about? I know it didn't take much with Professor Keith, but why go all the way back there after the party to quarrel with him?'

'It isn't that odd to call on him at that hour of the night,' Bonar explained. 'He often worked late, and I was usually welcome. I knew he'd be up making up, as he saw it, for wasting his time at the soirée.'

'Completely mad,' muttered George, but no one seemed to agree with him.

'I wanted,' said Bonar, choosing his words carefully, 'to discuss my prospects. I had heard some talk that he wanted me removed from the post of his assistant – you've probably heard that, too – and I wanted to make sure my position was sound. You can blame your good bunkwife for that,' he added to Charles.

'What, her homemade wine made you bold?' Charles grinned.

'In more ways than one. I was bold enough to tackle Professor Keith on this delicate subject, but I wanted to do it, to clear matters up, because I was at last bold enough to ask Mrs. Walker for the hand of her daughter.'

'You blackguard!' cried Thomas, leaping from the settle so fast he knocked his tankard over. Ale poured from the fir table in a dark brown pool. George scuttled backwards, guarding his clothing. 'You contemptible gileynour!'

'Ach, marry the mother, Thomas, if you're going to marry one of them,' said Bonar with almost a smirk. 'She likes you better than Patience does, anyway.'

'I'm not going to stand here and listen to this!' A fine spray of spit escaped his lips in his fury.

'Then sit down, Thomas, and leave it, eh?' said Charles, tugging at Thomas' threadbare coat.

'I will not. I'm going home for my dinner. It may not be much, but at least the company's better.' He tugged his gown off the heap by the fire, tumbling the rest on to the straw on the floor, and stamped over to the door. Then he turned, and made sure his voice was carrying well. 'And who is it in this town knows the most about poisons, then, eh?'

With that, he vanished into the rain.

'Well, you, I suppose,' said George helpfully to Allan Bonar, then shut his mouth abruptly as his mind started working. Allan stared at him. Charles picked up his and Bonar's gowns, Bonar's black and crumpled, and George's cloak. Then he tried to make his voice as unchallenging as possible.

'So what happened, anyway? When you went to see Keith?'

'Oh, he was all right at first.' Allan turned deliberately from George's apologetic blush. 'He seemed even to be quite cheerful, as if he had a weight off his mind. He had some sweetmeats in his study, and a jug of claret, and he offered me some. I knew I'd had plenty and I just took a sweetmeat, sort of trying to soak up some of the liquor.'

'Which kind did you have?'

'The crystallised fruit things. They looked less chewy than the others, and I wanted to give myself every chance to talk sensibly and clearly, despite Mrs. Walker's wine.'

George and Charles exchanged glances: in Charles a great bubble of tension burst slowly, seeping relief all through him. The crystallised fruits were George's, and only one had been missing – that must have been the one that Allan Bonar had eaten. There remained the problem of the missing cantharides from the package he had bought for George, but just for now, he could live with that.

'Are you interested in this or not?' demanded Allan Bonar, finishing his ale. Thomas' was by now mostly on the floor. Bonar raised his hand to call for more, then realised he had no money left. 'Let's go back to my bunk: I have a bottle of claret somewhere.'

They gathered up their gowns and George's cloak and wrapped up well before venturing outside. They were at the other end of South Street from the West Port, where Bonar's bunk was, so they set off briskly, finding themselves working against the wind. Conversation was difficult, and Charles was wary of pressing on with it in the hearing of strangers. Instead, they waited until they were established in the parlour he and Thomas had examined only yesterday, with the odd leaves and

216

mysterious bottles. Bonar swept papers off a bench and waved to them to sit down while he looked for the claret.

'Anyway,' he said as he moved bottles back and forth, peering at the contents, 'it turned out he had been trying to have me removed – I'm still not clear why, but you ken what he was like. Anyway, I told him what he could do with his damn' job – I'm surprised no one came to see what we were shouting about, but maybe they knew better than to disturb him – and I stamped off down the stairs and out into the street and I walked.'

'Where to?' asked George, whose expertise in random walking had been honed in these last few days.

'To Glasgow, as it happens.' Bonar stopped to watch their looks of surprise with satisfaction. 'Not all the way, ken. I walked most of the night and waved down the mail coach in the morning. I have a friend in Glasgow, see, at the University there, and I thought maybe I'd be able to find myself a tidy post there, thumb my nose at Professor Helenus Keith and marry Patience. My friend was less optimistic, though: I stayed with him on Saturday and Sunday, and I took the mail coach back again yesterday.'

'So how did you not hear about Keith, then?'

'I didn't want to see him at once, so I went straight to my bunk. The coach was in late, anyway. My bunkwife's not that well – too many sweets, gives her heartburn – so I just told her I was back and went off to my bed, and worked myself up to see the great high heidyin this morning. Well, I saw him all right, but I think his thoughts were elsewhere.' Bonar had gone, like everyone else, to see the corpse after his shocking discovery. 'D'you know, I think I'll even miss the old man,' he said. 'I can't say we were like brothers, but he was a great scholar.'

They digested this in silence for a while. Bonar finally pulled a dusty bottle of claret out of an empty flowerpot in the corner of the empty fireplace, and wiped out three cups, and they sipped at the wine. Charles, his conscience provoked, tried hard to think of good things he had known Keith say or do, but found that all he could remember were Keith's temper, his arrogance, his bullying, and his self-aggrandisement. So far he

217

could not think of anyone who had known him who had not benefited in some small way from his death. It was quite an epitaph: Professor Urquhart had probably already rendered it into Latin.

Anyway, did Allan Bonar's story really help at all? He had quarrelled with Keith and then gone to Glasgow. No one, presumably, had seen him leave the Professor's study, and no one had seen the Professor after he had left. Charles toyed with the idea of trying to establish the facts about the Glasgow trip, perhaps by finding someone who had seen Bonar on the coach, but on reflection there was no point. Allan could as easily have killed Keith as not, and gone to Glasgow as he had said, either way.

He needed to think about all of this, he thought, staring into the fireplace. The rain beat on the road outside but did not find the little windows of Allan's bunk parlour, tucked into thick walls. There were lots of questions, and not very many answers. It looked as if he knew now how the sweetmeats had made their way into the study: Keith must have gone and fetched them himself after his wife and family had gone to bed: the claret and the biscuits had already shown that he had a sweet tooth. George's sweetmeats had apparently been untainted, but some of the cantharides was missing – but Professor Keith had not died of cantharides poisoning. Charles thought back to Saturday morning and the scene in Professor Keith's study. He still did not know who had taken Keith's notebook, and why. Professor Urquhart seemed the most likely candidate: Dr. Pagan would surely have had no reason, and Professor Shaw ... well, he might have done it, of course, if he had felt that something in it might have harmed someone. But what?

It seemed that the Sporting Set were the only ones who had not had a clear opportunity to add poison to the wine. Everyone else had passed it at some point: Urquhart had even examined the jug. Professor Shaw had come back for his gloves, Allan Bonar had been near the jug on the landing and later in Keith's study. Thomas by his own admission had been near the jug for some time, waiting on the landing in the hope of seeing Patience Walker. Perhaps only the Walkers

218

themselves had lacked the opportunity at that point, though certainly not the motive: there was no question but that Patience Walker was the kind of girl who would be quite capable of slipping poison into a jug of claret intended for the man who was at the one time threatening her mother over the rent and preventing the advancement of her preferred suitor. Charles could quite clearly picture Patience doing it, and she certainly had the forethought to carry it out ... not a pleasant thought, when she lived in the same house as he did. And she would certainly know how to obtain arsenic: every good housewife did.

But then there was the question of whether or not the poison really had been arsenic. It was readily available for those who knew the routines of the College Chapel and Ramsay Rickarton's problems with the rats, but surely it was even easier to boil up, or grind down, or whatever they did in Chemistry, the last yew berries of the season? Particularly when the trees in question were at the end of the Keiths' garden, or looked at another way, branching over a common footpath. Most people would know, would have had it dinned into them as bairns, that yew was poisonous, but Thomas would have had the information laid out before him, and recently, too: he had studied its similarity to arsenic in his chemistry class, and his favourite seat was directly beneath Professor Keith's yew trees. The little slices of information kept coming back into Charles' mind, stacking up, spinning apart, sliding into mosaic patterns like the marble pieces on an Italian table. He was going to have to talk to Thomas. First, though, he had another call he needed to make.

He stirred and set down his cup, and George jumped. All three of them seemed to have been sitting in silence for ages: from the silly grin on George's face it was easy to see where his thoughts had been, but Allan Bonar's expression was less transparent, a wave of hair drooping to conceal his black eyes.

'I must be going, I think,' Charles said, trying to persuade himself that his afternoon looked appealing. He had an essay to write, he remembered, a translation to do, and some Greek to read, and for once no inclination to do any of it. He suddenly felt very tired.

'Aye, well, I'd better get on, myself,' agreed Bonar. 'There'll be a good deal to sort out over classes and things. It'll take a while.'

They stood, without enthusiasm. George looked for somewhere to put his cup.

'Oh, just stick it on the table, beside that wee white package,' said Bonar. 'What is that, by the way?'

'It's not mine,' said George.

'Wasn't it here when we came in?' said Charles.

'Was it? It's not mine,' said Bonar firmly. He stepped over and picked it up. 'It looks like an apothecary's package.' He opened one end carefully. Within the wrappings, which looked hastily assembled, was a fine white powder.

They looked at each other. Bonar's eyes were dark as pitch.

'I have no idea where this came from,' he enunciated clearly.

'What is it?' asked George.

'I think I can guess,' said Charles. 'Is there a way of finding out?'

'There's a chemical test. I can't do it here.'

'I'm going to see Dr. Pagan. Would he be able to do it?'

'Maybe.' Bonar held the package tight, then slowly passed it to Charles. Charles examined it.

'I think this is part of the one from the Chapel,' he said. 'But if you haven't seen it before, who put it here?'

'Someone who wants people to think I killed Keith,' said Bonar, as if he had no wish to say it.

'But who would want to do that?' asked George. Bonar and Charles met each other's eyes.

'I think I can guess that, too,' said Charles.

Dr. Pagan's house was in North Street, down the hill from United College, a modern house set right on the street with three steps up to the white front door proclaiming its importance and prosperity. It would have made Thomas feel inferior instantly. Charles reached up and rattled the knocker – no old-fashioned risp here – and waited politely on the street. Eventually a maid appeared, squinted at Charles' proffered card, took it and vanished. A moment later, with an almost tangible disapproval of students, she reluctantly showed him in to what appeared to be the doctor's study-cum-consulting room, though nothing tastelessly medical was on view. The maid took a last look around the room, memorising the contents in case Charles stole anything, and departed.

After five minutes, the dapper doctor hurried in, newly polished.

'Ah, it is you. I thought I recognised the name. I am sorry to have kept you. I was just changing to go back to the Keiths' for supper.' He smiled as though it were an unambiguously delightful social engagement.

'I hope not to detain you long, sir,' said Charles, wondering how well the supper would be eaten. 'A question occurred to me about Professor Keith's death. I hope you do not mind me asking: I do not study much science and the effect of poisons is not a subject with which I am familiar. A question has arisen in my mind, though: how is it that you can be sure that he died of arsenic poisoning, and not of, say, yew berries?'

'Well,' said Dr. Pagan, 'yew *berries* are not poisonous. The rest of the tree is, including the seeds inside the berries.' Charles showed his surprise. 'Yes, another common misconception. But yew bark, or the seeds, or the leaves ... Both they and arsenic would produce nausea, stomach pains, that kind of thing, and the vomiting and flux we know happened. Of course there's the burning throat in acute arsenic poisoning, which is probably why he drank so much. On the other hand, yew is reported to dry the mouth. The convulsions, the way he had fallen, I suppose are more common perhaps in yew poisoning, but then it is not impossible that they could occur in arsenic poisoning, either. The stomach pains, you see, can be acute, and a certain amount of, ah, *writhing*, is almost inevitable.' The doctor, neat as ninepence, looked as if he would never be provoked into writhing.

'Does one act more quickly than the other?'

'It depends very much on the dose given. Either can kill within hours.'

'And how can we tell that in this case it was arsenic, and not yew?'

221

Dr. Pagan looked thoughtful.

'Well,' he said slowly, 'to be perfectly frank, you have raised a few doubts in my mind. Are there yew trees about? Oh – at the end of his garden, of course. Oh, dearie me.' He seemed fairly complacent about his possible mistake: after all, whichever diagnosis turned out to be correct, the prognosis was still the same. Professor Keith's quality of life was not likely to be much affected either way.

'But how could we find out? It might help – people – work out who the murderer is.'

'It might indeed.' Dr. Pagan drew out his large silver watch and thumbed it open. 'I'm afraid I have no time to pursue this now. However, you might try Jamie Corsane, the apothecary on Market Street. He was given the claret jug to examine. If it was yew, it's a vegetable kind of thing he should be looking for. Now, if you'll forgive me ...'

'Of course, sir. Thank you very much for your time.'

Dr. Pagan disappeared as neatly as he had arrived, presumably to carry out some last essential burnishing before his supper. The maid showed Charles out, leaving him in no doubt that she would be sweeping the hall forthwith. If she could have checked his pockets for stolen goods he was sure she would not have hesitated to do so.

Outside, the rain pattered once more on to his trencher and soaked secretly into his gown. He blew out mournfully, taking shelter under the eaves while he tried to remember where Corsane's apothecary shop was. Then, avoiding the worst of the puddles, he set off.

He was just about to turn in to College Wynd when in the distance he saw a familiar figure, moving slowly despite the rain. It was his brother George. Changing direction he carried on up North Street to meet him.

It was not the George of that morning, setting out for the funeral, full of cheer and purpose. This was instead a dejected George, who barely saw the ground he stared at, who did not notice when passing carriages sprayed him with mud from their wheels. Even his boots had lost their shine. He did not see Charles until he was almost upon him.

'George! What on earth's the matter?'

'Nothing,' said George, not fooling anyone. 'Ach ... nothing. I thought I might go home today, actually.'

'Well, you'd better get on then, before dark.'

George looked up at the sky as if the possibility of night had not previously occurred to him. A large raindrop hit him in the eye.

'And you'll be drowned before you reach Guardbridge in this weather, for heaven's sake. Stay till the morning.'

'My back's breaking sleeping on that chair.'

'You haven't complained about it before.' Something had clearly gone wrong at the Keiths': nothing else could have thrown George into this despair, and Charles was sure it would not last long. 'And in the morning, remember to pay Mrs. Walker for your keep and the horse's stabling.'

George grew petulant.

'Even you don't want me to stay. I'm just an inconvenience to you.'

'George, just go back to Mrs. Walker's, change your clothes and ask for a hot cup of chocolate. I'll be back as soon as I can and we'll discuss it all then. There's no sense in standing out here in a downpour.'

'Hot chocolate,' said George thoughtfully, but with much less heart than he would usually have managed.

'Come on: I'll walk you through to Market Street and leave you there for now. I'm off to the apothecary's ... George,'

'Hmm?'

'That cantharides you asked me to get for you in Edinburgh.' Charles began walking, to be less easily overheard. 'What did you do with it?'

'Do with it?' George was bewildered. 'I never saw it. Where did you leave it? At Letho?'

'No, I brought it here by mistake. It was in my parlour.'

George shook his head.

'I never saw it,' he repeated. 'To tell you the truth, I'd pretty much forgotten about it.'

'Maybe it's best that way,' Charles muttered. They had reached Market Street. 'I'm off down this way. See you later.'

'Mmm.' When Charles turned away, George was still looking thoroughly puzzled.

223

The apothecary, Jamie Corsane, had withered legs from youth and the kind of hard face that grows out of too much limping. He spent most of his day on a high stool fitted with little wheels, so that he could reach the shop's counter and pull himself about to fetch the large glass and earthenware jars that lined the shelves, disappearing into semi-darkness. Charles had always loved apothecary shops, with the mysteriously abbreviated Latin on the glinting jars, heavy mortars of graded sizes, little brass weights on the delicate scales with even stranger names than the jars, and a scent in the air that seemed to combine fresh cleanliness with an underlying darkness.

'It wasn't arsenic,' said Corsane, after Charles had explained that Dr. Pagan had sent him. 'No metal in it at all, bar the jug itself. Nobody tellt me to look for yew.'

'Will you be able to? I mean, do you still have the dregs you examined?'

'I do. Yon constable's no been round yet to fetch it. Wait here now a minute.' He wheeled himself back from the counter to a high table behind him where he pulled a dustcloth off a bright brass microscope. Taking a taper to a candle burning in the darkest corner of the shop, he lit a lacemaker's lamp, the kind where the water magnifies the light, and tilted a mirror at the bottom of the microscope towards it, manoeuvring it minutely to focus the best light through the little slide above it. He stared down the brass eyepiece, and Charles longed to do the same. Then he opened a very large leather-bound volume beside him, flicked through the pages, glanced back down the eyepiece and back again at the book. Charles caught a glimpse of longhand writing and little watercolours before the book snapped shut.

'It's yew,' said Corsane, 'right enough. There are tiny wee bits to it that I've only ever seen in yew before. That'll put the constable's wee head in a fair guddle. Does it help you and Dr. Pagan?'

'I think so, thank you. Now,' he added, drawing the little package from Allan Bonar's bunk out of his pocket, 'can you tell me what this is?'

Jamie Corsane took the package, sniffed it, and laid it down on the counter.

'Arsenic,' he said, firmly. 'What's this, an examination?'

'No – how can you tell so easily?'

'Because those are my wrappings. I sold it to Ramsay Rickarton at the United College. Now, how are you?'

'Fine, thank you, thank you. I'll tell Dr. Pagan.'

'Happy to help you,' said Corsane, dismissing him.

He had helped Charles, certainly. Charles just wondered how much help this was all going to be to Thomas.

The students who lived in the college were wisely avoiding their damp rooms on a day like this, and most of them were huddled next to the fire in the dining hall, even though dinner was long over. There was an unmistakeable aroma of rabbit in the air. Some were studying or writing out their dictata in fair copy books; others were playing cards, and one had a scruffy copy of an Edinburgh newspaper from several weeks before. Henry Barchane, the son of a soldier from Perth, said he had not seen Thomas since dinner, and the others agreed. Charles asked if he had mentioned going to the library, but Henry gave it as his opinion that Thomas had been too bad-tempered to let near a book, and he had muttered something about walking things off. Charles sighed: that could mean West Sands, or East Sands, or the more sheltered walk along the mill lade to the south of the town, or, if he was lucky, Thomas' favourite bench under the Keiths' garden wall. Charles decided to try that first.

The rain had eased again, and it was easier to see other people on the street. Keeping an eye open for red gowns, the first person Charles saw was not Thomas, but Boxie Skene. Under his gown he was dressed in funereal black.

'You weren't at the Keiths' today, were you?' Charles asked, greeting him.

'Not at the Keiths', no,' said Boxie sheepishly, 'but I did go to the kirkyard. I know we didn't kill him, but I still feel bad about it.'

'I know what you mean,' said Charles. 'The night of the party he almost seemed to be friendly to you.' It had struck him as strange at the time, but he had only just remembered it again. Boxie was frowning, too.

225

'Yes, I never did find out what that was all about. I should ask Peter Keith, I suppose, but now doesn't seem like the time. Peter was very pally at the party, and then he took me off to meet his father, and it was like some kind of interview for a job. I don't know what they were up to.'

'Maybe looking for a replacement for Allan Bonar as Keith's assistant,' suggested Charles. 'Look, I'm walking round to the cliffs to see if I can find Thomas: do you want to come? Allan Bonar's storming ahead in the race to win Patience Walker, my bunkwife's daughter, and Thomas is a bit downhearted.' Charles liked Boxie when he was on his own, and thought that two of them might diffuse Thomas' wrath, if it was still strong. Boxie glanced up at the clock on Sallies' tower.

'Aye, I'll come. I don't much fancy being back at our bunk just now. Picket cowed is not a happy sight to see, and Rab's as thick as mince.'

They walked almost in silence to Castle Wynd. Charles was thinking ahead to his meeting with Thomas, trying to decide what to say to him, what to ask him that would help him to work out what Thomas knew about Keith's murder. He would have to calm him down about Patience and Allan Bonar first, of course, and that would be difficult enough. And if Thomas was not on his favourite bench, which would be the best place to try next?

As it turned out, however, Thomas was on his bench. They saw him as soon as they turned the corner, but did not call out, not wishing to give him time to develop his sulk before they reached him. He was leaning back against the wall, legs tucked under the rough seat, staring up at the sky: it was only when they came up level with him that they saw the pool of vomit on the ground beside him, partly diluted by the rain, and saw how his clenched hands had ripped the worn wool of his gown. His eyes were open, but the rain dripped into them unheeded from the dark yew trees above. Thomas was dead.

Chapter Twenty

Over the next few days, more people came to see Thomas than ever had before.

The constable and a couple of Rickarton's junior janitors had moved him first of all: it did not seem right for him to be stuck there in the rain, and it was a public pathway which he was, to some extent, obstructing. He was taken unobtrusively back to United College, through the garden gate on the Scores, but there was a small, silent reception for him there already as if the news of his death was breathed in by the town along with the sea air. The students who had been in the dining hall earlier stood haphazardly by the door to the students' stair, watching warily. The Principal and the Chancellor, hurrying across the college yard in damp gowns, removed their trenchers at the sight of the rough stretcher: Thomas lay on it covered in his scarlet gown, trailing darkly over the sides. The bearers paused, not sure where to go. The Principal stepped up and turned back the collar of plum velvet, staring for a long moment at the rough face below, while the students jostled silently for a view. Then he laid the collar back neatly, and with a nod dismissed Thomas from his keeping.

'I shall write at once to his father,' he said. 'You may take him to his room, I suppose.'

Charles showed the way, with Boxie and the other students tagging behind. Thomas had had a small study with a bed recess, nothing much: his clean shirt and underwear lay on a bare shelf, along with his books – mostly borrowed. The basin and ewer belonged to the college, as did the worn sheets and blankets. On the stool that served as a bedside table lay a Bible and a book of sermons, and a candlestick dribbled with ill-smelling tallow. Charles ran a hand through his hair, trying to feel something, pity, guilt, grief, but nothing would come, not yet.

Dr. Pagan, shiny and new, came to visit Thomas in his dingy old room straight from the delights of his supper at the Keiths'. He told the constable carefully that it looked like arsenic poisoning, but that it was extremely difficult even for experts to identify it without an analysis of the stomach

227

contents. The constable, used to stolen chickens and short weights at the market, and the occasional brawl when the Black Bull closed, went a little green and asked if the doctor would be good enough to arrange such an analysis with Jamie Corsane. Dr. Pagan agreed cheerfully, and nodded goodbye to Charles, almost winking.

The students assumed that Thomas' father would want to come and take him home for burial. When the doctor and the constable had gone, they gathered together, half in and half out of Thomas' tiny room as though they could involve him in the discussion, and settled a system of taking turns so that Thomas would not be left alone. A coffin would be something to be decided on by powers greater than they, Thomas' father or the Principal, but there were other ways they could be useful. Thomas had no mirror to cover, but no curtain, either: Henry Barchane fetched a table cloth from the dining hall and he and Boxie tacked it up over the little window – white, they knew, was the next best thing to black. Charles said he would bring some of his own store of candles back later, and one of the tertians fetched one for now. The tablecloth was thick and cut the evening light out very efficiently. Boxie suggested awkwardly that Thomas ought to be laid out properly, which made them all stare blankly at their shoes – no one wanted to volunteer for that one – until Charles remembered Mrs. Nicolson, the midwife, and said that he would try to find her. Then they solemnly contributed what coins they could, to purchase a keg of beer for the watchers, and took an oath each not to drink more than their share. It seemed to be as much as they could decently do, and shaking hands with unfamiliar, adult formality, they went their separate ways, leaving the first pair of watchers settling down, uneasy and as yet beerless.

It was someone else's job to fetch the beer. Charles went in search of Mrs. Nicolson, and eventually tracked her down to a prosperous-looking cottage by the mill lade south of the town. She agreed to come if she was not called away at once to Mrs. Shaw's time of trial: if she was, she would send her niece in her stead. Satisfied, Charles went home to fetch candles.

To his surprise, Mrs. Walker was just about to put his supper by the kitchen fire to keep warm. George had finished his, and was managing to exude a sense of smug irritation, pleased to have cause to complain about Charles' lateness and not the other way around. Mrs. Walker seemed prepared to be irritated, too, but something in Charles' expression must have made her think again. She stopped halfway to the parlour door, and looked at him carefully.

'Thomas Seaton's dead,' said Charles, still too dazed himself to show any consideration for her possible feelings. She gasped, and swayed. Patience, quicker than either man, steadied her and guided her gently back to her seat at the supper table. Even she had paled.

'How?' she snapped, before her mother had recovered the breath to speak. Charles, seeing Mrs. Walker's shock, managed to speak more gently.

'He – it seems that he might have suffered the same fate as Professor Keith.'

'Poisoned?'

'Indeed.'

There was a long silence while they took this in. Mrs. Walker poured herself what must have been the last half-cup of tea in the pot: it came out thick and black, and she swallowed it down in a gulp, the cup clattering again on the saucer. George asked,

'He didn't, er, do it himself, did he?' Charles stared at him. 'I mean to say, he was pretty upset earlier.'

'Upset? What made him upset?' asked Mrs.Walker sharply.

'Oh, he and Allan Bonar –' George broke off, focussing suddenly on Patience. 'They had a bit of an argument, after the funeral.'

'What about?' asked Patience, as if she thought she could guess the answer. Whatever she thought, it did not seem to please her. George sat with his mouth open, head so full of the truth he could not think of a convincing lie. Charles was beyond helping him: he had not even sat down, and he could feel the muscles in his legs tightening in turn to hold him up as he swayed.

'Never mind that now,' sighed Mrs. Walker. 'Charles, you'll want your supper ... it's maybe too cold, though.'

It was, but Charles ate it anyway, too tired and hungry to wait any longer. He felt better when the last flake of pie and smear of pigeon gravy was scraped from his plate, and when he had taken a small glass of brandy at Mrs. Walker's insistence. He even felt strong enough to do his duty by Thomas, and defend him against a charge which would probably feature often enough in local gossip.

'The constable wanted to know if Thomas had – had taken the poison deliberately,' he said at last. 'He thought it would save him a good deal of trouble if Thomas had done it in remorse after killing Professor Keith – public hangings cost good money, you see,' he added sourly.

'He wouldn't have done it. Not ever, neither himself nor poor Professor Keith,' breathed Mrs. Walker, aghast at the very thought.

'He had nothing about him he could have taken the poison in,' said Charles flatly. 'Dr. Pagan smelled brandy about him, and it looks as if he must have taken it in that.'

'Maybe he threw it over the cliff,' said George, looking apologetic. Charles eyed him.

'You know Thomas couldn't throw baps to a bairn.' He sighed. 'Besides, Thomas thought Professor Keith had been poisoned with arsenic.' He ignored the puzzled looks of those around him. 'I must go back soon: we are to sit with the body by turn, until his father comes to take him home.'

'Will you be gone all night?' asked George. 'Only, remember I'm away in the morning.'

'Aye, you can have the bed, George. I'll be in about three in the morning, so I'll take the chair for a change. I'll try not to waken you.'

The dead hours in a dead-room were dark indeed. Charles had drawn Boxie as his companion – Picket and Rab had not been around to join in the rota, no doubt to their relief – and the pair of them sat by the light of two of Charles' precious store of wax candles, stunned by how much their lives had changed in the course of only a week.

'Tuesday,' said Boxie, as if he could not believe it.

230

'Well, Wednesday, now.' Charles peered at his watch. 'This time last week –'

'This time last week we were in a howff in Edinburgh,' said Boxie bleakly.

'I was at home in Edinburgh, asleep in bed,' said Charles, not quite truthfully. He had in fact been lying awake thinking of how to evade his father at Letho, but there was no sense in going back to that now. He had hardly thought of his father over the last few days.

'If I hadn't told Picket that stupid story from school about the Spanish fly,' said Boxie, 'none of this would have happened.'

'It would: it's just that Alison wouldn't have been ill. You didn't poison Keith, by accident or otherwise, and therefore I suppose you didn't poison Thomas. Oh! If I'd been with him no one would have had the chance to poison him!'

'The trouble is that Picket can make you feel so clever, so necessary to his schemes. I don't know where the ideas come from: I suddenly think of something to do, like hanging a skeleton outside his gate, and I blurt it out and I see that gleam in his eye, and for about half a minute I feel so proud of myself! And then, of course, I start thinking about the consequences, and I could bite my tongue off.'

'The consequences, indeed.' Charles caught the word. 'You see all I could think about was the consequences. I thought Thomas had killed Professor Keith because of the living, and because he'd made him look stupid, and maybe even to punish him for his treatment of Mrs. Walker, but all I could really think about was that he had all the knowledge and all the chance to do it. And then he tried to make Allan Bonar look guilty by leaving arsenic in his bunk, and I realised he couldn't have done it, unless he was being really devious, because it wasn't arsenic. And I was going to talk to him about the whole thing, but all I could think of was the consequences, as you say, and so I kept putting it off, leaving him to sulk while I found out more and more in order to accuse my friend ... If I'd just gone after him, if I'd stayed and talked with him –'

'If, if, if, it's always if,' Boxie agreed. 'If Professor Keith had not been such an obnoxious, self-righteous, arrogant man

231

no one would ever have killed him. As it is it was just a matter of time. As I see it, someone was going to do it some time and we should just leave it at that. Let him who has no guilt in his heart cast the first stone.'

Charles tried to think of anyone with an abundance of innocence.

'Professor Shaw, then, or Mungo Dalzell. And yet even Professor Shaw ... no, that's ridiculous. Whatever the provocation, Professor Shaw would never kill anybody.'

'You're right there.'

They stared for a moment at the corpse, as if it might sit up and offer an opinion: Thomas had rarely been short of them. Mrs. Nicolson, or her niece, had done her best with him. He looked as freshly shaved as he ever had, and a napkin held his mouth closed, white as the pillow and his freshly laundered nightgown. He was laid flat with a black sheet pulled straight up to his chest, his arms outside and down by his sides. The neatness was not Thomas, any more than the sallow complexion. The straw hair looked like a wig borrowed for the occasion from someone with a larger head. Charles sighed.

'Beer?' Boxie asked, and poured two cups from the unstoppered flask. They sipped at it, trying to make it last.

'Was that the whole of Picket's plan, then, to drug Alison Keith into an indiscretion?'

'I think so. I wouldn't have agreed if I'd known: I thought he was going to use it on Barbara, the maid.'

'She would have been equally ruined. Maybe more so.'

'Yes, I know.' Boxie looked shamefaced. 'But the difference was that I loved – love – Alison Keith.'

Good heavens, another one, Charles thought, but just managed not to say. What did Boxie and George see in the scrawny girl? Charles began to wonder if he was missing something.

'Of course, there's nothing I can do about it, not for a long time yet. My father would never let me take on a wife at least until I'd served my apprenticeship – I'm to be an advocate, you know, like him.'

'That would be a good prospect for the future, though,' said Charles, thinking that on the whole George had less to offer. Advocates were the nobility of Edinburgh: few fathers would object to allying their daughters to the Scottish bar. 'Had you spoken to Professor Keith?'

'I'd hardly even spoken to Alison. I brought her presents, sometimes: the bracelets she was wearing the night of the party, those were from me. You probably didn't notice them. I don't think I noticed such baubles until I started to imagine how they would look against her lovely skin.'

Charles swallowed hard, and tried to think instead of Patience Walker or the girl whose shawl had blown into that tree. He did not want to think about Alison Keith's freckled, bluish arms. It grew quiet in the stuffy room, and they could hear the soft hiss of the beer cork, the candle guttering in the draught from the tiny empty fireplace, and the rats scrabbling behind the panelled walls. Leaving Thomas' corpse unattended would have led to more than just a lack of respect for his spirit: the rats were probably as tired of rabbit as the students were.

Their watches ticked loudly and not quite together, making an urgent double sound that stopped them from entirely relaxing, and made them think that the time was passing more swiftly than it was. Charles found his eyes closing, and pinched himself hard on his earlobe. Boxie's eyes had closed. Charles settled back on their shared bench, trying not to shake it too much, and applied himself to thought.

Thomas had not murdered Professor Keith. Even if he had, he would certainly, definitely, never, never, never have killed himself, so there was still a murderer about either way. The fact that yew had almost certainly been used for both murders pointed to the same killer being responsible for both, unless he himself, the doctor or Jamie Corsane, the apothecary, were the killer. But who would want both Thomas and Professor Keith dead? What possible gain could Thomas' death afford anyone? He had no money, no influence. He had perhaps secured himself a parish, through the courtesy and patronage of Lord Scoggie: perhaps someone else had wanted it? Charles knew of no one. Other students were perhaps heading for the church, but could afford to spend a year or two as assistants, first, or wanted a forward-looking city parish, or hoped to take over a parish from their own father. No one, as far as he knew, had as urgent a need or desire for a parish as Thomas.

But Peter Keith had been considered for it. Now, there was an interesting thought. Peter Keith, at least periodically, hated his father, and he would have studied, some years ago, the same chemistry course as Thomas with Allan Bonar, had considered medicine, had been brought up with the facts and methods of natural philosophy. What had he been doing in the garden on the morning his father's body had been found – the garden where the yew trees grow? Why would his sister not speak to him? And had he sent someone back to Mrs. Walker that Saturday to return her forfeited brooch?

Peter certainly looked likely: he was destructive, violent and unbalanced, and he might well have felt that his powerful father could only be brought down from a distance, with poison. But Charles was going to be more cautious, this time, and think through some other ideas as well. It was important to find the right answer, not simply one that fitted.

Rough hands on his shoulder woke him.

'Three o'clock,' whispered Henry Barchane, 'and our turn. I hope you left us some ale.'

Charles and Boxie staggered outside into the college yard, where a single torch spat above the gate to the street. Charles wished he had thought to bring Daniel, and then saw a light flicker in the gateway itself. It was Daniel, sent to fetch him.

'Good boy, Daniel. We'll just see Mr. Skene back to his bunk first.'

Shivering and dull of thought and speech they walked to Mutty's Wynd and on to South Street, reassuring the watchman with an attempt at a courteous greeting, fumbling keys in the lock. Mrs. Walker, wrapped in several thick shawls, had cocoa ready and Charles and Daniel drank it down swiftly. Within a few minutes they had all retired, though some fell asleep again better than others.

George left for Letho straight after breakfast, and paid his bills to Mrs. Walker who tried to refuse his money. George could be charming, though, when he thought Charles was

234

watching him. His horse was saddled and his various accoutrements, including the new cravats and gloves he had needed to buy while in St. Andrews, were neatly packed and rolled, and his fine boots burnished like walnutwood. The Walkers, Charles and Daniel all came out on to South Street to wave him goodbye, but he left without a backward glance, and Charles, with a shrug, took Daniel to a Latin lecture.

After dinner, Charles and Boxie had another turn at sitting with Thomas. Boxie was late but Charles had only just sat down when he heard footsteps on the stairs. The voice that accompanied them was not, however, Boxie's.

'... a little surprised to see you here, madam.' Professor Urquhart's unmistakably honed tones slid ahead of him.

'We had to pay our respects, of course. Thomas was a frequent visitor to our little house. And I thought that if we came now, when dear Charles was to be with him, it might be less awkward.'

Charles was already on his feet when Mrs. Walker entered, followed by Patience and Professor Urquhart, whose outstretched arm held the door for them. As a minister's widow, Mrs. Walker was a practised dead-room visitor, but this death had upset her more than most. Charles lent her an arm across the tiny room to the bed recess, and steadied her politely as she wept a little. Her hand in its neat black glove held Thomas' stiff fingers tightly for a moment, before she moved back to let Patience take her turn. Then they sat on the bench, the only seat in the room, side by side and doleful. Patience was not so hard that she could not feel even this death keenly.

Professor Urquhart drifted over and touched the corpse in his turn, staring down at it analytically.

'A tragedy,' he remarked at last.

'Indeed.' Mrs. Walker had her handkerchief out now, but she was not uncontrolled.

'Particularly when he had just secured a great deal of his future, and greatly to his satisfaction,' Professor Urquhart added.

'How do you mean?' asked Patience, eyes narrowed. The Professor arranged himself against the wall beside the shelves.

'Lord Scoggie had agreed to present him to a vacant parish he has in his gift. Not a grand place, perhaps, but prosperous enough: he could have been ordained to it soon after his degree examinations this summer.'

'Oh, the dear, dear boy,' sighed Mrs. Walker, between pride and despair.

'Indeed, as you say.' Professor Urquhart's smile said nothing at all. 'Lord Scoggie's patronage, too, is a recommendation in itself. He is most careful as to who is to receive the benefit of his gifts. Professor Keith and I had the honour to be invited to dinner and to stay the night at Scoggie Castle two weeks ago to discuss that, and other matters. A great friend to the University.'

A fortnight ago, thought Charles glumly. He had not even been sent to Edinburgh by then. No one had been poisoned, no one had bought any packets of Spanish fly, and the world had seemed a brighter, less complicated place. Why had all this happened?

'Still, as they fall, so shall they rise,' added Professor Urquhart. Mrs. Walker evidently took this as some reference to death and salvation, for her face assumed a pious look, until Urquhart went on. 'Thomas here has had bad fortune, but Allan Bonar, with whom I think you are also acquainted, has been very lucky. It seems that his future is quite settled.' He eyed Patience with a look on the near edge of decency.

'In what respect, sir?' hissed Mrs. Walker. Patience had gone white.

'Oh, in that he is to be Professor of Natural Philosophy now, of course. He was always named to be appointed to the chair when Keith went, and now he has both that security and the relief of no longer having to work, if you'll forgive the indelicacy, for a thoroughly obnoxious man.'

Charles watched in fascination. There was no doubt that Professor Urquhart knew the exact standing of Thomas Seaton and Allan Bonar in the Walker household: Urquhart knew every scrap of gossip from Cupar to Earlsferry. Just as it looked as if Mrs. Walker was going to walk out in angry confusion, he stooped a little and peered at the neck of her chemisette.

236

'What a charming miniature,' he exclaimed. 'And if the likeness is as good as the technique, the original must have been a fine gentleman indeed. A relative, perhaps?'

The three mourners left, still discussing the brooch, abandoning Charles to the impression that he had just been the audience to some amateur one-act play. Had Professor Urquhart taken the notebook from Professor Keith's study that morning, with the body still on the floor? It was exactly like him, bold but sly, and Charles could not believe that it could have been anyone else. But what could he have wanted it for?

'Thomas, my friend,' Charles addressed the corpse, 'If you were still alive, I'd suggest a little housebreaking, and you would look shocked, and that might even be the end of it. It would certainly be the end of me if I were caught. And I'm not even sure I could do it on my own. Stupid idea, anyway. And here's Boxie, at last.'

Boxie was not alone. Mungo Dalzell had joined him in the yard, and had also come to pay his respects, hurrying, like everyone else, to do so before Thomas' father might come and whisk the body away for burial. He brushed the black cloth with his fingers, a look of deep sorrow on his long face, and sat on the bench with Boxie and Charles, to wait out some of their wake with them. A chink of light showed from behind the improvised window curtain, and outside in the college garden they could hear the thump and slice of spades and the click of pruning shears, life going on. In the midst of life, thought Charles again, we are in death.

Chapter Twenty-One

It was all very well for the men still in college, Charles thought with a deep, early-morning disgust. When they had finished their turn sitting with Thomas' corpse, all they had to do was to stagger back down the corridor, or at most up some stairs, find their bed and collapse into it. It hardly required consciousness. He and Boxie, on the other hand, had to brace themselves against the cold night air at three in the morning, find their ways home, then unwind themselves from overcoats, scarves, gowns, hats and gloves before they could sleep – although leaving them all on was tempting. But as usual, early on Thursday Mrs. Walker had set and lit a fire for him in his bedchamber, so he made the effort and undressed, splashing water over his face from the jug and basin waiting for him. He found his nightshirt and tunnelled into it, struggled for a moment with the bedclothes, then blew out the candles and sank instantly into sleep.

His awakening was by every standard rude. Into the midst of a confused dream about Patience Walker and a carrot pudding there broke a sound like a cannon, and he was propelled from his bed in an undignified scramble to find himself standing, heart pounding, crumpled, unwashed and unfed, before the towering figure of his father.

It was unlikely that the effort of climbing the stairs, or even of riding here fast after an early breakfast at Letho, could have made Mr. Murray's face quite that shade of scarlet. No: he was furious – so furious, in fact, that for a long moment he seemed lost for words. Charles used the time to assess the space between his father and the door, to decide that he himself could not fit through it, and to resign himself to whatever was to come.

'So, it is true,' said Mr. Murray at last. His jaw seemed to be set solid. 'George finally dropped your name into conversation last night at supper, forgetting, presumably, that you were still believed to be in Edinburgh. And here I find not only that you are guilty of the grossest disobedience and deception, but also that you are wasting a fine morning by lying late abed, and not even pursuing the studies you affect to

238

find so essential to your wellbeing! What have you to say for yourself?'

Charles found he was winding his fingers abashedly into the side hems of his nightshirt, and stopped. This would not do. He had a life and responsibilities here, and he was not going to abandon them, not until he had at least seen Thomas' killer brought to justice. He would have to stop acting like a little boy.

Not meeting his father's eye, he stepped across to a stool and reached for his stockings.

'Do not dare to ignore me, Charles. I will have none of it.'

'Indeed, sir, I was gathering my thoughts.' It was true.

'You have betrayed my trust in you. What about the business for which I specifically dispatched you to Edinburgh?'

'The business with Mr. Simpson the agent? I completed it and returned the papers to Letho. Mr. Simpson assured me that they were not urgent.'

He was momentarily distracted by an odd smell near the fireplace, where the ashes still smouldered. In the back of his mind he made a decision to investigate it later, and pulled on his breeches. Now that his nether quarters were covered by something more than the folds of a cambric nightshirt, he felt more confident, but his father was more angry than ever.

'Not urgent? Nor urgent! You would take the word of a mere notary over that of your father?'

'But sir, you believed me with good will to be in Edinburgh all this time, enjoying the season. How have the papers become more urgent now that you find I have been all this time in St. Andrews?'

He could not believe he had said it. For a frightening moment, his father went white, and did not seem to breathe. Then, all at once, his colour returned and he let out a long, controlled sigh.

'Look, Charles, in all other matters I'll grant you have been obedient to me. You learn reason here, don't you? Then put that reason to good use. Let us come to an agreement and no more quarrelling. You can stay here till the end of the term. I'll meet all your debts, pay off the Walkers, even visit Alison

239

Keith if you would sooner not face her yourself. I hear her father's just died, so she won't want to be upset further. Then come home at the end of term and let that be the finish of it.'

It was a tempting offer: a peaceable compromise. Charles blinked at Alison's name but said nothing about it yet – he had no wish to betray George, even if George had let him down.

'I only intended you to stay at University for a couple of sessions anyway, enough to meet people and make connexions, enough to be apprenticed to an advocate if you wished it. There is no need for a gentleman like you to be a Master of Arts.'

'But that's what I want,' said Charles at last, slowly. 'And I cannot leave. One of my professors is dead, and now my friend is, too. I cannot leave until all this is sorted out, and until I have graduated.' He met his father's eye, then pulled his nightshirt off over his head. Through the muffle of the cambric, he heard a sharp sound, then a crash.

'You're as stubborn as your mother!' shouted Mr. Murray. He had snatched up a notebook from Charles' windowsill, and hurled it into the fire. It crackled, then roared.

For a moment it was the only thing moving in the room.

Charles knew there was no sense in reacting. The way he and his father both felt, it would have meant a fight, one he wanted neither to win nor to lose. He made himself breathe evenly. It looked like one of his Greek notebooks – the Aristophanes dictatas, perhaps. He could replace most of it, he told himself firmly, unclenching his hands. He could not afford to lose control. Though it seemed likely that his lack of reaction was going to make his father more angry rather than less: he wanted a fight.

Somewhere downstairs he could hear Patience singing as she did her share of the housework, then a few inaudible words in an anxious tone as her mother hushed her. In the hearth, the remains of the notebook sank in the ashes. Charles reached for his shirt and pulled it over his head, tucking in the tails, then ran a brush through his hair. He felt better already.

'May I ask,' said his father, retreating into sarcasm, 'what your living will be if you persist in staying in St. Andrews? For I shall no longer support you, you can be sure of that.'

A good question, Charles thought. He did not think he would be very welcome amongst the herring gutters. Shrugging on his plain waistcoat, he draped a cravat round his neck and sat to pull on his boots.

'I shall find employment of some kind.'

'Oh, yes? As what? A mewling minister? A pathetic, bullied tutor, half in the family, half in the servants' hall? What place is that for a gentleman's son?'

A very proper and traditional place, thought Charles, for the son of a gentleman who no longer chooses to fund him. Feeling daring, he stood and turned his back on his father to tie his cravat in front of the misty mirror above the washing table. How was it that good manners were sometimes the hardest habits to break?

'Why now?' he asked eventually. 'You have dismissed my studies as a waste of time before, but as long as I have not lapsed in my practice at fencing and boxing you have had no objection. Would you rather have me useless and expensive around Letho – like George?' he added, with a hint of vindictiveness.

'You are useless and expensive,' his father growled, 'but you are not even at Letho to learn the ways of the estate.'

'You've been teaching me the ways of the estate since I was five,' said Charles. 'What is different now?'

His father looked at the floor for a long moment. So he has been hiding something, Charles thought. His father still stood by the door where, apart from a swooping attack on the exercise book, he had stood since his arrival. Charles, his cravat tied and pinned, turned to face him. Mr. Murray tapped his gloved finger once on the top of his cane, as if giving himself a signal.

'I want you to marry,' he announced.

'Well, I know, at some point –'

'Now. Her name is Mawis Skirling. You have met, I believe.' Charles frowned. 'At the Assembly Rooms in Edinburgh. Mrs. Thomson agreed to introduce you.'

The hefty farmer's daughter he had danced with during his brief stay in Edinburgh, that must be her. Oh, no: he would not marry her.

241

'I remember. Why her?' he asked, sounding more calm than he felt.

'I know her father. He is an immensely rich man with only two daughters: the fortune will be divided between them and might be used as well in Letho as anywhere else. The elder daughter has recently married an earl.' Despite everything, the assumption was loud in his voice and manner that Charles was going to do exactly as he was told. Charles took it slowly.

'The earl's standards must be lower than mine, or the elder daughter was a good deal more handsome than her sister.'

'Where do looks matter? We are talking of a marriage beneficial to both families.'

'Not only looks were lacking, though. I should prefer to marry a woman of some grace and intelligence.'

'Intelligence!' Mr. Murray snapped. 'I married a handsome, intelligent woman and what did it get me? An equally handsome, intelligent son who doesn't recognise a good match when he sees it and won't leave off his damn' books to do his duty to his father and his house!'

'I will not marry her,' said Charles with emphasis.

'You will if you want to stay under my roof.'

'Then I shan't stay under your roof, either.'

'You would not dare to defy me in both marriage and study.'

'I would, and I do.' Charles pulled on his coat. He was fully dressed as he faced his father, and noticed for the first time that he himself was the taller, by an inch. 'I shall remain here at St. Andrews at least until I have graduated. I shall not marry Mawis Skirling, and wish her a more congenial partner in life. I shall find myself employment, should it be sweeping the streets. I shall not take another penny from you, sir.'

'You will never survive. You, in employment? A feeble bookworm, spoilt from the day he was born? No one would employ you so much as to carry his hat and gloves!'

Charles opened his mouth to respond, but there came a knock at the door.

'Go away!' yelled Mr. Murray.

'My decision, I think,' said Charles sharply, and passed him to snatch open the door to the stairs.

242

'A letter, Charles dear,' said Mrs. Walker hurriedly. 'Pay me later, dear,' she called back as she vanished discreetly down the stairs.

Charles looked at the wrapper. The seal, which he did not recognise, had a small coronet on it. He broke it.

'What is it, then?' snapped his father, emerging from the bedchamber doorway. Charles read quickly through the short letter, and could not for the life of him keep the grin off his face as he turned back to his father.

'It is a letter from Lord Scoggie,' he said. 'He asks if I should like to take up a post as his private secretary. Will you be staying to breakfast, Father, or do you hurry back to Letho?'

His father left in awful silence after breakfast, and Charles set out for his lectures. His feet seemed hardly to touch the ground, and he could think of nothing but what he had done, sometimes in elation, sometimes in terror. He passed the bakery, the candlemaker, the flesher, all trickling their particular scents into the stream of the cool, dry wind, but all he could smell was the pulse-racing odour of bridges burning.

In his waistcoat pocket, well pushed down for safety, was Lord Scoggie's letter. He had had the unfounded fear that his father would sneak back to his bunk and destroy it, and that Lord Scoggie would never send another. His reply would have to be carefully considered and in his very best hand – thank heavens he still had some of his father's heavy writing paper left, for he could not afford anything to match it. He longed to tell someone of his good fortune and immediately thought of Thomas, but that was no longer possible, and for a moment he felt a shiver of guilt that he should be so happy while Thomas, who had longed for Lord Scoggie's patronage, could not be there to enjoy his share.

Perhaps it was fitting, then, that the nervous smile was wiped off his face as he arrived in the yard of United College just at the same time as Thomas' father.

Charles knew him at once, though he had never met him. Thomas Seaton elder had the same unevenly shaved complexion, the same awkward look of not feeling as if he belonged, so familiar to Charles from his dead friend, so much so that a sick feeling of seeing the dead walk swept over him for an instant. The man was not alone: with him were two who could have been his brothers, and a young lad of fourteen or fifteen, perhaps the brother David Thomas had sometimes mentioned. All four stared about them, up at the grandly shabby buildings: in all the time Thomas had been here they had never seen the place. It was a privileged place, not for the likes of them, they would think, and too far to travel when a journey meant expense and no income. Thomas would have gone home with tales of his strange new life, an alien land with a currency in books and learning, the stuff of fireside tales on a winter night, not of real life.

He was about to offer help or directions when Ramsay Rickarton appeared: he had evidently already seen the visitors and gone to fetch Professor Urquhart from his rooms. The Professor was already in the yard and approaching solemnly.

'Welcome, welcome, though I wish it could have been on a happier occasion,' he said when he had introduced himself. Thomas' father seemed bewildered: he had probably never met anyone quite like Christopher Urquhart before anyway.

'We have brought a coffin, Mr. Urquhart,' he explained, and his two brothers indicated the long box they were supporting on its end. It was already pinned with black cloth, and wrapped for the journey in sacking. They began to take the sacking off, unwinding it and folding it before the wind could catch it. Professor Urquhart nodded, a quizzical look on his face.

'Thomas' body is in his room: someone will be happy to show you. Then you will want a meal after your long journey,' he said at last, 'and of course we have rooms for you for as long as you wish.'

'You are kind,' said Seaton gruffly – Charles could see exactly how a young man like Thomas could grow into an old man like his father. 'But we have eaten, and we would leave as soon as we can. It is a long way home.'

'Um, indeed,' said Urquhart. Certainly it was difficult to know what to say: the impression was that the Seatons wanted nothing to do with the college – and indeed, who could blame them? But the professor did not like to be lost for words, and as he cast about for inspiration the first thing he saw was Charles.

'May I present Charles Murray, younger of Letho?' he said smoothly, drawing Charles over with a look. 'Murray was Thomas' closest friend here, and had the misfortune of discovering Thomas' ... fate.'

Charles bowed obediently, and Thomas' father returned an echo of Thomas' own hapless bows. His gaze, a little blankly, ran quickly over Charles' shabby gown but decent coat and gloves. He appeared to be dredging something from his memory: Thomas had probably spoken of his closest friend.

'Will you step up with me, then, sir?'

'I would be honoured,' said Charles, and turned to help carry the empty coffin. The brothers already had it shouldered, though, with the ease of practice, and instead Charles led the way across the yard to the students' quarters and up the familiar stairs to Thomas' room, trying to remember and point out worn steps and awkward corners to the strangers. Professor Urquhart nodded in satisfaction as they left him.

'We arranged a rota so that he would not be left alone,' he explained, as he stood back to let the others enter. 'All the students in the college joined in. Professor Urquhart brought the flowers and the brown paper.' He did not add that it was in Professor Urquhart's own interest, living so near by, to use such means to keep down any unpleasant odours that might arise as the corpse waited to be collected.

'There's some ale still, if you want to toast the – Thomas,' said Henry Barchane, the student on duty, hospitably. When they had taken it in turns to touch Thomas' hand, the Seaton brothers took the ale automatically, passing one tankard amongst them till the boy, Davie, took the dregs. Charles glanced around the room, making sure they had forgotten nothing.

'Would you like us to leave you alone here for a while? You are welcome for as long as you need.'

'No, sir, we should get on,' Thomas' father decided, 'though you are kind. Is there a minister who would say a prayer over him when we have him kisted?'

'I'll see who I can find,' said Henry amiably, and hurried out. The other student on duty with him seemed to be trying to melt into the walls out of the way. The brothers stood awkwardly, but declined a space on the bench by the wall. Instead, they silently packed Thomas' few belongings into a roll, which one brother slung across his shoulder. In a surprisingly short time, Henry returned, with the Principal, who was, as was customary, ordained. In the security of his robes he glanced around the shabby student room, as if carrying out an inspection. Charles performed the introductions, and the Seatons seemed to shrink still further.

'You do us much honour, my lord,' muttered Thomas' father.

'Oh, dear, no, I'm not a lord, and anyway,' said the Principal, moving efficiently from modest denial to responsible regret, 'a prayer is the least I can do for you in your grief. The death of one of our students is always a terrible blow to our little community, but in this case it is especially so. Rest assured that we will do all we can to bring his murderer to justice.'

'You may do what you will, sir,' said Thomas' father, without rancour. 'I have lost my son: it was the Lord's time to take him, so I cannot question, though indeed I mourn his loss.'

Looking slightly reprimanded, the Principal drew himself up and took a step closer to the bed.

'Are you ready to kist him?'

The Seaton brothers manoeuvred the coffin into position and removed the lid. Folding the sheet back from Thomas' body, they took him gently under his shoulders and knees, and lifted him into the coffin, straightening him tenderly and tidying his shroud, making him presentable. They made sure the coffin was steady on the bed, then stood back, hands folded and heads bowed, ready for the Principal to begin his prayer. When he was done, the brothers stepped forward once more with the lid. Thomas' father touched his son's forehead once with the tips of his fingers, then between them they slid the lid into place and one brother quickly fitted the screws, shiny against the dull black cloth. From a roll tied to his shoulders, Davie tugged out a mortcloth and one of his uncles shook the

246

crumples out of it, then laid it over the coffin. The brothers glanced at each other, and gave a sort of communal shrug. They arranged themselves by the bed and lifted the coffin once more, now with its designated load, Davie taking his share like a man at the foot end. They took the coffin as carefully as they could, murmuring the same warnings to each other as before regarding uneven steps and narrow doors, and Charles, Henry, and the Principal, followed them outside to the yard.

Under a damp sky, whipped by the wind, Professor Urquhart stood where they had left him, but the rest of the students had collected near him, on either side of the gate. When they saw the coffin appear, the crowd drew out into two lines, billowing gowns making it hard to tell one figure from the next. The Seatons paused to shoulder the coffin, and Davie adjusted a wad of cloth on his side to even the load. The mortcloth caught the wind and was pressed precisely into the shape of the sharp boards beneath. The Seatons stepped forward, and at the same moment a student from the College choir gave the note. At funereal pace, they sang the old student song, *Gaudeamus Igitur*. 'Let us rejoice while we are still young', ran the Latin, 'for after joyful youth, after miserable old age, we shall dwell in the earth.' Thomas had not had a very joyful youth, thought Charles as he joined in, and he would never have an old age, but somehow the words seemed appropriate.

One verse, sung solemnly, saw the sad procession cross the yard and disappear out of the gate, and the Seatons, taking their son with them, began their long walk home.

Chapter Twenty-Two

The other students left the yard in twos and threes; Ramsay Rickarton nodded stiffly to no one in particular and returned to his little office by the gate, and Professor Urquhart, replacing his trencher, spun in an elegant swirl of gown and headed for the stair to his rooms. In the shadows of the Cage, Mungo Dalzell could be glimpsed, pale face smeared with tears, edging back into the Chapel.

For a few moments, Charles stood still. Above the yard, seagulls called bleakly to each other, their cries twisting and swooping in the wind, and echoing off the stone walls and high slate roofs. There was no other sign of life: if you did not know, you would almost think the place a ruin, long deserted, abandoned to the wind and the sky.

Feeling as empty and dry himself, he turned at last and made his way in Professor Urquhart's wake. Automatically he patted the pocket where Lord Scoggie's letter was still hidden: he needed to talk to someone, and he needed some advice, and he needed, he remembered suddenly, to see Professor Urquhart's rooms and to observe them a little more closely than before.

He remembered that had not visited Urquhart's rooms since he had been there with his father, and as if his father's presence was haunting him he had a sudden clear vision of that morning: seeing Mungo Dalzell scuttling away from his father, finding Professor Keith out, though his door unlocked, and visiting Urquhart so that old Mr. Murray could terrify him. The damp, worn staircase was the same, the mould on the walls and the uncertain sconces, but now the office door at the top of the stairs was firmly shut. Odd, he thought, on reflection: Keith had announced that he was keeping valuables in his office after the various attacks on his house by the Sporting Set, yet he did not lock his office door. He turned to Urquhart's unprepossessing entrance.

'Mr. Murray, come in,' said Urquhart, his gown and trencher now discarded across the back of one of the sofas. Without them, a visitor could appreciate his finely cut coat and deep red silk waistcoat. 'There is to be no Latin lecture today,

248

I'm afraid, if that is what you are seeking.' His face seemed pale against the richness of the room's palette.

'No, sir – that is, I did not expect one. I came, and I hope I do not disturb you, to speak about a letter I received this morning, and perhaps to ask for some advice.'

'Ah!' said Urquhart, 'I believe I may know about your letter. But pray, sit down and I shall heat some spiced wine: that yard is damned cold for standing round, and the occasion was not one to warm the bones.'

He busied himself at the fire, which needed building before a quantity of wine could be heated. Charles took the opportunity to glance about him, trying to take in what seemed likely to be important details: none of the windows in this room was open, and all looked latched on the inside. Urquhart had not locked the door after Charles had entered, but he probably did do so at night, and Charles could only envisage himself housebreaking by night. In fact, he wondered, when it came to it, if he would ever see himself housebreaking at all.

'So – this letter.' Urquhart called him back to the present from the putative future. 'May I guess that it might have been from a certain peer of our mutual acquaintance?'

'You are quite correct,' said Charles, not entirely surprised. Urquhart made it his business to know what was going on, and he had admitted to being a dinner guest of Lord Scoggie's. 'He has been kind enough to offer me a position as his secretary.'

'And do you intend to take it?' The Latin schoolboy's rhyme read that '*nonne* expects the answer yes, *num* expects the answer no.' If he had been speaking in Latin, Professor Urquhart would have used *nonne*. For the first time, Charles hesitated.

'It is a very desirable position,' he said slowly. 'The more so for me, as at present I find myself – at odds – with my father. However, I am not clear as to whether Lord Scoggie would prefer me to start immediately or not. And if he does not, I, er, need something with which I can support myself until the end of the session, or graduation, anyway.'

249

He did not feel very comfortable talking about money, and he could not meet Urquhart's eye. Awkwardly, he pushed himself out of the sofa and paced around the room.

'Did Lord Scoggie name a salary for this desirable position?' asked Urquhart, returning to his tending of the fire. He had brought brandy over to the hearth and set it near the flames to warm.

'He did,' said Charles, and after a moment named it himself. Urquhart glanced up and smiled.

'You are not used to such matters as salaries, are you?' he asked. 'Have you worked out what you need to complete the session?

Charles had, and he knew it off by heart.

'The whole year costs about sixty pounds,' he said, 'including fees. The last term would be about twenty, then, but cheaper in coal and candles in the summer. I don't need any more books,' he added, firmly, 'but I also have to find examination fees. I think twenty-five would be safe.'

Professor Urquhart laughed, and Charles looked down, mortified – and froze.

'Oh, my dear Mr. Murray,' said Urquhart quickly, 'I had no intention to ridicule you. You mention this sum with the ease of one who has always asked and it has been given unto him, but few young men of your age, I think - your late friend Mr. Seaton, for example – would speak it with such equanimity.'

'Then you think my case is hopeless?' Charles said slowly. Urquhart straightened with care and looked at him, and Charles began to pace again.

'Not hopeless, exactly.' Urquhart left the brandy to see to itself and moved over to the window that overlooked the yard. He paused for a moment, drumming his long fingers on the sill. 'Professor Shaw is supposed to be on duty this week, using the office next door, but Mrs. Shaw has finally had the child, so Mungo Dalzell has agreed to deputise, but he hates this building and never sets foot in it. Damn the man: I need to speak to him, and he must be around somewhere.'

'I think I saw him go into the chapel after the Seatons left,' said Charles, hoping to return to the subject of his university career. It would at least distract him from the fact that in his perambulation of the room he had found the notebook that had vanished from Professor Keith's desk: it was on a small, ladylike writing table near the window where Urquhart now stood.

'The chapel, eh? That fits: he seems to have taken up residence there these past few weeks – soon be holding lectures there. At least the roof's sound. Pour a couple of glasses of that wine, would you?' He arranged himself more comfortably at the window, almost as if he perceived Charles' interest in the notebook. Charles tried to look relaxed, but he began to know what a cat feels like when the mouse is just out of reach. His hand shook as he passed a glass of punch to Professor Urquhart, and himself returned to the sofa.

'Well, as far as I know, whatever it might say in your letter, Lord Scoggie wants you to finish your year here. He likes the style of having 'M.A.' after his secretaries' names.'

'Then he has other secretaries?' asked Charles.

'Not at the moment,' was the rather vague reply. 'Anyway, you can clarify that in your acceptance letter – if you decide to accept.' He glanced out of the window again. 'As for supporting yourself during this last session,' he went on, 'you could always consider borrowing against your expected salary. The letter from Lord Scoggie should be enough, but if it isn't, I can always write a covering letter to go with it. Then you pay it back out of your salary when you take up the post.'

Charles swallowed.

'I don't like borrowing,' he said tightly.

Professor Urquhart smiled at him.

'Neither a borrower nor a lender be, eh? Rates of interest, dishonest lenders, the shame of debt – puts you off, I dare say?'

'It does, sir.'

'Well, it needn't – but if I could get hold of Mungo Dalzell I could get the cash for you now. The man on duty holds the discretionary fund, a bursary set aside for emergency funding for students close to graduating. Some of the staff put it together, and the last Principal made a considerable donation. None of us likes to teach someone for four years and then see them fall at the last jump just because of a little pecuniary difficulty. Oh! There we are! I'll be back in a second,' he cried, hurrying away from the window and off to the yard outside.

For a moment, Charles sat still. It seemed very rude indeed to check the notebook when Professor Urquhart was trying to sort out money to support him for the next three months. On the other hand, if it meant not having to break in like a murderer himself ... in an instant he was off the sofa and across the room to the desk. He glanced out of the window, keeping his head low. Mungo had paused in the middle of the yard and turned – Urquhart must have hailed him, and there, Urquhart appeared. Ramsay Rickarton, stopping at the door of his office to talk to his grandson, still smart in the new breeches Charles had noticed before, watched them. Charles' mind raced. Sybie's brother in new breeches, a few days after Charles had seen Mungo come out of this very building. Mungo had run Sybie over. Mungo never went into this building. Professor Keith was on duty that week and had left money in his room, but had apparently left the door open. The money was stolen. Mungo had killed Sybie ... Mungo, racked with guilt ... Mungo, looking as if a weight had been lifted from his heart ... Sybie's brother in new breeches and a fine beef stew scenting the thin air of Heukster's Wynd. Mungo must have stolen the money and given it to Sybie's mother, as a – what, as compensation? Stolen money?

But maybe it explained something else, too. Professor Keith had mentioned money and valuables, and what more valuable than the brooch he had forced poor Mrs. Walker to hand over in lieu of her rent? And the brooch was so mysteriously returned, and not by Peter Keith. What if Mungo Dalzell had seen the brooch, too, and decided to make reparation there? It would be like him. But stealing money ...

Outside, Mungo Dalzell and Professor Urquhart were still deep in conversation, Mungo with his arms crossed to hold down his gown, Urquhart constantly adjusting the curls on his wig, unprotected, in his haste, by a hat. Charles dragged himself away from this speculation and turned to the notebook on the table. It was definitely the same as the one purloined from Professor Keith's desk on the morning of his death.

Reaching out one delicate finger, Charles opened it and held the cover so that he could just look inside.

It appeared to be Keith's diary. Charles flicked the thick yellow pages to the later entries, and saw at once why Professor Urquhart had removed it.

'This evening I believe the evidence was irrefutable,' it read, in Keith's black hand. 'Urquhart pays every attention to my wife. I should not wonder but that the activities of those repulsive students was somehow arranged by him in order that he might have some time with her out of my sight, though he seems to manage that often enough as it is. Others must also know what is going on. Am I to be made a laughing stock? I think not.'

Charles glanced back at the yard. Mungo Dalzell was just disappearing through the gateway, and Urquhart was nowhere to be seen. With an agility that he ought to have thanked his father for, Charles leapt neatly over the back of the sofa and was sitting in it, to all appearances relaxed, when Urquhart opened the door.

'Mungo Dalzell will write a note and release some money for you – at fortnightly intervals, if that is convenient for you? We don't carry as much as twenty-five pounds all at once, you know,' he added, sarcastically. Charles rose and thanked him solemnly, and with absolute sincerity, though he hardly knew what he was saying. 'Never worry, never worry. It is a charity, so there is no question of an actual loan. But remember it, when you have come to happier terms with your father: I am sure you will be generous to your old *alma mater*.'

'Indeed I shall, sir, to the best of my ability,' Charles agreed happily, and meant it, little realising how often Professor Urquhart had heard the same words before from students he had never heard from again. Urquhart sighed, and paused before the mirror to make repairs to his wig. 'Thank you for the punch, sir: I had better be going.'

'Congratulations on the letter from Lord Scoggie, anyway,' was Urquhart's parting shot. 'Don't be so excited you forget to reply.'

This time, the yard outside could have been ablaze as he crossed it, and he would barely have noticed. Though he picked his way automatically over the worn paving slabs and patches of rough ground, all he saw in front of him were the pages of Professor Keith's diary.

'Urquhart pays every attention to my wife.'

The question was, he realised suddenly, was it true? Was Urquhart paying attention – an innocent enough phrase on the surface, but full of a very specific meaning – to Mrs. Keith, or was Keith the kind of man who imagines such things? Charles had not known him well enough personally to have much idea. But how likely was it that Urquhart was paying attention to thin, nervy Mrs. Keith, mother of two grown-up children? Of course, she did have money of her own, and once she had been intelligent and might struggle to be so again, but how could there be any attraction there? On her side, perhaps there was the pleasure of spending time with someone other than her husband, but again Urquhart must be as old as she was, and had, moreover, a reputation for ... for what? It had never been entirely specified, but there were always jokes going around the student body about young men who had been 'corrupted' by Urquhart, though the only one Charles could think of specifically was Peter Keith ... perhaps that was connected? Perhaps Peter Keith had had extra tuition from Urquhart to cover his mother's association with Urquhart? Certainly Peter Keith and his mother were very close.

He forced himself to stop and look about him, for his mind was about to run away with itself. He had walked, he realised with a shock, to Thomas' favourite seat, where he had been found dead. All visible traces of the event had been washed away. Charles looked about for a moment, as if expecting to find murderers behind every rock, but there was no one in sight. He sat, warily, and in a moment his mind was off again like a dog in a field full of rabbits.

If Professor Keith had discovered that his wife and his colleague were – Charles tried not to picture anything too intimate – friendly, what would he do? He might divorce her, but that would be extraordinary and expensive. The only people Charles had every heard of divorcing their wives were

254

earls, and even Professor Keith's social aspirations hardly reached that high. He might send her away, force her to live in some secluded spot for the rest of her days, or he might try to use his influence on the Senate to have Urquhart sent away. The first would be better, he decided: Urquhart had to stay for at least term time in St. Andrews or he would eventually lose his post, though that could take years. Keith could expose them both, but that would also affect his own standing. Charles sighed: he did not envy Keith's situation. On the other hand, he did think the professor had been a little over-suspicious: Urquhart would never stoop so low as to use the Sporting Set to further his cause. But would he use poison?

If it had been arsenic, Charles would have had little difficulty picturing it. Urquhart lived opposite the Chapel and had a ready supply, and would have known all about it from his familiarity with its use in ancient times. Yew, however, was a different matter. The idea of Christopher Urquhart picking delicately through old berries and bits of twig at the end of Keith's garden, or here under the wall, was ridiculous, let alone the notion of him boiling them up into something he could put into a claret jug. But –

Charles was so shocked by his idea that he sat bolt upright, and stayed that way until he had thought the thought clearly through. What about Peter Keith? Would he have done it at Urquhart's direction? Charles himself had seen how Urquhart had influence over the boy, and Peter was certainly not, at the time, on good terms with his father. Could Urquhart have used him? Peter could have told him about the claret jug on the landing, and might even have suggested yew, from his classes with Allan Bonar. Charles could not see Peter having the presence of mind to do it all on his own, even if he had the ideas, but with Urquhart behind him, prompting his moves ... Urquhart could even have returned Mrs. Walker's brooch, which it would have been easy for him to remove from Keith's office beside his own rooms in college. He had certainly made a point of noticing it the other day when they had both come to pay their respects to Thomas' body. Charles could see Urquhart not quite being able to resist letting people know how clever he was.

If this was all true, there was another question. Did Mrs. Keith know? He tried to remember the day Urquhart and Professor Shaw had questioned her, in order to present her information to the burgh officer – well, when it came down to it, Professor Urquhart did the questioning, as he would have known would happen if he was with Shaw. Yes, even that fitted. He was there early next morning, with Shaw as an unimpeachable witness, to make sure that everything had gone to plan and to tidy up any loose ends, like the diary. And perhaps Alison knew as well, for hadn't Peter complained that she had refused to see him? Perhaps she knew, and had not wanted it to happen. Yet she had seemed to spend time comfortably enough with Peter, her mother and even Urquhart at the funeral. Perhaps they had eventually talked her round: after all, surely she had been treated as badly by her father as the rest of the family.

The more he thought about it, the more it all fitted into place. The Sporting Set and the Spanish fly was all just coincidence, or perhaps not, in a way: Professor Keith's soirées were well-known, and for either the Sporting Set or Urquhart to strike on an evening when there were to be plenty of people in the house made sense. Now there were only odd little things to account for, like why Urquhart had not destroyed the diary straight away, and why he should have given money from Keith's desk to Ramsay Rickarton's family ... and why Mungo Dalzell had been coming out of the door to the staff stair when Urquhart said he never went in there. Why, since he was sitting here, had Thomas been killed – had Peter Keith wanted the parish after all? And even if Charles was sure, sure to the point of proof, that this story was true, how would he prove it, and to whom? The burgh sergeant? The Principal? Suddenly he wanted to ask his father's advice, and swallowed hard. This independence business was harder than it looked.

He rose and stretched. It was almost dinner time, and he had a letter to write. Maybe Lord Scoggie could advise him, he thought, but decided that now was not the right time to approach him on the subject.

Dinner was pigeon pie, and Charles found that his various worries had done nothing to dull his appetite. Mrs. Walker and Patience seemed to be regarding him anxiously, and he did his best to be bright and cheerful: they were probably worried about the morning's confrontation with his father, and indeed, it suddenly struck him, about their own income.

'I am sorry you were distressed this morning, and feel I owe you an explanation,' he began, and told them of Lord Scoggie's offer and Professor Urquhart's help for the rest of the session.

There was, he saw, a certain look of relief that passed between mother and daughter.

'And you wish to stay here,' Mrs. Walker repeated, making sure.

'Of course, Mrs. Walker: there is no better bunk in the town. I did consider, I admit, moving somewhere where I should cook for myself, but now I am happy to be able to stay.'

'Cook for yourself ...' A shudder ran dramatically over Patience's shoulders, and Charles laughed.

'Yes, it was not a happy prospect – particularly in the presence of this pigeon pie.'

'And you are not to be married?'

'Married?' Charles was taken aback.

'It's just – Mr. Murray said ... something ...'

But there was a rattle at the risp, and Patience rose to answer the door, breaking the moment.

'It's a note for you,' she said, returning, and set it by Charles' plate. 'It's from Alison Keith. The man is waiting for a reply.'

She sat again at the table. Neither she nor her mother looked at each other, in a very pointed way. Charles stared at them for a moment, then slit open the note.

'Dear Mr. Murray,' it read, 'I should be very much obliged if you would be good enough to call on me this evening, at around half past five. Your friend, Alison Keith.'

'I'll just speak to the man,' said Charles, and hurried to the door. The Keiths' man stood outside, thoughtfully propped against the house wall.

'The answer is 'yes',' he said.

'Very good, sir,' said the servant, and pushed himself upright. He was off down the street in a second, and Charles, wondering what Alison Keith might have to say to him, went back inside.

It was about four now, he thought, hearing the bells of Holy Trinity almost immediately. He would write the letter to Lord Scoggie.

Up in his rooms, the odd smell he had noticed that morning was stronger. He opened all the windows, then thought for a moment and closed them again, sniffing to locate the source of the smell. Eventually he traced it to a loose skirting board near the fireplace in his bedchamber. A moment with his pocket knife, and the board was free.

Behind it was a scene of desolation. In a small aperture that had clearly been their home, four dead mice lay, in various states of decay, while in the midst of them lay little fragments of a familiar white wrapper, on which you could still see one or two little globules of black shiny cantharides. He should have guessed. George had used none of the packet Charles had bought for him, but it had proved a very effective vermin poison.

Chapter Twenty-Three

It was still a few minutes to half past five when Charles found himself once again at the stern iron gates of the Keiths' house. He made himself walk to the corner of the road and back, slowly: it was as much a curse always to be too early as always to be too late. At last, feeling he had looked foolish for long enough, he advanced up the familiar gravel drive and rang the front door bell. He heard it clang distantly, but he had to wait a few minutes before Barbara opened the door. Though she looked as tired as he had seen her at the funeral, there was a cheerfulness about her that he was sure he had never noticed before: Professor Keith would never have allowed it.

'I wish to see Miss Keith, please,' he said. 'I am expected.'

She took his card anyway, but in a few seconds returned to show him in to the downstairs parlour with the French doors.

The evening had turned chilly but no fire had yet been lit, and the parlour, shady now, was cold. Alison Keith was wearing a spencer over her black mourning gown, in a brown and gold Paisley weave, and her thin shoulders were hunched. However, she stood and curtseyed well enough, and even favoured him with one of her wide, nervy smiles. Charles instantly felt uneasy.

'You are well, I trust?' he asked.

'I am much improved, thank you, sir: I am pleased no longer to be a worry to my friends.'

'You have many kind ones, I am sure.'

It was formulaic, but there was a tension in the air. She had not sat, and pressed her hands together, rubbing them slowly as if it would help her mould the right words between them. At last she drew breath, but at that moment the door opened. Mrs. Keith entered, her mourning by comparison spruce and sharp, and glittering with her usual rings. She was tying her bonnet strings.

'Oh! Mr. Murray – what a pleasant surprise! I was just about to go out – down to see Chrissie Shaw and the new baby, you know. Will you not come?'

'Mamma, I have no wish in this world to see a mewling infant!' For a second, Alison was her father. The very air was shocked. Charles swallowed.

'I heard it had arrived safely,' he said, trying to smooth over the moment. 'Professor Shaw must be delighted.'

'I believe he is,' said Mrs. Keith with enthusiasm. 'Ah, there is nothing like a baby!'

There was a pause, then Alison said,

'Mr. Murray and I were about to take a walk along the Scores.'

'Oh? Were you? Very good, very good.' She smiled at Charles. The smile did not help his nerves. 'Well, I shall be off, then.'

She pulled a pair of gloves from her reticule and tugged them on over her rings, kissed her daughter on the cheek, and waved at Charles, and was gone. It was only then that it occurred to Charles that she seemed remarkably relaxed at the thought of her daughter walking out alone in the evening with a young man.

'Shall we go, then?' Alison asked, with another grin. 'I shall just fetch my bonnet and pelisse.'

She returned very quickly – Charles had only had time to wonder if he was to run some errand to George for her – wearing a brown velvet pelisse and small matching bonnet. Mourning could not always stretch to a warm winter coat, of course, but Charles was surprised that it could not in this household. Thin in the soft brown, she looked like a weasel, and he had to turn his instinctive laugh into an approving smile. He hoped she would not smile back.

'Come,' she said, 'I have hardly been out of these grounds for days, and I can bear it no longer.'

She seemed too anxious to walk slowly, and in a minute or two they had retraced Charles' steps to the corner and were on the Scores. There she relaxed a little, and folded her hands behind her, forcing herself to walk more easily. Charles matched her pace.

'Have you seen much recently of your brother, Mr. George Murray?' she asked, as cautiously as a swimmer easing himself into cold water.

'I have not seen him since ... oh, only yesterday. He left yesterday for Letho.'

'Time seems disjointed, does it not?' She sighed. 'I – this is very difficult for a girl! I do not know what to say!'

'Do you wish me to carry a message to him?'

'No! That is – look, he gave me – gave me reason to think that he might feel ... an affection for me.'

'I believe I am not betraying a confidence to say that he does, or did two days ago,' Charles agreed.

'I sent him away,' she admitted. 'I thought – but now ...'

'Forgive me.' Charles had waited for her to go on but she had drifted off dismally. 'But do you care for him?'

'Oh, no! No, no more than as a friend! But what is that to the consequence? Your father forbids him to marry me!'

'Who told you that?'

'Mr. Murray himself.'

'My father? He wrote to you?'

'No, no, he called. This morning. I was barely out of my bed but he said it was urgent, so I dressed and hurried down, and – and – he was very rude indeed!'

Charles sighed.

'I fear that was my fault. I had angered him, and he was probably still furious when he met you. He certainly was when he left Mrs. Walker's house – but I thought he had gone straight back home to Letho.' Charles knew he had upset his father, but this was outrageous behaviour even for him. 'I do apologise for this. It does not reflect well on my family.'

'"You will never marry my son." He just kept shouting it. In the end we had to have the manservant show him to the door. Barbara was in hysterics.' She walked faster again, roused by the memory.

'Oh, Lord, I am sorry,' Charles groaned. 'This is awful.'

'But why does he hate me so much? My family is not beneath yours, and I have a good dowry ... has he heard something?'

'What could he have heard? It hardly brings disgrace on you that your father met his death unnaturally. No: I think the trouble is that – oh, you may as well know, though I doubt it will make anything better. He thought that I was courting you,

261

not George, and he is at present trying to arrange my marriage to someone else. Whoever you were, if you were anything less than the sister-in-law of an earl, you would have appeared less satisfactory than his chosen candidate.'

'I see,' she murmured, though she sounded confused. Her remarkable eyes were downcast.

They walked on a little, then she turned.

'I should like to walk back by the cliffs,' she said. 'Do you mind?'

'Not at all, if you do not,' he replied, thinking of the bench where Thomas had died. She glanced at him.

'A place where someone has met their fate is not always to be avoided,' she stated, as if quoting someone. Charles nodded, and they walked for a little in silence. His own thoughts were busy, and at last he said,

'Professor Urquhart has been very helpful to your family, I think, since Professor Keith's death.'

'He has, indeed.' She seemed relieved to change the subject. 'He is a kinder man than he allows people to think.'

This was more perceptive than he had expected.

'But he has been a friend to your family for some time, has he not?'

She agreed.

'He has visited a good deal. He and Mamma are very friendly,' she added innocently, 'and he is very good to Peter. When my father – he and Peter used to have the most terrible rows, because Father knew just how to upset him. Professor Urquhart was the only one who could calm him down.'

'He did not care, I think,' said Charles carefully, 'for your father.' He would have been surprised, now, to find that Alison was part of the conspiracy he had surmised, but she might still know something.

'He did not, I know.' She gave a little laugh. 'But I could have wished better on him than finding my father that morning. Barbara was with them but they had gone ahead of her, but she said Professor Urquhart reeled back as if he was hit when he saw inside Father's study. Professor Shaw sagged against the doorway. Then they pulled the door closed and wouldn't let Barbara see in. I missed all this,' she added, slightly sadly.

262

Why would Urquhart have been so shocked? Had he told Peter to use the poison, but not said when? Had he not expected to see Professor Keith's body in such a state? Surely he was not innocent.

'I wish I could have known who had killed him,' Alison went on. 'Do you know I thought for a little that Peter had done it? My own brother? If he had struck him with the poker or stabbed him with the carving knife at dinner, it would have been obvious, but Peter is not really cool-headed enough to use poison! That is more Picket's way ...'

'Indeed,' said Charles. 'But what made you decide finally that Peter had not done the deed?'

'Well ... Mr. Murray, you have been very kind, and I think I must tell you. Indeed, I wonder that you have not guessed already – I am sure Mr. Murray your father has.'

'What?' She had stopped, and they turned to face each other. Thomas' bench was nearby, but neither felt the inclination to sit on it.

'Your father does not intend, then, to marry George off?'

'My dear Miss Keith,' said Charles kindly, 'I am sorry, but my father is a proud man. I think it extremely unlikely that, after what you told me about this morning, and the way things are in the family at the moment – my family, that is – that he would allow George to marry you, either. Besides, George is only seventeen.'

'Is he? He seems older.'

'No, he's just bigger.'

She smiled, tight-lipped. To his alarm, she seemed to be starting to cry.

'I had hoped that dear Boxie would take me, but his father wants him to wait until he has served his apprenticeship, and that is too late for me.'

'Too late?' Charles was feeling extremely thick.

'Yes.' The wind pulled back her pelisse, showing her thin, sickly figure. 'You see, Mr. Murray, I am with child.'

'You –' Charles could think of nothing to say, nothing at all. All he could think was that his father would not let either of his sons touch her at all. It would not be a helpful thing to say.

263

'But why – why can't you marry the father?' he managed at last. She was crying, now.

'Because he's dead. And because – because – because I hated him, and he did this to me, and –'

'You mean he forced you?'

'Yes! And Papa stood by me, and helped me, and was trying to find me a husband, and that's why Peter would never have killed him now! Never! I needed him!'

Memories were flashing through Charles' mind: Professor Keith at the party, drawing Boxie out for a serious conversation ... Boxie and Peter fighting in Mutty's Wynd.

'Did Peter think Boxie was the father?'

'Oh, yes, Peter is always so impulsive. When I was poisoned he thought I'd done it myself, taken lily of the valley to make – to make the baby go away. He even went to see if the plant was still in the garden. No, he heard Papa and me talking but he didn't hear all of it, and he jumped to the wrong conclusion.' She sobbed audibly, digging in her glove for a handkerchief but not finding one. He drew out his own and handed it to her absently.

'But if Boxie wasn't the father, and the father is dead, you say, who was it?'

'Didn't you realise?' She drew a breath, glancing at the bench by the wall. 'It was Thomas Seaton. Thomas Seaton,' she drew another breath, 'raped me.'

'Never.' Rudeness did not occur to him. The world lurched. 'When?'

'In the cathedral, the day of the last Senate meeting.' The tears raced down her face, forgotten as she came at him, urgent, insistent. 'Papa had said something to him – he kept muttering about Papa, all the time. I couldn't - He was covered in tea, and he was so angry, so frightening. You have to believe me. I have to convince you. Listen to me. He –'

'All right, all right.' Charles' head was humming. He could see Thomas doing it, that was the trouble. He could see hair on a filthy gown. A lot of things suddenly made sense. 'But that was only a few weeks ago. How do you know –'

'I just know, all right? I'm expecting a child. I know, my mother knows. And no one will marry me!'

264

She took another step forward and fell into his arms, furious and sobbing, clutching the folds of his cravat in long, thin fingers. Holding her, he stared beyond her at the empty bench, and felt sick to his soul.

Chapter Twenty-Four

'Hi! Get your hands off her!'

Running footsteps, a cry of anger: for a moment Charles thought it was for someone else. Then he felt a rough hand spin him by his shoulder. Alison broke away, open-mouthed. George stood there, panting and furious.

'I might have guessed it!' he cried. His face was scarlet. In his hand was a sharp fencing foil, and it was not there for appearances' sake.

'George! What are you doing?'

'I'm going to kill you!'

Alison gave a little cry. In an instant she was round Thomas' bench and behind George, on the grass between the path and her own garden wall. In the same moment, George lunged.

'George! George, I'm unarmed!'

'I thought of that,' his brother spat, and seized another foil from his belt. For a horrible second, Charles thought he was going to attack with both of them: he even saw the thought flash through George's mind, too. Then George tossed him the second foil. 'Defend yourself, then.'

The foils glinted dully. There was a moment of stillness: gulls called distantly, and the sea below the cliff to Charles' right hissed a little. A crow, smooth and black as a caltrap, flapped to land on the garden wall by the yew trees. He watched them in silence. Then George touched his foil to his forehead, and began.

They had fought before, many times. They knew each other's strengths and weaknesses. They had fought angry, true, but never as angry as George was now. The world folded down to one small section of coastline, and two brothers fighting on it.

George thrust, aiming for Charles' chest.

'Quarte,' thought Charles blankly, parrying, though the force of the thrust made him step back. George followed fluidly with another attack, this time lower, but George's low attacks tended to be weaker. Charles pressed the blade off, leaving the thin foible end twanging. 'Parry octave,' he mumbled, unable to help himself. Reality was elsewhere.

'Father told me,' said George, lunging again. 'He said you intended to marry,' he took a breath, and attacked once more, 'Alison.'

'I don't,' said Charles sharply. Alison herself had not moved. Charles was being driven down the path, backwards towards the harbour. He was having the worst of it so far: George was always better at fencing. 'He thinks I do because I won't marry Mawis Thing – whatever her name is. Ow!'

George had hit him on the arm. It was not an official target, but George was not playing by the rules. Charles resisted the urge to look at his arm, and lunged, hitting George on a waistcoat button. But returning to guard he over-compensated for his lunge. His foot hit a tussock of grass on the cliff side of the path. He fell.

'Well, if you don't,' George panted, following up, 'want to marry her, why were you here with her in your arms?' His blade was at Charles' throat. Charles took a breath, and pushed it away with his free hand, scrambling up.

'She was upset, you fool. Stop this, George.'

He was on the rough grass now, a few feet from the cliff edge. His back was to Alison: he could not see her reaction. George followed him, attacking quickly now so that the blades sang.

'Upset? Who upset her? You?'

Charles was backing into the wind now. Even if he attacked, the folds of his gown encumbered him. He needed to turn the fight round. But to pass George on the path side he would have to pass his left side, George's strong point. On the other side was the cliff.

'I didn't upset her. Father did.' He kept parrying George's blows, but George was quick. 'Father told her she couldn't marry his son. He meant me, but she thought it was you.'

At that George stumbled. Charles took his chance and darted past on the cliff side. George could not pull his arm around in time.

'This is all you, all your fault,' he cried. 'If you had done what you were told –'

'You helped me! You said you wanted me to stay here!'

'Not beyond reason.' George's anger seemed to be waning. Two quick steps brought Charles forward and drove George back, and Charles had an instant to look about him. Alison had moved across the path to the cliff side, behind George. She would need to shift out of the way in a second, Charles thought. 'You made him angry,' George went on. 'If he hadn't been angry ...'

'He would never have let you marry her anyway.' Charles pressed home his advantage, then saw a movement behind George. 'No!'

George spun. He was quick enough, just, to see Alison step out over the cliff.

For a moment she was suspended there, brown velvet billowing round her. Then she vanished.

'Alison!' cried George. 'Alison! I'm coming!'

'You can't go down the cliff, George,' Charles snapped. 'Come on: we can climb down at the Castle and work our way back.'

They ran, foils forgotten in their hands. The path to the Castle inlet was empty and they hurtled down it. The tide was high.

'The water might have saved her,' panted Charles. 'Come on, this way.'

They staggered across the rough sand to the rocks, the jagged diagonal ridges of teeth angling out of the high water. Charles had to slow down: their boots were tough, but not made for this. Recklessly, George plunged on, but even so he soon came to a place where he could go no further. Knee deep in water, breeches soaking, he clutched at the cliff beside him for support.

'Alison!' he cried, a long, desperate cry. 'Alison!'

But only the gulls replied, echoing him in the wheeling air.

'The lifeboat!' said Charles suddenly. 'We could get the lifeboat!'

He hardly remembered their run back up the steep path, sodden and heavy, and along the cliff top to slither down to the harbour. They were shouting to the fishermen before they could even see them at their nets, and before they knew it the heavy lifeboat was on the water, eight strong oarsmen slicing the waves, well-practised now at their work.

But though, at George's insistence, they beat up and down the dangerous shallows below the cliff for two hours, they found nothing. At last, pleading the failing of the daylight, the boatmen turned for home, and the coxwain lit a lantern in the stern.

Almost immediately George cried out.

'There!'

Expecting to see only seaweed, Charles and the coxwain turned – and gave the order to stop. George helped to lift her, heavy with velvet, into the boat, a dark and dripping bundle with a face as pale as seafoam. There was no room to lay her flat: George, after a moment, closed the remarkable dark blue eyes with a tender touch, and held her in his arms, for the first and last time, for the slow journey home.

Back on shore, Charles found coins for the subdued lifeboatmen, and helped them pull the boat up the slipway. It had had a sad christening. Then he returned to George.

Charles did not tell him about Alison's conversation with him. There was, as yet, no point. Later, it might be a comfort of sorts, or at least an explanation, but now it might only hurt more, and once said could not be unsaid.

He walked with his brother and the heavy, wet burden he carried, up the hill from the harbour and to the gate of the Keiths' house. There he stopped. George looked at him.

'You don't want me with you, do you?' Charles asked. *Num* expects the answer 'no'.

'No,' said George. He leaned against the gateway, and looked down at Alison's lifeless face. 'I shall go away for a while, I think. I'm sorry I attacked you, but I don't want to see you.'

Charles nodded. For the first time, he noticed that George had grown up. He felt they should shake hands, or something, but George's hands were otherwise occupied and perhaps it

269

was just as well. Instead, he bowed, and at George's answering nod, he turned and went.

He did not go back to his bunk. His wet clothes and squelching boots called for some kind of explanation, which at the moment he had no wish to give. Instead, he found himself back on the cliff path again, as though, by being there, he could work out what had happened, and find an explanation for himself.

Darkness was falling with the slow, steady draining of light that happens in the north. No crow waited on the wall now, but the gulls still called farewells over the sea as it faded from view. He looked at Thomas' bench, but did not want to sit on it. Instead, he propped himself against the wall, hugged his wet gown around his shoulders, and stared out at the dusk.

He had fought with George, and with his father. He had lost his friend Thomas, and then lost him again when he discovered what he had done to Alison. He felt angry, and drenched with loneliness.

He had been standing there for some time, though he had no idea how long, when a movement caught his eye and he heard footsteps on the path from the direction of the harbour. In a moment, the dim shape resolved itself into a short man in a hat and cloak, and then further into Mungo Dalzell. He peered at Charles, who reassured him.

'Good evening, sir. It's Charles Murray.'

'Thank the Lord for that,' said Dalzell amiably. 'I thought I was about to be set upon.'

'Sorry.'

'Not at all, not at all. What are you doing here, anyway?'

'Oh ... just thinking.' Charles was evasive. His thinking had been very specific.

'Well, if you're going to be thinking for a while longer I'll take a wee rest here in the safety of your presence – if I'm not disturbing you?'

'Not at all.'

Mungo sat on Thomas' seat, and stretched his legs out in front of him. He propped his chin on the handle of his stick.

'I've walked in from Kinkell Braes, do you see, and I've a fair way still to go. There's a good family there I visit from

270

time to time. He was a fisherman but he broke his back and cannot walk, and sometimes she's hard put to find food for the bairns.'

'You're a good man, sir,' Charles acknowledged.

'Oh!' Mungo laughed. 'For all I've said I might just visit them and help myself to any food they have! Careful what people say, Charles: they could be telling the truth, all right, but hiding it well.'

'True enough, sir.' Charles paused for a second, feeling for a more metaphorical foil than the one still by his side. He was already on guard: he tried a tentative thrust. 'But you are a good man, sir – so why did you take money and a brooch from Professor Keith's office?'

He felt Mungo's shape tense in the dim light, and found that his hand had gone to the real foil.

'Now, who told you that?' Mungo asked, but his voice was shaking.

'Nobody. I worked it out for myself.'

'I see.'

'You gave the brooch back to Mrs. Walker, which gave her, I may say, considerable pleasure. You gave the money to little Sybie's family, to Ramsay Rickarton's daughter. But what I can't understand, sir, is why you stole it? Forgive me, sir, but would the reparation not have been the greater had you given from your own money?'

Charles could just see Mungo Dalzell's face. He looked tired, and a little sad.

'The reparation,' he said, 'was not strictly mine. Yes, I was mostly responsible for little Sybie's death. It was the worst day of my life, the worst moment, and what it must have been for Ramsay and for his daughter I cannot imagine. No money makes reparation for the loss of a bright young life like that to those who are left behind.'

'Indeed, sir,' said Charles, feeling he had been boorish.

'Their situation, however, came to my attention at the time of the funeral: respectable but terribly poor. Ramsay gives invaluable service, but he is paid little. The house that the daughter lives in, like that of your Mrs. Walker, is owned – or was owned – by Professor Helenus Keith.'

'Oh.' Charles was beginning to add up some facts.

'The reparation, then, was his, only he was not making it. Dear me, I sound very self-righteous, do I not? And I have no right to, none at all. Quite the reverse.'

Charles suddenly remembered the conversation he had had with Professor Shaw on the day of Sybie's funeral. Mungo Dalzell, Shaw had said, was an antinomian. He was a justified sinner.

'I begin to see,' he said slowly. 'You could take it upon yourself to put this right because you are one of the elect? No matter what you do – forgive me if I have misunderstood this – you will be saved, and go to Heaven.'

'Ah,' and he could hear the kindly smile in Mungo's voice, 'not quite right. If I were one of the elect, then yes: but if I were one of the elect, of course I would not do such things.'

'But if you're not ...'

'Oh, I thought I was.' Mungo looked out to sea, wistfully. 'Years ago a preacher visited my family and told us we were all elect, though he prayed with us for many hours to find this out. I am sure he was right about my parents and my sisters – they were all good people, and worthy to proclaim His name – but I am afraid that with me, he made a terrible mistake.'

'How did you find out?' asked Charles, thinking to himself that if he had been told he was a chosen one, he could not feel inclined to question it.

'You see, it was when Sybie died,' Mungo Dalzell explained. 'When Sybie died, I felt terrible. I prayed and prayed, and at last I became convinced that she, at least, had been one of the elect, so that at least was a weight off my mind. But to bring such sorrow to her parents, her grandfather – how could I have been the cause of this if I was elect myself? And then I began to realise that I was not, could not be, had never been.'

'It's a long step from that, though, sir, to stealing money.'

'Well, yes. For a while I was simply shocked, and then I began to wonder. After all, the Lord had chosen the rest of my family, so why not me? He must have had some purpose in *not*

272

choosing me, and I had to work out what it was. I prayed a good deal – I fancy Ramsay Rickarton was nearly going to polish me along with the brasses, I was in the Chapel so much!'

'Indeed, it was noted,' Charles agreed. He wanted to smile, but he knew now what was coming.

'Well, I realised that I was here to do a few things that the elect could not,' Mungo went on, 'and that was when I made my reparations.'

'But then you found, did you not,' Charles broke in, 'that others were being blamed, that Professor Keith thought that Ramsay Rickarton had stolen the money, and was going to accuse him.'

'Professor Keith was an opinionated bully,' said Mungo mildly.

'Hated by everyone, persecuting the students, tormenting his family, riding roughshod over his tenants. So you killed him.'

'I did,' said Mungo in a small voice. 'Nobody else could have. So I did.'

Charles let out a long breath.

'It was easy, at the time,' Mungo went on, before Charles was ready to hear him. 'People like me: they don't recognise my sin. They tell me things, they like having me bustling around, being helpful. I helped Allan Bonar with some of his experiments, and I learned about yew. I didn't want to use arsenic, though I knew it was in the Chapel. I was afraid of putting blame on Ramsay again. I helped tidy up after the soirée. I had every chance to put the yew in the claret jug. Barbara told me it was for her master. People tell me things, you know. It was easy. I was doing the right thing.'

'But then it wasn't so easy. Complications arose, didn't they?'

Mungo sighed.

'I nearly died myself when I heard you say Alison Keith was ill, too. But nothing is ever straightforward. I cannot imagine how I thought that I was only here to remove one person from this life.'

'Thomas found out it was you.' If he tried, Charles could remember his old anger over Thomas' death.

'No, not at all, as far as I know.' Mungo sounded surprised. 'In fact, I found out it was him. Alison Keith's child, you know – do you know? I forget who knows what, these days.'

'I know about that,' said Charles sourly.

'I overheard Peter Keith and his mother talking after the funeral. I was – helping clear up, you know?'

'So you killed him, too.'

'I had a flask with me in case I met him – I knew he often sat here. It had brandy in it, not that I touch it. He drank it down greedily. I stayed a little, for although I had heard accounts of what happened to Professor Keith I wanted to see – how much they suffered, I suppose.'

Charles swallowed hard. He did not think he would ever come to this cliff path again, should he stay the rest of his life in St. Andrews.

'He had to go, you know, particularly when Lord Scoggie gave him the parish. How could he be allowed to become a minister? A man that takes out his hatred of another man on a poor, defenceless girl? He was foul, foul. I cannot bear to think of it. But the evil must look at evil, I suppose.'

'And have you anyone else in mind, now that you have disposed of these two?' Charles asked cautiously. He had stayed so still against the wall he could feel each grain of the sandstone against his back.

'Not at present, I think,' said Mungo, after a moment. He sounded cagey.

'You know I'll have to tell someone about this,' said Charles, pushing himself resignedly away from the wall. He could just see Mungo Dalzell's shoulders slump a little. He paused. 'We could just go and see Professor Urquhart now, if that would suit you.'

Dalzell sighed, just audibly.

'I suppose I'd better. After all, I'll meet my punishment sooner or later, regardless of what I do now, so I might as well make your life easier, eh?' He gave a little smile, straightened his shoulders, and preceded Charles off along the path back towards the Scores and United College.

It was only a moment or two later that they heard voices coming up the path behind them, and turned to see the swinging light of a lantern advancing towards them. People on this path at dusk were rare enough, in Charles' experience, and they both stopped to see who it was. The answer was not long coming.

'Ooh! It's the Grey Lady of the Pends!' came Rab's voice, slurring very slightly.

'If it is she's gey far frae home the night,' Picket remarked, also not entirely distinctly.

'It's no, anyway,' came the inevitable third of the trio. Boxie added a touch of sobriety to the proceedings. 'It's Charles Murray.'

The lantern came nearer and in a few seconds they could all see each other clearly.

'Oh, and Master Dalzell,' added Picket, bowing – with difficulty, for Rab was holding him up by one stringy arm. 'Your honour, it's an honour, our honour, on our own two feet ...' He giggled and straightened. 'Just about, anyway. Here we all are.'

'You're out and about again, then?' Charles asked.

'We've been at the howff at the harbour: we don't want to drink at the Black Bull yet,' Boxie said shortly.

'The howff at the harbour!' Rab repeated, seeming to find it hilarious. For a dangerous moment, he and Picket staggered back and forth across the path: fortunately it had left the cliff edge a little way, and the worst they could do to themselves was to fall flat.

'Listen, Murray, we heard something down there,' Boxie drew Charles a little to one side, leaving Mungo adrift with Rab and Picket. Boxie's face was out of the direct lantern light, but Charles could see that his eyes were wide. 'We heard some very bad news: I wondered if you knew anything about it, for someone matching your description was talked of.'

'Mr. Irving, are you quite all right?' Mungo Dalzell was asking, as Rab recovered from his hysterics.

275

'I think I know of what you are speaking,' Charles murmured. 'Alison Keith?'

'It's true, then, is it? She is lost?'

'She is drowned, it is true.' He put a hand out to Boxie's arm. 'We found her quite quickly, but there was no life left in her. George carried her safely home.'

'Mr. Dalzell-yell-yell,' Picket enunciated, 'tell me, what are we to do now? Our whole reason for life gone, gone in a second! Well, a few hours' writhing agony. Whom are we to torment with our jests now?'

'Jests!' reiterated Rab, and laughed again. 'Aye, they were good enough! Writing agony – that's what I get all the time! Awful pains in my hand!'

'Aye, he cared for her, too.' Boxie seemed to have heard enough from his erstwhile friends this evening, and every word from Picket made him wince. 'Well, it seems neither of us was meant to have her, and she is gone to a better place. He'll be feeling it badly though, I should say?'

'Very much so, indeed,' said Charles, thinking of George's face at the gate to the Keiths' house.

'Mr. Picket, you are not well. You need another drink,' he heard Mungo Dalzell say in his soothing voice. 'Here – I have a little flask here in my pocket.'

'They said she – she stepped off.' Boxie's voice shook.

'I don't know how they could tell that,' said Charles evasively. 'The first they knew of it was when – *don't touch that!*'

How could he not have noticed? Why would Mungo Dalzell, teetotaler, be offering Picket a drink from his little flask? He had spun round without even thinking, but Picket had the flask to his lips. He upended it, pouring the contents ungraciously down his lanky throat. He swallowed, and swallowed again, his adam's apple bounding and lurching like a separate being. Mungo Dalzell watched in wonder, open-mouthed. Rab, caught in the moment, was frozen in mid-cackle, before the flask crashed to the ground. Rab swooped and caught Picket as he fell.

276

'What – what in the name of damnation ...?' Picket gasped, speaking as if his lips and tongue burned each other. His breathing was harsh.

'Rab, get the doctor,' snapped Charles, flinging himself down beside Picket. Boxie hurried to his other side.

'What is it?'

'It's poison – the poison. Yew. Oh, he must have had – it must have been strong. Hold on, Picket, Rab's going for the doctor. We need to make him sick.'

'Sick? What – vinegar, he needs vinegar, that's what will make him sick.'

Charles looked across at Boxie.

'And have you any vinegar about you?'

'No.'

'Well, then.'

'Would water make it weaker?'

'It might, but we don't have any water, either.'

They heard footsteps, and looked up. It was Rab.

'Er, where's the doctor?' Rab asked. 'Only, I was running along, and it suddenly struck me I didn't know where.'

'For pity's sake!' Charles spat. Picket's face was blotchy, grey and red. His mouth hung open, his hideous teeth yellow in lurid gums. 'Get Dr. Pagan. Far end of North Street.'

'What about water?' Boxie cried. Rab was already on the move. Boxie called him back. 'Get water first! The well at the top of Heukster's Wynd. He needs water, fast!'

Picket squirmed and writhed, trying to claw at his throat and his stomach all at once. Then his face grew desperate, and with a horrible twist he spewed out vomit, over himself and the ground around him. Boxie and Charles had instinctively whipped backwards. Picket fell back, groaning.

'That will have done him good,' said Boxie, but Charles was not so sure.

'Thomas and Professor Keith had both vomited,' he muttered. Boxie's face was shadows, the lantern set down beside him at Picket's head. He whisked it away as Picket twisted again, shuddering, mouth wide in a search for cool air on his burning throat.

277

'Where the hell is Rab?' Boxie hissed. Picket opened his eyes, but there was nothing human left in them. Suddenly his body was wracked with another fit. His face was a demon's face, white bone planes and black shadow, his eyes glittering. His back arched, feet lashing out, the fragile joints springing. Then he fell back, and was silent.

'He's – gone?' Boxie sounded bewildered.

'I think so.' Reluctant to touch him, Charles opened one loose eyelid. There was no reaction. 'The doctor will say.'

'We should put something over him, just in case.' Boxie stood up. There was the sound of running footsteps. Rab appeared out of the darkness.

'Water!' he cried, and tipped a wooden bucket over Picket's head. It splashed in a great fountain about them, washing vomit away down the path. Boxie hurled himself at Rab.

'He wasn't on fire, you great fool! He's dead!' He beat on Rab's chest, as if he could drum the information into him. Rab stood still, as if he did not notice, and stared down at Picket's body.

'Dead? You mean, really dead?'

'Really dead. Really, really dead.'

Rab walked round Boxie and crouched beside Picket, touching his hair.

'Why?'

'Damn it, Mungo Dalzell,' cried Charles, and snatched up the lantern. It jerked back and forth, sloshing light around the path, the walls, the seat, the glint of the flask on the ground, and Picket's corpse. He held it high, and took two steps forward. On the edge of the cliff was a small, neat figure.

'Mr. Dalzell?' he called. The figure, looking down at the sea, turned back for a moment to stare at him.

'My task is finished, I think, Mr. Murray. It will be less trouble this way, and as you know, it has to be faced sooner or later. No, don't come any nearer: I wouldn't want you to fall, too.'

He turned back to the cliff edge, and took a little jump.

Boxie was beside Charles before they heard the splash.

For what seemed like eternity, there was only the sound of the sea. Then, above them, a late crow flapped coal-black wings in the darkness, and vanished into the yew trees over the wall. It was home.

The Murray of Letho Series
by Lexie Conyngham

Knowledge of Sins Past

Scotland at the beginning of the nineteenth century. Scoggie Castle is cold and grim, but a refuge to the disinherited Charles Murray. Then a series of mysterious deaths shakes family and servants alike, and splits the local village in two. Murray is thrown once more into the midst of murder, but who has the answer in this dark rural landscape - the pig-lovers or the pig-haters? *Knowledge of Sins Past* is second in the Murray of Letho Series.

Service of the Heir

Charles Murray is in Edinburgh when tragedy strikes at the heart of his family. But in the midst of obligation, is everything quite as it seems? The deaths of a lawyer and a servant not only draw him down to Edinburgh's grim underclass, but make him reconsider his elegant society friends. Who kills – and who gives the orders? *Service of the Heir* is the third in the Murray of Letho series, set in Georgian Scotland.

The Murray of Letho books are also available for Kindle readers at Amazon.

Printed in Poland
by Amazon Fulfillment
Poland Sp. z o.o., Wrocław

26144218R00161